Whisper Of A Tryst

A warm breeze blew in through the open French doors, beckoning her to answer its call. Rising slowly from the bed, she stretched languorously and stepped out onto the balcony. She had no fear of being seen nude. Alastair slept soundly in the room across the hall and she had locked her door before retiring.

Anna stared up at the full moon winking down upon the silent grounds below. Closing her eyes, she reveled in the delicate sea breeze cooling her heated body. "Oh, James, my love. Where are you?"

"Anna—"

Her eyes flew open. Was he here? Impossible! Then she recalled her first days in the old house. James appeared in the mirror's reflection and his voice called her name in the arbor. Was it his ghost?

Tenderly, long invisible fingers stretched over her breasts and the pressure of a man's naked form pushed against her from behind in a most familiar way. She would know his touch anywhere.

"James, help me. I want to come back." Was she insane? Whispering into the moonlit darkness as she melted into her phantom lover's arms?

Bristly whiskers tickled her ear and a deep voice hushed her fanciful illusions. "In the arbor, my love. 'Tis the secret."

He was gone. Anna sensed the instant he left her. A cold chill ran up her spine. She must be mad! It was crazy to believe in ghosts. Or was it? The evidence was only in her mind, but she felt it in her heart as well. James was calling to her through time in the only way he could—his ghost—a mere shadow of his former stalwart self

Other Works from The Pen of

Christine Poe

Heroes And Hunks ~ 2002

Twyla Twitt hires photographer Brad Denton for a road trip to launch her new magazine for women about men, in an attempt to save her late father's newspaper. Brad is the perfect hunk—until he tries to become Twyla's hero.

Quixotic Fantasy ~ 2003

Writer Georgette Jones is a widow raising three teenagers. Her hottest date is with the computer and the fantasy heroes she creates. Country star Colt Ryder sings about love, but in real life the novelty eludes him. Winning the perfect woman's love is like chasing windmills, until he meets Etta Jones.

Wings

WHISPER OF A TRYST

Christine Poe

A Wings ePress, Inc.

Paranormal/Time-Travel Romance

Wings ePress, Inc.

Edited by: Lorraine Stephens
Copy Edited by: Gail Simmons
Senior Editor: Pat Casey
Managing Editor: Elizabeth Struble
Executive Editor: Lorraine Stephens
Cover Artist: Chrissie Poe
Cover Painting by Jim Warren

Wings ePress Books
http://www.wings-press.com

Copyright © 2001 by Christine Poe
ISBN 1-59088-967-1

Published In the United States Of America

December 2001

Wings ePress Inc.
403 Wallace Court
Richmond, KY 40475

Dedication

This book is dedicated to the memory of
my brother Bruce,
who was a true hero in his fight against lung cancer.
We shared a love of nature, animals, and children, and his zest for a
simple way of life lives on in my heart.
May he rest in peace

Acknowledgements

I want to thank Jim Warren,
for the use of his beautiful artwork "On A Clear Day";
B. J. Haynes and the late Lorraine Stephens
for their belief in my work;
my family
for their love and moral support;
and my wonderful husband Will,
who truly is the "Captain" of my dreams.

One

Anna Bentley awoke drowsily to a firm masculine body pressing intimately against her. The whisper of his tender lips caressed her neck in nuzzling little kisses. Her breast tingled to the touch of his large callused hand massaging it to full titillation. She sighed dreamily as her mind suddenly came to total responsive awareness. Her eyes flew wide open only to reveal the empty moonlit bedroom. She sat bolt upright and searched the room's dim corners. Surely, no dream could be so vivid?

"Why me?" She rubbed her temples in complete frustration.

Once again, the same highly erotic dream had disturbed her sleep. It meant something significant. Her nocturnal lover was trying to tell her something. Maybe it was time to move on with her life, give up the past and begin anew. She tossed back the bedcovers and walked over to the open window. In the distance, she could hear the pounding surf calling to her poetic soul. She sighed. She wanted a place to belong and someone to love her. Not just anyone. She wanted the kind of man who existed only in her dreams and a love to last for all time.

Anna took a step back toward her bed and paused. Catching her eye, a long white envelope glowed in the moonlight as it lay on the nightstand. She reached down to pick up the letter. Postmarked from Mendocino, California, the short letter held the answer to her future.

She thought the letter a joke at first, but last week she had called the attorney's phone number and he told her it was legitimate. She had inherited an old Victorian home in Mendocino County at a stranger's bequest.

~ * ~

"Oh, my!" Anna's startled gasp brought the young attorney immediately to her side in the entry hall of the old house. They stood in curious contemplation before the portrait of a middle-aged man. The strong magnetic pull she felt toward the life-sized image nearly took her breath away.

"Do you like oil paintings?" Mr. Thornton asked, straightening his tie. He glanced quickly around the hall before his attention settled upon the portrait.

"Not usually," Anna said with a sigh, wondering why the man was behaving so oddly. Sure, the house had a musty smell from being closed up, but it wasn't all that bad. She fiddled with the end of her tawny blonde braid as she returned her gaze to the alluring painting. "Who is this guy?"

"Perhaps he was the first Duncan, a sea captain. Uh, as I understand it, he lived here at Duncan's Point until his tragic death at sea...late eighteen hundreds, I believe."

"To die at sea—how awful!"

She scrutinized the man in the portrait. A distinguished gentleman in a dark suit stared back at her, looking nothing like a salty old sea captain her creative imagination would dig up. His aura gave off an authoritative air that he must have emanated in life, whether on land or at sea.

Unruly chestnut hair fell in waves about a ruggedly handsome face, making him seem vaguely familiar. A sensual smile tilted up one side of his mouth creating a slight dimple in his left cheek—a very roguish dimple that bespoke of a teasing nature. His unusual sapphire blue eyes twinkled with laughter, making her wish she could sample his charm in person. In fact, his whole expression held a mischievous sparkle that tugged at her heart.

She heard a strangled gasp at her side and turned in time to observe a worried expression cross Mr. Thornton's peaked face. She had been so caught up in her detailed examination of the portrait that she had completely forgotten her companion. The poor man! He looked about ready to exit the house at break-neck speed.

"Are you okay?"

He blinked several times and nodded. "Y-y-yes. I'm—I'm just fine."

Quite unexpectedly, goose bumps rose on her skin. She was not a bit afraid, but something was definitely going on in here. Her five senses were running in chaos. She had never visited this particular old house before, yet she felt welcome. A strange sort of welcome, almost like a homecoming.

Mr. Thornton cleared his throat to a froggy croak. "The Duncan family made their great fortune in logging, an extremely lucrative business in the 1890s, as I recall my California history."

For the moment, Anna didn't care a hoot about history, only the odd sensation silently filling her soul. She rubbed her small icy hands across her bare arms and turned back to face the attorney. It was peculiar how he could more or less ignore the undercurrent in this house. Another glance at his pale face told her she was wrong. He appeared to have his fear under control, but he was definitely fearful of something.

Glancing around, she wished she could understand the complex emotions assaulting her senses. Not that the house was haunted, she didn't believe in ghosts. Still, there was something chilling, something a bit elusive floating in the air about them. It was almost as if the place had feelings of its own.

All in all, if she really was the sole inheritor of this piece of property, it would be a wish come true…a place of her very own, far away from the crowded city. She would have a beautiful home overlooking the scenic Pacific Ocean and surrounded by lush green pine trees reaching for clear blue sky. She would be in heaven.

A sudden heavy scent filled the room around them, its aromatic intensity nearly stifling. The startled gaze of the attorney let her know he could smell it too. Their eyes met just as an icy gust blew through the hall. They both looked up toward a tinkling noise coming from high above them. Suspended from the ceiling of the wide curving staircase a huge three-tier chandelier caught the sudden air movement. Hundreds of tiny crystal droplets crashed restlessly together in a cacophony of sound.

"Who would abandon a wonderful old place like this and leave it to me—a perfect stranger?" She inquired as the noise slowly decreased in volume.

"Y-y-you know, I can't tell you exactly who your benefactor is, Ms. Bentley. Didn't you say you were adopted? Perhaps someone from your biological family kept tabs on your whereabouts over the years." A nervous cough caught in his high-pitched voice and he politely turned away until he had gotten it under control.

"Are you sure you are quite all right, Mr. Thornton?" She watched his face pale even more in the shaft of yellow sunlight shimmering across the hall from the front door's oval window. He played anxiously with the keys in his hands, feeding her suspicious nature. "If I didn't know better, I would say you think this place is haunted. Do you?"

"No!"

His quick retort fell short of the truth. A grown man afraid of an empty old house made her want to laugh. She suppressed the rude urge and waited patiently for his upcoming explanation.

"I have a bit of a chill, that's all," he said, stuffing his fists into his bright red blazer pockets. "It has nothing to do with this house."

"Oh? Is that why you're so jumpy?"

His gaze shot erratically around the room like a Ping-Pong ball. "You must remember men are much braver than women."

"Only if we let them be." Anna released the light laugh tickling her insides. She truly could not help herself. Now she understood the near petrified expression on his face. "Mr. Thornton, I honestly think you believe in ghosts."

"Hardly!" He blinked several times, and then attempted to cover a fake cough with his fist. "Now—as I told you before—the last person to live here was a direct descendent of the Duncan family. A medical doctor who went away quite suddenly about a year ago."

"All the more reason to suspect foul play." Anna tossed the braid over her shoulder and placed her hands on her hips getting ready for battle. It didn't seem fair he would not tell her from whom she had inherited the property, or even why she was selected. "How did your law firm hear about this house if the doctor disappeared?"

"The family attorney handling the estate turned it over to us. Of course, it took a bit of time to locate you in the vast Bay area." He pulled at his snug white shirt collar and loosened his perfect herringbone tie. He was breaking out in a cold sweat.

"I really think you should sit down," she said, sincerely feeling sorry for the man. "You are beginning to look like a ghost yourself. Let's go into the parlor where you can rest for a while."

"No—thank you." He looked a little sheepish. "To be quite truthful, Ms. Bentley, I have heard a few rumors about this place. Apparently, the house does have the reputation of being haunted. You know, stories about lights turning on at night, that sort of thing. All the usual stuff that circulates when a house sits unoccupied for any length of time." He grimaced as he peered nervously into the parlor.

Anna hid her smile of amusement. She didn't believe in the supernatural. She didn't understand the odd sensation she was experiencing at the moment or the drafty entry hall, but she was probably just picking up on the attorney's hard case of the jitters. She did want to become more accustomed to the house itself, so she decided to move in as soon as possible.

She looked him straight in the eye. "I really like the old house, Mr. Thornton. Can we take a quick look upstairs before we leave? There must be an awesome view of the sea from the balcony."

"Y-y-you go…go on upstairs. I'll wait for you right here," he croaked softly, settling down in a white wicker chair next to the front door.

Anna headed for the wide oak staircase, not bothering to coax him any further for his company. She wanted to inspect the rest of the house, with or without his guidance. It was obvious he would not tell her what she wanted to know about the previous owners or their mysterious link to her.

Drop cloths covered the larger furniture pieces in all the upstairs rooms, except the master bedroom. She stood on the threshold and glanced about the room. Either someone had left in haste or they still lived here because the bed had that "slept in" look. A pair of French doors leading out onto a wide balcony drew her farther into the room. Through the windows, she could see a pine tree grove enclosing the estate with giant rhododendron shrubs framing a magnificent ocean view.

She reached for the shiny brass knobs on the double doors, only to find them locked. In heart-felt disappointment, she turned her attention back to the interior of the room. The dark oak, four-poster bed took up an entire wall. A sailor's wooden trunk, complete with weathered leather straps and an ornamental brass lock, set at the foot of the massive bed.

A curious sensation overcame her as she stood admiring the old sea chest. She shivered and rubbed her forearms, though the room was not a bit cold. A light laugh escaped her throat and she quickly covered her mouth with her hand. How silly! Why should the old house be affecting her sensitivity so much?

She glanced over her shoulder to see if Mr. Thornton had followed her upstairs after all, but there was no sign of him. She wondered if he was running for his car with winged shoes on his feet. There was something a bit unusual about the house, but it wasn't frightening by any means. The big city-bred attorney was far too much of a nerd to look beyond the obvious. The old country house had once been loved and well cared for, and poignant memories of its past inhabitants lingered on in the atmosphere. That was all—period.

Anna continued her scrutiny of the pleasant bedchamber, admiring a tall chest of drawers and an armoire opposite the bed. An ornate roll-top desk stood beside the French doors. It would be the perfect place to sit down and write for hours upon hours.

A large yawning fireplace caught her attention next. Adorned with multi-colored polished stones, the fireplace practically glistened in the room's filtered sunlight. She ran her fingertips slowly over the smooth surface, admiring the detailed workmanship. The wide oak mantel's edges were carefully engraved in a delicate rosebud pattern. Above the mantel, a large rectangular section of pale yellow rosebud wallpaper appeared less faded. A missing painting perhaps?

A comfortable, high-back chair sat on a thick woven rug before the gray slate hearth. The chair was the only piece of furniture in the room appearing well worn. She imagined long winter evenings by the fire, warming her bare toes and snuggling up against a tender lover.

Shaking off the room's dreamy ambiance, she walked over to the French doors again. Could it be she was related to the previous owners of this house? Or maybe she was simply ready for the adventure of writing and her active imagination was already working overtime.

She twirled around in a circle and grabbed for a spindled bedpost, giggling and feeling breathless. This would be the perfect place to write and the perfect place to recuperate from her recent bad marriage. What a disaster! There had been no one to turn to for advice while her entire life turned upside-down. She had stumbled through the nasty divorce only to discover she was the weaker sex in only one area—she couldn't lie.

Anna returned downstairs looking for the attorney, but didn't find him until she walked out the front door. The pale-faced man sat on the grass in the late afternoon sunshine, his back to the house. She touched him on the shoulder. He swung around with a startled gasp. His light chuckle didn't fool her. He was a total bundle of nerves. She smiled and watched his tension ease away.

"I do love the house, Mr. Thornton. Are you positive it's really mine?

"It's yours all right—every bit of furniture and every last garden plant. The whole thing is yours. The furniture, the house and thirty-five acres of land right down to the sea." He fumbled with a set of keys as he scrambled to his feet and hurried up the porch steps to lock the front door. He sighed with obvious relief to have accomplished his duty. "It is a great old house, isn't it?"

"Great doesn't even do the house justice," Anna whispered. "...It's totally fascinating."

With the sun's warmth outside it was hard to imagine the chill she had felt within the old house. She eyed gentle spiral wood posts holding up a long, broad balcony above the porch. Ornamental cobwebs filled all the corners. Delicate woodcarvings dripped like icing from the roof's edges. She found it difficult to believe the previous century's artistic talent and yet, here stood solid proof. Victorians may have been prudish and conventional, but their creative talents remained unsurpassed.

Deep wooden steps led up to a wide veranda. A beautifully carved, but slightly weathered oak door held a lovely oval glass window, etched with a dainty flower border. She loved the scalloped panels adorning the ornate house, just like a storybook gingerbread cottage. A multitude of windows in various shapes and sizes winked down at her. Tiny hexagon panes, stained with flowers and designs, brought a smile to her heart. She had wished for a place like this once—a long time ago when her girlish dreams were still untarnished.

Her heart beat faster with building anticipation. "I can hardly wait to move in. I have never really had a place to call my own."

"That's great, Ms. Bentley. Oh, I do apologize for my odd behavior earlier. I don't know what came over me in there, but I felt like I was suffocating."

Anna watched him wipe a handkerchief across his sweaty brow. It was not terribly hot outside, not even in the direct sunlight. Men weren't usually so sensitive. She hadn't felt anything particularly bad about the house. A little drafty maybe, especially in the entry hall, but the beauty of an old house was well worth a few faults; occasional drafts, lights that turn on by themselves, and things that go bump in the night.

Brave men, eh? She was glad there wasn't a man to complicate her life anymore. Brave or otherwise, being burned once was enough. Men simply were not born monogamous; it was not part of their "macho" criteria and it certainly hadn't been part of her ex-husband's. Nowadays men wanted to be fussed over and pampered.

Sometimes she wished she had lived in the Victorian era when women were cherished, respected, and treated like real ladies. Women in the past wore such feminine clothes. They were modest, pleasantly courted, dearly protected and treasured for merely being women. Why did everything have to change so much?

~ * ~

Friday was a glorious day for moving. A blustery sea breeze blew across Anna's face and tugged at her long braid when she stepped out of her car. She finally had a place where she belonged. It would be better if someone was here to share in her excitement, but she didn't really need any help moving. She hadn't brought much with her: two suitcases of clothes, two boxes of writing materials, and her beloved typewriter. She brought only the bare necessities.

By late afternoon, she had everything unpacked and her typewriter sat on the roll-top desk in the master bedroom. All she needed now was a little inspiration. As a freelance writer, she knew an idea would hit sooner or later. In the meantime, Mr. Thornton had given her all the house keys and she was eager to see where each precious key belonged.

Her first goal was the French doors leading to the balcony. After trying each of the dozen odd-shaped keys with no success, she cursed in frustration and headed for the narrow attic stairs. Her curiosity itched after having found the attic locked on her first visit. There was no telling what treasures lay hidden in an old attic.

To her surprise, the first large key she tried unlocked the small arched, attic door. The door creaked loudly on heavy hinges as Anna carefully pushed it inward. She was instantly assailed by the musty smell of age. She closed her eyes for a moment to quell the ripple of excitement buzzing through her, and then took a cautious step forward.

A large, sticky, very dusty cobweb floated down upon her. Her piercing scream echoed in the narrow hallway. Sputtering with disgust, she swiped at her face and quickly closed the door in retreat. The attic room would definitely have to wait until she could hire someone to help her clean things up.

She hurried down the hall to the bathroom and splashed cold water over her face in a feeble attempt to calm her shattered nerves. Only a few cobwebs, yet she had screamed like a paranoid pledge on sorority hell-night. Spiders. She hated spiders—or even the idea of them crawling around on eight creepy legs. She towel dried her face and looked up into the mirror to pick the remaining cobwebs from her hair. Her reflection showed emerald green eyes opening wide with surprise. Directly behind her picture sharp image a shadowy male figure appeared.

Anna froze in place. She blinked once—twice. He still stood there; staring back at her with his arms folded across his broad chest. A curious smile played softly upon his full lips. He gave her a flirtatious wink.

She swallowed hard, gathered up her courage and spun around to confront the unexpected intruder. No one was there! She exhaled slowly, not realizing she had held her breath. He had seemed so real. Yet, he was gone. Poof! Only the lingering image remained in her mind of a personable face with a sexy lopsided-grin.

Anna snapped her fingers. "Bingo!"

She knew where she had seen his face before. Her heart pounding double time, she left the bathroom and ran down the wide sweeping staircase. She came to an abrupt halt in front of the massive oak-framed portrait and released a small cry.

"Oh my God—it's him!" Except for his clothes, the dark chestnut hair and piercing blue eyes were those of the man in the mirror. At least the man she thought she had seen in the mirror, or had she indeed just seen a ghost?

Curiously, Anna studied the well-done oil painting in more detail. The man wore a black pinstriped suit with a blue brocade vest, a popular style around the turn-of-the-century. The jacket lay open, revealing a delicate gold chain looped loosely from a buttonhole on his vest to a small watch pocket. His white shirt looked starched and his black necktie was perfectly tied into a western bow.

He looked every bit the Victorian gentleman. His casual countenance gave off an air of humor to what must have been a devilish personality. Had some lucky female caught this fabulous example of masculinity? A shiver tumbled through her, almost in answer to her whim. She did not feel fear exactly, but a deep yearning. For what…a hundred year old ghost?

Smiling to herself, Anna met the magnetic eyes of the man in the portrait. She knew who to keep in mind if ever she needed a scoundrel for a character in a book. He could charm the tan socks off a Rottweiler with that exact expression; an expression captured by a talented, unknown artist from bygone days.

On the spur of the moment, she decided to go for a walk. She had seen enough of the old house for the day, and she was tired of being indoors on such a sunny afternoon. Setting the heavy key ring aside on the hall table, she picked up her sweater and tugged it on over her light cotton jumper. She felt curiously compelled to visit the ocean and fill her lungs with fresh sea air.

Anna crossed the sloping lawn and followed a row of huge pink azalea bushes through a lovely overgrown grape arbor. Wandering farther along the worn pebbled path, she eventually reached a row of pine trees edging a cliff high above the sea. The path became more rugged and layered with brown pine needles, crunching softly beneath her feet.

A gust of salty air greeted her. Freedom filled her soul and a curious feeling of familiarity crept into her heart. Or maybe she just wanted to belong so badly, she would do anything…anything to belong somewhere, to someone who loved her. Lofty pine trees cleared abruptly from the grassy bluff and far below lay a rocky cove dotted with tide pools. A beautiful sandy beach stretched southward, caressed by endless waves.

She took a deep breath of misty salt air and shouted to the world. "It feels great to be alive! It feels great to be here! It feels great to be *me!*"

An echo followed her shout down to the shore and out to sea. She closed her eyes and tried to absorb all the wonders of nature assailing her senses. Warmth from the distant fiery sun tingled softly upon her face as waves washed over the rocks below, playing a soothing melody to her soul. Gulls soared high above with graceful speed. They called to each other in mournful cries, carrying her thoughts to places far away. If she didn't know better, she would think there was magic in the air. So many things had happened to her lately, things that were changing her way of life…perhaps forever.

The setting sun nestled gently on the horizon, encouraging her to stretch out on the grassy bluff and enjoy the moment. She undid her braid, shook her head, and ran her fingers through her hair. The wind whipped long tendrils about her body and into her face, making her giggle. *If she could only capture this day and hold it in her hand....*

Anna opened her eyes and smiled with contentment as a cool breeze brushed gently through her unbound hair. The half-round sun dipped the last of its steamy brilliance into the sea as a typical light summer fog crept slowly in across restless waves. She shivered, recalling history and the many shipwrecks along the Mendocino coast. Rocky shores, steep cliffs, violent rainstorms and fog had shaped the uneven coastline she loved so much, into a cemetery for ships. She envisioned the seamen who had attempted to conquer stormy seas and navigate thick gray fog banks. Now those truly brave, dedicated and hard-working men made their women proud. Good men who broke their lovers' hearts when they went down with their ships.

She wondered if the first Duncan had left a lover behind when he died at sea. How painful it must be to lose a loved one in so tragic a way, never to see them again. She sighed as her heart filled with deep sentiment. Incredibly magnificent in its wild beauty and unpredictable power, the ocean could be deadly and it was far too easy to forget its treachery while enjoying the peace it brought to her soul.

Not at all eager to leave the beautiful sunset, but eager to cast off her melancholy mood, she stood slowly. Her gaze scanned the seashore one last time. Wrapping her sweater closer about her, she followed the pebble path back toward the grape arbor. Daylight turned quickly to dusk as she entered the enclosed area. She paused for a moment to allow her eyesight to adjust. The heady scent of moist, fertile earth and thick, leafy vines heavy with ripe fruit filled her senses.

"Be still, lass," growled a low masculine voice.

Anna stopped mid-step. She placed a hand over her heart as if the motion could still its exhilarated beat. Horror stories flashed through her mind about secluded old houses, lonely women and their vulnerability to predators.

"Who's there?" Her voice squeaked.

"Shh! Be still."

The husky whisper came from close behind her. For some absurd reason, Anna could not turn around. Fear eased into her as smoothly as high tide washed over a sandy beach. Without warning, her head felt stuffed with puffy cotton. She put her hands over her ears and shook her head in an attempt to lighten the weird effect. There was no one in the arbor with her, still she hesitated to budge even one inch. Her mind sought an answer to the strange feeling overcoming her.

In her line of peripheral vision, she caught a vehicle's bright headlights as it pulled up to the house. A familiar driver sat behind the wheel of a shiny black BMW. Oh God, how did her ex-husband find out where she had moved? He climbed out of the car with something bulky in his hands. He stumbled on the gravel drive as though he had been drinking again and slowly made his way up the steps. He knocked several times on the front door, then glanced down at his watch and set the bundle on the wooden porch swing. Whistling a tune, he strolled unsteadily back to his car, started up the quiet engine and sped away down the long tree-sheltered drive.

Anna shuddered in relief. A silly thought dawned on her out of the blue. The unknown entity had stopped her in the arbor just long enough to keep her presence from being revealed to her ex-husband—but how? She found she could move freely now and did so, making her way across the lawn. Uneasiness slipped quickly away leaving her merely curious as she approached the old house sitting in total darkness.

She reached inside the front door and snapped on the entry light, before turning back to see what the nemesis had left on the swing. The package sat nestled in a natural woven basket: a chunk of Colby cheese; a large stick of beef salami; a fresh loaf of French bread; and a chilled bottle of Chablis, a red bow tied neatly about its neck.

A romantic dinner for two...what's the big jerk up to anyway? Was he attempting to be a charming suitor now that he had nearly ruined her life? Thank heavens her ethereal friend had seen fit to watch over her. She picked up the gift-laden basket and entered the house, feeling compelled to look at the portrait again.

Anna stood before the painting. The man's bold image could have walked out to greet her. His intense gaze seared right into her soul. Was he more appealing each time she stared up at his likeness, or was her mind making up romantic fantasies again?

"Was that your voice in the grape arbor?" She inquired softly, as though he could hear every word. "Were you warning me of Dan's unwanted presence? Well, kind sir, you definitely saved me a hellish evening. Thank you very much."

She glanced down at the table to retrieve her keys and noticed they were missing. She was positive she had left them there. A tiny thought nagged at her brain. Perhaps the ghost had removed them. Now she was really becoming carried away with all this—this illusory stuff. Yet, she felt so alive for the first time in a very long time.

"You mischievous man," she whispered, catching his life-like gaze. "What in the world are you up to now?"

With a smile warming her heart, she turned away and headed for the kitchen. She flipped on light switches as she entered each room. Laughing lightly, she set the basket on the kitchen countertop. How silly to feel so self-conscious. She was safe here and she belonged. This glorious old house was entirely hers, and so was the handsome devil who haunted it.

Two

Mendocino, California ~ 1880

"There's a storm coming in from the west, sir," the first mate called out to the captain as he joined him at the helm. "Jock says we can outrun it."

Captain James Adam Duncan put the brass spyglass to his eye and focused to the West. "Aye—and is Jock the captain now?"

"No, sir," William Mayhew immediately explained. "Jock was only suggesting—"

"Blast it all, man!" The Captain's inner turmoil rose quickly to a raging fury. "I'll not have orders thrown about by my own officers!"

William stood at his side; nary breathing a word, his lean body fighting the rolling deck as his brown eyes studied the sea.

James softened his harsh tone as he watched the young man beside him squirm in discomfort. "Tis I who will give the orders on board this ship. Now make haste to come about, William. Sure and we'll beat the bloody storm."

William turned away, but not before James caught the wide grin spreading across his first mate's dark bearded face. They both knew Jock McDonald was right. He was oft times right when it came to matters of the sea and her wiles. James remembered meeting Jock when both men were mere cabin boys, barely beginning their careers as men of the sea. They had remained good friends ever since, even though they argued a bit now and then.

A loud crack of thunder brought the robust Jock himself to the helm. "Do ye hear that, James?" Concern evident in his every move, the second mate stood as solid as a mighty oak, gazing in the direction of the fast approaching storm. "Why aren't we turning about?"

"We are, Jock, we are." James eyed the giant of a man beside him. "Is it yer ship to command now, Jock?"

Thunder rumbled ominously in the distance, its fierce wind lashing around their steadfast forms. Silence fell between them as they turned their gazes skyward to study the forthcoming storm.

"James," Jock's tone held warning as he spoke, "...ye know I can sail this ship as good as the next man. Perhaps a wee bit better."

"Aye," James agreed, watching the sails and trying not to grin at his friend's discomfort. Jock shouldn't be telling the crew what to do, nor giving his advice without seeking the captain's agreement first, even if he was right in his prediction. Jock knew it well, yet he still gave orders to the crew.

Jock gripped the side rail and nodded toward William. "I was only teaching the young lad a few things."

"Were ye now?" James met Jock's steady blue gaze without a blink.

"Aye!" Jock glared back in defiance. "If ye weren't always having a wee drop now and then, ye would be here to do it yerself!"

James looked away before his friend could read the guilt written on his face. Jock's remark had hit too close to home, much like the cannon shots that had nearly sunk his ship back in his privateering days. He tried not to touch the bottle, but it did help to ease the burden of long nights. "Ye know I'm not a drinking man, Jock!"

"Aye, so ye say, and I'm a bloody dance hall doxy! Be truthful to yerself, man."

"Ye ornery bugger! I would not drink so much if I could stop the dreams, and well ye know it." Running long fingers through his tousled hair, James bellowed the first order to change the ship's dangerous course. "Ready about, William!"

Standing at the wheel, William measured the timing of a slight ruffle in the royals high above them. "Ready about!"

"Lee-ho, down helm!" The captain paced the rolling deck as William echoed his command, barking the order to the crew on deck and in the rigging. The dark blue sea churned restlessly. Thunderclouds thickened quickly in the late afternoon sky.

Jock stood aside as the ship's wheel spun toward the direction of the wind. "Maybe Cookie has a cure, James?" He stepped forward and gave a hand at the wheel to steady the listing ship. "He cured young Nathan's bout o' scurvy, ye'll recall."

"Aye. So ye want me down in my bed, is it?" He released a loud laugh as he visualized the hot-tempered cook who doubled as ship's surgeon. "Cookie would love to get his bloody hands on me. Ye would like that, too, wouldn't ye, old man?"

Jock chuckled and nodded. "Aye."

Absorbed in the task at hand, James watched a young seaman haul up the spanker to force the ship into the approaching storm. A great flapping of canvas drowned out all other noise as the wind suddenly dropped from all sails. The ship's speed slowed as she swung across the wind to change course.

He waited for the bowsprit to cross the direction the wind was blowing before he bellowed, "Mainsail haul!"

"Mainsail haul!" William's voice boomed out in echo across the deck.

James checked the rigging in the masts above. Resembling a spider's web, the rigging was an intricate ladder of ropes where deck hands worked to trim the yards, haul in braces, and sheet the fore and aft sails. The hands looked like busy little spiders high above the ship's sea washed deck.

Jock suddenly released the wheel to William's command and, cursing under his breath, jumped over the poop rail onto the quarterdeck to direct the young topsail boys in the rigging. "Blast it, lads! The lee-side! Pull to the lee-side," he shouted as he hurried across the rope-laden deck to assist.

A loud clap of thunder burst overhead, jolting a boy on the maintop. He lost his grip and fell to dangle limply over the yardarm. James left his position on the helm, quickly reaching the unconscious youth. Jock carefully helped lower the boy to the wooden deck.

James' overall physical examination was quick and accurate from years of sailing. "Thank God, 'tis but a few broken ribs and the wind knocked out of him. Take him below, Jock. Cookie will see to him."

"Aye. And when will ye be seeing Cookie yerself, James?"

"Do yer job, Jock, and leave me be." He had no time to argue right now. High above them wind filled the main and mizzen sails. He turned around to call out a final order to William, "Let go and haul!"

"Let go and haul," echoed William at the wheel.

James watched the foremast sails release and the deck hands haul in the braces to take in slack. The ship successfully turned about and, once again under full sail, headed away from the violent storm. Pride filled his heart at his crew's good work. Long hours on deck had taken their toll on the crew's strength and he appreciated their hard labor. He yawned, feeling his energy wane as well. He made haste to get below and rest before he would be needed topside again.

~ * ~

Great long tentacles wrapped securely about his struggling body. The giant octopus' wet, slimy arms extended to well over thirty feet and its enormous head glistened silvery-blue in the pale moonlight shimmering across the water.

Fear swallowed him whole. Tearing violently at the carnivorous beast's powerful suction, he wrestled to no avail. He gasped for a final breath of air as the hideous creature pulled him down beneath the glassy surface of an ink-black sea. Down, down the monstrous mollusk descended into the deep abyss...

"Och, no!" James jerked upright in his bunk.

Sweat poured off his furrowed brow and his ragged breath softened as he awoke slowly to his senses. He lay safe in his cabin aboard the *Ceilidh*. He shook his head to clear his muddled thoughts. Had that been himself screaming?

"Sweet Neptune! What a nightmare!" A shiver shot up his spine. He released a low whistle and ran long fingers wildly through his sleep-ruffled hair, damp now with perspiration. "Nay, I'll not go night swimming in the bloody sea again!"

Stretching the full length of his naked body, he stood and strode over to the cupboard where he stored a special bottle of Scotch whiskey. After pouring a full mug and downing it in several hefty gulps, he yawned and returned to the warmth of the plush quilt covered bed.

His eyes fell closed before he completed a second yawn.

Fair hair blew loosely about her shapely feminine figure as the beautiful specter floated above him, beckoning and luring him with her lovely charms. She held out her arms, welcoming him into them. "James," she whispered from delicate rose-pink lips. "James, my love—"

He mumbled a welcome response in his drowsy state. She had visited his dreams for a fortnight now. He knew not what her appearance meant, only that she filled him with a great need. His desire to be with her grew with each nocturnal visit. So much so that he would brave the worst nightmare just to experience a moment of her presence. Who was this illusive woman whose thoughts tangled so intimately with his?

~ * ~

Morning sunshine slipped silently through the window, spreading delicate lace designs across the comfortable bed. Anna yawned and sat up, thinking about the marvelous day blossoming before her. No more sorrow, no more grief. She had wasted too much effort already feeling hurt over her past marriage and all the mistakes. It was time to admit she was better off without the jerk.

There was so much to be happy about. She was free to be whatever she wanted to be; free to go wherever she wanted to go. With no one to rule her every move she could do just about anything her heart desired. A giggle escaped as she envisioned twinkling blue eyes and dark wavy hair. What an enigma he must have been in life to still be so enchanting more than a hundred years after his death. She sobered and stifled a yawn. How sad that she would never really have the opportunity to know such a man.

A faint sea breeze drifted in from the open French doors. She swung her slender legs out of bed, stretched like a well-rested cat and walked over to peer outside. How strange. She did not remember opening the French doors last night. Wait a minute! She couldn't have opened the doors. The keys had been missing when she returned from her walk. She distinctly remembered accusing the ghost of removing the keys from the hall table.

It was strange how she could think so calmly about the man's spirit who haunted this house. Thinking about him did not frighten her. Not one bit. She anxiously awaited his next magic trick—like opening the French doors. Apparently, he had a reason to want the doors open. Or had he been giving in to her fanciful wishes?

A thought flickered through her mind, urging her to view the portrait downstairs. She glanced in the oval mirror at her sheer nightgown. Maybe she should dress first. She chose a pale pink, sleeveless sundress from the armoire and slipped on her favorite pair of white tennis shoes. Brushing the tangles from her long hair, she plaited the thick blond tresses over her shoulder. She hummed a cheerful tune, feeling a little excited as she headed for the bedroom door.

Anna chanced a look up at the huge crystal chandelier as she descended the staircase. High above the entry hall the fixture sent quiet sparkles of light dancing across the papered walls. No draft whispered through the hall today, thank goodness.

She crossed the foyer and stood a moment, deliberately staring at the portrait. One hundred years or more—how could his presence still be so strong? The house welcomed her with his warmth, yet others were frightened away. A fiery blush of heat rushed to her cheeks as she recalled her erotic dream the night before. The same erotic dream she seemed destined to endure, night after lonely night. She didn't know who her dream lover was—until now. His image stared innocently back at her as though the rogue didn't have a clue what he did to her touchy female hormones.

She could not resist a delicious thought. How would he have kissed…tender and sweet or deep and plundering? She giggled softly. Lordy, her imagination was working overtime today. Yet, this was exactly what she needed. The urge to write had eluded her since her divorce. It was high time she returned to working again.

Maybe this old house truly would be the therapy she needed to get her career back in the groove. The sea captain could be just the man—or ghost—she needed to make her feel alive again. She wasn't leaving. A chance to live in a house like this didn't occur every day. She planned to enjoy living here—even if it was haunted.

Outdoors, a glorious shade of turquoise colored the sky. A mild sea breeze tugged at escaping tendrils of her hair. She wandered casually past bright pink and purple flowered azalea bushes. A true sight to see in full bloom, the delicate flowers gave off a heady fragrance uniquely all their own. She sighed as she walked along, feeling wonderfully carefree.

The arched trellis of the overgrown grape arbor stood in the garden, intricately interlaced with dark green vines. Anna couldn't resist the lure to look inside by daylight. Old wooden benches nestled snugly along the pebbled pathway. This would be the perfect place for an intimate little tête-à-tête. Near the middle of the bower, she sat on one of the weatherworn benches and slowly took in her surroundings.

Her gaze followed the crisscross latticework holding up thick grapevines, already heavy-laden with ripening fruit. Quite suddenly, everything went deathly still and an icy breeze blew through the leaves. Hairs stood up on the back of her neck. Someone was in the arbor with her. The air virtually thickened as an all too familiar aura surrounded her.

"Who's there?" Anna could not disguise the tremble in her voice.

Not really expecting an answer, she jumped to her feet when a deep voice whispered her name. There was absolutely no mistake. It was crystal clear.

"Anna..."

Some of the things this ghost did really unnerved her common sense. How in the world did he know her name? He could talk to her, move things around the house and appear in mirrors. What else could he do? She waited impatiently for his ghostly appearance because now she knew he was the man from the portrait.

"Can't you materialize outside the house?" Silly question. What would she do if he did materialize? Did she really want him to show himself? She swallowed hard. Maybe he was trying to frighten her away, but somehow she didn't think so. "Well, what do you want with me?"

"Anna...come back."

The deep voice sent a shiver of anticipation up her spine. He called to her with enticement, as one would call to a lover. Who was this man, this spirit, that she should be so drawn to him?

A warm wind rustled through the arbor. He was gone. He would not make an appearance this time. Disappointment quietly filled her senses, edged with a bit of frustration. She had not been able to—to what? Meet the man for Pete's sake? He was dead. Long dead. He had died at sea over a hundred years ago. Isn't that what the attorney had told her? She huffed and stood up from the bench, impatient with her fanciful daydreams.

"Sometimes I wish I could be a million miles away from my boring life." She took a step in the direction of the sea and hesitated indecisively. Then, as though someone guided her footsteps, she turned and headed back toward the house.

The genuine urge to write nudged at her subconscious. Ideas danced around inside her brain, teasing her like a dog coaxing to play Frisbee. She had not responded to the old familiar feeling in a long time. She certainly didn't bother to question a turnabout in her decision to relax and while away the hours.

Nipping a luscious purple bloom off a nearby rhododendron bush, Anna picked up her pace across the wide lawn. Wait a minute! She came to a sudden halt. Could this ghost possibly mess with her moods as well? Earlier she had been cheerful and full of anticipation for what the day ahead might bring. In the arbor a moment ago, she had been overwhelmed with mixed emotions. Now she had all the pages of history flipping through her mind like a giant catalogue of toys, inviting her to pick one and play for a while.

Anna rolled that tidbit of information over in her mind, but shrugged it off obstinately. Right now, she didn't care what motivated her, the ghost or her sub-conscious. She simply wanted to follow through with her desire to write.

She hurried toward the master bedroom. When she entered, she found the old set of keys atop the desk. The bright objects on the large worn key ring lay sparkling in the mid-morning sunshine. It had to have been the ghost returning them now that he had her attention. And he had her attention, all right. She was becoming obsessed with the notion of being haunted by the man in the portrait.

Shaking off the urge to laugh out loud at her infatuation, she crossed the bedroom to the multi-pane French doors and stepped out onto the balcony. She took a deep breath of tangy sea air in a futile attempt to clear her whimsical mind.

The faraway echo of waves crashing upon the beach made her remember her purpose in living this far away from civilization. She should not allow her imagination to run wild with thoughts of the supernatural—ghosts indeed!

Doubts crept into her heart. Anna wondered if she would ever find true happiness. She had no one really. No parents to turn to, no siblings to call, and no husband to love. But she didn't want another husband. Her ex-husband had been a first class jerk and, for the time being, she did not want to become involved with anyone else. Still, how would she ever overcome the intense loneliness filling her aching soul?

She shook herself out of her reverie. What was it about this house? She didn't feel fear, but something more obscure. It felt like stepping into a tunnel and not being able to gauge the distance to the other end. There was a purpose for being here, but understanding exactly what would take time. She would just have to accept things as they came.

Gulls cried out, flying in lazy semi-circles high in the sky above. Anna put a hand to her brow, her eyes scanning the beautiful landscape surrounding the house and its perimeters. She could see all the way down to the ocean. Her curious gaze strayed off shore to a large sailing ship with white canvas unfurled, making its way slowly along the blue horizon.

She remembered seeing an antique spyglass lying on the fireplace mantel and returned inside to fetch it. No matter what her mood, she never tired of watching the sea or a sailing ship under full sail. Standing close to the balcony rail, she put the long brass spyglass to her eye and carefully adjusted the lens.

Something was terribly wrong. Brilliant sunlight blurred her vision and her eyes filled with tears. She couldn't see a darn thing.

Weakness crept up her bare legs. Breathing became extremely difficult. Tight pressure strangled her chest, consuming her with panic.

Falling to her knees, Anna grasped the spyglass tightly to her breast as her stomach turned somersaults. Oh God, she was dying! Fear engulfed her every move. A piercing scream tore from her throat and she fought desperately to remain conscious as everything turned gray around her.

A loud crack startled her, sounding distinctively like a faraway clap of thunder. Her heart flip-flopped. The unnatural fog cleared as abruptly as it had begun. She could see, hear and taste...sea spray?

Anna pulled herself up to stand on weak knees. She held tight to the wide polished rail with one hand and gripped the spyglass possessively within the other. Very slowly, she became aware of her surroundings. Her heart pounded frantically within her chest and a squeaky cry escaped her lips. Her eyes grew wide in total disbelief.

Oh, dear God!

~ * ~

Thunderclouds grew thick and black as they dropped nearly to the sea's surface. Alert to the danger closing in about them, James shouted orders to Jock. He crossed the quarterdeck to check on William at the helm of the four-masted schooner. His first mate stood with legs spread wide, boots gripping the deck and a foolish grin upon his sea-drenched face. The sea itself was quickly becoming a torrent of wind-lashed waves, crashing over the deck and forcing the ship to a starboard tilt.

"Captain? How can it be we are entering yet another foul storm when we successfully outran the last one just an hour past?" William brushed the moisture from his face with the back of his hand. "I've never seen the sea quite like this. It's almost as though she's angry with our presence."

James nodded. "Aye, lad. 'Tis odd indeed to be running from one storm and have another come up from right off shore. Have ye noticed the way the wind is acting?"

"Aye, sir. The storm is circling about us."

"Tis strange, very strange indeed." He gave a hearty clap to William's back. "Just keep a steady hand at the wheel, lad. We'll soon be clear o' this one as well."

James endeavored to stay upright as the wretched storm swiftly enveloped them. Glancing aft, he watched Jock hard at work with the crew. His second mate was a fine seaman. He could not fathom why Jock would not command his own vessel. James was glad to have such an experienced officer. Without much sleep, he was finding it increasingly difficult to keep his mind focused upon his duties. He needed Jock's sharp wit to keep him going; at least until King Neptune saw fit to leave his slumber alone.

Haunted by the same terrible dream, he lay wide-awake most nights. He had not had a decent night's rest ever since he read the novel, *Twenty-thousand Leagues Under the Sea*. Now he knew all too well the terrors that lay in wait far below his ship in the salty ocean's depths. He could reason that he would never see a giant octopus himself. He could drown himself in whiskey and hope to sleep the whole night through without a nightmare. But no, his unruly subconscious played upon the writings of one very brilliant man and sleep was something that eluded him. His only consolation was the beautiful specter that appeared to rescue him from his torment.

James leaned against the rail and gazed out upon the wild black ocean swells, tossing his ship about like a bottle cork. He had never seen a storm quite like this one. The sea churned restlessly and there was a crackle of energy in the air about him. The dark clouds rolled within each other to form an opening.

A faint glow slowly appeared eerily out of the misty sea spray. He stared in amazement as a female shape took form right before his very eyes. He blinked and blinked again, knowing he had not touched a drop of whiskey all day. Sweet sea nymph! Had she come to haunt his waking hours as well?

~ * ~

Anna's panic subsided into astonishment. She no longer stood on the wide, shaded balcony of her Victorian home. She was in the midst of a crazy and totally reckless dream. She had to be! She would remember boarding a classic windjammer with yards upon yards of rope and canvas billowing in the wind.

She could hear men shouting as the ship fought to stay upright. The ocean's pungent smell assaulted her nostrils and she fought the urge to lose the contents of her queasy stomach. She glanced down at the smooth wooden rail beneath her hands. Water washed up over the ship's side, soaking her skimpy sundress and tennis shoes. She shivered and her teeth chattered. Struggling to keep her footing, she glared down at several inches of water covering the heavily polished deck.

This was no dream—it was a vivid nightmare! Her body was probably resting in a quiet room somewhere. Or maybe she had slipped and fallen off the balcony. No. That would cause severe pain, even death. She felt no pain, so she could be dead. Would everything appear this real if she was?

The wind beat against her slender body making it difficult for her to hold on to the rail. Fear seized her and she almost lost her grip. She shifted and got a better hold, looping her arm around the thick water-slicked rail. Salty gusts of sea spray washed over her, one right after the other. She wiped the stinging moisture from her eyes. Nausea flooded her senses.

"Ohhh—why me?" Anna groaned and shivered.

"Ye best get below, lass. We are nearly out o' the storm but the sea is still a wee bit rough," a deep voice shouted close by.

She whirled around, coming face to face with the virile man in the portrait. Dear God! She must be going insane. She needed a reality check, but she could not bring herself to speak. The spyglass slipped from her grasp, caught by the nimble sailor. She let go of the lifesaving rail and her wobbling knees nearly dropped her to the deck.

The brawny sailor took her firmly around the waist, pulling her close to his muscular side. "Tis sick ye are, lass? Come here, then. Ye should not be runnin' about in yer underclothes."

She couldn't find her voice. For the life of her, she could not figure out what had happened or why. Yet here he was—not a ghost and not a shadowy image in the mirror. He was a living, breathing man. A man who had no trouble walking on the slippery deck as they moved slowly along the rail.

He pointed toward a dark-haired man at the helm and spoke close to her ear so she could hear him above the clatter of the receding storm. "William is in charge this hour, so I have time to get ye below."

Anna buried her dripping face against his broad chest. It was really him! It had been his voice in the grape arbor. She must have died and gone to heaven. He smelled wonderfully of bay rum and fresh soap. Somehow, it surprised her. She thought he should smell somewhat...fishy?

Maybe this was a vivid hallucination, if so it was a darn good one. Even in her wildest fantasies, she couldn't do this well. Or maybe she could. All her recent research had supplied her subconscious with everything it needed to give her the best dream material possible. Everything here appeared so authentic, and so dangerous.

She peeked up at her rescuer's rugged profile. Now she knew how much she had indulged in her fantasies. She had really let her imagination run free this time. It must be her fascination with the old house—his house.

There was a perfectly logical explanation. She was fantasizing about the previous owner because she moved into his house, still furnished with his personal belongings. Studying his attractive face in the portrait had made her want to meet someone exactly like him, regardless of how she felt about romantic relationships right now. She couldn't deny that fact. Now she was experiencing the perfect dream. Her stomach rumbled as the ship tilted to the side and back again, rolling with the stormy sea. Maybe not so perfect a dream. She would wake up any moment. She was sure of it.

The sailor assisted her down a narrow stairwell and into a lamp-lit passageway, not an easy task with his arm firmly circling her waist. His touch warmed her and sent little shivers up her spine at the same time.

Down the dim passageway, she heard coughing and men's voices raised in anger. Two burly men burst out of a cabin and stopped in their tracks, their mouths agape. Her rescuer shoved her behind him, blocking her view of the other men entirely. She laid her cheek against his back and listened.

"Get yerselves above deck. I'll not find ye dallyin' aboard the *Ceilidh*."

"Aye-aye, sir!" One of the men responded as they moved swiftly past.

Anna peeked at the men in passing. Sailors for sure, but their attitude toward the man she was with showed respect for his authority. She was right in assuming he would demand attention. He downright ordered it.

"Come, lass. The lads will not be bothering ye now."

Anna looked up at his face as she moved back into the circle of his arm. Mixed feelings poured into her heart. He couldn't be all that she had imagined. She had envisioned the perfect male—at least perfect for her. She had always believed there was a perfect mate for everyone; only most people never found their other half.

They came to an alcove where he paused and opened a paneled oak door before signaling to her to enter. Light from the passageway only illuminated the threshold. She stepped cautiously forward into the cabin with her arms folded protectively across her chest. The large room's contents sprang to life as he lit a lantern on the wall. She looked slowly around, taking in every detail.

He picked up a heavy wool blanket and wrapped it around her shoulders. "Ye can sit on the chair if ye would like, lass."

Anna took him up on the offer and sat on the leather-cushioned chair, shivering in spite of the blanket's warmth. She didn't know what to say so she just watched him move about the room, lighting another lantern and opening a cupboard set into the wall. He removed a thick white towel and walked over to stand beside her.

"May I?" Ever so gently, he rubbed her soaked hair with the towel, leaving the towel and her long braid lying over her shoulder.

"Thanks." She used a corner of the towel to wipe her face and smiled, more to herself than at him. The towel held his masculine scent.

He smiled and crossed to a small cabinet set within the wall. Bringing forth a tall dark bottle, he poured a hefty amount of amber liquid into a large pewter mug. He returned to her side and carefully put the mug in her trembling hand.

"Thank you," she managed to mumble.

"Drink up, lass. 'Twill either make ye feel better, or help ye to rest…looks like ye could use a bit o' both about now. Ye are looking a wee bit pale." He pulled up a second chair and sat before her, swiping his long fingers back through his dripping chestnut hair.

"What is this stuff?" She sniffed the amber liquid and it tickled her nose.

"Just a bit o' barley-bree. Drink up now, there's a good lass."

The foreign lilt to his voice soothed her scattered senses. Anna took a sip of the lukewarm beverage, coughing as it blazed a fiery trail down her throat. Well, if it didn't kill her, the alcohol just might warm her. Anything was better than the salty taste of the sea. She licked the remaining moisture from her lips and glanced around the cabin.

A feeble source of light came from two small lanterns; one swinging precariously from a chain in the low, wood-beamed ceiling, and the other attached to the oak-paneled wall above the desk. Both flames flickered, swaying back and forth with the ship's movement. She caught a glimpse of the dark stormy sea through a deep, multi-pane window that ran along the stern. She was glad to be safe and dry below deck.

Her gaze scanned the authentic nineteenth-century detail of the cabin. This great illusion must be from the many hours she spent researching the history of sailing vessels. The nautical world remained strong in her heart and, evidently, very strong in her scattered brain as well.

A large wooden, leather-bound trunk positioned below the window struck her as vaguely familiar. The captain's table sat centered in the room, spread with charts, maps and other sailing paraphernalia. This was his cabin and that would make him the ship's captain. Her gaze swung around to face him. A blush of warmth crept up her cheeks when he stared back with interest.

Feeling self-conscious, Anna looked away. She inspected the bulky, wood-framed bunk bed. It extended out from the wall with strong chain supports attached to the ceiling. She could imagine getting a good night's rest upon the huge fluffy mattress, lulled into a deep sleep by restless ocean waves.

She pictured the man sitting before her stretched out upon the same bed, probably wearing nothing more than his skivvies. Her heart skipped rope and she was at a total loss for words. This was a purely masculine cabin, bold and organized, and as unique as the man himself.

All the while, the Captain remained quietly watching her, devastating her sensibilities. His ruggedly handsome face bore a deep tan and told of pleasant days at sea, long sunny days without a cloud in the blue sky.

She met his curious gaze again, daring him to speak first. After all, he must have as many questions as she did. Maybe he knew the answer to this strange situation she found herself experiencing. Dream or nightmare, it was all somehow connected with him, his house, and her extremely vivid imagination. So how did she get back to reality now that she felt like a fish out of water?

He broke eye contact for a moment to shake his long wet hair, spraying her with droplets of moisture. Then he reached across and borrowed the towel from her shoulders to dry himself. His dimpled smile enhanced the sparkle in his eyes as he examined her with open curiosity and silent amusement.

Wanton thoughts bolted rampantly through her mind as Anna recalled her erotic dreams. Taking another sip of the fiery liquid, she forced a quivering smile. There was no way he could know about her dreams. She should act normal and go with the flow. Even talking would be preferable to staring at the most attractive thing in the room, which just happened to be him.

Three

"Could you tell me where we are?" Anna asked with more than mere curiosity.

Dark eyebrows lifted in a most tantalizing way as the captain responded, "Off the coast o' Oregon, a wee bit more than we should be by now. We seem to have hit yet another wee storm coming from off shore. I've never seen the like and now the storm seems to be leaving us as strangely as it appeared."

"Oh." She shivered.

Casually stretching his long legs out before him, he paused to rub his jaw and eye her intently. "Do ye feel well enough to return to yer own cabin now, lass?"

"My cabin?"

"Aye." He sat upright and leaned closer, until only a mind-boggling ten inches separated their faces from touching. "Ye did pay passage to board the *Ceilidh*?"

Anna knew she didn't really belong on his ship, or in this dream, even if he didn't. She thought quickly to ward off his asking too many questions, questions for which she had no answers. Stall for time, that's what she needed to do.

"The Kaylee?" Her voice squeaked like a mouse. She could not breathe with him in such close proximity. He could be charming without even trying.

"Aye, my ship," he said, a glint of mischief in his eyes.

"What an interesting name for a ship."

"Tis Scottish. *Ceilidh* means a lively gathering o' highlanders."

"Like a party?"

He chuckled softly. "Aye. I suppose some would call it a party."

Anna swallowed hard and looked away. He was even more appealing in person than in the portrait. The artist who painted the captain's image had caught his teasing, dimpled smile to perfection. He had also captured the deep forget-me-not blue of his eyes. Somehow, just like the memorable flower, she didn't think she could easily forget this man.

His Scottish accent attracted her like a hummingbird to nectar. She loved to listen to him talk. For some reason she had forgotten how many people were foreigners to America during the eighteen hundreds. Mentally shaking off the spell he cast upon her, she concentrated on the matter at hand.

"It's a beautiful ship, by the way."

"Aye, lass." He set his hands upon his knees and cocked his head to the side. "Could ye be one o' the ladies traveling to San Francisco?"

Getting him off the subject was like trying to force a stubborn mule to move when it just plain didn't want to budge an inch. "Yes. That's right…I'm dying to visit good old Frisco again."

"I see." He raised his dark eyebrows in quiet contemplation.

"If this is your ship—that means you must be the captain?" She steered him away from the subject of her origins. What could she say anyway? This is only a dream, buster, so don't get technical on me?

"Aye…that I am. Captain James Adam Duncan at yer service." He flashed her a devilishly lopsided grin.

Her heretofore-resisting heart melted into a puddle of pure pleasure at his feet. No way could she have dreamed up such a hunk.

This whole thing was far too realistic a dream, but she refused to accept the possibility of what might have happened to her otherwise.

The captain refilled her mug. "I do not recall the other ladies being so scantily dressed. Be honest now, lass. Are ye one o' the crew's doxy? Have they managed to smuggle ye aboard without my knowing about it?"

"*Doxy?*" She felt a little shocked at his blunt suggestion. She understood perfectly what the old-fashioned term *doxy* meant. "You've got to be kidding? I'm not anyone's doxy! But, you are right, I don't belong on this ship."

"Aye, ye do, lass. I know why ye stowed aboard, but ye only had to ask. I can be very accommodating for the right price." The sparkle dancing in his eyes convinced her he was totally serious. He was a bit presumptuous, but serious just the same.

"Are you saying I came aboard this ship to seduce you?"

"Oh, aye," he replied. "Ye would not be the first."

Captain Duncan's face bore no sign of a joke. He was not the typical egotistical male. He was plainly stating a simple fact. He was so darned attractive most women fell at his feet, eager to do his bidding. Well, she refused to be one of them.

Anna stood up and sat back down, feeling the alcohol's woozy side effects in her movement. She met his steady blue gaze with a glare. "I should have known you were too good to be true. Somehow, deep-down inside, I knew you would be a womanizer."

"If ye are saying do I like the wenches? Aye. I like them well enough. Especially with a bonny figure like yer own, lass." He winked at her.

She nearly forgot his earlier callous remark watching his charming face. A flood of mixed emotions washed over her as she recalled her wish to be a million miles away from her boring life. Had fate seen fit to grant her wish?

"Honestly, Captain, I really don't have a clue how I arrived on your ship. I'm not sure of anything anymore."

"But ye must know yer name, lass." He leaned forward, placing his large weathered hands upon his knees. "'Tis bound to be a bonny name, as bonny as yerself."

She released a slight laugh, backing away from the intoxicating effect he had upon her. She wasn't sure which was stronger, the whiskey or the captain's charm. "Of course I know my name—it's Anna Bentley."

Feeling strangely confident, she took a big gulp of her drink and gasped at the fire filling her chest. She coughed, putting her hand to her throat. Maybe she should ask how potent the drink was and limit her intake.

"Anna," he repeated slowly, rolling her name over his tongue like sweet candy. "I like yer name, Anna Bentley."

"Captain, I am not here to seduce you. No matter what you may think," she announced boldly. "I don't know any of your crew—and I am definitely not a doxy!"

"My, but ye are a fiery wench!" He reached out to steady her as she attempted to stand. "But ye cannot be running about in yer underclothes, doxy or no. I'll have mutiny on me hands if the ne'er-do-well's on this ship see ye as ye are now, Anna." His gaze swept leisurely over her. "We best be finding ye something to wear 'til yer own clothes are dry."

James knew he should restrain his attraction to this wisp of a woman, but he could not help admiring her strength. She not only stood up to him, she showed no fear. She could be shy and sweet one moment, and as tough as a barnacle the next. He liked her soft feminine features when she smiled, and the way her sea green eyes sparkled with defiance when challenged. It mattered not how she had arrived, only that she was here with him at last. He held back his hunger to hold her, as well as the desire to brand her pouting mouth with a deep, plundering kiss.

She put a hand to her forehead, sighed wearily, and then proceeded to take another sip of the whiskey. "Barley-bree, huh? I feel so relaxed, so sleepy. I wonder—is it possible to fall asleep in a dream?"

"A dream, eh? Well, Anna Bentley, I think maybe ye best lie down for a wee bit. Seeing as how 'tis tipsy ye are," he said, carefully removing the mug from her hand and setting it aside on the nightstand.

He knelt in front of her and removed her shoes, not saying a word about their strange appearance. Nor did he comment on the odd-textured clothing she wore. He only wanted to make her comfortable before she caught a chill. "Now if ye want to remove your damp chemise, I'll be looking away so ye can do it in private."

Anna's mouth dropped open. He expected her to take her clothes off with him in the room? Then she smiled as he turned around and faced the wall. She studied his backside. Maybe cowboys were notorious for the way they looked in a pair of Wranglers, but she would bet dollars to donuts this guy could beat them all hands down in the tight-fitting pants he had on right now.

The thick black material stretched tight over muscular thighs and firm buttocks, outlining his long legs and trim waist to perfection. Her gaze strayed upwards. The damp fabric of his white shirt revealed strong broad shoulders, perfect evidence of exactly how hard he worked for a living.

"Are ye done, Anna?"

She nearly jumped at the sound of his voice and remembered she should be removing her wet clothing, not ogling his brute strength. She quickly did so and slipped beneath the crisp bed sheet. "Okay."

James turned back around, giving swift appraisal to the three scanty items on the floor at his feet. He raised a curious eyebrow, but again he did not question her. What she needed most right now was rest. He bent and tucked the blanket snugly about her before standing to his full height again.

He admitted he liked what he saw. She was the fairest woman he had seen in many a day. Her golden hair hung over the sheet and along her side like a thick twist of rope. He would like to see her hair free and flowing about her shapely form as it had been in his dreams.

Blast! She could not be the woman from his dreams. She could not have appeared out of the raging storm—but she had. She was here with him now. His gaze strayed upwards to her face. She lay quietly looking up at him with a dreamy expression in her eyes. He could not recall a lovelier sight.

Anna swallowed the hunger eating away inside her. To be here with this man was more than she had ever dreamed possible. She wanted to run her fingers through his thick damp hair and snuggle up against the broad expanse of muscles revealed by his half-open shirt, and then kiss those wonderful sensual lips.

Admittedly, she would be devastated if she awoke from this fantasy without first sampling one of his kisses. She shivered, struggling to control the erotic feelings he so easily aroused with a simple look. Geez, she was obsessed with the man. Blame it on the barley-bree, she mused with a silent giggle.

Feeling totally mischievous and very much aware of the effect she had on him, Anna gave him what she hoped was her most alluring smile. "I don't know what is going on or why I'm here, but thanks for sharing the warmth of your cabin."

The expression on his face alerted her that he was going to kiss her. She couldn't deny the spark of anticipation, nor the delightful shiver of excitement she felt as he hunkered down beside the bed and leaned slowly forward.

Another thought ran freely through her mind. What if he didn't stop at a mere kiss? The only man she had ever been intimate with was her ex-husband. Whether he liked to admit it or not, things had not been all that great between them. She had always wondered what it would be like to really let go with a man. Scream with pleasure and cry out in ecstasy, or to do whatever their passionate natures demanded.

A breath of space separated their lips and suddenly she froze, pushing against his chest with the palms of her hands. "No."

"No?"

"You heard me." She pushed a bit harder to keep him at arms-length. "You were about to kiss me and I don't want you to."

"Ah, but ye do, lass. 'Tis only a matter o' time."

James was sure the vixen did not know what an enticing picture she made lying naked in his bed with only a sheet and his damp clothing between them. His passion flamed for a taste of her soft full lips. He was drawn to her by more than mere physical need. It was a need beyond his understanding and he could not deny its power.

A light tap at the cabin door interrupted his thoughts. This was not a good time for company. He chose to ignore the request for entry. A moment later, William Mayhew opened the door. His dark trousers and white cambric shirt were soaked to the skin from the passing storm's intensity. The strapping first mate entered, followed promptly by lumber baron George Stenson, and his wife, Angelique.

James let loose his frustration over being disturbed, taking it out on William. "Blast it all, man! Can ye not see that I'm busy?"

"Begging your pardon, Captain." William's broad grin disappeared and he cleared his throat before continuing, "Mr. Stenson would like a quick word with you now that the storm has passed."

"Oh-oh." Anna giggled and rose up on her elbows to peek over his shoulder.

James pushed her back down again. "This best be important, lad," he grumbled for the first mate's ears alone.

He put his forefinger on Anna's lips to shush her. His gaze lingered longer than necessary upon her sweetly blushing face. Ah, but fate was cruel! A moment more and he could have persuaded her to accept his advances. He stood slowly and stretched, turning to greet his uninvited guests without a trace of embarrassment for being caught with a naked woman in his cabin.

"George, Angel," James acknowledged, a moment of impatience consuming him at their untimely visit. Still, they were his friends. He hastily set aside his desire for Anna and focused on his guests. The sooner he took care of their needs, the sooner he would be able to tend to his own.

Angelique's pretty face turned livid with discomfort. "James! I know you have a reputation with the ladies, but to keep your mistress on board the *Ceilidh*?"

George smiled ruefully and nodded toward Anna in the rumpled bed. "We will not be keeping you, James. I have a few matters to discuss with you about our special cargo before we arrive in port tomorrow morning. It can wait. I did not realize you had company."

"Well, I never! Aren't you even going to say anything, George?" Angelique poked her big burly husband in the ribs with a long perfect finger. "The wanton girl is naked!"

"Angel—" George warned softly. "This is not our business."

James cleared his throat. "I can speak with ye later this evening, George. I have my hands full at this time."

George chuckled. "I can see that you do, James."

"Won't either of you listen to me? She is not wearing a stitch of clothing!" Angelique's eyes narrowed with irritation as she looked from her husband to James and back again. "Well?"

Anna quickly pulled the sheet up around her chin. She wasn't ashamed, but she didn't want to stir up trouble. She felt wonderfully warm and glowing and possibly a bit tipsy from the large amount of barley-bree she had almost inhaled.

Fascinated with the new arrivals, Anna realized their style of dress encouraged the suspicion her mind refused to accept. Maybe somehow she had slipped backwards in time. She shook off the impossible notion and studied the newcomers with interest.

George bore a pleasant youthful face and the husky build of a lumberjack. His curly, dark-blond hair and shaggy beard added to his outdoorsy look, even though he wore a brown woolen suit. He did not appear the least bit upset at finding a woman in the captain's quarters. His mouth quivered with a smile he tried to conceal from his wife.

Angelique was as tall and graceful as she was feminine. Perfect dark brown curls framed her lovely oval face and her violet eyes sparkled with intelligence. She wore a full-length, soft-lavender dress with a short jacket of matching color.

Anna wriggled uncomfortably at the idea of wearing the stiff boning that bound Angelique from her breasts down to her slender waist. She grimaced at the absurd bustle on the woman's backside. Angelique appeared the picture of femininity, but she looked miserable, too.

Anna shivered. She wouldn't be caught dead in such confining clothing. She hiccupped, and then giggled, feeling the carefree effects of the barley-bree.

"George, this woman has been drinking, too!" Angelique quickly backed behind her husband, who in turn smiled cheerfully across at Anna.

Poor James! Anna giggled again. He could do little to defend her innocence. He had been so busy being charming that he had not considered how it would appear if she was found in his bed. Yet, the enticing scoundrel winked over his shoulder at her as he spoke in soft undertones to the Stensons.

Anna didn't quite hear all that he was whispering to his friends, but it had to be something about her. Her heartbeat quickened within her chest. She didn't like being the center of attention, but she didn't enjoy being ignored either. If George and Angelique were impatient enough to barge into the captain's cabin unannounced, then they would just have to live with feeling uncomfortable about it. So why was she the one squirming on the bunk?

Angelique held her small hand out to the captain. "Oh, James. I am so sorry! I thought the worst. Can you forgive me? And please accept our congratulations."

George slapped James heartily on the back. "I never thought I would see the day. All the female hearts in Coo's Bay are breaking this day. I say! Fine business, James!"

Anna laid back and stared at the ceiling...*all the female hearts in Coo's Bay. What's that supposed to mean?* She sat back up and glared at the captain as the meaning became perfectly clear. How could he do this? Because he was the captain and this was his ship, and somehow or other he felt compromised? She sighed in frustration and glanced across at the other sailor to see how he was taking the news.

William nodded in her direction with a curious grin, and then turned his attention over to the captain. "Sir, I'll be taking my leave now. I'm needed on the quarterdeck." He slipped quietly from the cabin, leaving its four occupants in uncomfortable silence.

James walked over and withdrew an amber bottle from the cabinet. He chuckled as a light mood settled over him, then carefully poured whiskey into three mugs.

"Tis time we drank a toast to my new bride," he announced, handing a mug to each of his friends.

James returned to Anna's bedside with a wink of conspiracy. He put her half-empty mug back into her hand, his fingers meeting hers. The slight touch was startling and he could tell she felt it too. She quickly looked away when he sat down beside her and raised his drink in the air.

"To our future together. May time bless our union and hold us as one in its hands," he toasted with a mischievous grin.

"To the future," George and Angelique declared in unison.

Everyone took a sip of the smoky-flavored Scotch.

James pretended not to notice when Anna elbowed him sharply in the side. He inched slightly away from her to avoid another jab to his ribs and offered her his most flirtatious wink.

"To the wonders of marriage." Anna's words slurred slightly.

She gulped the last bit of liquor with a devil-may-care attitude and dropped her empty mug onto the bed. She was fast becoming a lush, but who cared? This couldn't really be happening. She would wake up any moment now, never to sample one of the captain's amorous kisses. Frowning in disappointment, she could feel his heated gaze upon her. She looked up at him, knowing he could read what was on her mind.

He reached across her lap to clasp her hand in his with a gentle squeeze, and then he retrieved her fallen mug and handed it back to her. For some odd reason Anna couldn't explain away, she wished this dream would come true. She would love to be married to the most exciting man God had ever created, even if he did infuriate her by taking control of the situation without asking her advice first. Then again, he was the captain. He set things in order and commanded others' lives. That was his job.

"To my bonny bride, Anna," James said, splashing more whiskey from his mug into hers. "And to our good friends, George and Angel."

"To all of us," George toasted in agreement.

James swallowed the remainder of his drink, watching Anna over the rim of his mug. She had an ill-humored expression on her face and he wondered if he had given her a bit too much of the fine whiskey. He took her empty mug and set it aside.

Angelique nudged her husband's arm. "We will leave you two to your privacy now. Come along, George."

"Yes, dear. We'll talk later, James." George grinned as Angelique tugged at his sleeve impatiently.

"Aye," James confirmed, and then whispered to his friend. "Do not worry, George. I'll be sure to save ye a case o' my best whiskey." He turned and placed a brotherly kiss upon Angelique's cheek. "I do forgive ye, Angel."

The cabin door clicked closed behind the Stensons, leaving James alone with the angry young woman in his bed. He would laugh at her fiery expression, except he knew she was facing the dilemma of her unusual presence aboard his ship. He had just added to both their problems by announcing a phony marriage to his business partner.

"Are you nuts?" Anna hissed immediately. She scooted back against the wall, yanking the sheet with her to get as far away from his dazzling appeal as possible.

"Nuts?" James favored her with a rakish expression as he sauntered across the cabin toward her. "Explain yerself, lass."

"Why did you tell them a thing like that, anyway?" She was a little nervous to be the sole subject of his disturbingly close scrutiny. She wished he would go away and give her time alone to think about what to do. If there was anything she could do to get back to reality.

"I did it for yer reputation, Anna. Ye said ye are no doxy. I cannot let them think ye are now can I." He sat on the edge of the bed and put his hand under her chin, turning her face toward him. "I should not have had ye in my quarters. Not to mention the kissing we were about to be doing. Nay, I'll not shy from my duty as a man o' honor."

Anna felt hit in the head by the unrealistic logic of nineteenth-century reasoning. "Duty? Are you kidding? I hardly know you. I told you no, and I meant it."

"Anna, 'tis only a matter o' time. But as for yer clothes—"

"My summer dress is perfectly decent—in my time," her voice trailed into a whisper as she acknowledged her words. "I'm not from this time. At least, I don't think I am." Frightened by the strange inner turmoil rumbling to life inside her, she sought the comfort of his steady gaze. "Oh, dear God!"

James wrapped his arm around her shoulders when he saw fear dawn in her eyes. He kissed the top of her head, gently rocking her back and forth. "Easy, lass. Ye'll be all right now. I'll not let anyone harm ye."

Anna released a choked sob. "I don't know what happened up there on deck."

She couldn't control her pent-up emotions any longer. She buried her face in his damp shirt, crying her heart out in the silent strength of his embrace. His masculine smell and the warmth of his hard-muscled chest soon calmed her, soothing her troubled heart. Shock drained from her and acceptance seeped in quietly; there wasn't a thing she could do but let it be. Fate had seen fit to throw her a big one and she would just have to live with it. Gradually, she relaxed in his arms.

"There now, my bonny wee lass, I'll take care o' ye. What's this about yer not from my time? 'Tis the whiskey ye been drinking?"

Anna looked up into his soulful eyes, wiping tears from her cheeks. "I—don't know—hic—anymore. Maybe—I'm dead."

He leaned down and placed a sweet kiss upon her lips. A kiss so tender it left her breathless. "Tis alive ye are, lass. Ye feel warm and lovely in my arms."

He released a hungry groan and pulled her from the bed, sheet and all, onto his lap. A shaky smile was all she had time for before his lips returned to cover hers. His hands moved along the bare skin of her back. Exciting little tingles coursed through her. She let go of the sheet and slipped her arms about his neck to pull him closer.

Their mouths mated in pleasure and her heart raced to keep time with his. Kissing him was better than anything she had ever experienced. She hated to think what James could do to her if they went much farther. She didn't care. It was what she wanted, what they both wanted. She wanted to tear his damp clothes from his body and let him make love to her, long and passionately, here and now.

He was so devastatingly male. She loved his dark auburn hair that fell in thick waves to his broad shoulders. His smooth, well-muscled skin, bronzed from the sun, smelled pleasantly of bay rum. His eyes looked deep into her soul, making her feel strangely at home in this faraway place.

This morning seemed a very long time ago. If this was a dream then this morning had not really happened. Would it ever happen? If she had somehow traveled through time, how had she gotten aboard his ship from the balcony of the old house? Her mind reeled in desperate confusion.

Breathless from his kisses, Anna leaned away from his embrace. "Captain? What year is this?"

James was not sure if the bonny lass were sober, but he knew she was real—deliciously so. He decided to humor her, as if she truly did not know what year it was. "Well, Anna, 'tis the year o' our lord eighteen hundred and eighty."

Her sudden gasp made him think she might empty her stomach of the barley-bree. He should not be thinking of seducing her when she wasn't quite herself. He settled her back onto the bed and covered her with a dry blanket. "I need to speak with William for a wee bit. After ye have slept a while ye will feel a whole lot better."

He stood and smiled down at her. He was looking forward to getting to know her better. Right now, she needed to sleep off the whiskey's haze that seemingly left her a bit muddle-headed and then they would talk.

Calming the urge to give her one more kiss, he returned the whiskey bottle to the small cupboard and strode swiftly to the door. Once there, he paused and looked back over his shoulder at her. "It does not matter how ye came or from where, Anna Bentley. I only hope ye are here to stay."

With a last glimpse of her creamy shoulders peeking from beneath the covers and her full, kiss-swollen lips begging him to stay he slipped quietly out the door. His troubled mind went over the past two hours as he made his way across sea swept decks toward the helm.

Anna had appeared quite unexpectedly right before his very eyes. It was a good thing William had been busy at the ship's wheel, for her arrival was truly a shock to behold. Like a misty specter from the grave, she took the shadowy form of a lovely woman. She became so tangible she captured his heart and soul. He felt positive she was the same mysterious female who haunted his dreams.

When he held her in his arms, he knew she was not mere fantasy. Where had she come from…his dreams? That would explain her sudden appearance on board the *Ceilidh* while so far out to sea. Och, no! It was not truly possible—or was it?

Drawn to her in a way he had never experienced before, he dare not let her know he had seen her in his dreams. No, she would not likely understand. She might even think he was tricking her—or that he had gone totally mad.

Bloody hell! Maybe he was mad. He sure did not enjoy accusing her of sneaking aboard his ship to seduce him. He had even called her a common seaside doxy. He would not blame her if she wanted to leave, but their first kiss had been fatal to his heart. He could not let her leave him now.

His dangerous thoughts unnerved his usual ability to control his emotions. How would he explain to her what had really happened? He could not. Yet, the memory of her sweet kisses and the way she had responded would linger upon his lips. Aye, and in his mind, keeping away the blasted damp chill of the summer storm and haunting his soul as never before.

~ * ~

Eighteen hundred and eighty! Anna closed her eyes and shook her head in disbelief. There was no way she could have traveled back in time. Time travel was not physically possible, even though scientists and romantics had dreamed of accomplishing it somehow, someday. Still, the fact remained she was aboard a vintage sailing vessel with a man who had lived more than one hundred years before she was born.

Anna sighed wearily and stared at the closed cabin door. She did not know how long it would be before the captain returned, but she couldn't stay naked in his bed. Easing slowly to her feet and dragging the bed sheet with her, she looked around for something to wear while her clothes were drying.

She threw back the heavy lid on the captain's trunk and discovered a pair of black wool pants and a white collarless shirt. Without hesitation, she slipped out of the cool sheet and pulled on the warm heavy pants.

Giggling, Anna noted they were quite large around her small waist. The captain's long legs and wide waist would fill the same pair of pants to perfection. She bent to dig farther into the deep trunk. Straightening up slowly, she examined a big red silk scarf for a possible belt.

James opened the door to his quarters and paused inside the entry, folding his arms across his chest with sudden interest. What was the vixen up to now? She was much too busy rummaging through his trunk to notice his arrival. He turned and silently closed the cabin door, slipping the lock into place. He knew he should announce himself, but he wanted to see what she was doing first.

The lass stood naked from the waist up, her silky back and creamy shoulders inviting his touch. His eager body filled with desire as a growing need possessed him. It had been a long while since he had enjoyed the intimate company of a woman and he had never found one as attractive as Anna Bentley.

Anna felt a familiar tingling at the back of her neck. She peered cautiously over her shoulder, releasing a surprised gasp when she saw the captain leaning casually against the closed door. She quickly covered her breasts by crossing her arms over them. A feeble attempt to disguise their fullness was better than allowing him to freely ogle her nudity.

"Did you ever think to knock, Captain?" She scolded him with as much dignity as she could muster under the circumstances, only to see his eyes sparkle and dance with amusement.

He could speak a thousand words with those magnificent eyes. With her back to him, she finished tying the scarf around her waist and held the shirt up to cover her bare breasts. She turned slowly to find him still studying her.

"You should leave, you know." Her heart skipped a beat at his brazen curiosity. "I do like my privacy."

"Aye…that I know. But 'tis amused I am to be watching ye. Now what do ye think ye are doing wearing a man's clothes, lass?" His long strides brought him quickly across the cabin to stand like an immovable bronze statue directly in front of her. He was close, far too close.

Anna clasped the shirt even tighter against her bare chest, a futile attempt to dissuade the fiery longing in his eyes. "My nudity was causing a crisis in your cabin, or don't you remember? So quit complaining."

"Nay, I'll never complain. 'Tis a lovely body ye have, Anna." James leaned forward, lowering his voice to a mere whisper. "There's no need for ye to be so shy."

He cupped her face in his hands and placed a tender kiss on her forehead. His lips trailed a gentle pathway down her cheek, teasing her senses to startling awareness. She closed her eyes and released a contented sigh, leaning into him as his mouth brushed hers in feather-light caresses, teasing and promising.

A sharp knock at the door broke the spell of intimacy between them. James released her reluctantly and stepped back. He ached to make love to her this very moment. His face flushed with heat as he steadied his anger at the second untimely interruption.

"Cover yerself, Anna." He swept her back into his embrace for another quick taste of her honey-sweet lips. "Ye have my promise to finish this later."

A deep blush flooded her cheeks in response. She pulled the long-sleeved shirt over her head and tucked it into her baggy pants. "Am I presentable?"

"Aye." All he could respond with was a low growl. Presentable? He had preferred her earlier attire—absolutely nothing. His frustration at being disrupted from what had been the foreplay to seduction was barely in check. He opened the cabin door to find his first mate waiting patiently, a smile threatening to break his sober expression.

James set his personal life aside and took on the countenance of captain. "Step in, William."

William Mayhew was a strong, well-built young man whose appearance oft-times resembled a pirate. He wore his black hair caught neatly into a braid at the nap of his neck and a full dark beard covered his square jaw. The ladies found him extremely pleasing, which only made it more difficult to locate him when in port. But then James had his own weakness when it came to the ladies. Only right now his weakness strayed toward a green-eyed lady whose loveliness outshone all others.

William paused just inside the door. "You wanted my report, sir?"

"Aye, I do."

"I feel as though I am intruding where I am not wanted," William admitted, nodding toward the far side of the cabin where Anna stood. "I can come back later, sir."

"Nay." James had ordered him to check in before relieving Jock at the helm. He also needed to clarify his relationship with Anna, before things got out of hand and numerous rumors spread about the ship. "I need to be talking to ye on a personal matter, as well, William."

William smiled and nodded a greeting to Anna. "Evening, Ma'am."

"Hi. Sorry about earlier."

William coughed into his fist. "I understand, ma'am."

James glanced over at Anna. His heart raced at the sight of her simple beauty. Even dressed in his clothes, hanging loose about her feminine curves, her appeal had not diminished. Her long golden hair lay over her shoulder in a loose thick plait, falling well past her breasts to caress her small waist. She bent to roll up the long trouser legs. The sight of her round derrière, outlined to perfection by the black wool, caused his blood to thicken with desire. He shook his head before he lost track of what he should be doing and turned his attention back to the task at hand.

Gesturing for William to sit at the table, James offered him a drink. "Take a wee bit o' spirits to warm yer insides, William."

"Thank you, Captain." William smiled across at Anna and raised his mug to her. "Here's to you, lovely lady, may your marriage to the good captain be fruitful."

"To Anna." James raised his mug in agreement before downing its contents.

William turned obediently to his drink and took a lusty swallow, then set the mug aside. "It's been far too long a voyage this time, sir. I don't remember your lady boarding."

"Do ye not?" James chuckled. He did not recall her boarding in the usual manner either. Her boarding had been unbelievable, but it had happened right before his eyes.

"The sea is calm now, sir," William said, switching the subject to his report. "The *Ceilidh* weathered the storm well, as usual. We should reach Mendocino on schedule, and Jock says he can handle the helm for a bit longer. He says for me to tell you to get some needed rest, Captain."

"Does he now? Drink up, lad." Not even Jock taking control of the ship could muster his temper at this time. His gaze strayed over to Anna. She looked more delicate and ethereal than ever as he watched her pace the far side of his cabin.

Refilling William's mug and then his own, James stretched languidly before revealing the truth to his trusted ship's mate. "There's a wee matter o' privacy I'll be needing to share with ye, William." He glanced from his first mate to Anna and back again. He cleared his throat. "The lass and I are not legally wed. 'Twas a necessary tale to tell the Stensons. Angel needed to believe the marriage already done for Anna's sake. I plan to make amends and marry the lass when we reach Mendocino."

"My compliments on your exceptional choice, Captain. I cannot say you have ever made a bad choice, but this time you have excelled."

"Aye, 'tis a match made in heaven." He winked mischievously across at Anna and expelled a low chuckle at the menacing glare she shot him in return. The wee feisty minx! Her sweet lips betrayed her vexed feelings. He would enjoy enticing her to follow her heart's true desire.

Four

Anna shifted restlessly from one foot to the other. She had a queasy stomach and desperately wanted out of the cabin. Her eye caught the captain's and she looked away from the meaningful intensity of his gaze. The nerve of him to discuss her as though she were not in the cabin, then turn and flirt with her so openly. The man was a true rogue. Granted, he was the best-looking rogue she could ever dream up, but a rogue nonetheless.

"I believe I would like some fresh air. If you'll excuse me, gentlemen." She held her head high as she sidled past the table where the two men were sitting with their drinks.

James caught her hand in his strong grasp, pulling her to a halt by his side. "Nay, never alone, lass. I have warned ye about my crew. Jock, Cookie, and William here...ye can trust. But the rest o' the lot ye cannot trust at all." He stood up beside her, lacing his fingers through hers. The intimate contact felt good and he tugged her closer. "Come join us, William. 'Tis like to take the both o' us to keep her steady on her feet."

"Aye, sir." William stood, wiping the grin from his face with the back of his hand.

"Are you insinuating that I'm— hic?" She paused to catch her breath, "...drunk?" James guided her gently out the cabin door, a smile curving his lips at her protest. "A wee bit, love. Ye are not used to good Scotch whiskey, I'll wager."

"Nor to the sea," William added as he joined the captain in assisting her up the steep narrow stairway.

Anna wasn't quite prepared for the ice-cold blast of salt spray that assaulted them upon reaching the upper deck. Wiping her dripping face with her hands, she cursed under her breath. Standing beside her, the two stalwart men broke out in hearty laughter.

"I thought you said the storm was leaving us, William." She pulled away from his steadying hold. Reeling sideways, she gripped the rail firmly just before the next wave washed across the deck to drench her completely. This was not at all enjoyable. She wasn't sure what was rolling more, the ship's deck or her quivering stomach.

"Tis common to be sick, Anna. Lean over the rail when ye feel the need." James wrapped his arms around her from behind and held her secure against him. "I'll not let ye fall overboard, lass. Yer safe with me."

Anna was about to curse him when she looked up over her shoulder and saw genuine concern in his deep blue eyes. Damn, the rogue! Why did he have to be so sexually desirable and sweetly compassionate, too? He bore all the qualities she envisioned in a good man. A man who could hold her interest and be her equal. But James didn't exist in her time and she still wasn't sure how she arrived in his.

"Thanks." She managed a weak smile as waves of pain and nausea rumbled to the surface. She leaned forward over the rail. "Ohhh—"

James held her around the waist with one arm, while his large hand rubbed her back in comforting circles. She wanted to turn around in his arms and take in the full measure of his concern for her well-being. Before she could move an inch, a weird sensation crawled up her legs making her limbs tingle. She was about to faint. Darkness crept over her senses and she leaned heavily into the captain's strong embrace.

~ * ~

Dawn's first light shadowed the captain's cabin as Anna opened her eyes. Stretching leisurely, she nearly purred in blissful contentment. She was warm, snug, and cozy. Her tired eyes fluttered closed. She simply needed a few more minutes of sleep. Curling up on her side, her feet rubbed against something hazily familiar. She reached out a hand and felt the warm bed beside her—and a long naked thigh.

Suddenly wide-awake, she popped into an upright position and scowled down at Captain James Adam Duncan, lying soundly asleep and snoring softly. She had the undeniable urge to shove him right off the large bunk. How dare he climb into bed with her? Wait just a darn minute. She could not remember getting into bed herself last night. He must have put her here.

She stretched and rubbed the back of her neck to soothe its stiffness. Her hands touched the soft wrinkled fabric of the shirt she wore—his shirt. With a gasp of realization she peeked under the covers, her legs were perfectly bare. So were his. In fact, so was every last steely male inch of him.

James observed her through thick lashes. He knew she was awake having felt her movements against him. Now she sat with the most perplexing expression on her blushing face. The temptation to pull her into his arms was strong. Only with a great degree of self-control was he able to resist his quick rising interest in her closeness.

"You low-down, rotten jerk!" She beat her small fist against his bare chest. "What do you think you are doing in my bed?"

No sense in pretending he was asleep any longer. "Have ye lost yer bloody mind, lass?" He brought his arms up in self-defense, lowering them only to glare back at her. "Tis my bed we are sharing here—or do ye not recall?"

Her face flamed with passion. "I remember, all right. You tried to get me drunk with that damned old barley-bree!"

"Aye." He sat up with a frown. "Do ye know cursing is not very ladylike, lass?"

Anna's temper rose to the limit. Men were always the same, no matter who, what or where they were. It did not matter how much he appealed to her physically, she needed some space and she needed it now.

"I did not get ye drunk, Anna. 'Twas the sea that made ye sick."

"You tried to take advantage of me—don't deny it."

"Advantage o' ye?"

"Oh, never mind!"

Ah—but she was lovely when angry. James grasped her firmly about the waist and held tight as she struggled to remove herself from his bed. Her silky body was still warm from sleep and her loose blond hair wrapped around them like a velvet cloak.

"Is it vexing me ye are, lass? Or would it be my passion ye are wanting?" He didn't give her time to argue. He pulled her down on top of him, his lips meeting hers in an intoxicating kiss.

Anna gasped and placed her hands on his firm-muscled chest in protest. The movement brought her thigh against his hard arousal, throbbing in time with her traitorous heart. His warm lips upon her mouth set her body aflame. His masterful hands explored her burning flesh, holding her prisoner on top of him. He nibbled tenderly at her ear, coaxing her to relax and enjoy the sweet bliss.

She moaned in near surrender. An incredibly passionate lover like the captain did not come along every day. To yield to his undeniable charm would be pure heaven. She had long since denied herself ever feeling like this. With sudden reckless abandon, she resigned herself to his seduction.

"Please," she whimpered softly against his jaw.

James slid his arms easily around her small waist, pulling her firmly against the length of his masculine frame. He rolled them over on the bed. To hold her in his arms was temptation at its best; to make love to her would be conquering a dream.

"Anna—" His lips pressed lightly to hers at first, and then gently he covered her mouth in tiny nibbles. An expert at persuasion, his kiss slowly became more demanding, exploring the intimate hunger of their need for each other.

Anna reached up to run her fingers through his thick hair and groaned pleasurably when his kiss deepened in response. Her reaction to him shocked her, yet she could not pull away. He was the raging fire and she the delicate moth. And like a moth she was drawn to him, his lightest touch consuming her in passion's flames.

The whisper light caress of his lips was a delicious hypnotic sensation and she responded to him eagerly. She wrapped her arms around his neck and pulled him closer, succumbing to the sweet aphrodisiac of his lovemaking. She knew this enticing rascal from the portrait in the old house. Masterful seduction was his hallmark and she was about to be most willingly seduced.

James marveled at the strange new feelings coursing through him. His mouth moved tenderly over hers, devouring its sweet softness. He wanted more of this beautiful temptress…much, much more. His body pressed against her soft curves like a sailing ship upon a turbulent sea. Only she was the sea nymph luring him with her siren's song, and he was the conqueror battling a stormy sea of passion. Her uninhibited responses and her delicate lips beneath his own left him yearning to sample all of her seductive charms.

Anna squeaked with pleasure as they rolled again and she found herself astride his hips. He continued his romantic assault on her heated skin, moving her up and down with the pressure of his hands upon her thighs. She shivered in delight. His lips left her mouth to trail kisses down her neck, pausing to nuzzle her sensitive skin before easing down the vee of her shirt.

Wait! She was not prepared to roast by the flames of desire, only to be discarded along with the ashes after his interest waned. She pushed away from him, panting with need. "No—please."

His questioning gaze met hers, his tumidity a pulsing promise between them. "Do ye not like it, lass?"

"We can't do this," she said in a strangled whisper. Was this only a moment's lust she was feeling, or was her heart truly becoming involved? She couldn't tell with him in this close proximity. She needed time to think, away from his passionate touch.

"I am not so sure I can stop." James studied her face, his physical frustration mounting. "Tis not what I want, Anna, but what ye want o' me."

He lifted her from him with ease, plopping her down upon the bed, and swung his legs over the side. Running his fingers through his hair, he stood bare-naked and stretched his arms above his head. Then he stood for a moment, staring out the stern window at the glorious sunrise and fighting to control his raging need for the woman in his bed.

Anna tried to look away, but her gaze was drawn to his large sinewy frame. Built like a Greek god, his skin appeared smooth and bronze in the early morning light. He was not a bit modest, either. She watched as he reached for his pants hanging over the ladder-back chair. He turned around, giving her a full view of his evident sexual need for her. He didn't even stop dressing when he caught her watching him. Instead, his lopsided smile became smug and he winked at her, the handsome, taunting rogue.

"Do ye like what ye see, lass?" His low timbre voice teased her unmercifully. "Tis yers for the taking."

"Get lost, you arrogant beast!" She threw a pillow at him, embarrassed because she enjoyed checking him out. She couldn't have resisted if she had tried. His soft chuckle reached out to her and she found herself smiling back. She shook her head, trying to dispel her wayward thoughts.

"Is there anything I can get ye before I go on my rounds?" James hoped she would relent and let him show her the wonders of the flesh to be had within his arms.

"I need a bath," she requested suddenly, moving to the bed's edge and dangling her shapely bare legs over the side in temptation. "I feel gross."

"Gross?" He tucked his long white shirt into his trousers, and then looked up at her again. "Ye mean ye feel dirty."

Her gaze met his with limpid green defiance. "Yes, that's exactly what I mean. I'm all salty and I smell—" she paused to pull her shirt up and sniff it. "I smell like a liquor store—among other things—and it's gross."

He raised an eyebrow at her curious expressions. "If 'tis a bath ye will be wanting, then we'll get ye one." He bent down to pull on his boots. "Can I ask ye something, Anna Bentley?"

A cautious smile lit her face. "Sure."

"How is it ye come to be here? Do ye know?"

She shook her head. "I don't know how time travel works, but that must be what happened to me. This can't be a dream or I would be awake by now."

"Nay, 'tis not a dream. My life is real enough." He wished he could ease her pain of not knowing. What did it feel like to travel through time? Did she leave family and friends behind in the future? There was so much he wanted to ask her and so much he wanted to know. "I cannot explain it m'self," he admitted.

"Nor can I," she whispered sadly, turning away from him.

James reached for her, pulling her back against his chest and encircling her in his arms. She didn't resist, but leaned more fully into him. Bending over her shoulder, he placed his cheek next to hers and smiled. Her silky skin brushed against him and she released a troubled sigh. He closed his eyes, soaking in her feminine presence.

He loved her sweet smell, much like the lavender that grew in the highlands of Scotland. She did not smell gross to him at all. He wanted her to feel more at ease on his ship and in his time. If she wanted a bath he would order a bath for her, but he did not want to let her out of his embrace just yet. He needed to hold her for a wee bit longer.

"Can ye tell me what ye do remember, Anna?"

Anna stared out the stern window and relaxed comfortably into his strong embrace. "I remember standing on the balcony and looking through the old spyglass at a sailing yacht. My eyes began to hurt, my knees went weak, and I think I fainted. When I came to my senses I was hanging onto the ship's rail with water washing over me and then—you were there." With her last words, she turned in his arms to face him.

"A spyglass ye say? Did it have any markings?"

"A sailing ship, I think."

James released his hold on her and crossed the cabin to his desk. He opened an ornately carved wooden box lined in purple velvet and withdrew a long brass spyglass. "This was my father's, and his father's before him. 'Tis part o' my heritage."

"It's your spyglass?" Anna had only held the nautical instrument for a few moments, yet knew it was one and the same. She backed away and sat on the edge of the bed, shivering as an eerie chill raced up her spine.

"Aye." James sat down beside her. "My great-grandfather was an Admiral in King George's navy. He helped the English defeat the Dutch at Camperdown in 1797. King George gave him the title o' Viscount for his services, as well as this wee token o' his royal appreciation." He offered the unique spyglass for her inspection.

"I don't want to touch it." Anna pulled back from the shiny brass instrument. She studied his face as he continued to explain more about the curious piece. He was very proud of his genetics. She admired that in a man.

"Do ye see the markings, lass? A ship under full sail is Clan Duncan's heraldic badge. The Latin inscription *Disce parti* means, "learn to suffer." 'Tis a fitting motto for my family since the English ran us out o' Scotland after they had declared peace with our clan."

"Where did you find the spyglass? I thought I dropped it."

"Ye were holding the spyglass when ye appeared in the mist. I always keep it here in my quarters. 'Tis a tie to my father and sort o' my good luck charm. Ye see—there's a bit o' legend passed down with it. 'Tis said the owner can find his true love, wherever she may be. Though I did not think ye would have to travel through time to find me, lass."

Anna let his words sink in. It wasn't logical—therefore it couldn't be. She jumped to her feet and nervously paced the floor, biting back the sob that threatened to tear from her throat. Her mind did not want to accept the cold facts of her surroundings.

"Are you telling me that the spyglass brought me back in time?"

"Anna—" He stood and reached for her.

She backed quickly away. She could not let him touch her. His power over her emotions was much too strong. Escape was her only thought. Pushing swiftly past him, she threw open the heavy cabin door and ran blindly up the stairs, tears coursing down her cheeks.

James wanted to stop her, wrap her in his arms and make all her troubles go away. He wanted the impossible. She accepted for herself what had happened. Being pulled back to his time from the distant future must have been quite a shock to her senses.

He stared down at the spyglass in his hand. Could it be possible the legend was true? Was Anna the woman meant to capture his heart? She had come through the portals of time to appear on his ship. He was the first to see her, and immediately recognize her as the woman who haunted his dreams.

James walked over and set the spyglass back in its case. He opened the bottom drawer of the desk and slipped the case carefully inside, then shut the drawer, and turned the key in the lock. He dropped the key into his pocket for safekeeping. Something told him he must prevent Anna from ever touching the spyglass again. Considering her fear of the article, he was sure it would be safe locked within his desk.

His heart skipped a beat at the thought of her name. He had to find her before she attracted the unwanted attentions of his lusty crew.

~ * ~

Breathlessly gaining the sunlit deck, Anna paused and glanced around her. Wind blew gently at the sails above as the ship headed in toward land. Steep bluffs loomed in the distance. It would not be long before they reached port. She wasn't quite sure whether it was a good thing or not. Her mind refused to accept the obvious and yet, her heart had already grown quite fond of the sea captain.

Earlier she had been so sure everything was just a figment of her wild imagination. Now things appeared much too real. The antique ship was in excellent condition. The burly men scrambling around the rigging and cleaning the deck all wore authentic outfits of nineteenth-century sailors. This could still be a movie set, but there were no cameras or film crews. There was nothing to do but to accept the truth—she was in the past.

A dreadful fear flooded her senses. No one would really miss her. Other than the attorney, no one even knew why she had left San Francisco. Dan had tried to appease her by leaving the house-warming basket, but she had not even acknowledged its receipt. Besides, he was such a jerk he would probably never attempt to find out why she didn't respond. He would just go on his obnoxious way and, hopefully, he would never bother her again. Maybe she wouldn't have to worry about it. After all, she didn't have a clue how she would get back to the twenty-first century.

A seagull flew overhead and cried out its mournful cry, echoing her mixed emotions. Lost at sea or lost in time, it was an unsettled feeling. She lowered her gaze back to the ship and her heart tumbled in her chest. The captain appeared at the top of the stairs. His face looked troubled until he spotted her.

James reached her side and gathered her into his arms in a possessive gesture. "Are ye all right, lass? I thought ye might throw yerself overboard. Anna?"

She laughed softly through a heavy flow of tears and wiped nervously at her cheeks. She was so confused and so frightened. But it did feel comforting to be held in his strong embrace. She had no wish to back away, or to seek an answer to the how and why of what had happened.

She looked up and saw his concern, and knew she should try to explain. "I had to see up here for myself. I'm really here aren't I? It's really 1880."

"Aye, lass."

"James—you are real too. I saw you in my house—or your house. Anyway—first I thought maybe I had dreamed you up or something. You know, because I saw your portrait and you were so darned handsome and all. Well, then I wanted to write about you. The way you might have been when you were alive. Good Lord, I was only fantasizing. I honestly didn't mean for this to happen."

"Anna, 'twas meant to be. We have no control over the matter."

She smiled and looked into his eyes, lingering tears still upon her cheeks. "Do you really think so?"

"Aye, lass, I do. I also think we should go below to continue this discussion. Ye are not properly dressed for company right now."

She stepped back from his embrace and noticed the curious stares of his men. "Oh yeah—I guess you're right. Sorry."

James slipped his arm protectively around her. In his large cambric shirt that hung well above her knees, she looked quite appealing. He pulled her closer, hugging her to his broad chest in an attempt to cover her charms from his lusty, gawking crew. The desire to protect her overwhelmed and surprised him. He grinned and nestled his face against her soft cheek.

"Let's get below, Anna. Ye will catch yer death." He signaled William to join them and guided Anna toward the ship's stern as the crew looked on in rapt interest.

William caught up with them at the stairs, a smile showing his amusement. "You know, Captain, this is the first time the crew has seen you fuss over any woman, whether a brazen wench or a beautiful lady. I think they wonder at your sudden change in behavior."

"Aye, they might."

William chuckled. "They have been asking if the domineering, devil-may-care rogue they signed on with has gone a bit soft for the lady."

"I do not need any of yer teasing at this time, William. Help me get the lass below so I can see to her needs. The crew should be busy at their tasks and not wondering about the capabilities of their captain."

James held his temper in check, not wanting to upset Anna. He would see to the curious questions of his crew later. The men enjoyed a hearty laugh, he knew, but he would not let them laugh at Anna's expense.

Upon entering his quarters, James led Anna over to the bed and wrapped a blanket around her shoulders. She shivered and smiled up at him. He bent to brush his lips against her forehead, and then turned to his first mate standing quietly at the door.

"Thank ye for coming, William. Anna would like a bath and breakfast would be in order, as well. Stand a guard at my door, if ye will. Pick a man ye can trust, for now 'tis well-known Anna is aboard. They need not know she is anything more than a common wench, aboard to indulge in my pleasure. 'Tis a more likely thing for them to believe. But let them know, I will not have her touched by the likes' o' them."

"Aye, Captain." William accepted his orders and turned to leave, pausing before closing the door. "Captain? Will you be wanting me to see to the unloading of the special cargo in port?"

"Nay, lad. I'll be above shortly to see to that."

William left and James turned to face Anna. He had laid claim to her in front of them all, and it bothered him that the crew was well aware of his prize. Her safety was of utmost importance. He had no doubts that he could protect her, as long as he was nearby, but his crew, of fifty seasoned seamen, was sometimes a rowdy lot. They would not understand her unique situation and could be too randy to control—especially if they saw much more of her lovely charms.

He reached down and took her hand in his, careful not to overstep his bounds after their last encounter in his bed. His heart ached for what she must be experiencing. To have lost all things familiar would be devastating. At the same time, his heart filled with complete happiness. He knew without a doubt she had captured his very soul.

"Captain?" Her scratchy voice was barely a whisper.

She looked so fragile to him now. Was it because she had accepted her fate, or because her wind-tousled look brought a quickening to his blood? She was even more beautiful with her long golden hair flowing freely to her waist. Her small hand trembled slightly within his. When she smiled up at him, her bewitching green eyes stole his heart.

"I've been wondering," she said softly, "...what is it you do? William said something about a special cargo? Are you a pirate?"

His deep laughter filled the cabin. "Pirate? Is that what ye think me to be?"

Her eyes grew large. "Are you?"

"Nay." He grinned at her innocence. "Though I have experienced the way o' it, 'tis not to my liking to be hung from a blasted yardarm. 'Tis the lumber trade I deal in, lass. The *Ceilidh* transports lumber up and down the northwest coast. Sometimes we sail to the Sandwich Islands, as well."

"Sandwich islands? Oh yeah—Hawaii."

"Aye, George calls it the territory o' Hawaii."

"George?" Anna rubbed her cold nose with the blanket edge and yawned. There was so much to learn, especially if she didn't want to make a fool of herself and stick out like a sore thumb. "You mean, the same George who was here...works with you? I thought he was just a friend."

"Aye, George is a very old friend. He runs the lumber mill and takes care o' the affairs on land. I do the shipping and receiving. And we share the profit o' this very good trade." He touched her cheek with his palm and brushed away a lingering tear with his thumb. "Are ye feeling mended, lass?"

Anna shook her head in negative response. Her skin tingled from the slight touch of his large rough thumb rubbing across her cheek so tenderly. She wanted him to go on telling her about this strange new life in 1880. His voice was soothing and his accent entertaining. She had never felt such powerful male essence before. Without a doubt, she knew she didn't even need the whiskey to have him intoxicate her.

"I don't think I will fit in very well in your time."

"Ye can if ye try. Ye have the knowledge o' yer past to guide ye." He shifted position and stared down at his black leather boots. "Can ye tell me what 'tis like in the future, Anna Bentley?"

How could she explain the future? What could she say to him so he wouldn't think she was totally bananas? She didn't want to frighten him with tales about machines resembling huge monsters. Or try to explain complexities of the marvelous inventions that made her daily life so easy in comparison to his. A life she had taken for granted. Her futuristic knowledge would only frustrate her in this era where everything was so basic.

"The future is very different, Captain." She removed her hand from his and settled back on the bed. She lay staring up at the ceiling, as though just thinking about her own time could take her back. "In my time machines do almost everything for you. All you have to do is turn them on and off. Electricity runs almost everything. Some things are solar powered and then there is gas—" her voice trailed off as she noticed the wondrous expression on his face. "You don't understand a thing I'm saying, do you."

He glanced away, then back again. "Och, 'tis pulling my leg ye are. Ye are saying that people do not work anymore."

She giggled. "Oh they work all right—just in a more mental capacity. Hard labor still exists, too. There are many things that make life more comfortable, easier to tolerate the everyday trivial chores."

He nodded. "Go on, Anna."

"Well, we have huge flying ships called airplanes, or jets, actually. Jets carry people clear across the country and even around the world in a matter of hours."

"Like birds, ye mean?" James felt awkward asking, but could not imagine a form of transportation resembling the feathered fowl. He could not conceive the miracles Anna mentioned, but he loved to watch her face light up in memory of what she knew so well. "Do they have wings?"

Anna's eyebrows rose in uncertainty. "Well, yes. Most airplanes resemble birds in flight and they do have wings. They're made of metal and powered by—" She stopped when she saw his amusement over what she was trying to describe. She could almost sense his next question. "No, Captain, they don't have feathers. They fly high in the sky using the wind for support, much the same way your ship uses the sea for buoyancy."

He rubbed his chin thoughtfully. "Tell me more, lass."

"We mostly travel in cars—horseless carriages? They travel much faster than the fastest horses, but people still keep horses for pets, racing and shows. Probably the worst thing about the future is that this beautiful free country becomes so over-populated people have no place to live."

"Why not build more houses? We have lumber enough to build most anything."

She would be treading treacherous ground if she brought up the damage men like George Stenson wrecked on the prime virgin forests of the great Northwest. "There is not enough land in the right places, unfortunately. Everyone wants to live in or near the big cities."

"Aye, 'tis why San Francisco is growing so fast."

"Yes. San Francisco gets huge." Her thoughts wavered for a moment. San Francisco had yet to be devastated by the 1906 earthquake and the terrible fire that leveled the proud city. She swallowed hard, not wanting to predict that one for him.

He leaned back on the bed with her and crossed his arms over his broad chest. "Tell me more, Anna. This future o' yers sounds a bit exciting."

"The future is exciting, I guess. It's stimulating. It's full of miraculous inventions, but it's fast-paced and sometimes violent. Terrible world wars go on for years. People turn on each other— families and friends." She felt out of her league trying to explain her way of life and the awful reality over-population brings. "It doesn't sound like a very desirable place, does it? Yet, in many ways, the future is a wonderland."

"Is nothing the same as now?" He asked, his voice turning husky.

The day of the lady and gentleman was long gone. People were too busy making money to be bothered with family life, teaching manners and all the qualities of a more peaceful time. She became a writer to escape the daily drudgery of forcing herself to do something she didn't want to do. She did not want to shatter his dreams too soon.

"Maybe love—and greed. Some things never change, Captain."

"Aye," James agreed solemnly, studying her somber face. He watched her mouth and wanted to taste her sweet lips again, but knew she must have time to adjust to her new life before he complicated it any further.

"Don't look at me like that."

"Yer saying ye want me to leave?"

"I'm saying it makes me nervous. I have never been looked at quite the way you look at me, that's all."

He chuckled. "Tis lovely ye are and I cannot help m'self."

"Flattery will get you nowhere so behave yourself."

A loud knock at the cabin door disrupted her thoughts. She followed the captain across the room to the door. Two young boys, probably no older than twelve years, carried in a large wooden barrel cut down to become a bathtub of sorts. They left the cabin, returning a few minutes later with buckets of steamy water.

Anna sighed at the crudeness of the barrel filled with boiled seawater. She put on a cheerful countenance and tried not to show her discomfort at the primitive appliance. Water was water and she definitely needed a bath. She thanked the boys, sighing with relief when they left. Now she needed to get the captain to leave his cabin for a while so she could bathe in privacy.

James stood at his desk with his back to her—feigning interest in a chart spread across the desktop. Who did he think he was fooling? She would not allow him to stay in the cabin, no matter how nice a guy he was. She had already been intimate enough with him, losing all sense of right or wrong where he was concerned.

William knocked and came in bearing a large wooden tray of food. He set the tray on the captain's table and smiled at Anna. "Hungry? There's enough food here to feed you and half the *Ceilidh's* crew, as well. I don't know what Cookie thought he was doing. Sometimes he feeds us as if we are on one of his old cattle drives." He laughed and his friendly face lit up with humor. He nodded to the captain, leaving with a mischievous grin.

"He thinks we're bathing together!" Her cheeks flushed pink as she stood with her hands upon her hips.

James raised an eyebrow, enjoying her embarrassment. "Maybe we will, lass. 'Tis not such a bad idea." He ducked as a book flew across the cabin, nearly hitting him full in the face. Laughing heartily, he taunted her to get closer.

Her eyes flashed with fire and she bent to pick up another book. "You, my overly attentive captain, can leave while I take a bath. If you wish to bathe after me then that will be perfectly fine."

"Ah, but ye are a bonny lass when ye are angry." He crossed the room to the door. With his hand on the brass knob, he looked back over his shoulder. "My crew has done without me these past few hours. Now what do ye suppose they will be thinking if I do not show my face on deck until we reach port?"

She threw the second book as he stepped out the door. He chuckled and closed the door behind him, cutting off her spiel of unladylike curses.

Five

Anna's anger passed quickly after the captain left the cabin. Just thinking about the teasing expression on his face brought a smile to her lips. He enjoyed sparring words with her. Admittedly, she enjoyed it too. She loved hearing the Scots lilt in his deep voice when he spoke to her. The more excited he became the more pronounced his accent.

She wandered over to the table and examined the tray of food. Even though she was not hungry, she decided to taste the eggs and potatoes, leaving what looked like a shriveled up piece of salted beef untouched. She did not want to hurt anyone's feelings. After all, someone had made an effort to make her feel welcome.

As she sat eating her breakfast, she wondered if the captain had eaten or if she had been the cause of his missed meal. She recalled his hearty laughter and the way his lips formed an undeniably sexy, lopsided grin. The story about his great-grandfather proved his emotions ran deep and he was not afraid to express his true feelings. How different he was from most men in the future. There was no honest comparison. He would outshine them all, from his gorgeously built body to his warm vibrant personality.

A blush of heat rushed to her cheeks. She could not get him out of her mind. With a determined sigh, she stood and stripped off the captain's shirt, then climbed into the large tub of warm water. Good thing she was small. She sat with her knees bent just to fit within the cramped confines of the wooden barrel. Relaxing down into the steamy liquid, she let her eyes fall shut.

It felt so good to unwind and pamper her tired nerves. She may never understand what had happened to send her back to 1880. She didn't know if she would be whisked back to the future, or if she would remain here for the rest of her life. Only time would tell. Those words had never held such poignant meaning.

"Och, are ye done now—or are ye falling asleep in my bath?"

The captain's lusty voice boomed into the silence, shaking Anna out of her reverie. She sat up and hugged her bare knees to her exposed bosom before she looked over her shoulder to find him standing so close he could undoubtedly see everything. She didn't even know how long he had been there while she lay daydreaming about him.

"You are incorrigible! I thought I asked you to leave."

James smiled with nonchalance and folded his arms as he leaned against the closed cabin door. "Aye, lass. Ye see, I forgot my sextant and it seems William needs to use it."

"That's a crock!" Anna slid a little deeper beneath the water's surface. "Why are you ogling me? You would think you hadn't seen a woman naked before, and I doubt that's even a remote possibility. So get your darn sextant and leave me alone!" She looked away, trying to regain her composure.

"Oh, aye. I've seen naked women before, Anna. But none as beautiful as the woman in my bath right now." He stepped nearer as a roguish grin spread across his suntanned face. "Would ye like me to scrub yer lovely back for ye?"

"No! If you get any closer I'll scream." She tossed in the threat with a glare, daring him to move. He was big enough to overpower her without much effort—she knew it and he knew it, too.

James paused a few steps away from the tub. "Go ahead and scream, lass. My men would only think I was having a wee bit o' fun with ye." His expression changed, suddenly becoming more serious. "But 'tis willing I like my women. I will not bed ye, Anna, unless ye are willing."

He removed the sextant from its case and strode purposely from the room, leaving her staring after him in awe. He was unpredictable. He was a total mix of charm, manners, rogue, and devil. How in the heck was she supposed to calm down and relax, when he constantly had her nerves on end?

She situated herself more comfortably in the tub and closed her eyes. He wanted to make love to her—not force her. The mere notion sent a shiver of delight right to the core of her femininity. Damn. She reached for the large cake of soap and hurriedly washed herself before he could return to tempt her again.

She stood to dunk her long flowing locks into the tub as she soaped them. The old-fashioned soap left a foamy coating on her hair that was difficult to rinse away. It was different from her special salon shampoo and conditioner, but at least she would smell a whole lot better.

As she dried off with a soft towel, she could not resist a secret smile. She had never felt such deep passion within herself. The captain need only look at her with those deep blue eyes filled with potent desire and she was trembling like a young schoolgirl.

~ * ~

Mendocino in 1880 was a bustling little coastal port, filled with lumber schooners and brawny sailors. The town appeared different from the quiet little seaside community in the twenty-first century. Anna stood on the quarterdeck dressed in a fresh white cambric shirt and a large pair of black twill pants—compliments of the captain. Admiring the growing industrious town of yesteryear in its glory day, she released a long dreamy sigh. The experience was better than any history lesson. Sights and sounds of a lost way of life surrounded her in Technicolor; sort of like having her own tour guide to walk her through the late nineteenth-century.

"Everything all right, ma'am?"

Anna whirled around to find William standing close behind her. "Fine, William, thanks." She smiled with relief; glad it was the first mate and not one of the sailors she didn't know. The captain's warning about his crew stayed with her and she was constantly aware of their watchful eyes.

William had taken her on a stroll earlier, introducing her to the most important crewmembers, from the quartermaster to the ship's carpenter. She would never remember all their names, but his effort did help to make her feel more at home.

For all his good looks and intelligence, William was shy and awkward in his exalted position. Jock seemed a better man for the first mate's job, yet the captain encouraged this young man of twenty-two to do the best he could.

"We'll go ashore soon. Best you return to the cabin now. It gets pretty busy on the lower decks." William scratched his full beard. "Course, you belonging to the captain and all, he will likely be around to watch out for you."

Anna caught the glint of humor in his dark eyes. She tossed her long, loose hair back over her shoulder to blow freely in the warm sea breeze. "The captain does not own me, William."

He laughed. "He told me you suffer from delusions."

"What?" She held onto the rail for safety. Every time the ship hit a wave, she lost her footing. "I don't know what you mean."

William's spread-legged stance kept his balance as the ship hit another swell. "He's made his claim in front of the whole crew. He's not a man to back down from what's proper, Anna, even if it means sacrificing his freedom to save your honor."

"My honor? Why, you are as bad as he is. I am not marrying the man because I slept in his cabin—and that's final."

"He said you were no common doxy. Are you telling me you are?"

"No! Geez, I'm simply telling you I have no desire to be married to the captain." Another swell rolled under the ship and she grabbed the rail with both hands to stay upright. "I'm serious, William. The captain will not have his way in this."

He burst into robust laughter and strode away, leaving her wondering just how much he knew about her and the captain. Had he guessed her secret, or had James told him she was from another time?

If William knew he sure didn't let on that Anna might have another choice besides marrying the captain. Was everything so cut and dried in the nineteenth-century? She decided she wouldn't let the thought ruin her day. She was too excited to experience 1880 to waste her time solving riddles. Inhaling a deep breath of salty sea air, Anna closed her eyes and tried to recapture the earlier sense of belonging to this special place in time.

On the distant shore, she could hear the clatter of horse's hooves as they pulled heavy-laden wagons along the pier. She could smell fresh fish from vendors selling their goods along the boardwalk, mixed with the fragrant scent of the pine forest drifting out across the bay. Sailors' shouts filled the air, men of many nationalities, as they worked hard at their lot in life.

The small clapboard buildings crowded together along Main Street didn't look much different from their present day counterparts, except for the horses tied to hitching posts outside. Unique storefronts boasted wide wooden sidewalks and brightly painted windows, sparkling like diamonds in the afternoon sun.

The port was busy with seafaring activity from transport dinghies to large four-masted schooners like the *Ceilidh*, most in various stages of unloading lumber. Anna watched with curiosity as ships fought for places to drop anchor in the dangerously crowded harbor. She marveled at the talent it took to maneuver the great sailing ships around without hitting each other.

Several tall clipper ships sat lined up along the docks. Even with their sails down and their masts like huge toothpicks dotting the summer sky, they were impressive. Piles of rough-hewn lumber cluttered the docks, as more was unloaded from newly arrived trade ships. Horse-drawn wagons with long beds lined up to haul finished wood to its storage destinations. Later the lumber would be shipped on to San Francisco and other far away ports by James, or some other seafaring captain in the trade. Maybe the lumber would travel as far away as romantic Hawaii—oops—the Sandwich Islands.

She smiled at her slip of thought.

Excitement heralded their own ship's arrival in the shouts and cheers going up from the men on board. Her thoughts were so busy she almost didn't see Jock wave at her from across the deck. She raised her arm to wave back, but he had turned around and missed her acknowledgment.

Earlier she had nearly driven Jock crazy with questions. After being introduced to him and left in his company while the captain and William went over their cargo, she tagged along at his side as though he were her mentor. She wanted to know every little detail about the ship and the skills of sailing. Jock proved he was a brilliant tutor. One thing she learned was that the captain required organization on board the *Ceilidh*. James was a very organized man.

William bellowed orders from the helm until Anna thought he would go hoarse. She watched in fascination as crewmembers rushed about in what looked like organized chaos. In preparing to unload their own heavy burden of redwood shingles and railroad ties, each man had his position and job to do. Jock's job as second mate was to see the crew follow through with swift and accurate maneuvers.

A warm and gentle coastal breeze picked up, blowing her long damp hair into dry wispy tendrils. She felt so free, so utterly fresh. She looked around the deck for a sign of the captain. He had left her alone since her bath, except when he sent William to fetch her and show her about the ship. Maybe he thought she was still upset with him for sneaking up on her earlier.

James approached quietly behind Anna. Long golden-blond strands of hair tickled a path across his clean-shaven cheek. Absorbed in the crew's activity surrounding her, she did not even notice him. He leaned close to her ear and whispered, "Time to put ashore, lass."

She swung around to face him. "Oh! James—you scared me."

A smile lit her whole face and he could not help touching her lips with his fingertips. He wanted to place a kiss upon those sweet lips, here and now. Resting large hands upon her slender shoulders, he gave her a gentle squeeze. "William can finish what needs doing. I have yet to find us a place to stay ashore this night."

"Don't you sleep on board your ship, Captain?"

"Oh aye, I do sometimes." He held her at arm's length and captured her attention with his steady gaze. "But this night is very special."

The desire in his tone made Anna's skin tingle. "Why?"

"Tis not every day a man takes a bride."

She looked down at the deck and shook her head. "Why do you persist in this marriage business?"

She could disappear as quickly as she had come into his life. The idea of having James hold her and make love to her was not distasteful—far from it. She resisted the magnetic pull between them for both their sakes. It was wild and crazy just being close to him, almost as though he was the eye of a hurricane waiting to consume her with his power. When they kissed, he did consume her and everything stood still for a perfect moment.

"Can ye not feel the magic between us, Anna?" His arms slipped around her, pulling her into his embrace. "I cannot tell ye how it came about, but ye were meant to come to me. I feel it in my heart, lass. Aye, even in my very soul."

Tears trickled down her cheeks at the fresh honesty of his words. She leaned against his chest with a frustrated sigh. "Don't, Captain. Don't even talk like that. Dear God—I don't really belong here. I can't expect to stay forever."

"Ye just need a bit more time." James brushed his lips against her soft hair as he released his hold on her. He gazed down into her dreamy eyes. She had cast a spell over him, and he was powerless to resist. "Do ye believe me, lass?"

"I don't know," she answered softly.

He wiped her tears away with his fingertips. "Do ye want to go back then—back to yer own time?" He did not know what he would do without her. He had held her and he had kissed her. He could not let her go. He would fight to keep her.

Anna couldn't answer him. Did she want to return to a place where no one loved her? No one would even miss her in the future. If only she could be sure her attraction to this charming Scotsman was enough to hold her here. She looked up at him, but didn't have time to answer. The Stensons were coming toward them, full speed. She braced herself for the onslaught of their Victorian conversation, hoping she could respond the way she should for a woman of their time.

"James, so glad we found you!" Angelique took hold of the captain's elbow. "We were wondering if you two have a place to stay. It is your honeymoon, isn't it?"

"Oh, aye." James' charming crooked grin fell into place.

Anna felt as though she were acting out a scene in a play. These people thought she was married to the captain. How would they react if they knew she had only shared the captain's bed? Not very well, she feared. Angelique had already accused her of being the captain's mistress. Her heart fluttered with desire at the idea of becoming the captain's lover, but her mind refused to let go of the facts. Marriage was not something in which she was successful.

Angelique turned to George and he nodded in agreement. Her face lit up as she spoke. "We would love to have you stay with us, James. We have simply too many rooms and never enough people to enjoy them."

James looked from the Stensons to Anna. She appeared rather surprised but made no effort to respond. "Would that be pleasing to ye, Anna?"

Her eyes met his for a moment. She glanced away and then back again before she answered. "Yes—it will be fine."

James wasn't sure what he read in Anna's eyes, but knew they had to find a place to stay the night. His partner was making a generous offer. Lodgings were rarely available at this late time in the day. He turned back to the Stensons. "Are ye sure ye will not mind?"

George chuckled. "You know Angel, James. She loves to fuss over people. You would be making my little wife mighty happy if you will come. We'll put you in your own wing of the house so you will have all the privacy you need, eh?" He nudged James' arm, meeting his gaze with a sagacious grin.

Angelique took Anna by the arm, continuing her non-stop chatter. "It will be so nice to have another real lady in the house. I fear California has far too many shady ladies at the present time." She paused for breath. "James told us the misfortune of your trunk falling overboard while loading in Coo's Bay. I understand all your lovely things were quite ruined. I have so many beautiful dresses and I simply cannot use them all. Since we are of a similar size, I would love to give some to you. A wedding present?"

Anna was surprised at her generosity. No one in her time would give away expensive clothing and not expect something in return. She nodded her head in shy agreement; embarrassed at the tall-tale the captain had subtly constructed to cover her sudden appearance and lack of luggage on board his ship.

"Thank you, Angelique."

"Please, call me Angel. I have the feeling we will be the dearest of friends." She turned to her husband, looping her arm through his and flashing him a radiant smile. "We'd best be off, George. We are to have company and there is simply so much to be done."

George tipped his top hat to the captain and Anna in farewell, shrugging his shoulders as he was led away and forced to listen to the excited plans of his chattering wife.

Anna watched the captain's friends disembark—their valet and maid following promptly in tow. A large luxurious carriage with a magnificent pair of black horses undoubtedly awaited their arrival.

"This century seems so romantic," she said with a sigh.

"Ah, Anna, 'tis very romantic. And 'tis sure to be a bonny wedding night, as well." James winked down at her, a mischievous grin crossing his face. He slid his arm around her waist and pulled her close. "Ye will not be sorry. I'll be very gentle with ye."

How dare he assume she would be a part of his charade? The Stensons were good people and she did not want to take advantage of their kindness. Her quick temper flared and she turned her fury on him.

"I still haven't agreed to marry you. And if you think you can force me into marriage, you will be waiting until horses fly, dude." She pushed out of his arms and fled down the narrow stairs to his quarters below.

James pondered her confusing words. Waiting until horses fly? What a strange thing to say to a man. He shook his head at the preposterous possibility of horses flying, even in the distant future. And what the bloody hell was a dude?

James was about to follow Anna when William signaled to him. He would have to wait until later to find out what ailed her. He had to prove he was sincere. And they needed time alone together—before she had to deal with polite society.

~ * ~

In the captain's cabin, Anna searched for her discarded pink dress as her smoldering anger climbed into a rage. Why was he so totally impossible? Boldly assuming she would submit to his seductive charm—it irked her to think men were all the same. James was no different after all. He was an egotistical, charming, take-charge-of-everything male.

She recalled admiring his portrait in the old house. Had fate intervened, sending her back in time to experience what she had only fantasized about? Could love be the force to determine her destiny?

The heavy cabin door flew open with a bang. Anna jumped nervously. It wasn't passion's flame shooting from the captain's eyes; it was pure, unrestrained anger. She straightened her shoulders and stood her ground. "What do you want?"

James slammed the door shut behind him. His thoughts boiled over with pent up emotions. He was determined to make her understand exactly how he felt about her. Her shocked expression made him smile. So, this feisty minx did have a weakness? She was just a wee bit afraid of him. His anger cooled swiftly and heated desire took its place.

"What do you want?" She repeated haughtily.

The element of surprise was so effective; James could not resist going further with his scheme. His voice grew husky as he moved in on his lovely prey. "Ye know what I want, ye wee bit o' booty."

Anna acknowledged his hands clenched into fists. He looked mad, all right, real mad. Unconsciously, she backed away from him until her legs bumped into the bed frame. "Maybe I don't want what...what you want, Captain."

"Aye, lass. And just maybe ye do."

She gasped as he swept her into his arms. He laid her down upon the bed, his virile body hovering over her. His warm lips paused mere inches away, filling her with trembling fear that quickly turned into sweet anticipation. He nuzzled sensual kisses to the curve in her neck and up along her jaw to her cheek—temptingly close to her waiting mouth. Gently nibbling at her skin, he slowly moved his mouth to cover hers.

Anna pushed at him, ignoring the sexual hunger igniting like wildfire within her. "Don't you have any decency? Get off of me."

"No." James continued to bath her skin in delectable little licks, refusing to stop no matter how much she struggled.

Images of the self-defense class she had taken flashed through her mind. Did she dare try to get the upper hand in this situation? Not conceiving the extent of pain she might cause him, she thrust her knee upwards as she had been trained. She hit him full in the groin and his face contorted in anguish.

James fell to her side. A miserable groan escaped his throat. His hands immediately covered the throbbing area between his legs as he rolled into the fetal position. Bright bits of light flashed through his brain as the pain increased to its maximum. He panted and gasped for breath, waiting for his vision to clear.

Anna leaped up from the bunk. "Oh gosh! Are you okay? Captain?"

Quick as a cat, James grasped both her wrists. He pulled her down on top of him; their overheated bodies lying so close together that their hearts beat as one. "Are ye mad, Anna Bentley? Ye will never do that to me again, or ye will get the bloody thrashing ye deserve!"

"You wouldn't dare!" She struggled in his grasp, unaware her subtle movements rubbing against his sensitive body were doing little to argue her plea. "You are a real barbarian aren't you? You think because you are so darn sexy I will gratefully fall into your bed—full of lustful desire. What are you going to do if I don't submit to your barbarous ways? Make me walk the plank?"

"Tis not a bad idea," he agreed, rolling them over so she was beneath him. He loved the feel of her silky skin and the fullness of her breasts pressing against his chest. His manhood bulged between them, throbbing in blissful pain for release. Ah, but he needed this woman in so many ways.

"Scoundrel! Pirate!" Anna glared up at him. "You are the one who is mad."

"Aye, my wee bonny lass. I'm mad for the taste o' ye, and the feel o' ye in my arms. The desire in yer voice when ye growl at me in anger does naught to distract me, but makes me want ye all the more. Ye are mine, Anna Bentley. Accept yer fate." He lowered his mouth in a hungry kiss—a kiss that told her he was in control.

The attack on her senses caught her totally off guard. Anna melted into the passion he awoke. She responded to his advances with rising flames of intoxication. His large weathered hands took liberties to explore her body. She relaxed her arms and he released her wrists, only to settle more firmly between her legs.

The masculine smell of him made her senses reel. She ran her fingers among the dark curls of hair peeking through the opening of his loose shirt. She longed to see every inch of him again, and this time she wanted to touch, too.

James groaned, kissing her cheek in light whispers. His fevered lips inched along her jaw to nibble her ear. "Anna, m'dear, ye have done me in," he said softly, feeling a bit breathless. "I've never felt this way before. Sweet sea nymph, I want ye!"

"Captain—" Her sigh echoed with passion.

"Ye will not call me Captain. 'Tis James ye should be calling yer betrothed." His mouth covered hers in a lengthy kiss as he fought to control the need he felt bursting within. "Och, I've no desire to wait," he panted, with a tender touch of his lips to hers. "Tis too tempting ye are. Say ye will wed me this day."

"James—" Anna smiled, cupping his endearing face between her palms. He couldn't seriously fall in love so fast, could he? "I need to think about this. Don't you see what we're messing with here? It's a paradox. How do we know this can work between us without something happening to alter either now or the future?"

"Paradox? 'Tis strange words ye use, Anna." He licked at her ear, relishing the pure joy of caressing her responsive body.

"A paradox is a contradiction. An unbelievable event." She giggled. "For Pete's sake!" She pushed at his chest and he rolled to the side. "Something impossible happening even though it can't happen—it's like it does. Don't you see?" She sat up on the bed, putting some space between them and breaking the sensuous spell he had over her.

"I know what ye are saying, Anna, but who is Pete? Do ye speak o' someone from the future, lass?"

Anna fell over in peals of laughter. She held onto her sides as they cramped from delight. He was so open and so incredibly honest. The whole silly idea struck her funny bone again and another bout of laughter erupted before she could stop it. Then she noticed the dour expression on his face and immediately sobered.

James moved into a sitting position at her side. "Laughing at me, are ye? 'Tis yerself who is from another time, and still ye make fun of me for not understanding yer ways."

"I'm sorry. I didn't mean to hurt your feelings. I suppose it would be a natural thing to mistake what I meant, if you didn't know the slang expression. 'For Pete's sake' is like a curse of exasperation, it's used a lot in my time."

"So Pete is not a person of yer acquaintance?"

She giggled again. "Right. It's just a saying to vent frustration. You must have a curse or two hidden up your sleeve."

"Aye," he said with an acknowledging grin. "But I hope ye will never be hearing them, lass."

Anna adored every detail of the larger-than-life male at her side. She almost hated to admit how much she liked the man, and how physically attracted she felt toward him. Her gaze lingered over the length of his impassioned body. His arousal was still extremely evident, though slightly impaired by their recent conversation.

"Do ye want me to court ye proper, Anna?" He asked suddenly.

"Court me? You mean, you have given up the silly idea of having to marry me just because I happened to be naked in your bed when visitors walked into your cabin unannounced?"

Anna knew the Victorian age had strict moral standards, nearly to the point of being prudish. How would he deal with his potent emotions, stay within propriety's reins, and still get what he wanted? The idea positively intrigued her. She waited patiently for his response.

"There'll be a marriage between us, Anna. What I'm saying is to slow down a wee bit. Ye must accept me as I am. Ye will not be thinking to leave me for yer own time once we are wed. I will not allow it."

"I have no control over leaving, James. I don't know what forces brought me here, or even if they'll interfere again. That's what I keep trying to tell you. I can't marry you. I don't really belong here." How could she make him understand? She met his confused blue-eyed gaze. "Look, marriage is a legal matter drawn up on legal documents passed down through time. We can't take a chance of altering the future."

Anger flashed across his features. "Ye will not be leaving me."

"I may not have a choice."

"Aye, ye do. If ye wish to stay, we'll make it so."

Anna threw her arms into the air in surrender of the preposterous argument. "Leave it to me to be obtuse when it comes to time travel."

He looked at her curiously with a raised brow.

She knelt beside him on the bed. "You are the most exciting man I have ever met. Don't you think I would stay if I could?"

"Aye, and ye will." He grinned his infatuating grin.

Crossing her arms, she shook her head in disbelief. "Stubborn."

James leaned over and pulled her back against him, enjoying the feel of her safe in his arms. "I am proud to be captain o' this ship. I've worked hard for many a year to build my fortune. My life is good. My crew—a gang o' bold hardy lads who respect my wishes—are the best seamen along this coast." He rubbed his jaw thoughtfully before continuing. "Anna, I cannot leave my time. I'm asking ye to leave yer time—forever."

"I don't know that I am able to do that."

"All I ask is that ye consider it for now. Ye may never be able to return, and then again, ye may. I feel something here, Anna. I know yer ability to come to me from so very far away must have a purpose. I can only trust my instincts and they tell me to watch out for ye. Maybe that's all, but my heart tells me 'tis not."

Anna shivered, but she wasn't cold. "Maybe your heart is wrong."

"Aye, and maybe 'tis yer heart that will not listen to reason." He released her then, stood and crossed to the door. "I only know there are some things we cannot understand and we must learn to accept them as they are."

"What if I can't accept them?" Her stomach wrenched at the wounded expression upon his face. He hurt deep inside, but somehow she didn't feel she was the only cause for his ailment.

"It will be a great loss—for both o' us." He nodded farewell and walked out, quietly closing the cabin door behind him.

Anna stared after him in silent contemplation. For the first time in her life, she had someone who cared about her, someone who put her welfare above his own. She wouldn't be lonely anymore. Being with James made her feel alive and special. If she could remain here, she would have the answer to her prayers. The kind of life she had always dreamed about living. Maybe she should tempt fate and accept the captain's love. Would that be accepting things as they are, or would she be foolishly attempting to believe in miracles?

Six

Two strong brown packhorses, loaded down with goods in leather and canvas bags, waited on the dock. Anna, skittish with excitement, stood on the boardwalk near two golden-colored horses that were saddled and ready for departure. Earlier, James had received a message from George requesting a meeting at the lumber office on the dock. James returned to the ship a half-hour later and informed her he needed to take care of a few things at their logging camp. He gave her the choice to go to the Stenson's to await his return, or to accompany him to the camp.

Not wanting to offend Angelique, but wanting to spend time with the captain, Anna agreed to tag along with him. She enjoyed being with him and she couldn't wait to explore an authentic nineteenth-century logging camp. James assured her they would visit the Stensons in a day or two, and then she could see how the townspeople lived.

Anna found the Victorian age fascinating; being a nineteenth-century history buff, she had studied the period in great detail. Now she could sample history first hand. She might even fit in without too much conflict, and with James watching over her no one had questioned her sudden appearance aboard the sailing ship. Things would be more difficult when she met polite society. She would have to behave, speak and dress like a Victorian woman.

She tapped her foot impatiently, glanced across at the small, wood frame building, and wondered what was keeping James. She was eager to begin their journey. Maybe she should try to get on her horse while she was waiting. She wasn't much of an equestrian, but she could handle a horse for a short ride.

James smiled as he left the shipyard office. Today was the start of a weakling shore leave for himself and the crew. Only this would be a week to remember long after he returned to sea. His ship, his lumber business and his vow of revenge had always taken precedence over leisure. Not this time. This time pleasure would be his for the taking. He must wed the vixen who had stolen his heart or get her out of his blood for good.

He caught sight of Anna and grinned. She was having difficulty in mounting her horse. Dressed in his trousers and shirt, she had one foot in the stirrup and one flying off the ground as she grappled desperately for a handhold on the saddle horn and cantle. She dropped the reins in her effort to mount the horse. At least she stood on the left side of the beast, or she would have been kicked by now. He chuckled under his breath. She made an amusing sight. Yet he knew there would be nothing amusing about her temper if she did not succeed soon. He hurried over to her side, grasped her small waist in his big hands and lifted her easily into the saddle.

"Thank you, James," she said, smiling across at him as he mounted his horse. "The horse was not being very cooperative."

He chuckled. "Oh, aye. But ye said ye could ride, lass."

"I can. I'm ready whenever you are."

James met her challenge with a nod. "Then let's be off." With a touch from his booted heel, his horse trotted steadily along the docks.

Anna followed his example. When they reached the end of the long pier, they turned eastward and headed up the well-worn bridle path running along the edge of the bay. The narrow path led them over the grassy headlands. With the horse's steady gait and her bottom bumping up and down in the saddle, Anna became more than a little uncomfortable in a short amount of time. She couldn't keep her bottom from bouncing in the saddle. The last thing she wanted to do was complain. James would only take her back to town and she wanted to visit the camp.

High on the top rise of a grassy bluff, James paused for a few minutes while Anna took delight in scanning the breathtaking view below. The sea lay at low tide and the afternoon sun shimmered off the water in rays of sparkling iridescence. He glanced over at her with a tender smile. She could not resist returning his smile with one of her own. She was happy. She owed a lot to this man already— more than he would ever know.

James could tell she was not accustomed to horseback the way she arched her tired back and tried to keep her lovely bottom up off the saddle. He admired her for not complaining. Most women would be whining by now, but then most women would not think of riding a horse astride like a man in the first place.

"We can stop for a bit, if ye have a mind. There's a bonny wee waterfall ahead that reminds me o' the Highlands." He nudged his horse into a slow walk, knowing she would follow suit.

"James?" Anna tried in vain to get her horse to move again. The mount was as stubborn as a mule and for all she knew about horses it was a mule. "James—wait!"

What did one say to a horse? She had ridden a horse only once before at a riding stable where a trail guide had shown her what to do. She found letting her horse follow other horses in the pack was the easiest solution. Those horses seemed to know the trails with their eyes closed. But this was the open wilderness—wild and untamed.

"James!" Her panicked shout carried over the trail to the tall rider far ahead. She felt a little silly, but at least he heard her.

James turned in the saddle to see Anna tugging on the reins of her horse. The stubborn animal stood with all four hooves firmly planted on the ground while it enjoyed nibbling on the tender sweet grass growing at its feet. She shrugged her shoulders at him in pure female helplessness and braved a timid smile.

He managed to keep his humor under control as he approached his stranded riding partner. "Ye said ye could ride a horse, Anna."

Her cheeks flushed becomingly as she blew a strand of hair from her face. "I said I had ridden a horse before, and I have, just not this one. Are you sure she's not a mule?"

"Oh, aye. I wonder now, does the horse know o' yer grand equestrian experience?" He had a difficult time hiding his smile as a look of utter confusion crossed her features.

She glanced around the grassy headland stretching all the way to the forest's edge. "It's all this green stuff. It's way too distracting for her. They must not have fed the poor beast this morning."

James laughed heartily. "Come on, lass. We'll find a proper place for yer horse to feed and for ye to take a bit o' rest." He took the mare's reins and led her behind him, chuckling to himself all the while.

Wild flowers covered the headlands in brilliant color and nestled beneath the tall green pines in casual bouquets, so different from the future. Most of these beautiful trees were gone now, unless they stood in established national or state parks. Anna loved the bright orange poppies and lavender sea-daisies swaying in the mid-day breeze. She loved the heady scent of pine trees mixed with the salty tang of sea air.

She wanted desperately to stop and rest, but James kept riding. They traveled farther up a secluded fern covered gulch, through tall pines of various sizes and species. James finally turned to her and pointed ahead to a clearing in the trees. Relief washed over her. Sore was a mild description of how her bruised bottom felt.

"You said you had a cabin," she hastily reminded him as she looked around. There wasn't even an outhouse in sight.

"Aye, I have." James dismounted, dropped his horse's reins and turned to help her down from her sturdy mount. "Come on, lass."

"Why are we stopping here?" Anna obstinately pulled away from his touch. She felt tired and cross, and just a little upset it was taking so doggone long to get to the cabin. He said earlier they would reach camp before nightfall. She wanted to know exactly how much more she had to endure before they would reach their destination. She wasn't about to dismount until they arrived.

"Tis the wee spring I mentioned. My cabin is not far now."

"Where?" Her lips pouted with pain when she shifted in the saddle. "I see no cabin in sight and we have been riding for hours, James."

He ran his fingers through his ruffled hair. "Is this a game ye are playing, lass? 'Twas yer idea to come along. I could have left ye with George and Angel."

"I thought we were headed for your cabin."

"Aye, we are. 'Tis less than half an hour's ride from this very spot." He kicked at the ground with his boot toe, and then reached up for her again. "I thought ye might enjoy a wee bit o' rest. Ye recently told me yer horse is very hungry."

Why was he so gallant? Anna could not stay angry with someone who was trying so hard to be kind and considerate. She contemplated her options—there were none. She was stuck out in the middle of nowhere with a stubborn horse and an equally stubborn Scot.

"It's really that close?" Her hopes at being able to sit on something soft for a change helped her to cope with a short delay. Besides, waterfalls were beautiful. She was also exhausted and quite thirsty. The clear water in the pool below the falls appeared cold and refreshing, and hopefully safe to drink.

"A wee thought has suddenly occurred to me." He stood back and crossed his arms, a mischievous glint in his eyes. "Ye might only want me on account of my money."

Anna shook her head in disbelief. Sometimes his arrogance went too far. "Your money? Why on earth would I want your money? I want to go to your cabin, that's all."

He cocked his handsome head. "Aye, that's where my money is hidden."

"James—read my lips—I do not want your money." She wiggled uncomfortably in the hard saddle. She felt like jumping down and running away from this silly argument, but she doubted her legs would carry her far.

"Why do ye want to go to my cabin so bad, eh?" He lifted a dark eyebrow in speculation. "Maybe ye read somewhere in that distant future of yers that I had a wee bit set aside for the reclaiming o' my father's lands in Scotland. I'll tell ye now, its purpose is naught for anything else. I'll have my way in this, Anna. Wed ye or no, 'tis only right I reclaim what is mine from the English."

Sunlight caught the highlights in his hair, making it sparkle like burnished copper. She sighed in frustrated defeat. How could she care about such a block-headed person? She no more wanted his money than she wanted to marry the man. Somehow, this entire situation was getting way out of control.

"James, I'm not sure this is right for us."

He grumbled and looked her straight in the eye. "I know 'tis right for us, Anna. 'Tis yer feet that are chilling."

She laughed. "Are you saying I have cold feet?"

"Aye, a block o' ice would melt sooner than ye will warm to the idea o' our marriage." He frowned and glanced at the waterfall before looking back at her with that teasing sparkle in his eyes.

She giggled with zest and pointed at him. "You have a sense of humor!"

"Did ye think me boring, lass? Well then, let's liven things up a bit." Without further ado, he grasped her around the waist, removed her from the saddle and swung her up over his shoulder. He strode calmly to the deep pool beneath the falls, stopping right at the water's edge.

"James? You wouldn't?" She looked down at the serene water that had appeared so inviting only seconds before.

"Ye should not taunt yer future husband," James said solemnly, dropping her bottom first into the icy-cold water. He stood back and laughed heartily. She was a true sea nymph, after all; teasing and alluring, and about as seductive as a dripping wet female could be.

She came up sputtering. "You dirty-rotten...I'll get you back for this one, James Duncan!"

He held out his hand to the sopping wet beauty, admiring her curves beneath her wet clothing. The white fabric clung to her unbound breasts highlighting nature's perfection. He found it difficult to speak. She was lovely no matter what her predicament.

"Do ye need some help, lass, or did ye want to swim a while?"

Glaring up at him, Anna pushed dripping strands of hair away from her face. The pebbled bottom of the pond was slippery with moss and she lost her footing just as her hand reached his. She held on tight, trying to reclaim her balance, but to no avail. All she succeeded in doing was making James' position on the mossy bank's edge more precarious.

James fell face first into the pool beside her. He sat up on his knees, shook his hair out of his eyes and laughed. Finding their current situation equally as humorous, Anna laughed too, until her sides ached.

"James! We'll never dry out!" Fire burned her cheeks when she saw the lusty gleam in his eyes. She struggled to her feet once again. His gaze swept the length of her drenched body and settled upon her breasts. Her nipples pebbled under his scrutiny and goose bumps broke out along her arms. She sat back down to his level and stared at him—eye to eye. She couldn't help the smile that tickled her lips.

He grinned and pulled her up with him, carefully stepping across the pool's slippery rock bottom. She almost tripped on the baggy pants hanging off her hips, but he caught her against him. Reaching safety at last, they fell to the moss-covered ground and hugged each other amidst peals of laughter.

"Ye are a bonny lass, Anna," James said softly, touching her cheek with his fingertips. "I have not had fun like that in a long, long time."

He studied her moist face, ran his fingers over her pouty pink lips, and then gave in to temptation. His mouth covered hers in a kiss that began gently, only to burst into a fiery caress of passion. His hands explored her shapely curves, while rolling them over so she was beneath him. He watched her expression as drips of water from his hair tip-toed across her face.

She blinked and pushed at his broad chest. "No, James. Stop it right now."

He released her and fell to the side. "Don't tell me ye cannot enjoy yerself."

She stood up and tried to straighten her clinging wet clothes.

"Ye want me, Anna. I can tell when ye kiss me."

"I want you, all right. But wanting great sex isn't enough." She looked down at him with sincerity. "We have to be in love, James, really in love. What we are feeling here is pure lust. You know, and I know it."

James got to his feet and pulled her into his arms. Gazing down into her limpid green eyes, he knew what he saw there was the first stirring of love. He only had to persuade her to relax and open up her heart to him. Lust! He knew well what lust felt like and the feelings he had for her went far deeper than mere lust.

"We are in love, lass. Can ye not see what is in yer own heart?"

Anna stared back at him in awe. Yes, she felt a little flicker deep down inside, but she also looked at life realistically. No way could she fall in love with him. She did not want to take the risk. She could wake up tomorrow in the future.

"Nothing is in my heart right now, James. Yes, I am physically attracted to you. But that just isn't enough to build a marriage on. Take my word for it, okay?"

He cocked his head to the side and peered at her from beneath thick lashes. "Ye are wrong. I can see this will be a rough journey for ye, lass. I have my own opinion o' how ye feel. I can wait a bit longer."

"You are too darn stubborn for your own good, you know," she argued. "I don't want to hurt you, James."

"Aye, ye do...but enough o' this *clishmaclaver*. I know what I know. Ye will be my bride soon enough." He stepped back from their embrace, but continued to study her in reserved silence.

Anna smiled and boldly studied him right back. She loved the way his sexy eyes could talk. He wanted her, and the thought thrilled her to her toes. But an emptiness needed filling within her, and she didn't know if she would be able to stay in 1880 and start a new life. She could be whisked back to her own time, at any given moment, and never see James again.

A great shiver ran through her. God—she would miss him. She didn't know all the answers, but the idea of leaving him unexpectedly tore at her heart. A sob escaped her throat and she quickly turned away. Tingles ran up her back and goose flesh tickled her skin. She didn't want to leave—she knew that now.

James stepped up behind her and turned her about. He wrapped his arms around her; hugging her against him so hard, she could barely breathe. She could feel how much he cared. His every pore cried out to her. She dared not look up at his face. He would know he was right.

"Anna, say ye will wed me, lass. It may be the only way to keep ye here." He tilted her chin up and studied her tear laden face

A glazed look of despair appeared in her eyes. "I'm so frightened, James. I don't know why this happened. I mean, what is the purpose of my being here? I'm a realist, the kind of person who needs forthright answers."

"Aye, Anna. So am I." He did not know what he could do to calm her fears. He shared them too—especially the fear that she might return to the future. "Tis safe ye are for the moment, lass. I'll not be letting anything harm ye. And I'll do my best to help ye find the truthful answers ye seek."

Anna sighed and relaxed in his strong, comforting embrace. They stood close, incredibly snug in each other's arms, watching the last rays of sunlight filter through the trees and dance upon the trickling waterfall. Safe for the moment, his tender concern bound her to the past in a way nothing else could.

~ * ~

Exuberant shouts, smiles and laughter welcomed them as they rode into the logging camp just before dusk. The gloaming James had called it—a peaceful romantic time of evening. A time meant for lovers and lovers' trysts.

Anna groaned as big burly men surrounded their horses. The heady scent from the giant pines, nor the beading sweat upon the horse's flesh could cover the pungent smell of unwashed bodies. She looked around at all the unshaven faces before her.

Most were men, except for a few teenage boys, and all ranged in size from big to huge, each with their own style of clothing. Some wore old worn-out suits resembling a Halloween costume picked up at the Salvation Army. Others wore coveralls or baggy pants held up by leather suspenders. Their heavy muslin shirts sun-bleached and worn, and the rolled up sleeves, bared their thick muscled arms. Lumberjacks. She could think of a name or two to add to that distinctive title.

James dismounted and greeted each of them, one by one. Anna was grasped firmly around the waist by a large set of hands belonging to the tallest man she had ever laid eyes upon. She recalled stories of Paul Bunyan from her childhood days. This could be the man in the legend.

"My name's Burns, ma'am. Michael Burns." A wide grin split his blond bearded face, displaying a row of pearly white teeth. He was an attractive giant of a man.

"Michael is my bull-buck," James explained, stepping up beside her where she still hung mid-air in Michael's strong hands. "He oversees the men and assigns them their duties." He glared a warning at the powerfully built man who was even taller than his own six-foot-two frame. "Mind yerself, Michael, and I'll introduce ye. This—is Anna Bentley."

The title bull-buck fit Michael Burns perfectly. He bellowed a cheer and swung Anna around in a full circle. He was at least seven feet tall and extremely well developed. Muscles rippled across his broad chest, visible even through his buttoned cotton shirt.

"It's nice to meet you, Michael." Anna smiled. "Could you put me down, please?" She felt as light as a feather in his hands, but it was an uneasy feeling to be so trivial in comparison.

Michael set her firmly on her feet and nodded at James over her head. "She's a beauty, Jamie!" He slapped James heartily on the back, nearly propelling him forward.

"Aye, she is at that." James lifted the saddlebags off the horses and looked around at the group of curious men. "Ye will all get to meet her in the morning, lads. Right now she's a wee bit weary from the long journey on horseback."

James led Anna through a small stand of young Douglas Firs to a tidy-looking log cabin, nestled at the edge of the woods. Inside, the cabin was cozy with a deep fireplace, a small table and two chairs, and a large, lodge-pole pine bed covered in heavy quilts.

"Wow, this is great! I really didn't expect anything so nice." She moved over to the hutch and icebox to examine their contents. "Oh, cool—a block of ice! I can't believe how simple things are." She turned to him. "Are you hungry? There's even some food in here."

James closed the distance between them in two long strides. "Ye need not worry, lass. We have a camp cook by the name o' Martin who'll see to our meals."

She pulled away from the teasing lips about to descend upon her own. "You don't trust me to cook, do you?"

"Are ye saying ye can?"

"Of course I can. Just show me the microwave and I'll—" her voice trailed off as she saw the question in his eyes. "I'm joking, James. But I can cook."

She moved across to the hand-tied rug before the fireplace and lifted a carved-wood candleholder from the mantel. A cute pinecone design decorated the outside edges and the handle formed the letter C. A half-burnt beeswax candle waited for a flame's touch. No electricity, no light switches. No power. Ugh.

"We should get the candles lit before it gets too dark. Can we have a warm fire?" Anna plucked at her damp shirt. "I'm still rather wet—aren't you?"

"Aye, we'll light the candles, Anna. Aye, I'll build a fire, and aye, my clothes are still a wee bit damp as well." He was beside her again and he was not about to let her escape this time. "But, all I want at this very moment is a taste o' yer sweet lips."

A loud series of knocks with rowdy laughter following came from outside the cabin door. James cursed under his breath and looked down into Anna's half-closed eyes. If only he could get her to admit her love as freely as she expressed her passion.

"I'm thinking we'll not get much peace this night." He crossed to the door ready to be testy as he swung it open.

A stout, dark-skinned, little man stood with a big pot held firmly in his grip. "Ah, James, it's good to see you. Michael told me you had come." He leaned out around James to peek into the room. "He also said you had a lovely lady with you. I thought perhaps you would enjoy my hot fresh minestrone."

James chuckled and shook his head. "Martin, ye know me well." He stood back with a gallant bow and waved the cook to enter.

Quickly following Martin came several more lumberjacks, one with more food and three of them were carrying wood. Michael followed with a bottle of wine. He ordered the fire and candles lit. The men jumped to do his bidding. A young boy with a jagged scar on his face threw a plain cloth over the table and, using the dishes in the hutch, quickly placed settings for two.

Martin set the soup tureen in the center of the table, then hurried over and bellowed out the door. Soon another boy, lanky and shy, rushed into the cabin with a long loaf of fresh baked bread wrapped in a creamy linen towel.

Anna's stomach growled at the wonderful smells filling the cabin. She had not eaten since leaving the ship hours before. A smile brightened her face as she walked over to the table, feeling like a princess at a royal banquet.

"James? Come on, this is wonderful." She stood eye to eye with the little cook. "My name is Anna. Thank you, Martin. Everything smells delicious and I'm half starved."

Martin glared at James with parental concern etched on his face. "You starve the pretty lady, James?"

"Oh, aye. Can ye not see how weak the lass is?" His devilish grin gave him away and they all laughed cheerfully. "Anna is right, 'tis a very nice thing ye have done for us, Martin. On such short notice too."

Martin beamed with pride. "You are more than welcome, both of you."

Michael grabbed the two young boys by their collars and nodded for the other woodsmen to follow. "Enjoy your dinner, Anna. Jamie, I'll be seeing you later at the bunkhouse, eh?"

Anna looked over at James as he sat down at the table opposite her. He was leaving her alone in the cabin their first night in the wilderness? No way!

A myriad of expressions crossed his face before he answered his friend. "Aye, I'll be bedding down in the bunkhouse."

"You aren't leaving me alone all night?" Her surprise was nothing compared to the devastation she felt over the loss of his company. "James?"

Michael chuckled.

James was ashamed he had not told her. It was not any more proper for them to sleep together here in the camp than it had been on his ship. On board his ship, it had been a matter of protection. His randy crew might have taken advantage of her. Here, it was the morality of the situation. He could trust the lumberjacks. Many already had wives or sweethearts. Some of them had even worked with his father and his uncle. They had known James since he was a wee lad of ten—long before he went to sea.

"We have a bit o' time before bed, lass. Time to talk. That is, if these well-wishers will give us a moment o' peace." His eyebrow rose with significance and he motioned to his friends to leave.

Michael headed out the door, a wide grin upon his face and his two young charges in tow. Martin left the cabin last of all, assuring them he could supply more soup if needed. When the cabin door shut behind the generous group of men, Anna leaned across the table and tore a chunk from the warm bread loaf.

"You are not leaving me alone in this cabin, you know," she said. "There's not even a lock on the door."

"Anna, 'tis not proper for me to sleep in here with ye, even if we are betrothed," he countered smoothly. He spooned a ladle full of soup into her bowl.

"We are not betrothed."

He smiled his charming lopsided grin and spooned himself a bowl of steaming soup too. "Aye, ye keep reminding me o' that. Yet, I beg to differ with ye. We are."

Not surprised at his comment, but ready to argue, Anna quickly swallowed a large bite of bread and nearly choked as it caught in her throat. She took a big gulp of her drink, then spat and choked on the raw bitter taste. "What the hell is this stuff?"

"Tis ale, lass. Do ye like it?"

She grimaced, shaking her head with distaste. "It's awful! It tastes like crap!"

James burst into hearty laughter. "I'll not believe ye have tasted the likes o' that. 'Tis a wee bit grainy I'll admit—"

"A wee bit? I may as well put dirt in my water." Taking a sip of the delicious vegetable broth to cleanse her mouth, she quickly forgot the ale and smiled up at him. "You've changed the subject again. My, but you're good at it."

He nodded acquiescence. "I'll not argue with ye. I want to come to an agreement before we return to Mendocino."

"An agreement?" She feigned innocence.

"Ye know what I want, lass. 'Tis only yer answer that needs changing." He took a lusty drink of ale and grinned across at her. "The sooner ye say yes, the sooner we can enjoy the pleasures awaiting us. I ache to take ye to my bed and ye know it well."

Anna swallowed hard. Her gaze met his and she forced a casual smile. She couldn't help the way her blood raced through her veins when he looked at her, nor could she stop the irregular pounding of her wayward heart. All she had to do was give in and say the three-lettered magic word. James would be all hers to enjoy, but for how long?

Seven

In the clearing, high above the giant redwoods, James watched a shooting star cross the late night sky. He made a silent wish. If only he could keep Anna beside him forever. He did not want destiny to intervene and return her to the future. He had to find a way to make her stay, but if he never won her heart...what then? He would be doomed to spend eternity lamenting for a love that was never to be.

What a strange twist of fate. James remembered his father telling him about the special spyglass. He wondered what his father would think about the spyglass bringing Anna to him across time. He would not allow fate to take her back, so he had hidden the spyglass in a locked drawer to prevent her from ever touching it again. He would do everything in his power to make her stay, now that she had come.

Anna appeared at the cabin door and waved cheerfully. The soft glow from the fireplace illuminated the cabin's comfortable interior behind her. She seemed more ethereal than ever—even dressed like a lad. She had changed into another pair of his trousers and a dry cambric shirt. He smiled and thought about how she must look to the men in camp.

Undoubtedly the lumberjacks assumed she had dressed in men's clothing for the long ride on horseback. He knew she was as at home in trousers as she was in a short, sleeveless dress. He wondered how the women of her time dressed every day. Did they all like to wear trousers as Anna did? He loved the way his trousers looked on her. The vision nearly drove him mad with desire and a raw heat burned deep in his loins.

"What are you thinking about with that smug grin on your face, James?" She walked across the clearing and snuggled up against him.

"To be honest I was thinking how much I want ye, Anna." He wrapped his arms around her, lowered his lips to hers and kissed her ardently.

"Then don't make me stay alone tonight." Anna watched the tree tops sway with the mountain breeze. "You can even sleep on the rug by the fire, if it makes you feel better."

He frowned down at her. "Tis not where I want to be."

"You want to stay in the bunkhouse with all those dirty men?"

"Watch yer tongue, lass. They may not bathe as often as ye like, but they are braw men. I'll not have ye hurting their feelings."

"I'm sorry. I guess I expected them to smell as good as you do." She made an issue of sniffing his freshly washed skin. Then she licked playfully at his furry chest, peeking through his open shirt.

"Yer not fair, Anna. I bathed in the stream because I'm courting ye. They would likely do the same if their women were here." His attitude was stern. He was doing his best to ignore her tempting seduction.

"Oh yeah? Then how come your crew keep themselves clean and they dress nice?" She pointed her forefinger into his chest. "I didn't see any of their women on board."

"Yer asking too many questions. I like my crew tidy and their clothes well mended. Not all captains require it."

He covered her mouth in a lingering kiss, hoping to distract her. She gazed up at him dreamy-eyed. He nearly changed his evening plans, but that would be accepting defeat. Something he was not prepared to do. Not yet. He grasped her around the waist and hugged her to his side.

"Kiss me again, James." She sighed and puckered up, raising her determined chin.

If he kissed her again they might not take a stroll at all. He could think of many ways to entertain her—none of which were options. A quick peck on her cheek would have to suffice for now. "Let's go roaming, lass."

"You know you didn't tell me what you were smiling about." She poked him in the side, pouting her full lips. "I have never known anyone who can change the subject so fast."

Anna waited for him to continue the conversation with an argument, or at least an excuse. He said nothing. Instead, he pulled her along with him into the woods. They followed a well-worn path with trees and shrubs cut away for foot-traffic. He stopped suddenly and she plowed right into his broad back.

"What?"

He swung around and covered her mouth with his big hand. "Shh! Look yonder, Anna. 'Tis a wee nasty badger."

She peered into the starlit clearing ahead and saw to her horror a large dark shape rooting in the dirt. "Aren't badgers really vicious?"

"Aye, if ye are dumb enough to bother the ornery buggers." He chuckled, but became serious when he met her gaze.

She glared at him. "Then why are we standing here?"

He bent and touched his lips to hers, causing her to melt against him. "Aye. Why indeed, Anna?" He took her hand in his and they took a shortcut through the trees, well out of the badger's path.

"James?" Her heart fluttered from his tender caress. "Where are we going? I thought by a walk you meant down the road or around the camp—or something normal—not a nocturnal romp through the underbrush with God only knows what kind of wild creatures."

James continued their brisk pace, knowing what natural beauty lay ahead. He was eager to share nature with Anna. "Och, 'tis romantic I'm being, lass."

"Romantic? Stomping through the forest in the middle of the night is romantic? You would never make a good Romeo."

He stopped in his tracks and turned to face her. "Aye, I have heard o' Shakespeare and his dashing Romeo, seems to me his fair Juliet was a bit more adventurous than ye are." His face was inches away. "Maybe I can change yer ways."

Her defiant gaze met his. "Ha! You don't consider time travel adventurous?" She tugged her hand away and headed back down the trail, spewing curses left and right.

"Anna?"

James watched her stomp away through the low-branched trees, ducking every now and then. She was the one who suggested exploring the wilds. He thought she would enjoy a hike up to the ridge above camp. The sea was visible in the distance and the subtle majesty of the huge redwood forest was awe-inspiring and romantic in the moonlight.

He was contemplating whether to chase after her, or let her run back to the cabin, when he heard an anguished cry in the woods.

~ * ~

Crashing through the forest in her haste to find the worn path, Anna stumbled over a tangle of dead branches. She landed face down in the ferns and groaned at the pain in her twisted ankle. When she tried to stand, she fell against a sapling pine and the supple young tree gave way, sending her tumbling to the ground again. She grasped the sharp edge of a rock to prevent her head from hitting the ground so hard. Warm blood oozed from her palm and she drifted into painless unconsciousness.

Michael came running down the path from camp. James pushed wildly through the pine boughs in the direction of Anna's scream.

He called out for his friend to follow. When Michael caught up, James was already kneeling over Anna's still form.

"I heard her scream. What happened?" Michael knelt beside them. "Is she all right?"

James was cursing himself for even bringing her up to the logging camp. He carefully felt over her limbs for broken bones and found none. "The lass has hit her head and there's a wee cut on her hand, but 'tis her ankle that needs tending." He lifted her carefully into his arms. "Is Douglas still at camp, Michael?"

"Douglas is in bed in the bull pen. Don't worry, I'll have him to your cabin before you reach it, Jamie." Michael hurried off toward the bunkhouse.

James' pace quickened when he reached the camp clearing and kicked the cabin door open, not bothering to close it after him. He gently laid Anna down upon the bed and wrapped a clean rag around her bleeding hand, then rolled up her loose pant leg. In the oil lantern's light he could see her creamy skin was already turning a deep purple. He pulled her modern shoes off both feet and hid them under the bed. That's all he needed, questions about the oddities of Anna's dress.

A burly, red-haired man rushed into the cabin with a hardy shove from behind. "Michael! Don't push. I always knock first."

"Not tonight, Doc. Jamie's girl is hurt."

Douglas moved to the bedside with his small black bag in hand. "James? What happened here?" He began examining Anna by taking her vital signs.

James was remorseful. He was about to tell Douglas what he knew about her fall, when her eyelashes fluttered. Pushing the burly older man aside, he cupped her face in his hands. "Anna?"

Her small hand came up to rest on his. "Oh, Geez, what a klutz! I can't believe I tripped and fell like that."

James smiled down at her and no further words were spoken for he covered her lips in a sweet kiss. "Tis sorry I am that I caused ye to get hurt, lass."

"It wasn't your fault, James. I simply tripped and fell."

Douglas pushed his way through to the bed. "My name's Douglas, ma'am. I ain't no doctor by rights, but I cured a lot of folks. Looks like you've got a twisted ankle here and, if we can get your fella out of the way, I'll take a look at the cut on your hand."

Michael took James by the arm and led him over to the fireplace. "She's gonna be right as rain, Jamie. Doc's good with sprains and cuts. Hell, he's fixed enough of 'em around here. A lot worse, too."

James smiled gratefully at his childhood friend. The two had grown up together and even though Michael was a year younger, they had been inseparable in their youth. When they reached their teens, they even courted the same girls. Then James turned to a life at sea and Michael went to work in the logging camp—the same as their fathers before them.

"Shoot! Is that a tear running down your cheek, Jamie?" Michael hooted in joy, slapping his knee with gusto.

"Och, man! Ye take me for a wee *bairn*?" James rounded on him with a playful punch to his middle. "Aye, too long a time since we had a wee sprattle, Michael. Now is as good a time as any, eh?"

Michael was grinning his brilliant toothy grin as he caught the offending fist before it struck home. "I'll fight you any day, Jamie. We always did enjoy a good round. Shall we go outside for this?" He was already removing his shirt. "I know how you wild Scots liked to fight with bare chests and bare fists."

"Aye," James agreed, glancing over his shoulder to make sure Douglas was taking good care of Anna. He crossed to her and placed a tender kiss upon her forehead. "I'll be outside for a wee bit o' sport, lass."

Anna grimaced in pain as the doctor wrapped her ankle. "I heard, James, but you said you two were old friends—ow!"

Douglas glanced up apologetically from his work, only to smile and continue wrapping her ankle until it was twice its normal size with the bandage.

"Michael enjoys a good fight. I've not seen him for weeks. I need to release my anger, Anna. Michael understands." James smiled and strode quickly from the cabin before she could say anything to make him stay.

"Anger?" She closed her eyes and sighed deeply. What in the world was he angry about? Her head pounded violently. Douglas' tender ministrations as he tended her wounds got on her nerves. With a weary sigh she looked up at the large man who was trying so hard to make her comfortable while he tortured her.

"So you're the one who finally caught our lonely James?" Douglas inquired as he dug through his little black bag.

Anna knew she needed a couple of stitches and she didn't care to see the archaic tools he would use. Watching was out of the question. She concentrated on something else. What did Douglas just ask her?

"Lonely James? You are not trying to tell me he's celibate?" She doubted the reality of her words. She giggled a little off key, then moaned in misery as the slight body movement made her ache from head to toe.

Douglas laughed, a deep rumbling sound. "Not that one by any means! Women fall all over him. Why, I even heard how they sneak aboard his ship to seduce him."

Anna moaned again, both from the pain of being stitched and smoldering jealousy. "You don't say. I thought I was his first woman."

He chuckled softly and jabbed her hand again with a needle that felt like a hot poker. "You'll need your sense of humor with James. He enjoys practical jokes." Finishing the last catgut stitch, he cleaned off the wound.

"Good Lord!" She screeched. "What the heck is that?"

Douglas' face turned beet red. "Carbolic acid. It only stings for a few minutes. It helps prevent infection. Your cut looked pretty clean, but I would rather be safe."

"Phew! It stinks, too." She covered her nose with her good hand. She felt like such a ninny. He was only trying to help her. "I'm sorry, Douglas. I didn't mean to yell at you. I appreciate what you've done for me, honest."

He patted her good arm and smiled down at her. "Anytime I can be of help." He closed up his bag. "You really should stay in bed for a day or two in order for the sprain to heal. And I believe you'll have quite a headache for a while."

"Great, I probably have a concussion."

Douglas looked at her with curiosity. "Yes, well, I'll talk to James outside. Very nice to meet you, Anna. I wish it could have been under different circumstances."

She reached out and grasped his hand. "Me too, Douglas, and thank you."

James walked into the cabin. "All done, Doc?"

Douglas nodded and took James aside to talk with him.

Anna watched from the bed and wondered what the two were avidly discussing. James glanced over at her with a sheepish grin upon his handsome face. She had the feeling she was the topic of their hushed conversation.

Douglas finished what he had to say to James, smiled again in her direction, and then took his leave. James crossed the room to her side with a curiously smug expression.

"What was that all about?"

"Och, ye will never believe what Douglas thought." He sat beside her on the bed. "He blames it on the knock to yer head."

"Are you going to tell me or keep me guessing?"

"Curious wee bugger, aren't ye? Aye, well he said ye told him I was celibate. Did ye really, Anna?"

She couldn't contain her giggles, even though her head throbbed more with every subtle movement. "Oh James, did he?"

"I do not see what is so funny."

"Sorry. It's just that, well, I was teasing him. Honestly, I thought he knew it." She struggled to wipe the smile from her face. "Is that embarrassing to you?"

"Aye, 'tis saying I'm not a virile man." James leaned down to nibble along her silken neck. "I've a randy reputation to uphold, ye know."

Anna placed her hand along his jaw and forced him to look up at her. "James, you are the most masculine man I have ever met. To believe that you couldn't tumble any woman into bed would be absolutely laughable."

"Aye?"

"Aye." She pulled his head down to place a much-needed kiss upon his lips. "By the way, he confirmed your story about women sneaking aboard your ship. I didn't do that, of course, but now that I've met you, I can see why they do."

"Ah, Anna. I love it when ye are so bold with me." He brushed tiny kisses all over her face. "I love the taste of ye, as well."

"Ummm, and I love your kisses, Captain." She relaxed under his sensual attack. Her ankle hurt like mad and her hand throbbed like crazy. Her head was exploding like the Fourth of July—and the best medicine in the entire world was his loving embrace.

~ * ~

Michael knocked on the cabin door early the following morning bearing a hand-made set of crutches. Anna was impressed by his workmanship. Carved, sanded, and made from fresh scrap lumber, they were unique in their design. He must have worked late into the night to make them specially for her.

"Gee, thanks, Michael." She compared them mentally to modern-day, adjustable, metal crutches and smiled. "They're so beautiful. Now I won't be hopping around on one foot like a klutz."

"Ye know how to use them?" James helped her to her feet. She was the most surprising woman he had ever known. When most women would take advantage of their injury to be coddled and pampered, she was desperate to be up and about.

"Oh yeah, I broke my leg once water-skiing...Ummm, I mean...sure, I've had to use them before. Mine were a little different from this pair, but these are great." Her embarrassed stammer covered her slip of tongue. Neither of the men said a word.

James coughed. Hopefully Michael was too busy admiring Anna's beauty to pay attention to her unusual words, but what in the devil was water-skiing? He would remember to ask her when they were alone. He watched as she moved awkwardly around the room demonstrating her new mobility.

Douglas peeked into the cabin. "Good-morning! How are you feeling, Anna?"

She smiled. "I feel great today, thanks to you and your excellent care." Stopping in front of him, she winked conspiratorially. "I feel good enough to take a tour of the camp."

"Ye will only hurt yerself again."

"James, I will not. We came all the way up here and I want to see how a logging camp operates. If you think I will miss seeing an important part of history—"

James took her arm and tugged her to his side. "Tis not history to us, Anna," he whispered in warning.

"Ornery bugger," she cursed, using one of his favorite expletives. "I want to see a nineteenth-century logging camp. Now, will you take me on a tour, or should I ask Michael to do the honor?"

James fumed with jealousy, but he knew he had to give in or she would do exactly what she pleased. "All right, Anna, I'll take ye around the camp."

~ * ~

Much to her dismay, Anna found herself being escorted by James—and Michael. James was not his usual cheerful self with Michael present. He seemed a little on edge, as though he needed to prove something to Michael. Was this their usual camaraderie?

She glanced up at Michael's seven-foot frame. He was extremely well built. His thick blond hair waved about his head and down the back of his neck. His fair full-beard hid the rest of what was a rather attractive face, but his crowning glory was his smile. A wide grin displayed a set of perfect, pearly-white teeth. He could charm a cobra with his smile, Anna mused.

Without even dwelling on it, she knew Michael was no challenge to her affections for James. Her emotions were already deeply involved with the brawny sea captain. Could it be a touching of souls? Time had not even been able to keep them apart. Had they known each other before in another place—perhaps another sphere?

Stopping at an overlook, Anna gasped in awe. A deep gorge lay far below where a raging river carved its way through mother earth, leaving behind large boulders that made a graceful playground for the water.

"James, I love it. It's all so beautiful in your time." She covered her mouth with her fingertips and giggled.

James scowled down at her. He reached for her good hand, but his competition was there first. His fists clenched in frustration. "Blast it all, Michael. Can ye not let us have some time to ourselves?"

"You've never minded sharing before, James." Michael wrapped a large arm around Anna's small waist. "Look yonder. That's the holding pond where we catch the logs until we have enough to float down river at summer's end."

The area around them was thick with ferns, scrub oak, and sapling pines. Anna took in the wonderful unpolluted smell of fresh crisp air. She looked down at the huge holding pond spread out below that would soon be filled with logs. When the fall rains came, the water's sheer force would send the logs spewing down river to the mill.

"How did you get all those logs into the river in the first place?" She looked up at Michael, squinting her eyes to see his face in the bright sunlight.

Michael was kind enough to squat down beside her as he explained skid roads and how they worked. "We live a rough life, but I don't complain."

James cleared his throat to get their attention. He stood with his back against a huge tree, arms folded in his usual observant manner, and an expression of pure irritation upon his face. She would have laughed, but knew he was truly losing patience with Michael.

Michael chuckled. "I'm only trying to make him jealous."

"You're doing a great job of it. But please stop. He is a good man, Michael."

"Ah, that's what I like to hear. He deserves a woman such as you, Anna. One that can see the good in him over his gruff and stubborn nature." Michael stood to his full height with a stretch. "Enough leisure for the day, I better get back to the men and leave you two alone."

Anna laughed softly. "I do believe that is exactly what the captain has in mind."

She stood watching as the friendly big lumberjack walked away through the forest. Strong arms slipped around her waist from behind and she leaned back against a warm, broad chest. James' touch was magic. No words were spoken as they swayed slowly back and forth to nature's quiet orchestra.

Birds chirped and flitted through the underbrush as they foraged for nest building materials and food. Wind whispered through the tops of the giant pine trees, sending their heady scent into the air. The faraway sound of the river below brought serenity to mind. Awkwardly, she turned around on her crutches to face him. Her eyes overflowed with joyful tears. She could no longer deny how she felt inside.

"I am happy in your time, James." She buried her face into his soft shirt.

"Aye. I was thinking that very same thing." He kissed the top of her head, and then tilted her face to meet his in a deep passionate kiss. "Is yer ankle hurting ye, lass?"

She had tried bravely not to show how much her foot was throbbing, but she had nearly reached the end of her endurance and she knew she should relinquish her tour for the day. "Yes, just a little. Can we go back to the cabin now?"

"Aye, 'tis a bonny idea." James gently lifted her into the cradle of his arms, shifting so she could settle the crutches on her lap. Then he easily carried her back through the forest.

Anna nuzzled her face against his neck, inhaling his wonderful masculine scent. For now she was completely safe in his arms, the threat of her ability to remain with him in 1880 pushed far from her troubled mind. She closed her eyes and let his delectable aura surround her.

~ * ~

A distinctive knock, three quick raps at the cabin door, got Anna up from her resting place on the bed. James sat at the dining table deep in concentration over his paperwork; he hadn't even noticed the knocks. Michael stood on the porch, a bouquet of bright wild flowers quickly wilting in his large sweaty hand.

"Hello, friend," Anna greeted.

"My heart still melts before your beauty, lady," Michael said handing her the flowers. "An apology is in order for tormenting you earlier in the forest. I'm more than happy for you and Jamie. I swear I've not a jealous bone in my body."

She smiled up at the giant of a man and couldn't resist a little stab at his good nature. "That's quite a statement—coming from James' biggest competitor."

Michael laughed with gusto.

James got up from the table and walked across to the door. "Good afternoon, Michael. I understand ye are just leaving."

Michael nodded. "Jamie, I've come to wish you well."

"Oh, aye? Ye sound to me as though ye still fancy a black eye."

"James!" Anna was surprised at his rudeness. She reached for his arm to pull him back, but he turned and swung a lightning-quick, hard fist right into Michael's smiling face.

Michael staggered backward, but kept his balance as he shook his head and laughed. "You'll have to do better than that, little Scot."

James hated Michael's nickname for him. His anger blew the fuse that had sizzled all day. He barreled forward, headfirst into Michael's washboard stomach.

Douglas mistakenly took that moment to appear at the cabin door. "Is everything all right in here?"

Anna smiled feebly and shrugged.

The two burly, struggling men fell backward into Douglas, who lost his footing and landed with a sickening thud, right smack on his backside. James and Michael landed on top of him, both swearing heartily as they crashed to the ground. The cursing, fist-swinging duo continued their fight with Douglas trapped beneath them. Douglas' fervent pleas turned to curses, but still the two ignored him.

Anna followed the fight scene to the door and watched in awe as they rolled off the porch into the dirt. She had never seen men fight with such raw violence. If their friendship went way back to childhood, how could they hurt each other like this? She glanced around at the growing crowd of lumberjacks who had come to watch the fight. Why didn't someone stop James and Michael, and rescue poor Douglas?

Douglas had been an innocent bystander, just coming by to check out the shouting match going on between the two men. Well, enough of this chaotic situation. If all these big muscle-bound men could only stand aside and encourage the bloody combat, then she would be the one to stop it. She pushed through the crowd on her crutches and reached the camp doctor where he lay sprawled on the ground, spitting dirt and sputtering curses.

She bent to help Douglas to his unsteady feet. She glared down at James, still rolling on the ground in a never-ending clench with Michael. "This is absurd. What in the world are you two fighting about?"

Anna hobbled with Douglas to the porch step and went in search of a cloth and some water. She carefully cleaned the scrapes on Douglas's face and retrieved his black bag from the bushes where it had fallen upon his unfortunate arrival. Listening to the loggers cheer the combatants on, she found the alcohol and cleansed the camp doctor's wounds.

Douglas grinned up at her. "He loves you, you know."

"What did you say?" She couldn't believe she had heard the older man correctly. Grimacing from the slight pain shooting up her ankle with every move, she repeated her question. "What did you say?"

The dusty fighters rolled by with limbs entangled, grunting and groaning as their big fists made contact with each other. She turned her back to them, hoping for a quick resolution.

"He loves you. James has never acted this way before. I've known him since he was just a boy, and a feisty one, at that. He's gone and done it this time. They say the bigger they are the harder they fall. In this case, that's exactly right."

Anna was too shocked to interrupt Douglas as he rambled on about the captain's many virtues. He didn't sound upset at all with the way the two grown men were acting, even after being unintentionally knocked down and beaten in their scuffle. She dropped carefully to her knees on the step beside Douglas.

"How can you be sure?" She asked quietly.

"Take a piece of advice, Anna. Grab the captain while you can. He's a fine catch and a good man, and he'll make an excellent husband." Douglas put his arm around her shoulder and gave her a fatherly hug. "You're the right one for him. He needs a woman to keep him in his place and put up with his wild Highland ways. Just don't ever let him tame you, you're wonderful just the way you are."

James won the fight and stood above Michael with a wide satisfied grin breaking the mask of dirt and blood on his face.

"Thank you." She tried not to blush at the sincerity in the doctor's words, but when she caught James devouring her with his unerring gaze she failed miserably. Heat flooded her face and she tried to concentrate on her conversation with Douglas. "I believe you're right, Douglas. I'll grab him right now, as a matter of fact."

She didn't get the chance to move.

James walked over to the porch, his cocky attitude overflowing. His lower lip was bloody, his fists cut and bleeding. "Twas a grand fight, Douglas. But I will not be needing yer medical attention." He took the porch step steadily and stopped short before Anna. He met her gaze evenly. "We're leaving now, Anna. Best we hasten or 'twill be too late to stay at the Stensons." Grasping her hand in his bruised and swollen one, he pulled her into the cabin and slammed the door.

Anna yanked her hand back, furious at his actions. "Do not presume to boss me. What you just did out there was uncalled-for. Michael is a nice man and you deliberately picked that fight."

"Aye, but he had it coming."

She shook her head in dismay. "No, James. He did not. Excuse me." She pushed past him and opened the door in time to see Michael struggling to his feet, wiping his reddened jaw.

He stood slowly and dusted the dirt from his clothes. "James is feeling much better now, Anna. I wish I could say the same. Damn, the man fights like the devil!"

"You could have beaten him, Michael, and you know it," Douglas said. "But it was good of you to spare his handsome face for his upcoming nuptials." He groaned as Michael helped him to his feet.

Anna stepped up to the two beaten men. "Look, I am so sorry about all this. If there is anything I can do to help—"

Michael laughed. "Sure is. Take the nasty little Scot back to Mendocino and wed the man, before he kills us all."

Douglas laughed too. "Good advice, Michael."

She smiled and shook each of their hands in turn. "Thank you both for putting up with his brutality. I'll take you up on your advice to get him out of camp, but I'm not so sure I want to marry a man with a temper like his."

Standing in the late afternoon sunshine, Anna watched the men walk away. She folded her arms and sighed. The beauty of the land escaped her as her troubled thoughts ran back over the fight scene. What kind of man was Captain James Adam Duncan? What drove him to such wild fits of rage?

Eight

James sat at the table wiping blood from his lip with a damp cloth. He was ashamed of the way he had reacted to Michael's mild flirtation with Anna. Now he wondered why he had gone into a roaring rage so quickly. He knew Michael was goading him, trying to make him jealous. He fell for it, harder and faster than he ever had before.

Anna was special to him, but this was not the way to win her affections. She was mad at him now, and he did not quite know how to approach her and apologize. He could hear the men's robust laughter out on the porch with Anna and wished he could join them. He needed to talk to Anna alone first.

He turned to see her image through the open door. She voiced her farewells to Michael and Douglas, and stood watching as the two men walked away. With her arms crossed, standing deep in thought, she looked alone and vulnerable. He waited patiently for her to come back inside the cabin.

The closed expression on her face told him she was not in the mood to talk, but he had to try. "Anna, I wish to speak with ye, lass."

"I don't want to argue anymore, Captain."

"So 'tis back to Captain we are now?" He stood, pushing back the chair and dropped the soiled cloth to the table.

"Look at you. You're all black and blue—and bloody. And why? Your temper is nastier than a great white shark." She crossed the room and picked up the cloth. Carefully, she dabbed at his face. Her touch felt heavenly. "I can't believe you would pick a fight with someone as nice as Michael. I'm glad we came here though, because now I know things could never work out between us. I abhor violence."

James' heart sank to the bottom of his shoes. "What are ye saying, lass?"

"I think I said it pretty plainly. What is it with you, all this crazy violence and uncontrolled rage?"

He sighed and winced as she rubbed a particularly tender spot on his jaw, just as her words nagged at his heart. "I suppose 'tis from my heritage. We Scots are a hardy breed o' man. We learn to fight before we learn to walk. 'Tis how we kept the English at bay."

"But in the end they won, didn't they?"

"Aye, they won."

She rinsed the rag in the washbowl. "Is that why you are so eager to fight? Because your family lost the battle with the English?"

He drew back from her touch. "I aim to set it straight, Anna, and to gain what is rightfully mine. No matter how long it takes. No matter the cost."

"How about if I say I will marry you—if and only if—you give up this senseless quest for revenge?"

He raised an eyebrow in amazement. "How can I give up what my father died for?"

"Do you want to die for it too, James?"

Her question was simple and right to the point. Would he be willing to die for his father's cause? Before he had met Anna, he would not even have hesitated in his answer. Now, he was unsure of where his loyalties lie. He only had to think of losing her—never being able to see, touch, or talk to her again. He knew without a doubt he would give up everything he owned to keep her.

He looked down into her green eyes, soft with concern for him, and felt a tightening in his chest. If he answered her now, would she withdraw her proposal, or would she marry him as she said?

"Hold still. Let me get some fresh water and clean you up properly." She busied herself with the water pitcher and cloth, and then returned to torture his wounds. "You didn't answer me, James. Is the question that difficult?"

"Are ye serious, Anna?"

She sighed. "About as serious as you are. You aren't in love with me. You might be infatuated with my difference from the women of your time, but you're not in love with me. Love just doesn't happen that fast and, if it does, it doesn't last. I speak from personal experience."

"Have ye been in love before then?"

"No. I know that now, but I had to learn the hard way. That's why, next time I want to be sure. I will not give my heart freely to just anyone, you know."

Aye, he knew. He had been battling to win her heart from the moment she arrived aboard the *Ceilidh*. After his earlier loss of control, he had slipped back a bit in her heart. It was time to ease off and take life slow with Anna Bentley. For win her heart he would, and still be able to keep at least one promise to his father. Continuing the family line was his worthy father's dying wish.

~ * ~

Mendocino was buzzing with activity when they arrived to return the horses to the livery stables. It was nearly dinnertime and people were rushing about to finish the day's activities before retiring to their homes. Anna stood waiting for James on the boardwalk, watching history in action with mild amusement.

"Here we are, lass." James appeared from the shadowy interior of the stables and slipped an arm around her waist.

Anna turned to see a large fancy carriage with a pair of horses hitched and waiting. Never in her life had she ridden in a horse

123

drawn carriage. She reached up and kissed James on the jaw, then hurried toward the vehicle.

The short ride on dirt packed streets was a bit jarring, compared to riding in an automobile on a paved highway, but she savored the unique adventure. The lush velvet interior, the soft tufted-seats and the coach's fancy detail made it easy to feel rich and pampered.

As they traveled along in the bouncing carriage, she peeked out the windows to admire the Cape-Cod style town with its short and narrow streets. Victorian houses were so gaudy with gingerbread trim and bright-colored paints they sometimes looked totally absurd.

She suppressed a giggle and pointed to a grotesque mansion on her right. "Oh my! James, look at that one."

He chuckled. "Tis the mayor's home, lass. He likes the color o' purple violets."

"And yellow sunshine," she added, noting the house looked more like an overgrown pansy than a dainty violet.

The carriage slowed to a stop. A beautiful example of the frivolous era stood like a proud painted lady. Anna marveled at the talent needed to build such an eccentric mansion. Her eyes widened as her gaze combed the structure. From the tall brass weathervane at its peak to the elaborately sculptured posts guarding the front porch, and all the etched windows in-between, it was perfect. A conception in cream with chocolate trim, it was definitely the most attractive home on the shady tree-lined street.

"Here we are at last," James whispered in her ear, while a footman unloaded his trunk from the carriage. "Ye promise ye will mind yer manners, now?"

Anna took the bait, almost too easily. She turned to him, ready to argue, and then saw the laughter in his eyes. "You, my dear captain, are the most despicable man I have ever known."

"Aye, I am a bit o' that, lass." He laughed heartily and winked at her. "But it does get me what I want in the very end."

"Do you always have to have your way?"

"Aye, when it comes to loving ye, I do." His arms slipped around her waist. His warm hug would have gone much further, but for the ill-timed arrival of the young footman opening the carriage door.

George welcomed them on the porch steps, greeting James with a bear hug and Anna with a kiss upon her cheek. "Anyone can see how much in love you two are. You simply glow with happiness. Welcome to our home, Anna."

James took Anna's hand with an understanding squeeze. Her blush told him she felt uncomfortable because the Stensons thought they were man and wife. It did not bother him because he knew in the end he would persuade her to become his wife.

The entry hall was enormous in size and Anna marveled at the heavily decorated room. Her gaze wandered from huge portraits lining the walls to a myriad of small tables covered with knickknacks. The home was an antique lover's delight.

A giant crystal chandelier hung from a high ceiling, revealing four-levels of stairs. The steps spiraled upward with ornate carved banisters just made for sliding all the way down to the highly polished, hardwood floors.

"Anna! Why, you're limping!"

Angelique's motherly tone startled Anna out of her state of awe. "Just a little. I tripped and fell in the woods."

"We've taken care o' her, Angel. She just needs to rest." James knew Angel. She would have to know all the details and would be unhappy James had chosen to drag his new wife up into the wilderness.

"You poor dear. We should get you off your foot right away."

"I feel fine, Angel, honest," Anna assured her.

"If you would like me to contact the doctor, please let me know."

"Thank you, but that won't be necessary." Anna was able to bear the pain from her swollen ankle for a short while and she hoped to get by without using the crutches Michael had made. Their simple existence seemed to keep James' anger simmering.

"You must want to freshen up after your long ride. Rosie will take you to your suite." Angelique motioned the black maid to lead the way.

"Tis a wee bit o' rest we could use, as well, Angel."

She smiled sweetly. "We'll have a lovely dinner and chat in a couple of hours."

George winked at his wife, then laughed when she responded with a slight blush. "Shall we tell them how we diverted our travel fatigue, my dear?"

"George!" Angelique's face turned as brilliant a pink as the gown she was wearing. She turned to Anna, ignoring her husband's playful taunting. "I will send Rosie up with an outfit for you to wear. Do you trust my choice, or would you rather come and select one for yourself?"

"I'm sure I will like whatever you choose, and thanks again for your generosity." Anna's voice was much calmer than she felt at this particular moment. She was amazed her modern-day language had not caused more problems. Her verbal slips of the tongue were almost impossible to control and she was sure the Stensons would notice.

"Shall we?" James lifted her into his arms and carried her up the long staircase, following the servant to their suite.

Anna gasped with surprise as they entered the large suite. She could only imagine the wealth it took to create such luxury. Her tired gaze noted the lavish decor in deep emerald green with touches of rose. Everything from the papered walls to the flowered carpet matched perfectly. Two tall French doors, draped by yards of emerald velvet pulled aside with gold tasseled ropes, framed a lovely formal garden below the balcony.

A romantic rose-colored brocade love seat sat invitingly before the stone fireplace. A fresh bouquet of pink roses decorated the center of a small mahogany dining table, their sweet scent highlighting the cozy atmosphere. Adjoining the main room on each end were two large bedrooms done in the same entrancing color scheme.

"His and hers," Anna whispered. "In case I have a migraine headache, hubby?"

James groaned in mock anguish and set her on her feet. "Yer a bonny wee package to carry, Anna, but mayhap I should have dropped ye on the stairs?"

"Humph! I'll ignore that remark, you scoundrel."

Rosie grinned from ear to ear. "I'm happy to see James has settled down at last. I been taking care of him since he was a boy." She reached out and tweaked his cheek.

"That'll do, Rosie," James said sternly.

Rosie ignored him as she continued speaking to Anna, "I've grown mighty attached to this young man over the years. You take good care of him, you hear?" Pushing open another door, Rosie proudly showed them the marvelous new addition called a lavatory.

Anna smiled in good-humored pleasure at the modern convenience. The room boasted a claw-foot porcelain tub and a pedestal sink with brass taps. A large oval mirror with flowers etched around the edges hung above the sink. A tall toilet sat beside the sink with a long pull-chain hanging down from a tank attached to the wall above. Still, the toilet was a huge improvement over the bucket on board the *Ceilidh*.

The tub sat already full of steamy, lavender-scented water. How on earth had Rosie known when they would arrive? "I'm first!" Anna blurted out enthusiastically, noticing the surprise on Rosie's face.

"We'll bathe together, Anna," James said softly with a twinkle in his blue eyes.

"In your dreams!" She whirled around and gave Rosie an apologetic look, remembering they were supposed to be happily married. "Sorry. I just want to stretch out and relax in the tub. Thank you for drawing the water for us. How did you know when we were coming?"

"Old Rosie knows many things." She clicked her tongue and headed for the door. "You two behave now. No more spats."

"We promise." Anna sighed, wishing she could recall the details of the women's rights movement. It would sure help her get through these priggish times. There were so many things to remember and so many things to learn.

James left Anna in the bathroom and walked over to the massive canopied bed. He ran his hand slowly over the deep pink, velvet spread. His thoughts were on seduction. One night alone with Anna in this bed and he was sure he could convince her of his love. Infatuation? Never. That was for young lads and old men, not for a man who knew what was in his heart.

Anna watched James with open curiosity. It was obvious what he had on his mind. She had never been pursued so ardently, or persistently, in all her life. It didn't really disillusion her to know how much he looked forward to their union in the flesh, as well as in marriage. Instead, she found herself looking forward to giving in to his erotic seduction. A shiver ran up her spine and down to her toes, curling them with sweet anticipation.

He turned around, catching her boldly studying him. His lips parted to form a tilted grin and a dimple appeared on his left cheek, tempting her with his natural charm. He held his arms out to her, appealing to her physical weakness for him.

"I know what's on your mind—and you can forget it. I want to have a real bath, enjoy a nice home-cooked meal and sleep in a soft wonderful bed." Her gaze met his in defiance. "Alone."

"Ah, Anna, ye are so bonny when ye are being stubborn." James sauntered toward her and encircled her in his arms. "I've been meaning to ask ye…what is a dude?"

She laughed lightly. His questions always caught her off guard. "Another one of my oddities, I suppose. I use the term endearingly, yet teasingly, much like you call William a lad. He's nearly twenty-three, James."

"Aye, he is. Old enough to be called a man, but young enough to make mistakes."

"So he is a lad."

"Am I a dude?"

Anna laughed again. "Heavens, no. Not really. I mean, I could never feel this way about..." Her voice faded away.

James was staring at her mouth. He wanted to kiss her. Was she simply stalling the inevitable? She wanted this robust man, more than she wanted any man she had ever met before, but she wasn't sure she could ever completely trust a man again. Looks were so deceiving, and so were lovers. She dropped her troubled gaze from his view.

"I'll not bother ye while ye have yer bath," he said in a deep voice filled with longing. "I'll take my leave o' ye now."

James could tell Anna was struggling with something that really upset her when she became suddenly quiet. Running a hand through his hair in frustration, he walked over to the bedroom door. He wanted her so badly he ached with need, but he knew he must back away rather than lose her.

"James?"

"Aye?" He turned and saw tears running down her cheeks. A moment later, she was in his arms. "What's this, lass?" He wiped her moist cheeks with his fingertips. "Are ye hurting?"

"Yes, but it's not my leg. I'm such a romantic fool. You are the best thing that has ever happened to me. I want to be loved by you— but part of me can't let go of the future."

"I can see how it would be difficult for ye. 'Tis not the same here, is it, lass?"

"No. The place I came from is where I really belong. This is like living in a fictitious world; it's too good to be true. I don't want to lose you. But I'm afraid that's how this will all end."

Anna buried her face against his shirt. She would always remember the wonderful masculine smell of him. He soothed her senses in a way nothing else could, as well as stimulated them to the point of no return. She didn't fully understand the yearning she felt deep inside, or the confusion it brought to her wayward heart.

"Ye belong with me, Anna. I'll not let ye go back to the future, but I promise I'll not let ye be hurt as well." James lowered his lips to meet hers in a tender kiss, causing the last of his resistance to falter. He needed her in the most intimate way, before she drove him mad with unleashed passion.

A breathless sigh escaped her lips. "James—"

He proceeded to remove her cambric shirt, followed quickly by his own. Curiosity peaked his interest at the soft fabric barely covering her lovely round breasts and wild excitement coursed through his veins as he reached out to caress them gently with his hands. He could feel her nipples harden with eager response to his touch. Their eyes met with shared desire.

He crushed her to his chest with a sensuous groan of satisfaction. Awareness dawned in her limpid green eyes as he bent to kiss her sweet lips again. A kiss meant to be tender. He was fast coming to terms that he could no longer control his physical need.

"Ah, Anna—"

She smiled up at him, panting nearly as hard as himself. "Good Lord, you're so much more than I ever bargained for in a man."

"Am I now?"

Her palm cupped his jaw. "Better than my wildest dreams, you rogue. Where on earth did you learn to kiss so well?"

"Do ye like it, lass?" He rubbed her bare sides with his hands, marveling in the softness of her fair skin.

"I love it. You're so sexy. Your technique is sending my emotions through the ceiling." She kissed his jaw, staggered kisses along his neck, and nuzzled his shoulder with gentle nibbles.

"Anna—say ye will not stop now." His hands grasped her round hips, pulling her snug against his rising need.

Anna giggled at the hunger in his deep voice and continued to run her fingers through his thick wavy hair. "Okay, Captain. I won't stop if you give up the foolish idea of avenging your father's loss. Let the man and his life rest in peace."

"Yer not playing fair, lass," he said, looking deep into her eyes. "Tis my father ye are talking about, his lands and all he worked for. Why should I give up and let the bloody English have what should be mine to pass down to my *bairns*?"

Her fingers stopped their caress and she pushed away from him. "If that's how you feel, then we aren't meant for each other. I want no part of a man who can't see straight for the jealous anger in his heart."

James eyed her cautiously. His hunger to possess her nearly blinded him. She was his and he knew it as well as he knew how to captain his ship. He had no doubt what was most important. A force of nature much greater than he had ever dared to challenge brought her to him. Now the golden opportunity was here for her to willingly agree to be his wife. He would have chuckled but it would give his lighthearted attitude away.

"Ye know how to work my mind, don't ye?"

"I've come to care about you and I don't want to see you hurt. I know for a fact Scotland will never rise again to be what it once was. There is no phoenix hidden in the dust, James. Give up before it's too late."

He contemplated her strange way of expressing herself for a moment. Aye, he knew of the legend of the phoenix and he knew too, Scotland's days of peace were at end. The British would never let them be free again and the Scots would never surrender.

Taking her hands in his, he tugged her back into his arms. "Ye mean ye will marry me if I do?"

Anna saw the glimmer of hope in his sapphire eyes. Could she really do this? What if she failed again? She bit her lower lip in contemplation. She really had few choices. It would be difficult to survive in his time without his guidance and support. Besides, she really did admire the man. As for sexual attraction—no one had ever drawn her in quite the same way James did. He was insatiable, uncontrollable, and perfectly wonderful.

"Okay."

His roguish grin was full of amorous designs. "Tomorrow? My need for ye is so grand I cannot get ye off my mind." He hugged her and tenderly kissed her cheek, then held her at arm's length. "Can I ask ye something?"

"If you promise to stop staring at me."

James grinned. How could he stop looking at her when she was so lovely? "What manner o' corset is this, Anna? Ye are barely covered." He took the straps of stretchy material in his fingers, lowering them down her bare shoulders.

"It's called a bra, a twenty-first century corset," she explained. "You look puzzled. Don't you believe me?"

"Oh, aye. 'Tis just that I want to kiss ye there and I cannot get inside. How do ye release the thing?" His gaze lowered to her breasts.

Anna wanted to refuse him, knowing her weakness for his touch. The temptation of feeling such an intimate caress by this man, who sent her senses practically reeling into orbit, totally overwhelmed her. It was innocent enough, as long as he could stop at merely fondling. For an answer, she released the front clasp holding her bra together.

A hungry growl escaped him as he led her to the bed. He sat on the bed's edge, slipping the lacy binding from her arms and pulling her closer until his lips softly touched a nipple. His tongue caressed the rosy flesh tauntingly.

She arched her back in ecstasy while running her fingers through his tousled hair. When he sucked the fullness of her breast into his mouth, she gasped aloud with pure pleasure.

"Oh, James!" The tips of her breasts tingled, sending silent messages to the core of her womanhood. "If you go on we won't stop."

"Aye." His mouth moved to nurture the other breast while his hand massaged the erect, moist nipple of the first.

She fought to maintain her common sense while her body betrayed her with burning flames of rapture. Bending to kiss his thick chestnut hair, she lifted his head gently away from her breasts. "We have to stop now, James."

James had no desire to put a stop to the wonderful feel of her soft yielding flesh beneath his touch. Throbbing with passion, his manhood pressed fully against his trouser seams. If he could not release his lust soon he would burst.

"Stop?" His mind spiraled into the depths of frustration. "Och, ye are so bonny, Anna. I did not mean to become carried away."

"Neither did I." She gazed down at him through pale lashes, her green eyes sparkling with desire.

"Sweet Neptune, 'tis release we both need, lass."

"Yes." Anna put her hands to her inflamed cheeks and looked away. "Victorian women are noted for their modesty, and I'm far too bold for these times."

"Ye can be as bold as ye like with me," he admitted, his large weathered hands tenderly clasping her shoulders. "But I'll not share ye with anyone else." He stood up and adjusted his pants.

Anna wondered how to tell him about her previous marriage. She would be careful in the way she approached it. Crossing her arms over her bare breasts, she pointed down at the significant bulge below his belt. "Something stuck, Captain?"

The teasing question brought a low chuckle from him as his eyes met hers in challenge. "Would ye like to fix it for me, ye wee vixen?" He pulled her into his arms and tickled her relentlessly.

"James! Rosie will be returning soon with clothes for me to wear."

Releasing Anna with major reluctance, James watched her walk toward the lavatory. She cast an enticing smile back at him, tossed her bra across the room, and seductively waved her fingers in a taunting lure. His heart soared heavenward as he followed her, pausing in the doorway to watch her discard the rest of her clothes. She released her waist-length hair from its braid and shook her head. Golden waves fell about her shapely, naked form. She looked up at him as he moved slowly toward her.

"Anna." He could not resist wrapping his arms around her, pressing her hard against his swollen desire. His lips met hers with fierce hunger and his hands explored the softness of her silky satin skin.

Anna could not believe the cataclysmic feelings exploding inside her. So, this was love...tender concern, burning passion and a blending of the souls in ecstasy. Dear God, why did it have to be this way? Why couldn't James have existed in her time? She wasn't even sure of the next minute, let alone the days ahead.

Could she stand to lose him now? If they gave in to their physical desires she would be even more attached to him. Her heart was in torment. She longed for James to make love to her. But to surrender her heart with the knowledge that their relationship could end at any moment was out of the question. It would only leave her mournful for a past where she might never be able to return. She stopped him before she succumbed to her body's wildly intense cravings.

"James—Jamie—not now."

"Tis my childhood name ye called me. Och, it sounds bonny when ye say it." He placed one last kiss upon her lips and sighed wistfully. "I'll leave ye be for now," he whispered softly, his palm resting lightly upon her left breast, "but my heart stays here—within ye."

Tears filled Anna's eyes at the rawness in his voice. She bit back a sob, knowing she had to be strong or things would get out of hand. She couldn't think of a word to say to him in his present torment, so she watched with a sad smile as he backed slowly away and left the room.

A cloud of melancholy drifted over her while she bathed and washed her hair. Her priorities were all messed up. She should be worrying about returning to her own time, not her involvement with the captain. Yet, he was always uppermost in her thoughts. His swashbuckling attitude and his roguish grin—even his warm Scots burr when he spoke—all worked to charm her heart and capture her very soul.

~ * ~

Anna answered the knock at the bedroom door, still wrapped in a large white towel from her bath. Rosie bustled in with a beautiful pink confection draped over her large arm, along with all the necessary undergarments.

Anna's spirits brightened. Wearing such exquisite clothing would be like being in a play. The gown was beautiful. Entirely hand stitched, the dress fastened up the back with tiny pea-sized buttons. The chemise and corset laced up the back as well. She suddenly realized she could not possibly dress herself.

"Can you help me, Rosie? I haven't worn fine clothes like these in quite a while." A great stretch of the truth, she mused, feeling a little like Alice in Wonderland.

"That's what I'm here for, ma'am. Don't you worry none. Old Rosie will have you dressed in no time." Her dark animated face broke into a friendly grin as she laid the dress carefully on the bed. She was a well-rounded, middle-aged woman with the kindest brown eyes and brightest white teeth Anna had ever seen.

An hour later, Anna stood fully dressed with her hair plaited and wrapped around her head like a crown. Rosie added a few dainty pink flowers to the thick braid and stood back with a smile to admire her amazing transformation.

Anna felt like a princess in the long flowing gown. White satin ribbons adorned the waist. The neckline dipped low with a sheer white lace inset extending up to the high collar. Delicate lace edged the puffed sleeves and covered the length of her arms.

"Wait until James sees me in this," she whispered, satisfied with her appearance in the exquisite dress. "Rosie, thank you. You have done wonders. Do you think anyone will notice I'm not wearing a corset?"

"Your figure is so perfect you don't need no corset." Rosie began straightening up the room. "That's why they wear them things...is so they has lots of curves. You're gonna drive your man to distraction without one. Just be careful when he puts his arms around you—that's when he'll know."

Anna giggled. She could not bring herself to wear the wire bound contraption no matter what the consequences. The multiple layers of clothing made her body feel trapped. Freedom of movement was definitely much easier in a cool summer mini-dress—or better yet—a bikini.

Gads, what would James think of a bikini?

~ * ~

James sat in a large wing chair with his black high-top boots perched on a dainty needlepoint footstool. He had dressed carefully, wanting to look his best for Anna. He chose white britches with a short, royal blue topcoat from his special landlubber's wardrobe.

"You're looking fine tonight, James." Angelique crossed the room to stand beside George at the fireplace. "You should dress formally more often."

"Tis nice of ye to say, Angel." He took a sip of Scotch. "But 'tis not generally to my liking to strut about like a bloody peacock."

George chuckled and held up his glass. "It's a good thing too, James, or there would be even more broken hearts along the coast."

Angelique gasped. "Mind your manners, George. Here's Anna."

All eyes turned toward the door as Anna limped into the parlor on her crutches. She blushed at the sudden attention. "Good-evening," she whispered.

James caught sight of the vision in pink and sat forward, dropping his feet to the floor. He had not realized what a beauty she truly was—until now. Moving swiftly, he met her halfway across the room. He set aside the crutches and took her into his arms. His gaze caught hers in silent conversation.

Angelique broke the spell. "Anna, you look positively beautiful! The dress was made for you. It fits your lovely figure quite nicely. Does it not, James?"

"Ye do the dress honors, lass." James bent to kiss her cheek.

His husky reply made Anna tremble in spite of her attempts to resist him. She recalled their earlier rendezvous in the bedroom and shivered with delight. Remembering her manners, she breathed a faint thank you in his ear and turned to face Angel.

"Angelique, I love this dress. Thank you so much."

"You are quite welcome. Now, let's all go in to dinner?" Angelique took the proffered hook of George's arm. "We have so much to talk about."

James winked at Anna and circled her waist with his arm, supporting her weak ankle. His simple touch sent her heart a twirl. She leaned against his side as he assisted her across the hall and into the dining room. Table seating was arranged with couples sitting across from each other, but being across the table from James was pure misery.

His tender gaze lingered on her, devouring her. It was difficult to concentrate on the delicious meal, let alone casual dinner talk. How could he stare at her and still carry on a normal conversation with the Stensons?

Anna blushed without knowing why she should feel so uncomfortable. The Stensons were wonderful people, who made her feel totally at ease in their presence. Captain James Duncan was a different story. He was like a dangerous whirlpool in the sea, threatening to draw her within his dynamic center and entirely absorb her with his potency.

"Is that right, Anna?" George stabbed a hefty mouthful of roast beef from his plate.

Anna blinked, turning her attention from her meal to the burly blond man on her right. "I'm sorry. What did you say, George?"

"I told them how we met, Anna," James explained solemnly. "And all about the tragic logging accident that took yer poor father's life."

Nine

Anna sputtered and choked on her food, dropping her fork to clatter noisily on her plate. "You—you told them what?"

"Tis still hard for her to talk about, poor wee thing." James winked across at her. "Twas good I was there to help."

Anna struggled for something to say. What the devil was he up to now? Her mind was so preoccupied with thoughts of him she hadn't been part of what was clearly an interesting topic of conversation. She was angry with herself for not paying closer attention. What in the world could she say that wouldn't make her a blundering idiot?

"Aye, she still has nightmares about it. Don't ye, Anna?" His somber expression taunted her from the safety of his position across the table. The devilish man was enjoying all this!

In a quick decision to go along for whatever reason, Anna was able to force a few phony tears. "I've blocked it from my memory, but it haunts my dreams every night." She wiped daintily at her eyes with her napkin. Thank heavens for high school drama.

"Poor dear! George, let's talk about something else. Can neither of you see how you are upsetting her?" Angelique patted Anna's hand. "It will pass, Anna. Be strong."

"I don't know what I would have done without James." Feeling like she was drowning in this little play of his, she stumbled on with her convincing lines. "He has been such a comfort to me." *But she wanted to strangle him!* "However, all that is in the past and better forgotten."

Seeing a need to change the subject, James coughed and pushed back from the long dining table. "Tis time to retire to the library, George. I feel in need o' a bit o' spirits."

Anna followed Angelique's lead and moved toward the dining room door. "Don't drink too much now, James. It's a beautiful evening and well…you know." She winked at him. His eyes sparkled with amusement and he got her message, loud and clear.

Angelique touched George's arm tenderly in passing. "We'll be in the parlor, dear."

She whispered to Anna, "They'll be quite busy for a while. I'm afraid George loves the Scotch whiskey James brought him. I'm not supposed to know, you see. It's a game we play. Shall we adjourn to the parlor? I have some wonderful new catalogs from back east, even Godey's Lady's Book. We can go over them together."

Anna's senses sharpened. She would need to be very alert to talk about present clothing styles knowledgeably so that Angelique would not catch on, but then she'd managed to deceive them all so far. She'd even made it through the captain's tall tale at dinner. Playacting was her new way of life, since falling backwards in time. She truly did not belong in this era, unlike the captain who enjoyed taunting her and testing her knowledge of the past. He was so vibrant and full of life, and he was the dickens to catch up to in his verbal escapades. He could unfold a drama faster than Shakespeare could; and he enjoyed the mischief he stirred up in doing so.

~ * ~

Anna sighed wearily as she paused on the stairs. Angelique had bid her goodnight and left to check on the household staff. Now all she had to do was make it up to the bedroom suite. She contemplated the rest of the steps she had yet to climb. Her ankle had felt okay while she was sitting, but now it was beginning to throb.

A loud burst of laughter escaped from the library below. The two men broke into yet another zealous song. She leaned over the rail and listened for a moment to the silly words of their drinking song, shaking her head with dismay at their immaturity.

Amazingly, a nineteenth-century man was not so different from the men of her time. Lusty, cocky, and too self-assured—they were all the same. She hoped James would come up to bed soon. Hopefully, he would still be sober enough to tell her just what cock'n'bull story he had made up for the Stensons' benefit.

Reaching their beautiful suite, Anna was surprised to find Rosie waiting patiently to help her undress. She greeted the kind older woman with appreciation. In no time at all, Anna wore a gorgeous diaphanous pale blue nightgown with her hair brushed out into waves cascading down her back and curling gently around her hips.

Rosie grinned mischievously. "I think James will be pleased with what he finds in his bed this night. You're a lovely bride, if I do say so myself."

"Thank you," Anna said with a tired yawn. "But if he doesn't get here soon, he'll find me fast asleep until morning."

"I'll see what I can do to break up the men. Don't you worry none." She closed the wardrobe door and turned to leave the room. "I'll be back in the morning to help you dress for the day."

Anna was exhausted. All she could do was nod acquiescence to the maid as she bustled out of the room. She sat on the bed and noticed the full moon for the first time, shining through tall open windows. The lure was too much to resist without getting a better view. Crossing to the French doors, she opened them and walked out onto the balcony. Her nightgown fluttered about her in the cool, sea-scented breeze. She reminisced of another balcony in another time—far, far away. What had really happened that fateful day?

She leaned against the banister with a heavy sigh, releasing the tormenting thoughts she had held at bay for so long. Gazing out over the dark pine forest below, its scent mingling with that of the sea, she pondered what the future held for her. Her heart felt weighted by the desire to make the right choice, if the choice was hers to make. She sighed again and let the summer evening envelop her in its comforting peace.

James found her standing on the balcony. His strong will sobered him in her presence, helping him maintain his masculine intensity. A low whistle escaped his lips at the fascinating sight of his lovely bride-to-be standing outdoors in the moonlight.

"Anna?"

She whirled around with a quivering smile. "Oh! You startled me, James."

"Are ye all right, lass?" Forgetting her beauty for the moment, he read distress in her expression and took her trembling hand in his, pressing a kiss to her palm.

"I was looking at the moon. Isn't it beautiful?" She did not realize the very same moon was allowing James a perfect view of her luscious curves through the sheer blue fabric.

"Aye, Anna, 'tis lovely." He couldn't keep his gaze off her. He wanted to have her right now, on the open balcony, under the bright summer stars. Scented lavender drifted by as the breeze played with her long golden tresses, teasing his responsive awareness.

Anna shivered, but not from the cold. He was staring at her, devouring her while standing so close she could feel his warm breath upon her cheeks. He smelled strongly of whiskey, with a slight touch of bay rum still lingering from his bath. If she moved an inch she would be locked in his passionate embrace, her strength drained from her by his kiss. It was more than she could endure not to freely enjoy his lovemaking. She must discover the purpose for her presence here in his time.

She shuddered as a horrible idea invaded her mind. Could she have died in the future, while being transported into the past, and somehow been spared the memory? She had to find out the answers to her questions. Becoming emotionally involved with James could be her undoing. She was not ready to commit with her heart, though physically challenged by his charm.

"Ah, Anna, ye drive me wild with desire, lass." His soft Scottish burr sounded throaty. He pulled her gently to him. "Can ye feel it?"

Groaning with a pleasant weakness, Anna relaxed against his warmth. The quiet strength of his hard body pressed against her through the thin nightgown. His ardent hands gently rubbed her hips and teasingly caressed her stomach, finally coming to rest on her tingling breasts. He nuzzled her neck with tender kisses, sending little chills down her spine.

"James?" Her voice was barely a whisper on the breeze.

Slipping the strap off her shoulder, he nibbled sweetly at exposed skin. "Aye, lass?"

Anna wiggled out of his fervent embrace. She moved purposely toward the bedroom beyond as she spoke in a ragged squeak, "We need to talk, James. Only you can't be touching me, or I—I can't think straight."

His eyes bleary with rapture, and a bit too much whiskey, James followed her into the room and sat on the love seat. Anna took the chair opposite him, her body trembling from his recent touch. For a moment neither spoke, except with their eyes in a silent telepathy, a flaming knowledge of their fervent desire for each other.

James lowered his gaze to her breasts, slightly visible through the flimsy material. He remembered hot kisses on erect nipples and her urgent response to his attempts at seduction. Sweet Neptune! Why did she keep putting him off? Running his fingers through his hair, he put his hands to his face and leaned forward onto his knees.

"Are you okay?"

He looked up at her. "Do ye know what ye do to me? 'Tis daft I have become. I cannot think o' anything else. Yer lovely face, yer womanly curves, yer laughter, and yer way o' sassing me. Ye have my heart, Anna. I cannot wait to bed ye and make ye truly mine, once and for all."

Christine Poe

Anna's pulse raced at his heated confession. She had his heart? The words he spoke burned into her memory. She would never forget this man or this moment, no matter what happened. At last, she had found someone who truly wanted her for the first time in her lost and lonely, unloved life. Her mind battled over the choices before her. Calmly, though she was sure her voice would tremble, she knew what she had to say.

"I must find out what happened to me, James. I can't exist in your century, not knowing if I still exist in mine." She moved to sit beside him on the love seat. "Do you understand my point of view?"

"Aye, lass. Do ye understand mine?"

The pure devotion in his deep voice made her sob and throw her arms around his neck. "Oh, James." She kissed him without reserve. "Hold me for a while, please?"

Not wanting to release her from his arms, James carried her to the turned down bed. "There's no need to ask. 'Tis an honor I'll surely treasure." He shed his clothing quickly, joining her beneath the sheets in the comfort of the feather bed.

Snug under the warm covers with her back nestled against his powerful chest, Anna recalled their dinner conversation. "James? What exactly did you tell the Stensons tonight?"

With only her nightclothes between them, James fought to resist the temptation he held in his arms. His manhood throbbed with desire against her firm round bottom. As much as he needed her physically, he could settle for having her close. He did not want to upset the special moment, nor risk losing her.

"Well now, I told them yer father was a logger. Ye were taking the men a bit o' lunch when ye saw the accident. Yer father, God rest his soul, was killed when an ox-drawn wagon carrying a load o' pine logs lost a wheel, fell over and crushed him."

She sat up in the bed and turned to face him. "Oh, James! How could you?"

144

"Tis a true story, Anna. I just changed the characters a wee bit."
He turned her back around and pulled her down under the covers
with him again. "I was only trying to cover the way ye suddenly
appeared in my life. They would not believe the truth."

"Do you mean to tell me somebody really was killed like that?"
Anna shuddered at the mental image of a huge log falling on
someone, let alone an entire wagonload of logs. "Good Lord! That's
horrible!"

"Aye, 'tis true. Only the lass married a friend o' mine in Coos
Bay. 'Twas him who saw the tragedy, not I." He nestled his face
into her neck with little kisses. "Did I tell ye, lass, ye smell o' the
Highlands?"

Anna giggled; she couldn't stay at odds with him. "No, you
didn't. Do I? It must be the bath soap Rosie gave me, it smelled
really nice."

He sniffed at her hair making her giggle even more. "The
Highlands are covered in heather and lavender. The two scents
remind me o' home."

"Scotland?" She didn't know much about the wild brave people
called Highlanders. She snuggled in closer. "Did you wear a kilt?"

"Aye, the bonny tartan o' Clan Duncan. 'Tis a proud man who
wears the plaidie." James sighed in reminiscence. Blue and green
wool, with white, red and black lines was Clan Donnachaidh's
unique pattern.

"I would like to see your Scotland. I mean, the way it is now.
I've never even left the state of California. But I'm an avid reader
and it's sort of like traveling—if you have a vivid imagination." She
turned a bit in his embrace so she could see the outline of his
features in the dim lit room. "Tell me more."

His lips parted in a contented smile. "There's an old Gaelic
legend: 'When God had finished making Britain, some fragments o'
earth and stone were left in His ample apron. With a smile, He

flicked them out and they fell into the sea to form the islands o' Scotland.' A bonny great land is Scotland.'"

Anna traced the curve of his ear with her finger. "Aye," she whispered, copying his burr, "and a bonny great Scot you are too, lad." Her lips pressed to his in sleepy affection.

"Anna? Will ye stay?" He tugged the blankets up around them, pulling her closer.

"Ummm." She loved the smell of bay rum. It would always remind her of James. She should answer him. But right now, it just felt good being held in his warm embrace. She simply sighed and drifted off to sleep.

~ * ~

Anna awoke and stretched with a long, luxurious yawn. Remembering the night before she felt the cool sheets beside her, but James was no longer there. She blinked the sleep from her eyes. A soft humming sound filled her ears. She sat up to see Rosie industriously cleaning the well-kept room.

"Good morning, ma'am. You sure does sleep late. Did I wake you?" She paused with her work-worn hands settled on her hips and smiled.

"No, you didn't." Clearing the frog in her throat, she stretched and covered a yawn. "Do you know where James is?"

"Sure enough. Him and Mr. Stenson went out early this mornin'." Rosie stood at the bedside; an understanding expression flickered across her pleasant face. "Don't you fret none. Your handsome young man will be back soon."

Anna frowned thoughtfully. James must have left to find someone to marry them. Damn, but he was a determined human being. She didn't care for Victorian morality one tiny bit. Forcing marriage on compromised women was barbaric. She wondered how many poor women were forced into loveless marriages in this century. Marriages innocently called a marriage of convenience— convenient for whom? It annoyed her to think men had such power over women. She didn't like the idea any more than she liked deceiving these nice people. James had told a few whopping tales last night and she had gone along, not knowing what else to do at the time. Now she questioned the wisdom of being his deceitful accomplice.

No matter what, Anna should be prepared for whatever James had in mind. She stretched again and reluctantly climbed out of the deep feather bed. After dressing in a pale-yellow frock, she sat down at the dressing table and let Rosie comb her hair. Smiling at her own old-fashioned reflection in the large oval mirror, reminiscences assailed her from early childhood. She looked like her great-grandmother, or at least the one and only photograph she had seen of her ancestor.

The small battered picture in the old photo album had been carefully preserved and passed down to her adoptive parents. She had snuck into her adoptive parents bedroom, searching for some small memento of her biological parents; something to bring their love back to her, something to comfort her in her great loss. That's when she discovered the photograph.

Anna had been only four years old when she contracted pneumonia and almost died. A few months later, she was told her parents were killed in a boating accident. Sometimes she wished she had died too, and then she wouldn't feel so alone. Her eyes brimming with tears, she looked up to see Rosie's sweet dark face puckered with concern.

"What's wrong, child? Am I pulling your gorgeous hair too hard?"

Anna wiped her tears away. "No. I was just remembering my parents." A convenient truth. "I'm okay. Thank you, Rosie."

When Rosie finished with her hair, Anna was surprised how pretty it looked pulled up into a full chignon. The thought lingered in her mind of her unique resemblance to her ancestor's photograph.

A solitary tear trickled down her cheek, the mirror mimicking her sorrow.

~ * ~

A few hours later, neither James nor George had returned. Angelique seemed a little reserved and Anna hated to quiz her on her husband's whereabouts, so they sat in the parlor pretending to look at yet more dress catalogues. Luncheon was served at two o'clock and the two women ate a quiet meal together.

Anna didn't know what to say about the untimely disappearance of their men. Instead, she tried to busy herself by checking out the huge library. When she came across a brand new copy of Jules Verne's famous Twenty-Thousand Leagues Under the Sea, she made a mental notation to show James. It was one novel she was certain he would thoroughly enjoy.

Anna walked over to the window and peered out through rain-spattered panes. A nasty storm had blown in sometime during the night and it was getting worse as the day wore on. Lightning in the distance lit up the darkened sky and Anna waited for the rumble of thunder to follow.

Angelique tapped politely at the library door and entered the room. "Anna, I have news. I am afraid it's not very good."

"About James?"

"There's no delicate way to say this." Angelique walked over to her and took hold of her hand. "James has had an accident."

Anna was confused. This couldn't be happening. "But, James isn't at sea."

"Late last night a few ships were riding out the storm off the bay when one of them came too close to the rocks. George left early this morning to get help from the men at the lumber mill and James went down to the bay to organize a rescue party. A sturdy rowboat went out to save as many men as possible from the floundering vessel. James was in charge."

"Oh dear God—" Her heart tightened in her chest.

Angelique clasped her hands as tears trickled down her cheeks. "When they tied up to the schooner a wave washed over the larger ship, breaking the mizzen mast in two. James was hit when it fell."

Anna's heart stopped beating for an instant, choking off her thoughts. Pain speared through her head in lightning streaks. She felt faint and ill all at once. "He's—dead?"

"Oh no! James is alive, thank God! He's been hurt, but I was not informed of how seriously. A messenger came only a few moments ago. I sent the maids to fix up his bed and I sent an urgent message to the doctor."

"I can't believe this is happening." Anna shook her head in total disbelief, and then turned to see her new friend's tormented face. "But it is, isn't it?"

Angelique's nod was affirmative. "These storms have a way of causing disaster. Every season we lose ships, and sometimes worse...we lose the men."

Anna felt as if her heart would break. Her stomach fluxed, trying to force its way up into her throat. God in heaven! Why did this have to happen now? If she lost James what purpose would she have met? Surely, she had not been sent back in time to see him die? James was injured, okay. But he was still alive. She wasn't about to lose him to the consequences of an unpredictable summer storm.

Angelique led her across to the sofa. "Anna?" She shook her shoulders. "Anna, please!"

Anna forced a weak smile, pulling herself from the painful trauma that held her captive. "I need him Angelique. He—he's the only person who has ever cared for me. I can't lose him."

"We'll do the best we can for him. I promise."

It was the last straw and Anna broke into uncontrollable sobs. She thought about their short time together, his hearty laughter, and his loving touch. She might never feel his strong arms or tender kisses again.

A sudden commotion in the front hall caught her attention. She hurried to follow Angelique out of the room.

Several sailors stood clustered at the door, delayed entry by the butler's interference. The housekeeper argued with the butler on whether to put James in the parlor to await the doctor, or to carry him upstairs to his bedroom. Angelique stepped in and gave orders in a brusque tone, quite uncommon to her gentle nature.

The men carried a canvas stretcher into the house and upon it lay James' still figure. Before they could take him upstairs, Anna dropped to her knees beside the pallet, tears streaming down her cheeks. "James? Can you hear me?"

She wiped blood from the small cut on his forehead with her handkerchief. He probably had a concussion. His left leg was bleeding profusely above the knee, obvious from the dark stain spreading slowly across his torn pants. An ominous-looking gash glistened in the lamplight through a ragged tear in the left shoulder of his coat. He didn't look good to her inexperienced eye. His unconscious condition was undoubtedly a godsend for the pain he would be feeling otherwise.

"Anna, let's get him up to bed," Angelique insisted. "We can tend to his wounds there until the doctor arrives."

George appeared from nowhere and slipped a supportive arm around Anna's waist. He led her up the stairs behind the men carrying the stretcher. She suddenly realized a few drenched and worried members of his crew were carrying James.

Once the able-bodied seamen had stripped James of his clothes and lifted him carefully onto the bed, they each expressed their regrets to Anna. Big burly Jock paused at her side.

"'Twas an unfortunate accident, lass. But we were able to save most o' the stranded men because o' James here." He looked down at the man he admired. "I know the captain's physical and emotional strengths, and I know he will pull through."

Watching nervously as George cut long strips of clean white sheets, Anna nodded. "Thank you, Jock."

She stood helplessly watching as a bystander, not really sure what to do for the terribly wounded man lying still and pale on the bed. Rosie came in with a steaming bowl of water. Angelique hurried into the room carrying an armload of towels, and a young servant followed quietly with a large tray of medical supplies.

Rosie put her arm around Anna's shoulder. "Come on girl! You'll feel a might better if you help with your man. He needs you now more than ever. He's gonna make it 'cause he's a strong one. He's seen worse trouble than this." She lifted Anna's chin with her forefinger. "You hear me, honey?"

Anna nodded, accepting her role as his spouse. She moved slowly to the bedside. She couldn't explain the turmoil raging through her. She couldn't lose James now. Not only was she beginning to build a dear friendship with him, but also he was the only one who knew of her plight. The only one who could help her. She trembled as she stared down at his naked body and saw the seriousness of his wounds.

George paused from blotting the steady flow of blood trickling out of the jagged tear in James' leg. "Would you put pressure on this for me, Anna?"

"Oh, yeah. Sure." Anna shook her head to relieve herself of the fear constricting her heart. The sight of blood oozing between her fingers did little to dispel her worry. Try as she might she could remember none of the first-aid course she had taken.

She watched George cleanse the shoulder wound with soap and water, then carefully bandage it with clean cloth strips. He did the same to the deep cut on the captain's forehead where a nasty bruise was already forming.

Lifting the compress from his leg once again, George sighed. "I wish I could say it looks better, but it's a mighty deep cut." He stood. "Damn! Where is Doctor Hobbs?"

Footsteps sounded in the hallway outside the door and Anna turned to see a remarkably attractive young man entering the room. Her gaze was drawn to him with a feeling of familiarity. Dressed in a plain white shirt and black pants that emphasized his tall lean form, he fit in with the wealthy style of the era.

He removed a broad-rimmed hat, revealing wavy dark brown hair worn tied back from his face in a queue. Setting his black leather bag down beside the bed, his deep blue eyes met her bold perusal. He smiled and a slight dimple appeared in his cheek.

"Alastair! We thought you had left for San Francisco." Angelique took his hands in hers and smiled gratefully up at him. "We sent for old Doc Hobbs, but he's out delivering a baby. I'm so glad you're here! Perhaps you can help? James has been hurt."

Alastair's eyes closed briefly to stop the train of thought running rampant through his mind. He smiled agreeably down at Angelique. "My ship was delayed because of the storm. Looks like you'll be stuck with me for a while."

He moved quickly to the bedside and began examining the patient. He refused to look back into the limpid green pools of Anna Bentley's eyes. He became so involved with treating James that for the moment his mind was curiously free of hampering thoughts. First things first, this man had to be saved.

Anna felt a strange emotion she could not explain. She watched as the skillful young physician carefully unwound bandages and checked the deep wounds. His long slender fingers fit his chosen profession. She could well imagine him doing surgery. He probed the vivid cut on James' leg, then released a sigh and dug through his medical bag.

"It's not as bad as it looks, Angel. He will need a large number of stitches, but I promise he will be up and about soon." Alastair found what he was looking for and stood to prepare a syringe. "Was there anything removed from the flesh wound?"

George stepped forward. "William pulled out a large wood sliver so he could wrap the cut to slow the bleeding before moving him."

"I thought so. Well, I'll give him a shot of tetanus and penicillin to fight infection, then I had better suture the wounds before he wakes." He moved with swift steady precision, injecting the first needle into James' upper arm and the second into his hip.

George cleared his throat and took hold of Angelique's hand. "If you will please excuse us, Anna? Rosie will assist if you need her, Alastair."

Anna paced the bedroom floor after the Stensons left, with only occasional glances toward the bed. The doctor worked tirelessly, his steady hands neatly stitching up the layers of flesh. She was amazed at his advanced medical knowledge and surprised to see the variety of instruments he carried in his black bag. Her mind became so preoccupied she didn't notice the method with which the doctor brought James to momentary consciousness, and was only aware of it when she heard him groan.

"James!" She hiked up her skirt and crawled up on the bed beside him, placing soft little kisses all over his whiskered cheek. Tears tumbled freely from her eyes. But to her dismay, he did not open his eyes or even respond to her touch. "What's wrong with him? I heard him try to say something."

Alastair smiled as he completed the bandaging with Rosie's adept assistance. "He'll be fine, Miss, or is it Mrs. now?"

Anna looked up, ignoring his question of her marital status, and wiped the tears from her cheeks with the back of her hand. "Are you sure he will be okay? I think he's in a coma or something." She glanced back down at James, so silent in the big feather bed.

A lusty laugh escaped the young doctor. "It wouldn't be the first time I saw someone slip into a coma from alcohol consumption, but I guarantee this is not the case here. His men must have poured a great deal of whiskey down him to ease the pain. He has simply fainted from the stress of what has happened to him."

"He's drunk?"

"Just a bit." Alastair put his supplies away. "He needs a couple days of bed rest and his bandages should be changed twice daily."

Rosie pulled the quilt gently up over the captain. "I will see to the bandages, Doctor. I done my share of nursing. Besides, Anna here, she's done had her fill of worry for the day. Maybe you could give her something to help her rest?"

Anna blushed with embarrassment at suddenly being the center of attention. "Rosie, I'll be fine now that I know James will be all right."

Alastair pulled a bottle from his bag and emptied two small pills into the palm of his hand. "Just the same, one or two before bed should help you fall asleep faster and feel more rested in the morning."

"I really don't need them. What about James? Won't he be in pain when he awakes?" She accepted the tablets anyway and slipped them into the deep pocket of her dress.

"I'll be back to check on him before I retire." He stood up and stretched. "I think he may need something by then."

Anna put her hand on his sleeve. "Thank you, Doctor." She met his gaze and a strange feeling tingled up her spine. *Déjà vu.*

"I am always glad to be of help. More important that I made it in time." Alastair nodded to Rosie, and then to Anna before slipping quietly out of the room.

More important that I made it in time? His cryptic words hung in the air, haunting Anna's thoughts.

~ * ~

Storm clouds shifted ominously to the east as the moon shone weakly through the French doors. Anna had chosen to sleep in the other room so she would not disturb James by tossing and turning all night. After several hours, she finally gave up the notion of a restful night's sleep. It just wasn't possible when she was so concerned about James.

She crossed the sitting room floor on tiptoe to peek into his shadowy bedroom. All was quiet. He slept like a babe. Too bad she couldn't get some sleep. She hadn't taken the little pills the doctor had given her. She knew full well her susceptibility to even mild tranquilizers and she wanted to stay alert in case James needed her.

Sighing with fatigue, Anna crept quietly over to his bedside and smiled down at his bruised but still extremely appealing face. His relaxed body let her know he was slumbering peacefully. She wondered if he would be fully awake in the morning. Leaning over him, she caressed his forehead with her fingertips. He didn't blink an eye.

"Oh, James, what are we to do?" Her soft whisper echoed in the quiet room. "I'm falling in love with you and we both know it can never be."

Alastair stirred from sleep in the dark corner of the room. Smiling, he listened carefully from his hidden position in the lounge chair. So, he was in time to help her too. He sighed quietly with relief. He had worried so much about his particular roll in the past, and yet...when the moment came he had moved through it with ease. James would survive this bad accident and live for many years to come.

Not wanting Anna to know he had overheard her, Alastair dared not move from the chair where his long body sat cramped from a restless nap. He watched Anna place her arm gently across the captain's chest. Her eyelids fell closed and sleep overcame her.

Alastair thoughtfully planned the approach he would use to tell Anna about himself. Deciding honesty would work best to explain the situation, he smiled and shut his eyes to the early hours of dawn.

Ten

James was still asleep when Anna awoke, so she went to the other room to prepare for the day. Rosie insisted she take a leisurely bath. Afterwards, the large black woman took her time in styling Anna's hair, all the while expounding on current gossip circulating in the servant's quarters, something about a notorious highwayman hiding out in Mendocino while he robbed stagecoach gold shipments.

Anna listened half-heartedly. Her thoughts were on the Scottish sea captain lying injured in the next room. It was all she could do to be patient. When Rosie finished her hair, she hurried across the sitting room to check on James.

Alastair stopped her at the door. "Good morning, Mrs. Duncan."

She looked up at his inquisitive face, realizing for the first time how tall he was. "How is James this morning, Doctor?"

His blue eyes lit with intensity. "The captain is doing fine. I just gave him a bit of a sedative and he's sleeping peacefully now."

"Sedative? You mean he was awake and you didn't send for me?" Her anxiety over James' condition was definitely wearing on her nerves.

"Momentarily, ma'am, only momentarily. He was in a great deal of pain. He needs rest more than anything else right now to fight off the danger of infection." Alastair took her elbow and led her over to the settee in front of the fancy marble fireplace. "Mrs. Duncan, I need a few moments alone with you. Could we take a walk around the rose garden after lunch?"

"James is okay, isn't he?" She met his steady gaze and a curious shiver ran up her back. What was it about this man? She wasn't romantically attracted to him, even though he was undeniably handsome. But she felt a strange familiarity she couldn't seem to shake. She racked her brain to think of a plausible reason, but zilch came to mind.

"This is an entirely different matter, but of vital importance. I assure you. Please say you will join me?" A twinkle in his eyes accentuated his wide, charming grin.

"If you feel it's important…" Such an odd feeling buzzed around inside her. Maybe it wasn't that he seemed familiar. Maybe it was intuition, foreshadowing things to come.

He placed his hand over hers. "After lunch then, Mrs. Duncan."

Anna studied his confident stride as he left the suite. What could the doctor possibly want to tell her? She shivered again and nearly tripped over a footstool as she rushed into the bedroom and knelt beside the captain on the bed.

"Oh, James! Why did this have to happen to you? I don't know how to act or what to do in this God-forsaken time without you. I'm feeling lost and frightened, and I need you so much."

Her whispers drifted into the still air. She was so worried about James. It tormented her until she could no longer keep a stiff upper lip. Tears rolled freely down her cheeks to splatter like fallen raindrops upon her soft green dress.

~ * ~

Lunch proved an onerous experience. Anna did not know the doctor was actually staying with the Stensons. In fact, she learned he would be staying on for another week or two. Her hopes were dashed in thinking she could simply avoid a confrontation with him. He would be present at all meals, as well as attending to James' medical needs.

Alastair caught her intense scrutiny of him and could not help but smile. He didn't expect to find she was a true beauty. Old tintypes were so misleading. He watched her nervously playing with her fork as she shifted her gaze toward George.

"This is not the first time one of our payroll shipments has been robbed, Alastair." George expounded on the plight of local lawmen and their efforts to catch the highway robber hiding in their midst. His face flushed red with fury. "Blast it all! This truly gets me riled. Why can't they catch the dang fellow?"

"Are they sure it's the same man each time?" Alastair's tone betrayed none of the excitement he felt within. He wished he could tell them what he knew firsthand.

Angelique spoke up, her pretty brow etched with worry lines. "He leaves a calling card."

"A calling card?" Anna suddenly caught up with the absurd conversation about a highway robber. The men chuckled and she couldn't help stealing a glimpse across the table at Alastair. He grinned back at her in the most disturbing way.

George cleared his throat, wiped his lips on his napkin and took a hasty sip of wine. "It appears the rascal leaves a fancy lace garter upon the leg of an innocent lady passenger, while his accomplice holds a gun on the driver and other passengers. Some have said he even steals a kiss."

Anna choked on her food as she stifled a laugh. A woman's garter must be very risqué to say the least! And he stole a measly kiss? Did the women know how lucky they were not to have been raped or beaten? The desire to giggle welled up inside, but she didn't want to appear rude or out of tune with the times. After all, Angelique appeared quite concerned.

"How gallant." Alastair's deep resonant voice sparkled with amusement. "Any other clues to this rogue's identity?"

"Alastair! The scoundrel actually lifts the lady's skirts to put the garter on their bare leg. Why...who knows what other liberties he has in mind? It's indecent to treat respectable ladies in such a fashion. I hope they catch him and—and—" Angelique's words trailed off as she put her hanky to her trembling mouth and abruptly excused herself.

"My dear? Excuse me, Anna...Alastair." George hastened to follow his beloved wife from the room.

Anna turned to see what the doctor's reaction was to Angelique's apparent distress, only to find him leaning casually back in his chair regarding her with a tantalizing smile. She did not want to be left alone with the doctor. No matter how humorous he thought the situation, she wasn't amused at Angelique's upset. Lifting her linen napkin from her lap and placing it beside her half empty plate, she stood with a frustrated sigh.

"I want to go see James. If you'll excuse me, doctor."

"Actually, I was just about to check on him myself." He stood up from the table and held out his arm. "Shall we?"

She raised her eyebrows. "Persistent, aren't you?"

He didn't respond. As she walked up the wide staircase, she heard him chuckle behind her. Damn, the man. He made her nervous and he knew it.

James was still sleeping peacefully when they entered the room. Anna crossed to his side and leaned down, placing a tender kiss on his warm forehead. He looked as though he were having a pleasant dream. His handsome face bore a wonderful crooked smile that slightly tilted his full lips, lips that had kissed her passionately, causing her body to tingle with desire.

Alastair stepped silently to her side. "He will be fine, Anna. You have my word on it as a doctor of medicine."

She let it slide when he used her first name. "I guess I know that. It's just so hard to see such a wonderful man all beaten and lifeless." She touched her fingertips to the captain's lips. "Later, I promise."

"Let's let him sleep." Alastair gently took her arm, surprised to feel a tinge of jealousy at her open affection for the captain. "Besides, you promised me a walk in the garden. Remember?"

She lingered a moment longer. "Yes, I suppose I did."

No one was about downstairs when Alastair and Anna slipped quietly out the front door. Walking slowly around the house, they followed a narrow brick pathway into the garden. The air was fragrant with the scent of roses after the recent bout of rain. It was almost unbearable. Rosebushes of every hue lined the walkway until it opened to a large, lovely gazebo built upon a rise.

Anna sat on one of the ornate stone benches, remembering to spread her full skirt to prevent wrinkles. "What is this important matter you wish to discuss, doctor? Hopefully, not the daring deeds of the scandalous highwayman?" She looked up at him and couldn't keep from smiling. The stories at lunch had been humorous entertainment.

"Actually," he said, sitting close beside her as he spoke in a soft husky voice, "...it's even more important."

Surprise replaced amusement. "More important than a gold-stealing rogue?"

"Could be. May I call you Anna? You may call me Alastair." He took for granted her silence was in acquiescence and continued, "Anna, what I have to tell you may come as a real shock." He paused to examine a small pink rosebud on the bush beside him. "You see...I know where you're from. I even know why you are here."

Shock was not the word for it. Was he for real? Did he honestly know about her trip through time, or was this just a ploy to get her to open up to him? She decided caution would be best. Act dumb, it always worked in the movies.

"I don't know what you mean."

He turned and eyed her carefully. "Do not play games with me. I heard you talking to James last night."

"I still don't know what you're talking about." A sudden sense of dread washed over Anna. "What is this? Some sort of sick joke?"

Alastair jumped to his feet and stood glaring down at her. "I want to help you. If you refuse to let me, then so be it."

Something made her reach out and grasp his sleeve before he could leave. She shrugged her shoulders lightly. "Please, doctor, give me some time to accept what you are saying."

"Time is exactly what I want to give you." His harsh look softened. "I know the secret of our voyage."

She shivered at his choice of words. "Our voyage?"

"Yes, Anna. I'm a time traveler, too."

A time traveler? Dear God, was there a chance she might return to the future?

"I have been stuck here for almost a year."

"Oh, no." She shook her head in dismay.

"Anna? Let me explain." He sat beside her on the bench. "It all started as a lark, really. I was on vacation from the hospital, staying at Duncan's Point with one of my colleagues, when we stumbled across a secret passage to a cave below the cliff. We were joking around about pirates and their hidden caches of gold when we found an old rusted door. One thing led to another and you know how adventurous our family is—"

Anna interrupted him. "Our family? I'm more than a little confused. I've never seen you before in my life."

"Of course you haven't. Now let me finish." He took a deep breath. "My friend and I decided to check it out. We never guessed that what we had found could really even exist. There are dozens of theories on time travel, but none of them can be proven. Yet here I am in the year 1880, decades before I was even born."

"Over one hundred years."

"Yeah." Alastair ran his long fingers through his already tousled hair. "We crossed through the door's threshold, stumbling along in the dark until we found a large opening in the stone wall. We could hear the sea. My friend flicked his lighter. We stood in a cavern with a deep pool, stretching the length of the natural room before us. Stacked in a hollowed-out area across the pool stood piles of old sea chests."

"Sea chests?" Goose bumps prickled her skin.

"Of course!" He jumped to his feet again and paced as he talked. "Curiosity demanded we see what was in the chests. We walked across the old wood planks bridging the water, and that's when it happened. It was worse than a tilt-a-whirl ride."

"I know the feeling." Her head throbbed at the memory of her wild journey through time. Was it possible he had traveled through time too? She studied his features as he paused to stare thoughtfully into space.

"I have had bad vertigo in my day, but nothing like this. My head felt as though it would burst and the screaming in my ears was almost intolerable! I lost my balance and fell into the pool." He turned to smile down at her. "I didn't know the same thing had happened to my friend, until I came to—lying on the cold stone cavern floor."

Anna's heart stuttered in awe. She knew exactly what he was saying. A spyglass didn't transport him back through the portals of time; it was a pool of water! "You say this pool is in a cave under the old house."

"Yes! It's amazing, isn't it?"

Questions cluttered her mind all at once. She chose carefully what answers she wanted to know most. If all he said was true, he must be the doctor the attorney told her about who had disappeared last year from the house she inherited. Pieces were falling together like a puzzle and her interest peaked to know more.

"What happened to your friend?" She brushed a wispy strand of hair from her face and waited for his response.

Alastair's thoughts turned grim. He did not want to speak poorly of the man he had once trusted with his life. "Greed does funny things to a person. He wanted to stay here, and I wanted to make sure we could get back. He promised to wait while I went back to get some supplies. It took me nearly a full day to gather together medical supplies and information I would use to navigate in the past. When I returned, my friend was gone."

"You mean he went back to the future."

He shrugged. "That's what I thought, at first. I left my things in the cave and returned once again to the future. I became totally drained from the time travel experience. I stayed in the house and slept for two days. When I felt better, I began making plans to find my friend. I researched history at the local library and the historical society in San Francisco. I looked up my family's genealogy, too. That's how I found Captain Duncan—and you."

"So you really are a doctor?" Anna sighed with relief. It was all becoming clear to her now. Everything she had seen him do, his actions and the way he expressed himself. He seemed so familiar because he was from her time. Simple conclusion.

He chuckled. "Yes, Anna. I am really a doctor."

"The medicine you used on James hasn't been invented yet, has it?"

He laughed outright. "How observant of you! The germ that causes tetanus won't be discovered until 1884, although, it will kill quite a few people before they find the proper vaccine. Dr. Fleming won't discover penicillin mold until 1928. Most of the medications I brought with me weren't made until the twentieth century, including the tablets of Phenobarbital I gave you last night."

"I thought they looked too modern." She pondered all he had told her. "How do I know you are telling me the truth?"

"I graduated from UCLA's medical school in 1996. I'm a general surgeon, specializing in cardiology. I wanted to help others, as well as James, while I was here in this century. But I never guessed how long I would be forced to stay."

A sudden upsetting thought occurred to her. "Will your helping heal the captain cause problems with history?"

Alastair started to answer, then thought better of it. How would she feel if she discovered James would have died without his help? Doc Hobbs was a nice old man who did his best to help people. With only a few months of medical school under his belt and a great deal of incompetence, Doc Hobbs was more like a kindergartner attempting to enter college.

Alastair had assisted the old man over the past several months enough to discover he didn't have the knowledge he should have as a medical doctor. He stubbornly refused to accept any updated knowledge, like disinfecting wounds and equipment sterilization.

"I feel pretty sure all this was meant to happen. Why, we're making history—you and I." He winked at her.

She surprised him when she socked him in the arm. "Are you nuts? Haven't you ever heard of karma?" She jumped to her feet. "Just answer me this—are we stuck here forever?"

"Too many questions. I think I've said enough for now." Becoming the professional doctor again, Alastair looked down at his watch. "I need to check on the captain again." He offered her his arm, slipping smoothly into the Victorian mode. "Will you join me?"

"No, go on without me. I need to think about all this." Anna settled back on the garden bench to think. So many questions left unanswered. One thing was for sure though—the handsome young doctor could be her return ticket to the future.

~ * ~

Alastair relaxed in the darkened room. He had been with James for quite some time, watching him sleep fitfully in restless bouts of pain. Throughout his torment, James called out Anna's name and each time it stung Alastair with regret. He had always imagined sharing a love as great as all time, one that could survive eternity. It had yet to happen for him and he wondered if it ever would.

Hell, he could make it happen. Couldn't he? This was like writing a darn book with the power to control the characters and the outcome of their situations. Alastair knew what had happened in his family history. Now he had the opportunity to make changes. But could he do it? Would he still exist in the future if he found happiness in the past?

A gentle knock at the bedroom door announced Anna's arrival. What was it about this woman that drew him so? Did his soul sense her importance to his very existence?

"Is he awake, yet?" Her face appeared strained with worry.

"No." His gaze took in her shapely figure accented by the close-fitted dress she wore. His great-great-grandmother was a knockout in any century. He cursed himself inwardly for such notions as he shifted positions in the small chair.

"Do you mind if I sit with him a while?" Without waiting for an answer, she moved to the bedside and gazed tenderly down upon the captain. "Isn't it unusual for him to stay out so long? I thought it could cause brain damage."

Alastair sighed and stood, stretching his cramped legs. "I am doing everything in my power to make him live."

"I know." She sat down in the overstuffed Turkish chair next to the bed. "I have thought about something all day. Are you the Duncan descendent who disappeared in the future?"

"Yes." He would have to tell her eventually, but he had hoped it would be much later. "When I found the journal in the attic, I knew I was destined to travel back in time and attempt to save my great-great-grandfather. He was dying from complications he received in an accident. This very accident, Anna."

"Oh no!" She covered her mouth with a dainty hand.

"The journals explain how a young doctor's timely arrival in Mendocino apparently saved his life. The doctor had amazing medical talent, especially for the nineteenth-century. I put two-and-two together. I already knew about the time pool. My training in advanced medicine would be the key to his survival. It had to be me, or I wouldn't exist." He pulled his chair closer to her and sat back down himself.

It dawned on Anna that by reading the family journals, Alastair would know for sure whom James really married. Her heartbeat quickened. Was she ready to hear the answer? Could she deal with the truth even if it was not what she wanted to hear? Curiosity overpowered her and she couldn't resist.

She leaned forward. "Do you know who your great-great-grandmother is?"

"Yes." He flashed a crooked smile with a twinkle in his blue eyes. "I was hoping you would not ask. You see...I need your help with a little matter. If I tell you all I know now, you may not trust me anymore."

Anna refused to be manipulated by this suave and persuasive rascal. "You forget, doctor. You're dealing with a woman from the twenty-first century, not a simpering genteel prude. Am I, or am I not, your great-great-grandmother? I'm asking because I need to know for an equally important reason."

His chuckle was devilish. "You could be, but there are a few things at risk here."

"I refuse to play your games!" She stood and gave him the evil eye. "If I have to find the information I seek by myself, I will."

"I beg to differ with you." He grabbed her arms, pulling her onto his lap. "Not only will you play my game, madam, you will do as I say. I hold your future in my hands, just as I hold you now."

"You rude, poor excuse for a man." Anna quickly brought her arms up with force and dealt him a hard blow to his chin with her right fist. She pushed off his lap and stood with a satisfied huff.

Alastair fell back, dazed by her strength. "Wild woman!"

"Do not threaten me." She folded her arms and turned to peek at the captain. Finding him still at rest, she stepped closer to Alastair. "You are the most dishonorable entity that has ever walked this earth."

"Not the most dishonorable, I assure you." He rubbed his chin. "Where in hell did you learn to fight like that?"

Anna ignored his irrelevant question. "I thought doctors had a code of honor." She watched his smile reappear and suddenly recognized it for the same roguish grin James himself so casually embraced.

"We do in medicine, but I never said I was an honorable man. In fact, I know I'm not or I never would have assisted Morgan." Alastair hit his forehead with the heel of his hand in absolute frustration. Damn! He could have bitten his traitorous tongue! Lack of sleep had made him careless.

"Morgan?"

"My horse," he lied.

Anna frowned. If she fought with Alastair and made him mad, maybe he would discontinue his treatment of James. She glanced over to the bed, reassuring herself James was still sleeping peacefully in spite of their whispered argument.

"I suppose you have done something illegal." She stepped backwards.

He stood to confront her, towering over her. "And if I have?" He quickly closed the short distance between them. "You know there are ways to make you cooperate."

"Don't threaten me. I warned you. I'm sick of overbearing men." Anna took another step backwards, bumping into the bedpost. She watched him closely with all senses alert.

"I forgot you were married before. Let's see—what was his name?" Alastair hit a raw nerve. She flinched, even before her beautiful eyes concealed what she was thinking. "Does the dear captain know about him?"

She shook her head. "No."

He grinned. "I would sure hate to be the one to break it to him. If you agree to help me, maybe I can find a way to hold my wayward tongue."

"You jerk! That's blackmail." Her fiery green eyes threw daggers at him.

If looks could kill, he might be deader than a doornail. He was winning and it was a heady thought. "All in the family, Anna, but enough of this verbal warfare. We will continue our conversation later." Nodding in her direction, he turned and strode swiftly from the room.

A horrible thought crossed Anna's mind. If she were to marry James, Alastair would be her great-great-grandson. How would she know if what she chose to do was right? What a nightmare! All she could think about was escaping from everything for a while. Her head throbbed with the beginnings of a tension headache. Moving toward the door, she glanced over at the captain. She was startled to find him awake and watching her. How much had he overheard?

"Anna?" His voice cracked as he whispered her name.

"Oh, James!" She nearly flew to the bed, covering his face with tiny kisses. Her fingers caressed his thick chestnut hair and gently rubbed his rough whiskered cheek. "How are you feeling?"

"Much better now, lass, since I've laid eyes on ye." He released a groan as he shifted his injured leg on the bed. "What were ye talking about with Alastair?"

Looking down at him, her heartstrings tugged. "We didn't agree on something. But you aren't to worry about it. I just want you to get better."

James knew more was going on than Anna wanted to admit. He had heard something about blackmail before his mind cleared and he opened his eyes to see Alastair storm from the room. "Ye look bonny, lass. A true sight for sore eyes."

Anna blushed. She stood at the bedside, fingering the creases on her pale blue dress. Her hair was gently slipping from the plait wound around her head, falling in soft tendrils about her face.

"You, dear Captain, must be looking through rose-colored glasses," she scolded with temperance as she carefully put a cup of cool water to his lips and waited for him to take a sip.

He leaned back against the pillows with a weary sigh. "Nay, 'tis only the eyes o' love." Beckoning to her with his index finger, he smiled and patted the bed beside him. "Come here, Anna."

"James you are in no condition—"

"Did I say I was? Ah, but yer mind dwells upon a lovely subject." He released a deep chuckle at her reaction. Pain shot through his head from the subtle vibration. Still, he managed to reach for her. "Tis only for a wee sweet kiss from yer honeyed lips that I'm asking."

She moved slowly into his embrace. "I've been longing to give you a kiss, but with a lot more passion than sweetness."

Careful not to jostle his injuries, he pulled her down beside him and felt his blood quicken. His lips covered hers in a tender kiss, a kiss promising to recover and be faithful. Aye, the promise was there to keep her in his arms forever if possible.

~ * ~

Anna wanted to discover the truth about everything Alastair had told her. He was holding back something important. The past should not be tampered with, no matter what had happened.

Still, she had so many unanswered questions on her mind. Was she supposed to remain in 1880 with James? And what about Alastair? Were their lives so intricately entwined? Would all work out somehow? The answers seemed to rest in the old house in the future, but she wasn't even sure it had been built yet. Now that she knew about the time pool, she was determined to return to her time and solve the mystery conclusively.

Without another thought as to what the consequences might be, she hurried quietly down the backstairs. Slipping unobserved through the fragrant rose garden, she stepped out onto the dusty dirt-packed street. Thank heavens the walk to town was short.

Anna inquired at the milliner's shop for the location of the stagecoach office. She only walked a couple of blocks to a small clapboard building with a huge sign above the door. Entering to the sound of bells, she approached the man behind the ticket window.

"I need a ticket to San Francisco," Anna said, trying to make her request sound calm, although her heart raced. She held in her hand the few coins she had found in the captain's pants pockets, hoping they would be enough to pay her fare. She had no idea of monetary value in her present situation.

A wizened old man with wiry gray hair, a ridiculously long mustache and bushy beard looked up at her from under the brim of his cap. His wire-rimmed glasses were so thick; Anna marveled that he could see her at all.

"A ticket to San Francisco, you say?"

Was he deaf as well?

"Yes," she confirmed, desperately wishing he would hurry before someone at the Stenson's noticed her missing.

She had told Rosie she didn't care about dinner. She wanted to rest and not be disturbed until morning. The kind woman had raised her eyebrows in curiosity, but left Anna to herself. Nothing was said about it being a little unusual to skip a meal, especially the last meal of the day.

"Well, there'll be a coach leaving for Gualala at four o'clock. That's in about fifteen minutes, young lady. You can catch one bound for Frisco from Gualala in a day or two." His smile was genuine. Apparently, he was doing his best to accommodate her.

"I'm not sure I have enough money for the fare." She spilled the coins out onto the smooth wooden counter, where they clattered and rolled, and landing in disarray in front of the surprised ticket agent.

His voice edged with laughter. "You're not from these parts are you, young lady?" Counting out the correct amount, he looked up at her. "You traveling alone?"

Caught unawares, Anna shifted uncomfortably from foot to foot. She held up her chin. "Yes. Is there a problem?"

"Only if the road agents get you. Make yourself a friend on board, a protector of sorts." His wrinkled fingers reached out and patted her hand as she picked up the remaining coins and put them back into her pocket. "Tell Jake Hardwick that Old Bill said to keep an eye on you."

Taking the overly large paper ticket from him, Anna gave him her sweetest smile. "Thanks, Old Bill. Where might I find this Jake Hardwick?"

"He's across the street having something to eat before the run. But that there's a saloon and nice young ladies won't be welcome inside." Old Bill scratched his head thoughtfully. "Why don't you just wait in here a while? I'll call to him when he comes outside."

Caught up in the feminine war of propriety again, Anna shrugged her shoulders and walked over to a long wooden bench. She sat down in her most prim and proper manner. Gazing around the room, she studied its sparse contents.

The wood paneled wall covered in WANTED posters, and numerous other notes, caught her attention. Not being able to resist a little excursion into real living history, she stepped up to the wall and began reading. Attempting to decipher the spelling and language from the Wild West criminal posters was a challenge to say the least.

She could not believe the infamous outlaws so glamorized in the future as 'sexy, handsome hunks' in books and movies, were in reality plain ordinary men. Some were young boys. A few were handsome and most were not.

She was surprised to see such a legendary figure as the charismatic gunman, Billy the Kid. His freshly printed poster hung dead center, right next to an article about Pat Garrett running for sheriff in Lincoln County, New Mexico. Was this an omen of things to come?

Another WANTED poster, this one faded with age, hung nearby. It bore the likenesses of Jesse James and Cole Younger, members of the notorious James Gang, who terrorized the West for more than a decade. Was it possible for her to exist in this age where bandits ran free—shooting people just to pass time? She shivered at the frightening notion as she heard Old Bill call to her from across the room.

Eleven

"Here comes Jake now, young lady." Old Bill pointed his gnarled arthritic finger out the door. "He'll take real good care of you. You'll see. Ain't nobody lived to brag about holding up one of his stages, no sir. He's faster with that old Winchester than any man around."

Anna looked past the ticket agent to see a tall, rugged young man in a weathered cowboy hat crossing the street. His blue jeans looked worn, his leather boots scuffed, and a faded denim shirt hung unbuttoned halfway down his chest. His neck bore the typical red bandanna. A six-shooter hung from a wide leather belt looking ominous, as did the long-barreled rifle held firmly in his right hand.

She suddenly remembered the WANTED posters in the room behind her. This was the wild old west. A shiver ran up her back. She was both frightened and fascinated at the same time. Jake drew nearer and she covered her mouth, surprised at his youth.

"He's so young!" She blinked twice. "I mean...to be carrying guns."

Bill's mustached mouth broke into a proud grin. "Nah, he's almost twenty-two. Been riding shotgun for almost five years now." He took her arm and walked her out onto the wide boardwalk. "He's single, too," he said, raising his eyebrows with a sly conspiratorial wink.

"Oh?" She tried to sound politely interested, as she met the sable brown gaze of the ominous gunman.

His long black hair hung straight to his broad shoulders, emphasizing his square jaw and tan complexion. A dark mustache settled between two deep dimples appearing at each side of his sexy, broad smile. She gulped when he came to a stance before her.

"Old Bill, who's this you got here?" Jake asked.

"This here is one of your passengers to Gualala. She's traveling alone, so I thought maybe you could keep an eye on her." Old Bill leaned against a nearby post with his pocket watch in his hand. He flicked open the engraved golden case with a grunt. "If you're gonna be on schedule, you'd better get your hide over to the blacksmith's and see what's keeping him. He should have had that horse shoed an hour ago."

"Hush, ye grumbling old codger." He turned his attention back to Anna. "Jake Hardwick, ma'am. You sure will make the trip a whole lot more interesting. Never seen such lovely golden hair and such attractive green eyes."

"She needs looking out for Jake, not your flirting ways," Old Bill said, while standing protectively at her side.

Anna swallowed hard. Was all this truly necessary? She could take care of herself, for Pete's sake. It was only a stagecoach ride. How dangerous could it be?

"This is harsh country for a lady traveling alone. I'd be right pleased to watch out for you." Jake tipped his hat as he spoke. "Just wish I'd taken up Molly's offer for a bath earlier. I don't smell none too pretty about now, sleeping with the horses like I often do. But I reckon I can fix that before we leave town."

She took all he said with a grain of salt. He seemed honest anyway. "Thanks, Jake. I'm Anna Bentley." Extending her hand in greeting and expecting a handshake in return, she smiled when he took her fingertips in a gentle squeeze. She didn't miss the appreciative grin, or the interest in his dark smoldering eyes.

"Anna. Pretty name. I'll see what's keeping Joe and pick up the other passengers on my way back. You just as well wait here, ma'am." Jake tipped his hat again and strode off toward the smithy, his long legs crossing the distance in minutes.

Anna turned around from staring after him and noticed Old Bill had retreated to his small office. She could not believe she had stood drooling over a stunning Jake Hardwick. Were all the men in this era so substantially appealing, or was she just meeting the cream of the crop?

She sat on the bench with a sigh. Her thoughts flashed back to James. She wondered how he was feeling about now, and if he had missed her yet. She hated leaving him, but she had to know what Alastair had up his sleeve. She satisfied her aching heart with a prayer for James. If Alastair were correct, then his presence would ensure James' recovery. One way to find out was return to the future.

~ * ~

James stirred restlessly under the covers, groaning as his movements brought fresh pain to his injuries. Afternoon was passing and evening shadows crept slowly into the room. He squinted and tried to focus, hoping to see a sea nymph watching over him.

The room was completely devoid of people. Something was wrong. He could feel trouble deep inside. He strained to sit up and heard Rosie's familiar voice in the next room.

"Mr. George, I done told you as much as I know. She told me she was retiring early and not to disturb her. I never knew she would up and disappear."

"I didn't mean to scold you, Rosie. I simply do not understand where she could be. She left without telling anyone where she was going. I've sent the stable lads around to inquire if anyone has seen her. We should—" His words trailed off as he noticed James, leaning heavily against the door frame.

Rosie turned to see what had caught George's attention and was the first to reach James' side. "Now what are you doing out of that bed? You ain't in any shape to be up and about yet."

George rushed to assist. "Of all the foolish things! We want you to recover, James. This is pure suicide."

"Where is she, George? Where's Anna?" Bright lights of pain shot through his head. His knees became weak and he stumbled, caught from falling by his sturdy friend.

"We think she may have stepped out for a walk and become lost," George said with a worried sigh. "I have some lads out looking for her as we speak."

James held onto his head and cursed in Gaelic. He focused on George, his voice raw with emotion. "I cannot lose Anna, now. Tell me she's safe, George. Tell me she has not left me for her own time."

"Let's get you back to bed, James. You aren't making any sense. I will find her. I promise." George led James back into his room and settled him carefully down upon the rumpled bed.

Rosie mixed laudanum into a bit of water and put it to his dry lips. "You just relax now, James. We ain't gonna let no harm come to your pretty little bride. Mr. George will find her."

"Blast it all woman! I'll not be drugged. I need to find Anna." James spat and sputtered over the medication, but Rosie was determined. She forced the bitter tasting liquid down his throat until he had swallowed it all.

George gave him a gentle pat on his good shoulder. "I'm off to find William. He'll know best how to locate Anna and bring her safely home."

James' last clear thought before the sleeping drug closed his eyes was of his bonny Anna. No one knew about her troublesome plight except him. Perhaps the force that had so suddenly brought her into his life had returned to remove her from his grasp, just when he needed her most.

~ * ~

Huge pine forests gave way to secluded meadows abounding with wild flowers, ferns, and blackberry brambles. Anna caught fleeting glimpses of the not-so-distant ocean through the trees. Reminded of her journey's purpose, she knew she had to go back to the future and find the Duncan family journals. From Alastair's story, the captain had yet to build his house at what would one day be known as Duncan's Point. She hoped she would recognize the right area. Would the coast look the same topographically in 1880?

Having grown bored with the lush scenery, Anna decided to study the other passengers in the coach. The well-dressed gentleman to her right sat cross-legged reading a folded newspaper. He seemed oblivious to the rolling motion the Concord coach made as it rambled down the rough-hewn road. She marveled that he wasn't getting sick. She had never been able to read while traveling in a car or a bus, and they had much smoother rides than the stagecoach.

Anna glanced across at two young cowboys with Colt .45's belted around their lean waists. One boy caught her studying him and blushed bashfully. He couldn't have been more than sixteen. Once again, she pondered the ease with which young men and boys openly carried firearms.

The fourth passenger wore tight black jeans tucked into black boots, a black dress shirt that lay open at the neck and a black bandanna tied loosely about his collar. Slung about his waist he wore a gun belt and nestled menacingly within its leather holster lay a long-barreled, wood-handled Peacemaker .45. A wood handled Bowie knife peeked out from his left boot top and a black wide-brimmed hat covered his face. He looked as if he was in control of life. Except for his long blond hair, he could have passed for the fictitious bandit, Zorro. He emanated danger and she was glad he kept to himself.

On top of the coach rode two more male passengers. No doubt they were cowboys too, from the quick look she got before they boarded. The driver was a gray-haired man who looked as though he wouldn't be able to handle a team of six horses, let alone get them all safely to Gualala. Jake Hardwick sat shotgun, setting her mind at ease with his presence.

Anna sighed and leaned back into the hard leather seat. Darkness fell, bringing with it thick coastal fog. The coach's rocking motion made her drowsy. Hazily, she wondered how much longer it would be before they reached their destination. Her bottom felt as though she had been joggled around for days, not just a few hours. Where was her Camaro when she needed it?

The coach slowing down brought Anna quickly to her senses. Her heart leaped at the idea of getting off what she now considered a nineteenth-century torture machine. Out the small window, she noticed the outline of a large frame building. Oh great—a way station. Why hadn't the old man told her the stage wouldn't go straight through? All she needed was to waste more time and have someone catch up with her before she accomplished her goal.

The coach stopped and a few seconds later the narrow door swung open. Jake held out his hand for her to grasp. "Ma'am?"

Feeling a little silly, her cheeks blushed with warmth as she looked down into his grinning face. She was even more embarrassed when his big hands circled her waist and he casually lifted her as though she didn't weigh an ounce. Holding her close for a moment too long, he released a deep breath that brushed seductively across her cheek.

"You smell right pretty, ma'am."

She tried to ignore the fact he was so darned handsome and focus on the matter at hand. "Thank you, Jake. Is this a way station?"

"Yep. I reckon some folks call it that."

She watched the other passengers leave for shelter in the nearby building. "So how long do we have to stay here?"

"We'll be spending the night here, ma'am." He wiped his bandanna across the side of his neck and tipped his hat back. "We go over the pass first thing in the morning."

"We're spending the night? Here?" Oh damn, more hurdles to overcome. She had to succeed in pretending she knew what to do while consorting with these seasoned frontier people.

Jake shuffled his booted feet and removed his hat before meeting her gaze again. "How come I get the feeling you have never done this before?"

"Most likely because I haven't. Traveling by stagecoach is rather new to me." Her mind raced to come up with a logical reason. "I usually travel by ship."

"Ship?" He cupped her elbow and escorted her inside. The room echoed with conversation and clattering dishes. He led her to a seat at a long wooden trestle table. "Even to watch the sea makes my stomach turn. My short-lived experience with sailing was years ago aboard a dirty old fishing boat. It took a mighty strong mind to overcome the potent smell from a hold chock full of fish."

Anna smiled in response and glanced about the large rustic room. Two more trestle tables stood against the outer wall, already full with passengers from the stage as well as several dusty horseback riders. Kerosene lanterns hung at intervals around the walls, accounting for the smoky torch-like atmosphere. The rough stone fireplace was stacked full with logs, casting heat all the way across the wide room.

The delicious aroma of venison stew and fresh baked bread mixed with the equally strong smell of sweat and unwashed bodies. A short, brightly dressed, Mexican woman served each person as they were seated. Apparently, the menu was the same for everyone—stew and red wine.

Anna missed having to pour over a restaurant's detailed menu for several minutes before making up her mind. Not having a choice in food didn't seem to upset any of the travelers here, though. They were happy to eat a hearty meal.

Anna sipped at the weak wine. They probably watered the wine down so it would go further, or maybe simply to ward off drunken brawls. Still, with cholera running rampant in the late 1800s watery wine was better than chancing plain water.

"Do you like the sea?" Jake's deep voice disturbed her musings. He played silently with his food, awaiting her answer.

Caught with a mouthful of stew, it was a moment before Anna could respond. "The sea? Yes, I guess so. Why do you ask?" Then she remembered what their conversation had been about as they arrived. He was still on the same track.

"You told me you traveled by ship. I thought you must enjoy it."

She did enjoy watching endless ocean waves and smelling salty sea breezes. They made her feel so vibrantly alive. Yet, she didn't really care to sail all that much. "My ex-husband was a sailor. I was expected to like it."

"You've been married?"

Anna smiled at his grimace. "I haven't seen him in a long time. He lives too far away." If he only knew how far! "We weren't happy and the whole thing was a big mistake." Feeling she had said too much already, she stared down at the half-eaten bowl of stew. She was no longer hungry, but yearned for some fresh air. "Excuse me, please."

Jake stood up, his deep dimples showing again.

She pushed back her chair in a hurry to leave the closed-in, stuffy room. "I'll be right back." She gave him a wavering smile and made a rush for the door.

"Ma'am?"

"What'd ye do, Jake? Make a pass at the little lady?" A loud hoot of laughter followed the stage driver's comment.

Anna stood at the end of the long porch looking back inside through a low, narrow window. She could hear the men's conversation through the open door. She watched in silent amusement as Jake threw down his napkin, took the last swallow of wine in his glass and stomped outside to join her.

"Bet he makes a pass at her now!" A husky voice shouted. Another round of laughter broke out through the crowded room.

Jake shook his head at the playful teasing. When he spotted her, he crossed the porch in a slow, easy saunter. "Sorry 'bout that," he said, rubbing his thick black mustache as he leaned against the porch post.

She smiled. He had a good sense of humor. "They like to tease you, don't they?"

"They do."

"It was all in fun, so I don't mind."

"I do." Jake stepped closer. "It's not proper to say such things around a lady."

Anna looked down at the ground, and then slowly up into his nonchalant smile. He was the kind of man who would make a woman's heart flutter just by looking at him. "It's really okay, Jake. They were just joking around."

"I would never make a pass at you."

Okay, so he didn't find her attractive. "I appreciate your manners, Jake."

He glanced back over his shoulder, and then leaned even closer. "Not that I would mind a sweet kiss or two."

Oh-oh! He wanted to kiss her. Now she'd gone and done it. How did they get off on this subject anyway? She wouldn't mind kissing a real old west hunk of a gunslinger, but her heart was truly involved elsewhere. She shouldn't have confided in him earlier about her divorce. Undoubtedly it was the same in any era—a divorced woman was easy prey.

"Jake, I already have someone special."

His smile faded. "Guess that means I better keep my mind on my work, huh?"

"Yes, I guess it does."

He coughed, and then grinned. "At least you're honest. I admire that in a lady."

"Thanks. I admire your sincerity, too, Jake."

He took her elbow and led her across the porch. "There's a few cots inside for the ladies. Men sleep on the floor. You won't get cold. Maria has plenty of blankets. I'll be here if you need me."

"Where will you sleep?" It was a normal question. She didn't think it would stop him cold, and she sure didn't expect to see sparks in his dark eyes when he looked down at her.

"Under the stars. I never sleep indoors." Jake released her arm and glanced around. "Are you afraid to be alone with all those men in there? You are the only female this trip."

She hadn't thought about it. A room crammed full of dirty hard-working cowboys and who knew what else? "I don't think I can stand the smell," she admitted with a frown.

His sudden burst of laughter startled her. "Are you saying you prefer my company to theirs?"

"Yes." There, that was simple enough. She looked up into his personable face. "Is that okay with you?"

"It'll ruin your reputation."

"My reputation?" Curse the Victorian age with its silly morals and archaic prudery. She wanted to sleep and she didn't want to deal with any more problems tonight.

"A lady might be compromised. Some people frown on that sort of thing." Jake rested his hand absently on his handgun.

She saw the subtle movement and remembered what the ticket agent had said about Jake being a fast draw. Well, she would rather be safe with him than closed in with a rowdy, grubby bunch of men. Men she didn't know the first thing about. The gentleman from the coach had retired to a quiet corner of the room upon arriving. Thankfully, the dangerous blond Zorro had left on horseback soon after the stage stopped at the way station. But she still couldn't face going back into the crowded room.

"I don't mind. Besides, I trust you, Jake." Anna watched his dimples reappear and for a slip of a moment, his face was as readable as an open book. Then he frowned and his brow furrowed as though deep in thought.

"You shouldn't." He turned and strode off toward the stables in back.

She watched him leave, wondering all the while if she was supposed to follow him or wait for his return. There were times her independence was a pain in the—

His smiling face peeked around the building. "Are you coming, or you gonna stand there all night looking beautiful in the moonlight?"

Beautiful in the moonlight? She hurried to catch up and couldn't help the smile that escaped. He was nice—in a mountain man sort of way. She wasn't afraid of him either, even though she had only met him today. He could be equally as dangerous as the Zorro dude on the stage, but somehow she didn't quite think so.

"My bedroll is on the coach," Jake explained, keeping a brisk pace that drew them across the yard to the huge barn in no time.

Anna followed his long strides, enjoying the cool night's fresh, crisp air. The stars were so brilliant, she imagined she could reach right out and touch them. Giant trees outlined the sky with pointed spirals reaching for the moon and the scent of fresh pine assailed her nostrils.

Feeling the pressing need to relieve herself, she looked around. She wondered where the toilet was. Probably in a dilapidated, stinky outhouse somewhere out back, but it was dark now and she couldn't make out the familiar shape anywhere.

Catching up to him, she grasped his sleeve. "Jake, I need to—"

"It's over behind that clump of trees. I'll take you in a minute," he said, as though reading her mind.

They reached the stables, dimly lit by oil lanterns hung right inside the double doors. Anna could hear snoring and figured even some men preferred the barn and horses to the overcrowded station house. She didn't blame them one iota.

Jake climbed nimbly onto the driver's box of the stagecoach and pulled a bundle out of the front boot. He jumped down and landed steady on his feet beside her. Their eyes met and held.

"Sure you want to do this? The ground is real hard, you know. There's always a snake or two—"

"Are you trying to scare me?"

"Do I?" His eyes twinkled with pleasure.

"I don't think we're talking about snakes anymore."

"You're right." He turned and walked away.

Anna ran to keep up with him. "Jake, wait!" Catching his sleeve again, she gasped for air when he finally slowed his pace.

He pointed a short distance ahead. "There's the outhouse. I'll stand guard over here. Don't be too long."

"You make it sound dangerous. Are there wild animals or savage Indians around?" She had no fear sleeping in the great outdoors, having camped out many times before. Sure, things were different a hundred years from now, but sleeping under the stars hadn't changed all that much.

"No." He chuckled. "So do you go in alone or do I escort you?"

"Alone, thank you."

She laughed at his teasing and entered the cramped confines of the weathered, wilderness bathroom. She held her breath to keep from smelling its pungent fumes. A deep black hole loomed before her with two splintery boards for a seat. She prayed she wouldn't fall in as she struggled with yards of dress material.

Jake was waiting for her when she exited the small cubicle. "Better?"

"The fresh air? Most definitely!"

He led her toward the back of the station house and showed her a deep wooden rainwater barrel. She washed her hands and splashed cool water on her face, then lifted her full cotton skirt to wipe herself dry.

A low chuckle rumbled beside her. "You are the most curious woman I have ever met. Do you always use your dress as a towel?"

"It's the only thing handy and I want to wash off the road dirt." She looked up and met his inquisitive expression. "Don't stare at me like that, and if you dare laugh again...why I'll stomp on your big booted toes!"

"I reckon you would. Well, let's bunk out over here. There's a meadow in the pines where it's a little softer on your backside." Jake led the way on a short walk into the forest.

It was a beautiful night. Starlight filtered down through giant trees onto a small grassy meadow. The soothing sound of the sea echoed in the distance. Jake rolled out two thick woolen blankets close together, then loosened his gun belt and laid it carefully between them.

Anna sat on one blanket and looked up at the stars. "It's so quiet when you can't hear all the traffic on the freeways." She realized her verbal blunder the minute the words tumbled out of her mouth.

"Traffic on the freeways?" Jake rubbed the back of his neck and eyed her for a quiet moment. "Lady, where'd you grow up?"

"San Francisco, why?" She half-hoped if she challenged him he would let it slide, but part of her knew he was too smart to do that.

"Just wondering what a freeway is, that's all." He looked up at the stars too. "So many things I don't know about in this world."

She swallowed hard. Should she tell him she was from the future and ask for his help? No. He would probably think she was crazy. "Freeway is just a word I made up for the busy streets. They are quite busy in downtown San Francisco, you know."

"Yeah, I know. I guess it is quiet here compared to Frisco," he agreed, settling down on the blanket beside her. He laid back and faced her, using his arm for a pillow. "Pretty too."

"It sure is if you're from the big city." Her dreamy gaze dropped from the stars to him. He wasn't talking about the scenery anymore. "Well, guess we had better get some sleep. I'm really bushed!"

Jake pulled a heavy blanket over them. "Good-night, Anna."

"Good-night, Jake." Stretching out on her side, she closed her eyes and waited for that blessed thing called sleep to overcome her senses. If she juggled much more conversation, she might expire from the effort of covering her errors.

~ * ~

The low hungry cry of a wolf broke the silence, startling Anna into an upright position. Her sleepy gaze scanned the dark woods. She didn't want to find the wild animal close at hand. She looked over at Jake who slept soundly. Men could sleep through anything.

Shivering, Anna knew she could not go back to sleep. She leaned over Jake's large form and touched his shoulder. Before she could say his name, she found herself lying flat on her back with Jake sprawled out on top of her and the tip of his knife at her throat. Then cold truth hit Jake like a ton of bricks, she saw it dawn in his eyes.

"You just about bit the dust, woman!" He rolled off her and sat up, cursing under his breath. Glaring at her through thick lashes, he spoke with a growl. "What in the hell do you think you are doing?"

"Well I sure didn't expect to be attacked by a mountain man!" She was angry, too. He nearly scared her to death. "You would have killed me, huh?"

Jake slipped his knife back into his boot. "Maybe, but damn! You just don't wake people up like that out here in the woods." He pushed his fingers through his tousled hair. "I didn't hurt you, did I?"

Her chin jerked upwards. "You could have. I was only trying to tell you I heard something in the woods. I couldn't sleep."

"Probably a bobcat, maybe a timber wolf. They don't come near people much." Jake yawned, his sleepy face dimpled and he reached across to slip his arm protectively around her shoulders. He pulled her into his embrace and hugged her close. "You were really frightened, weren't you?"

Anna buried her face against his chest. Jake was kind and gentle. His wit was quick and she enjoyed their carefree banter. Jake felt too good…too strong, too safe, and too sensuously masculine. She cried softly. Was it the night sounds or her emotional confusion? The sensation of hanging in limbo and not really belonging anywhere, washed over her.

The purpose for her journey was to confirm Alastair's fantastic stories. She was furious with him for meddling with the concept of time travel in the first place. When he told her he had to save James or the future would be altered, she felt pressed to do something about it. Now she was on her way to a place she wasn't even sure she could find—in a totally unfamiliar century.

She should return to Mendocino and let the chips fall where they may, but what if she really belonged in the past? If so, then she shouldn't try to return to the future. And if she did, could she be the one to ruin it all?

She pushed out of Jake's embrace. Closing her eyes, she pictured James. Sweet, incredibly handsome, hot-tempered, and terribly romantic, James held her heart. A warm blush of desire crept slowly up her cheeks and she knew where she belonged.

She wiped the tears from her eyes. "Thanks, I just needed a good cry."

"Anna? Are you all right?"

"I'm fine." She couldn't look into his eyes. His attraction to her disturbed her. He was very nice, but if anyone could keep her here, it would be James.

"You're sure?" Jake cupped her chin in his hand, and searched her upturned face.

"Yes, positive. Hey, you have a tender side, Jake Hardwick." She touched her fingertips to his rough cheek. "You're a great catch. Some lucky girl will be very happy."

Dimples quickly reappeared, telling her he was perceptive once again. "Are you saying you like me?

"Very much so. You're a good friend." She studied his shadowed profile. "And as a friend...may I ask a favor?"

His eyes twinkled with affection. "You honor me, little lady. Ask away."

"Can you hold me while we sleep? I can't stop thinking about what might be prowling around out there in the forest."

His deep chuckle filled the night air. "To think all I wanted was a kiss."

Stretching out on the bedroll, Jake held his arms out to her. "Come here, Anna. I will protect you from the wolves of the forest." He wrapped her in the warmth of his arms as they snuggled down beneath the blanket to sleep under the stars.

Anna thought she would never see the day when she would willingly depend on a man again. Yet, here she was over a hundred years from home, wrapped in the arms of a stranger, and not just because she was afraid of the dark. She was also afraid of what the future held for her, and if she was doing the right thing by trying to go back.

She needed Jake's strength and friendship. She had sensed his attraction to her, yet they had turned into friends. And rightly so, because there was only one man who refused to leave her heart. She closed her eyes and dozed off thinking of James.

Twelve

"Good-morning, Captain!" Rosie's cheerful voice called out from the adjoining room. "I'll be right in to take care of you. I'm just gonna put these things away first."

James opened his eyes a slit and groaned. He felt much better today and no way would he allow Rosie to give him any more laudanum. He scrambled out of bed, almost falling over in the tangled sheets. Limping in pain, he quickly disappeared into the lavatory. He smiled as he slid the bolt safely into place. The woman meant well, but he wasn't a lad anymore. Rosie still treated him as though she were his nanny, something she hadn't been for more than fifteen years. He never should have recommended the Stenson's hire her as their housekeeper.

He dressed in fresh clothes with minor difficulty, brushed his hair into the favored queue and proceeded to walk stiffly downstairs. His blasted leg still pained him. If he didn't exercise the leg, his muscles would become weak and he could very well lose mobility.

Gritting his teeth, he hoped no one would notice his struggle. No matter. He was going after Anna today. Nothing would keep him from it, not even a wee bit of pain.

~ * ~

James entered the dining room and was surprised to find the doctor sitting at the table, nursing a cup of coffee. Alastair looked miserable and exhausted, suffering the aftereffects of drunkenness no doubt. "Good-morning, lad."

Alastair squinted up at him. "You shouldn't be up and around yet."

"Ye do not look as though ye should be up and about yerself." James stood at the sideboard, choosing from the large variety of food. He sat down at the table, his plate piled high with ham, eggs, and crisp fried potatoes. "Ah, but 'tis bonny to have a wee bit o' real food. I'm feeling much better thanks to yer good work, Alastair."

Angelique entered the dining room, wearing a pale pink dress. It complemented her fair complexion and luxurious brown curls piled high on her head. She was an extremely feminine woman, full of extremely feminine ideas.

She planted a kiss upon his brow. "James! It's so good to see you up and about today. Is it not, Alastair?" She glanced over at the young doctor. "Oh my, George was certainly right. I can see your temperament is not at all pleasant this morning."

"Leave me be, Angel," Alastair grumbled.

James felt mischievous this morning. "Alastair, seems as though ye could use a wee bit o' doctoring yerself. Or are ye aware o' the fact?"

"I knew I'd rue the day I saved your ornery hide. Can't a man suffer in peace?"

James chuckled. Many a time he had found himself in the same kettle of fish, especially after a good night's drinking and bedding a lusty wench. But since Anna had come into his life, he had not even fancied another woman. Anna. Ah, sweet Neptune!

Angelique sat down at the breakfast table, waiting for the kitchen maid to fill her cup with warm tea. "You know you two resemble each other so much you could be brothers. I don't know why such hostility exists between you. You act as though you are about to go at each other's throats."

"Aye, maybe we are. Did ye ever think it might be our own business, Angel?" James tried to hold back his humor over the situation. He could tell Angel was flustered with the tension slowly building in the room, but he was not in the mood for her senseless female prattle either.

"Have ye heard anything about Anna?" James took a hearty bite of ham.

"George went for William last night and I have not seen him since." Angelique reached over and patted James on the arm. "George will find her. You don't need to go roaming about in your condition."

"Blast my condition! I'll not sit by licking my wounds, Angel. And I'll not rest 'til I find Anna!" Having finished his tasty meal, he stood to leave.

Alastair's arm shot out, stopping him. "Hold on there! You aren't going anywhere." He stood, keeping a firm grasp on James' good arm. "What's this about Anna?"

"She's run off and we do not know where she has gone. 'Tis all I've thought about for hours now." James pulled away from Alastair. "Where have ye been, lad?"

"Drunk, I guess." A worried look crossed Alastair's face. "I cannot believe she would go without telling someone."

James remembered the tail end of the argument he had overheard yesterday between the doctor and Anna. Alastair was upset over something. Could it be the good doctor knew more about Anna's situation than he was willing to admit?

"I am going to find her. Are ye with me, Alastair?"

Alastair looked his great-great-grandfather straight in the eye and knew he should not tamper with fate. Anna belonged here with the captain. Alastair was sorry he had confused her on making the right choice.

"Yes. I may even know where she has gone. I think we will need your ship, James. And if I'm right, you may just want to hit me."

"If there's a need I may give ye a hardy thrashing, but 'tis yer help I am wanting right now, Alastair." James kissed Angelique's cheek in passing. "Tell George I am taking the *Ceilidh* out o' port, with or without him."

~ * ~

Mendocino bay scuttled with activity. Yet, it took only half an hour for James to get his robust crew together, including rounding up George Stenson. The deck hands rowed them out to the *Ceilidh* while George filled them in with what little information he had uncovered overnight.

"Anna is on a stagecoach heading south for Gualala." George scratched his head. "She is alone and without baggage, something the station master found unusual. Old Bill remembered her because she's pretty and traveling alone."

William's expression revealed his concern over the matter. "We can be there about the same time by sail. Don't you agree, Captain?"

"Aye, we can at that, lad," James agreed. He gazed toward his ship, thinking about the voyage ahead as the skiff quickly closed the distance with ease.

Pulling alongside the sturdy vessel, James heard the boatswain bellow to the men on board. A rope ladder lowered over the side to accommodate them. James climbed carefully over the rail, receiving unwanted assistance from Jock. His stormy expression told the heavyset second mate he was not in the mood for pleasantries. None came.

William was next on board. "It's not good, Jock. He's lost Anna."

Jock rubbed his full bearded chin. "So that's the way o' it? I felt something amiss when I saw the signal from shore."

"Aye. That's the way o' it, Jock." James turned to his first mate when he saw George climb up the rope ladder. "Go ahead, lad. We best be on our way."

William nodded and called back over his shoulder, "Make ready to sail! Hoist anchor! Prepare to set a course south to Gualala!"

Jock put a hand on James's shoulder. "Are ye up to this, Jamie?"

"Aye, Jock. I will not rest until I find the lass." James turned and, with a weary sigh he wanted no one to hear, hurried to his quarters below. The throbbing pain in his leg was nothing compared to the pain in his heart.

James entered his cabin and glanced around. The last time he had been on board Anna was here with him. Her feminine scent remained in the very air he breathed. He sat at his desk with his log and maps spread before him in disarray. Bending forward, he placed his head into his cupped hands, his mind filled with unanswered questions. Was this a foolhardy journey to attempt? He didn't know for sure if they would even find Anna in Gualala. The possibility of her having returned to her own time was greater than he liked to admit.

William knocked on the open door before entering the cabin. "Captain? I have given orders to set sail, sir."

James never lifted his face from his hands. "Thank ye, William. Are George and Alastair settled in their cabins?"

"Aye, Captain."

James looked up at the fine young officer and forced a grin. "Let's hope we find Anna in time, eh?" He winced at the double meaning in his choice of words. If ever he needed a miracle, he needed one now.

~ * ~

Anna's second day on the overland stage started out worse than the first. Upon approaching a steep slope over the pass, the driver insisted they all get out and walk to the summit. It would be easier for the horses to pull their burden uphill with less weight. The rough, rocky road threw dust in their faces as they walked, even though the stagecoach rumbled up the incline a good distance ahead.

Jake walked beside Anna, instead of riding his usual position beside the driver to guard the gold shipment. No one should know about the gold shipments, yet every darned robber in California did. For the moment, he felt safe enough. The danger lay ahead in a stretch of dense forest below the pass.

"Damn, if I know why I take the stage! I hate walking uphill for a quarter-mile," the well-dressed older gentleman grumbled to no one in particular.

Anna giggled. She felt the same way about the long dusty hike. "At least the cowboys don't seem to mind," she whispered to Jake. She noticed the four young cowhands trudging along, sharing jokes as if they were out on a cattle-drive.

A gunshot broke through the morning's tranquility. Jake pushed Anna down at the side of the road and told her to stay put. He took off running uphill toward the stage and his good friend, Joe. The four cowboys seemed to have forgotten their guns as they all ran for cover amidst the roadside shrubbery. Amazingly, the older gentleman just stood frowning in the middle of the road as Jake passed him by. The frightening sounds of gunshots rang out from up on the pass.

Anna looked up to see the distinguished gentleman frozen to the spot. He must be nuts, or frightened right out of his common sense. "Hey, boy scout! Do you want to get air-conditioned?" She got his attention as another bullet whizzed by her head.

The gentleman stepped toward her with an odd expression crossing his face before he fell to the ground, his limp body landing inches away from her face. Not knowing whether the bullets came from friend or foe, Anna froze as her heart leaped into her throat.

"Holy crap! I wasn't serious, Geez!"

She jumped to her feet and ran, but not away from trouble. Her conscience told her to find Jake. He was up ahead and might need some assistance. Topping the rise of the hill, Anna came to a halt. Jake knelt on the ground next to the stagecoach, his left hand grasping a bloody shoulder. Two men with bandannas covering the lower portion of their faces sat astride black horses. Robbers holding up the stage!

One bandit held Jake at gunpoint on the ground, while the other waved his gun at Joe, who was still sitting on the driver's box with the reins held securely in his hand.

"Throw down the express box! Now, dammit!" The bandit's harsh request was rewarded moments later. He dismounted and walked toward the small chest, lying on the ground in a swirl of road dust.

A soft gasp escaped Anna's lips, catching the second rider's unwanted attention. His dark eyes lit with sudden interest, though his gun never left its deadly aim at Jake's chest. She immediately recognized her mistake in allowing herself to be caught up in a honest-to-goodness holdup. She must be crazy to have believed she could do anything. This was not a movie set. This was really happening and these men were heartless killers.

Jake turned his head slightly to see what had caught the road agent's attention. "Damn! Anna, go back!"

"Too late, my friend," came a Spanish drawl from the dark-haired rider. "Hawk, we have a pretty *señorita* come to join us today."

The blond bandit, Hawk, forced open the lock on the Wells Fargo box with a short steel bar. He lifted the heavy canvas bags of gold and deposited them into his saddlebags, before turning to see what his companion was saying.

Hawk's surprise was as obvious as his pleasure. He sauntered slowly toward Anna while his friend, still mounted and dangerous, directed the old driver to sit down beside Jake. "Well, I see we have a lovely young morsel to sample, Emil."

"Try it, buster." Anna glared defiantly up at him, daring him to touch her and at the same time praying he would just go away.

"You've got the money. Now, leave the lady alone." Needled with pain, Jake leaned back against the coach's wheel for support. Damn! He was never caught off guard before. He cursed himself for allowing a woman to distract him from his duty. Guilt filled his heart over having put Anna in the middle of a dangerous situation.

Anna shifted her feet nervously as recognition suddenly flooded her senses with the bandit's identity. "Why, it's you! You were on the stage with us yesterday, planning to rob this very shipment I'll bet!"

"So I was, sweetheart. I am pleased this opportunity has arisen. I never forget a lovely woman."

Though Hawk's face remained covered by the bandanna, she knew his scheming mind. He had casually ignored everyone on the stagecoach the day before while planning this escapade. His piercing gaze devoured her like an expensive chocolate.

"Stop staring at me." She heard Jake's deep groan in response to her words, but her stubborn gaze never left the criminal towering before her. She lifted her chin a bit higher and summoned all her courage. "You can't get away with this."

"I can and I will."

She stared him straight in the eye. "Your arrogance will be your downfall."

"And your sharp tongue will be yours. Now you will come with us." Hawk's arm reached out quickly, catching her before she could move out of his way. He grasped her in a steel-tight grip around the waist and threw her easily up onto the saddle, then mounted behind her. Glaring down at Jake and Joe, he spat out a vengeful warning, "If either of you has any ideas about following us, you will find yourselves dead and left for the buzzards."

Jake made one more verbal attempt to bargain with him. "Leave the woman, and take me. Wells Fargo will pay highly to have me safely returned."

Emil slowly pulled the trigger back on his long-barreled gun. "Now gringo, why should we give up this pretty *señorita* for a few lousy dollars we will get off the next stage anyway?"

Anna watched in horror as the dark Spanish bandit took careful aim at Jake. "No! Please don't hurt him! I'll go with you! Leave him alone, please. You've already done enough harm."

"Stop taunting, Emil!" Hawk's deep voice boomed from directly behind her. "We do not want the reputation of killers."

"Just thieves?" Anna could not help the note of sarcasm in her voice or the icy fear in her heart. They were common criminals, nothing glamorous or fancy, but very, very deadly.

Emil released a burst of devilish laughter. "I will spare these two gringos only for you, *belleza amor*." He tipped his black hat at Anna with a wink.

"One more thing—" Hawk reined in his horse and moved closer to the stagecoach. He tossed something at the two men on the ground. "Since I cannot leave the lady you may want to give the sheriff this...a token of my gratitude for his abundant generosity."

Anna saw what laid in the dirt before Jake. A garter—a fancy lace garter. Suddenly she felt faint. She was being abducted by a couple of highway robbers in the nineteenth-century, for Pete's sake. One of them was the very crook she had laughed at over lunch. The highway robber whose activities had so upset Angelique. Now Anna knew firsthand how helpless the other women had felt, even though none of them were abducted. So why her, because she had openly defied one of them?

"*Adiós, amigos!*" Emil shot his gun into the air, before both riders turned their mounts south and galloped down the road in a cloud of dust.

Anna hung on for dear life, her grip on reality swiftly becoming a thing of the past. A dreamlike quality enveloped her. Tormenting mental pictures of James lying injured and unconscious in bed, Jake sitting in a pool of blood beside the stagecoach, and the stranger on the road shot down where he had stood. Death was all around her and life had turned into a royal nightmare.

~ * ~

Anna awoke to darkness. Her head was pounding from the blow she had received when taunting the highwaymen. They had killed one man in cold blood, shot and wounded Jake, and kidnapped her like she was a prize cache of gold. She was not strong enough to free herself physically, but she sure could give them hell verbally. Of course, she never imagined they would strike her, but the one called Hawk did exactly that. They had stopped to water the horses at a stream and she just could not keep her mouth shut. That was the last thing she remembered about the frightening journey on horseback.

Gently, she rubbed the tender spot on her head as her eyesight adjusted to the dark room. Lying on an old wood and canvas cot, she could smell the ocean and hear the surging sound of the surf. She lifted her head to better view her surroundings. A dim oil lantern hung on the far wall, casting shadows across the floor. She staggered to her feet, took few shaky steps and fell to her knees.

"Dammit!" Her curse echoed eerily around her.

"Awake now?"

Hawk's cocky, distinctive voice startled her.

"Thanks to you, jerk, I have an enormous headache." She couldn't see anyone in the shadows, but knew he stood nearby.

Strong arms circled her waist, lifting her to her feet with quiet ease. He spun her around, holding her firmly against his broad chest. "I wouldn't have knocked you out if you hadn't gotten so damn sassy with me."

"Oh? Did you expect me to fall into your arms in grateful ecstasy after what you've done?" Anna peered up at him. She couldn't exactly tell how he was responding to her comments.

"You are in them now," he reminded her, tightening his grip upon her waist. "Don't tell me you don't like it?"

"I don't! You are nothing but a low-life creep!" She struggled and attempted to push away from him, but he held on tight. Recalling the move she made on James and his immediate reaction, she brought her knee up between Hawk's legs and caught him by surprise. He doubled over with a loud curse and a miserable groan.

Anna ran toward the shadows slipping on the wet cavern floor. She slid feet first into a pool of water. She heard her voice echoing off the damp chamber walls as water closed over her head.

Quickly, she resurfaced and swam to the edge, gasping desperately for air. Her head cleared and the dizziness passed. That was no ordinary plunge. But she didn't have time to figure anything out before Hawk suddenly appeared at her side. She pulled herself out of the illuminated pool onto a cold stone floor.

"Where are we?" An odd sensation overcame her, causing her to panic. Feeling trapped and at the mercy of this madman, she glanced quickly around. There had to be a means of escape, but it was much too dark to see beyond the glowing pool.

"You have to come back with me now. You don't belong here." Hawk reached for her, his voice low and threatening. "Come back into the pool, Anna."

Scooting back from the water's edge, she shook her head in defiance. "Are you nuts? I almost drowned in there! That's no ordinary pool." The words stuck in her mind. No ordinary pool. The time pool—of course! But how did Hawk know about it?

"Anna, you must not defy me. It's for your own good to return to the pool, now." He lifted himself easily from the cool water and stood before her, his clothes dripping wet and hugging his well-built body.

"You can't intimidate me. I know about this pool." She clambered to her feet, struggling with her heavy dress and layered slips of yesteryear. She felt like a true drowned rat and she hated the dark.

Hawk laughed heartily. "Exactly what do you think this pool does?"

Anger made her answer bold. "It's for time travel and I refuse to go back."

His sharp intake of breath expressed his surprise. "How did you find out?"

"Alastair told me." Her mind raced to discover the implication of this man knowing what he knew. Something tugged at her memory, but she couldn't place it.

"Alastair Duncan? Doc?"

"Do you know him?" She wrung the water from her heavy skirts.

"Know him? We went to school together. We discovered this time pool together. Say—" He grasped her shoulders roughly. "Where is Alastair?"

This was the friend Alastair had mentioned? "Why?"

His long fingers dug into her skin through the thin sleeves of her damp dress. "Never mind why. I asked you a question and I expect an answer."

"Let go of me or I won't tell you diddly-squat, mister!"

"Morgan." He released her. "My name is Morgan. I suppose you know what century we're in right now?"

"I thought Morgan was his horse." She frowned, realizing Alastair's deception. What else had he lied to her about? "Are we in present day?"

"We are. At least, we should be. Each time I've gone back and forth, I find I return to the exact same day I left. So, I end up losing no time at all. It seems the centuries run parallel to each other." He paused for a moment and she could hear him feeling for something in the dark. "So you are from the present too, and not from the nineteenth-century?"

"Yes." Anna felt a sudden elation at being back in her own time. And just as suddenly, remorse hit her like a brick. What if she couldn't get back to James?

"Who are you?" Hawk lit a candle set in the stone wall of the cavern.

At last, she could see him and there wasn't such a supernatural feel to their conversation, even if they were speaking of things she had never dreamed possible. "My name is Anna Bentley. I inherited the house at Duncan's Point. Right now I'm trying to find out the truth about the past."

"You must be the one who found the spyglass?" He acknowledged her acquiescence. "It was foolish of Alastair to leave it in so obvious a place. He knew the captain wanted to reach you. How does it feel to be wanted by a ghost?"

"How do you know about the ghost? Did he haunt you, too?" She shivered and wrapped her arms about herself for warmth.

"No." Hawk handed her a towel. "Alastair read all about how it happened in a journal. The captain knew you were coming...something about his dreams telling him. So he lured you into the past using the only method available—his subconscious."

Memory washed over her like a cool dip in the pool as she put pieces together. Her first glimpse of the old house had made her feel as if she had come home. The familiar feeling she had when she first saw the captain's portrait in the drafty hall. His deep voice calling her name in the grape arbor had protected her from a run-in with her ex-husband.

James told her he'd dreamt about her before she appeared aboard his ship and his spirit lured her to use the spyglass. Could his dreams have crossed over the barriers of time, the result causing her to hear voices and see ghosts?

Hawk snapped his fingers in front of her face. "Hey, are you okay?"

"Oh, yeah. Sure." She would be just fine, when she caught her breath and stepped back into reality from the Twilight Zone.

~ * ~

A warm fire crackled in the hearth as Anna sat wrapped in a woolen blanket on the thick woven rug, trying in vain to ease the chill from her heart. Dressed in a comfortable pair of old Levi's and a well-worn T-shirt, she watched Morgan as he put down the full food tray he had retrieved from the kitchen. She was surprised such an abundance of food remained in the refrigerator. How long had she been gone, two or three days…a week? It seemed like forever. How was James recovering from his injuries? And what had happened to Jake?

"Morgan? What were you doing in the past? I mean, besides the obvious bandit stunt?" She leaned back against the over-stuffed armchair, munching on her sandwich of cheddar cheese and sourdough bread.

Anna studied his arrogant face while he made himself a sandwich. He wasn't as rugged looking as James or Jake, but more chiseled like a model. He was a fair-complexioned version of the silver screen Zorro. His looks were striking. Unfortunately, he knew it.

"Just playing bandit." Morgan yawned. "It started as a game, but I became rather involved with my character." He sat beside her, stretching his long legs out before him.

"A character? Are you telling me that killing was a game to you?" How could the man be so charming one minute and so deadly the next?

"Not the killing. It started as a lark. I even had Alastair go with me a couple of times. It was his idea to give the garter token. Sort of romantic, you know? But then he said it was too dangerous. He wanted me to quit and return to the future."

"He was right."

201

"No. You are both wrong." Biting into the sandwich, he released a garbled laugh. He swallowed the bite with a gulp of soda. "Alastair thought he would be a gentleman. I just want the money. It is so incredibly easy."

Her jaw dropped open. "An innocent man was brutally killed, and you shot poor Jake. You are telling me you did it for the money?"

"I shot no one, that was Emil's fault. He is the dangerous one. He is the reason Alastair stopped helping me."

"I would say you are both very dangerous." She ran her fingers through her still damp hair and reflected how James did the same thing when he was upset. "Why would you want to rob and terrorize innocent people?"

"I loved to watch westerns when I was growing up. I acted them out with my younger brother. I always thought it was cool to be the bandit." He smiled at her and wiped his chin. "Don't you ever wish you could be something you are not?"

"That's my problem, Morgan. I want to know who I am. I came back to find the journals Alastair told me about." Setting her sandwich aside, she picked up an ice-cold soda and popped the tab. She cleared her throat and smiled. "Alastair could be my great-great-grandson."

Morgan choked on his food. "What?"

"I may belong in the past with James, or Alastair might not be born. I need to find some answers and quick. Will you help me?"

"You're serious?" Morgan glanced over at the crackling fire for a moment, deep in thought, and then returned his gaze to her. He understood her dilemma that much was obvious. He snapped his fingers. "Alastair said he had to save his great-great-grandfather. He did, right?"

She shrugged her shoulders. "As far as I know. Right now James is probably going crazy with worry wondering where the heck I've gone."

"Guess I made that a bit more complicated."

"Yes and no. I was headed here anyway. But I would have preferred a different means. Maybe a bit more gentle?" Anna studied his movements as he finished his meal.

He stood, dusting crumbs off his hands. "Did Alastair tell you where those journals were?"

"In the attic, I think. I tried to go up there once, but it was incredibly filthy. It looked like no one had been up there in years. Apparently, I was wrong."

He laughed, a generous lusty sound. "I may be crazy, but if you won't tell anyone what crimes I have committed I promise to help you settle your future—even if it's in the past."

Anna eyed him cautiously. Was he just a bit too intelligent for his own good? Rumor had it the most intelligent people always went over the deep end easiest. If he tried to trick her, was she smart enough and strong enough to avoid trouble? She surely hoped so, because it didn't look as though she had any other choice. He was here in her house, in her time, and all she could think about was how quickly she could escape the present and return to the past.

~ * ~

The schooner sailed into port at Gualala as the sun slowly melted into the blue Pacific Ocean. James stood at the helm, his hair blowing freely in the evening breeze. His thoughts were grim at the prospect before him. William stood at his side, more for support than duty. The two seamen had been friends for so many years; it was simply habit to console each other when times got tough.

"Gualala is not a big town, Captain. We will find her soon enough," William said quietly, reading his mind.

"Aye, William. Take the helm now, lad," James ordered. "I have a few things to discuss with Alastair before we lay anchor."

"Yes, sir."

James limped slowly across the deck, still favoring his injured leg. All hell would break loose aboard the *Ceilidh* if he could not get

Anna back. And it would be entirely his doing. He was a fair and just captain, but if the need arose, he could be tough and mean like the lowly pirate he was in the past.

Below deck in his comfortable quarters, James stretched his sore leg out on the chair opposite him and released a long overdue groan. Bloody hell! Why did he have to be injured at a time when Anna chose to disappear? Or did she leave because he was injured and might not have pulled through?

His shoulder was a bear to deal with and his leg taxed him greatly. The headaches pounding through his brain made him dizzy and uncomfortable with his judgment. He tried to rest as often as he could, without letting the others know how miserable he was. All he needed was Alastair knocking him out with one of his blasted medicinal concoctions. Best to keep the leg rested and say nothing. A short catnap would not hurt either. His thoughts drifted again to Anna. Where was the lass?

James must have dozed off for a bit. He nearly fell out of his chair when a light tap on the cabin door disturbed him. "Come in!"

George rushed in, his face alight with a broad smile. "Well James, looks like we are in luck! A lad on the docks knows Jake Hardwick, the man who rides shotgun on the Wells Fargo stage down to Frisco. It seems Jake got shot in a stagecoach robbery recently while protecting a young woman kidnapped by the highway robbers. It's the talk of the town. I don't know why we didn't learn of it sooner."

James leaned forward, eager to hear more. "Out with it, man! Was the woman Anna or not?"

"I am afraid we won't know until Alastair returns. He went to the hotel where Mr. Hardwick is laid up. He promised to send word as soon as he talks to the man."

James' agitation only added to the pain searing through his body. If Anna had been kidnapped that would explain why she had disappeared so suddenly, but it still did not explain why she was on the stage. He adjusted his leg to a more comfortable position with a grimace. "Good work, George. Thank you."

"Your leg, is it bad?" George frowned. "I knew it was too soon for you to be up and about. Alastair agrees with me on this, I assure you."

"Oh, aye." James tried to make light of it, but then realized to whom he was talking and just how well George knew him. "Ye will not tell Alastair, George. Or ye will find yerself swimming ashore. Do ye understand?"

George chuckled. "My lips are sealed."

James breathed a sigh of relief. "My leg has been paining me this entire voyage. My shoulder has been gnawed upon by a grizzly bear, and my head is no longer a part of me." He rubbed his muscled thigh with a wince. "Och, but 'twill all be worth it to see my lovely Anna again."

"Soon, James. Hopefully very soon."

James prayed silently that George was correct. He had never experienced such agony before, physically or emotionally. "Remember yer promise, man. For if ye breathe a word to the doctor, I will hang ye from the yardarm."

Laughter was generally the best medicine, but as George left the cabin, his mischievous chuckles disturbed James in a way nothing else could. He had the sneaking premonition his loyal friend was about to betray him.

Thirteen

Alastair burst into the captain's quarters, excitement running rampant through his veins. He had just returned from his visit to the injured stage guard. He was eager to inform James they were on the right trail, but the hardy captain was out like a light.

"George?" Alastair stepped up to take the captain's pulse. His breathing was slow and deep, as if in a drug induced sleep. "What did you do here, my friend?"

George grinned sheepishly. "He was in agony, Alastair. I didn't know when you would return, so I gave him quite a bit of laudanum to deaden the pain. It was a simple matter of slipping it into his daily ration of orange juice—citrus for scurvy and laudanum for pain."

Alastair frowned. The captain's reaction to George's caring interference might not be pleasant. "You realize he'll have our butts hanging from the yardarm for this little treatment of yours."

"He did threaten me, but someone had to help the stubborn brute. Still, he's not the pirate he was. Anna was doing a good job of taming the man before she disappeared. I just hate to see the captain's ornery side return."

"Good move, George. Let's hope you gave him enough to keep him quiet until we reach our destination—or we'll have hell to pay." Alastair turned to William, who sat quietly to himself at the captain's table. "Did you have a part in this?"

William shook his head, and then grinned as if he could not tell a lie. "Not exactly."

"Tell the truth Will, it was you who suggested we spike his orange juice." George wiped a flickering smile from his face. "It was a sorry thing to do to James, but I am sure he will understand how much we want to help."

"I am sure he will," Alastair agreed with a chuckle. "Since I am no longer able to gain the captain's attention, would you two like to hear what I discovered in town?"

"By all means." George pulled out one of the captain's cherished bottles of whiskey and three mugs. "We might need this. It's going to be a very long journey."

"I'm afraid you may be right, George." Alastair sat down, joining the two men, and told them all he had learned. For the time being, he held back Anna's unfortunate abduction by highway robbers, leading George and William to believe she was still safely traveling on her own.

"This whole road agent mess has Angelique in an uproar. I do believe my wife would like the patrolmen to hold a necktie sociable for the rogue."

"I'm not sure a hanging is in order. This is his first kidnapping, if indeed it is the same man." Alastair ran a forefinger around the rim of his mug. He hoped to hell they didn't hang Morgan. The foolish man was running the risk of being caught red-handed by his newest escapade.

"At least it was not Anna who was kidnapped," George said as though reading Alastair's guilty mind. He sipped the whiskey pleasurably and relaxed back in his chair.

William's eyebrows rose. "Someone was kidnapped?"

Alastair wondered where George had received his current information. The news had not even hit the paper yet. "It appears she went willingly, William."

Alastair had a hunch from the guard's detailed description that his old friend from the future was responsible for the abduction. What a curse of luck! Why on earth did the two time travelers' paths have to cross at this particular time? Morgan had picked up some bad habits recently, one of which was his scandalous behavior toward Victorian women.

"Most importantly, Anna is still safe on board the Frisco stage. That is what you heard...right, Alastair?" William swallowed the last of his whiskey and pushed his mug forward for more. "I mean, I would hate to think of the captain's reaction if he were to find her in harm's way."

"You forget we still have a gentleman bandit riding our highways, Will. If the man hasn't satisfied himself with one woman, who's to say he won't capture another?" George took a hearty swig of whiskey and set his empty mug aside. "Pray that Anna will not meet up with such a man. With her spunk and beauty who's to know what the rogue might do?"

"Ah, yes...the mysterious road agent who slips a sexy silk garter up a female's shapely thigh. Not the same man, I assure you. This rogue simply grabbed the woman and rode away, anxiously heading for a lover's tryst, I would assume." Alastair couldn't help the laughter rippling up inside him from the look on George's boyish face. "Calm down, George. I was only jesting. But I do have quite a tale to tell you both. It's one that must be kept between us three and not leave the captain's cabin."

"Now you have intrigued us, Alastair, there is nothing I love more than a good tale. Please...do continue." George poured another round of whiskey.

Alastair cleared his throat. "I know you will find it difficult to believe what I have to relate to you. I know you will think it a tale of a madman, but I assure you I am as sane as any man in this room."

William leaned forward. "We are willing to be entertained, Alastair. Go on and tell us your unbelievable tale."

"Yes. Okay, first things first. I have traveled through time from the future."

William nearly spilled his drink. "Alastair, it's not possible!"

"Tell us more, my friend." George eyed him skeptically.

Alastair told his story to the two stalwart men sitting before him. "I'm telling you all this because it is imperative we rescue Anna. You see...Anna has traveled through time, as well."

William's jaw dropped open. "Good Lord! It makes sense to me now. I know Anna was not a scheduled passenger on board the ship that stormy night. And yet, suddenly, there she was with the captain. I saw it with my own eyes."

George shoved his chair back and wiped his brow. "Pshaw! What you are telling us is a bit difficult to believe, Alastair. I think perhaps you may have sampled your own pain medications."

"It's the truth, I swear it. If you don't believe me, that's fine. But we must save her from the devil who has taken her."

"Hold on a minute! Anna was abducted yesterday?" George shook his head, drew a deep breath and exhaled slowly.

"Yes." Alastair drained his mug and glanced from one disbelieving face to the other. He would be taking a chance revealing the truth to anyone from this century. Other than a few great writers of the era, no one would ever even conceive such a thing could happen.

William cleared his throat. "The captain did mention to me once that there was something special about Anna. After talking with her I agree there is something a bit different than most women of our time."

Relieved, Alastair stood and gazed down at William. "You believe me then?"

"Yes." William turned and met George's astounded glare across the table. "I believe Alastair is telling us the truth. He's all the hope we have right now, George. Look for yourself the miracles he has performed on James. The man should not have lived with the amount of blood he lost that night. We both know it for the truth."

George harrumphed. "Physicians are skilled in saving lives."

"Not all physicians." Alastair shrugged and decided to go for it. "Look George, she is trying to go back to the future. It's my fault. I forced her hand, so to speak. I know who she really is and I would not admit it." He hesitated before dropping the second bomb in their laps. "Anna Bentley is my great-great-grandmother."

"Your what?" George and William bellowed in unison, both men jumping to their feet. They stared at Alastair as though he had truly gone bonkers.

Alastair smiled to ease their astonishment. "You heard me. I'm sorry I didn't talk to her more when I had the opportunity. I didn't know she would disappear. I wanted her to help me, but I honestly didn't expect this." Alastair poured himself another shot of amber whiskey and gulped it down in one quick swallow. "I think Morgan is more dangerous than I thought. If he discovers who Anna really is...well, I'm not sure what he will do."

William looked up from his drink. "Who the blazes is Morgan?"

"A friend. Well, he was my friend." Alastair went to pour himself another shot of whiskey.

George's large quiet hand stopped him, removing the bottle from his reach. He slipped the bottle back into the cupboard, and then returned to his seat. "I think we will all agree we have had enough spirits."

Alastair sat down wearily and glared across at the two men. "Morgan has become a little obsessed with this time travel stuff."

"Seems to be catching," William remarked astutely as he sat back in his chair. "You are not making much sense yourself. A moment ago you told us Anna was still on the Frisco stage. Now you are saying she has been abducted."

Alastair laughed, feeling a bit shaky and out of control. The potent whiskey was definitely taking its toll on his senses. He'd never been one to drink much and was easily inebriated. He had to tell these two men the entire truth before he passed out from too much alcohol consumption.

George eyed him carefully. "Well, is she or is she not on the stage for Frisco?"

"I lied," Alastair said simply.

"You what?" George jumped to his feet.

"I lied to you earlier. Anna was on the stage for Frisco, but she was also the woman abducted by Morgan. I am sure of it."

George paced the floor restlessly. "Suppose we believe you, Alastair? What next? How do we find Anna for our friend here?" He nodded toward the captain where he lay snoring in comfortable oblivion.

"I know where they are going. We can sail the ship to the cove beyond the point and find them there." Alastair sighed and ran his fingers through his hair. "I need your help in this venture, gentlemen. I've only confided in the two of you because I know you are the captain's most trusted friends. I know you care about Anna, too."

William straightened to his full height, placing his young weathered hands upon lean hips. "Well, gentlemen, what are we waiting for?"

George stood at his side with a wide grin. "What indeed."

A rush of adrenaline surged through Alastair's veins, reviving his senses. The rescue mission was underway, he only hoped they could arrive in time. He grasped the first mate's arm. "Are you sure you know how to navigate this ship without the captain?"

William's deep laughter echoed about the cabin. "With my eyes closed!"

Alastair could not resist taunting the younger man. "Blind man's bluff, eh?"

~ * ~

Blast it all to hell! Who had given orders to leave port? James stumbled to his feet, holding onto his pounding head. He moved over to the washbasin and splashed cool water upon his sweaty face. He was about to throw open the cabin door and call for his first mate, when William stepped into the room unannounced.

"Captain, you are awake I see. I was just coming to report, sir."

"William! What the devil are we about? Why have we left Gualala? Well? Speak man!" James bent to pull on his boot. The last thing he remembered was thinking George must have spiked his juice. He had been so groggy; it was almost akin to the way he felt after Rosie's medicinal ministrations.

"Sir, we may have found your wife," William stated plainly.

"Sweet Neptune! She's not yet my wife, lad. Nor will she ever be, if we do not find her soon!" James cursed under his breath as he struggled to pull on the second boot. His shoulder jarred in miserable pain and he cursed even louder.

William bent to his knees, lending a hand. "Alastair thinks we have found her, sir. We'll be dropping anchor off the coast where there's a cave...well, I'll let the good doctor tell you all about it."

"Alastair?" James met William's unsteady gaze. "God's teeth! What could that rascal be hiding from me?"

George peeked into the room, and then walked in as if he had been invited. "I thought I heard you bellow, old man."

"The devil ye are, George. Ye put laudanum in my juice, did ye not?" James accused, giving him the evil eye.

"You are a very stubborn man, James. You needed a good rest, admit it." George argued, emitting an easy chuckle.

"Oh, aye. I was in a wee bit o' pain." James hobbled over to the mirror. He forced a comb through his thick hair using his good hand. He winced at the muscles that argued in his stiff shoulder during his simple ministrations. Tying his hair at the nape with a leather thong, he looked a wee bit better than he felt. "Now tell me what's going on, George. A man takes a wee nap and, before ye know it, his ship's not his own."

"Alastair will be here in a moment to tell all. Are you feeling better, James?" George eyed his business partner with concern. "We were thinking about leaving you on board ship whilst we go ashore."

"Not bloody likely!" James was once again the hardened and capable sea captain, though his anger tipped more toward piracy now. "Tis Anna ye are to be finding. Ye will not try to stop me from going along to do what should be done."

"No one is trying to stop you, Captain," Alastair announced as he sauntered into the spacious cabin. Good thing he knew what kind of man James Adam Duncan really was, because the look the enraged captain shot him would make most men shake in their boots. "We need to make haste, gentlemen, if we are to beat high tide and reach the cove's shelter before dark."

~ * ~

The old heavy attic door moved inward, creaking loudly as Morgan pushed against it with a grunt. Anna stepped back, anticipating more cobwebs. Morgan coughed as a thick dust cloud descended upon him. He fought his way gallantly through and motioned with his hand for Anna to follow. The dark stairs groaned under his weight as he paused looking back over his shoulder.

"Come on," he coaxed.

Anna hesitated to join him for more reasons than the obvious filth and cobwebs. She could not explain away her reluctance, but it was almost like being forewarned. "Morgan? Why don't you find the journals and bring them down here?"

He chuckled. "What? Deprive you of this great adventure? Never!" Reaching out, he grasped her hand and pulled her along behind him. "Come on, brave up. If Alastair could do this so can we."

A rusty pull chain dangled from a precariously hung light bulb at the top of the stairs. He tugged on the chain to illuminate the shadowed room. The large drafty attic was full of antique furniture covered with yellowed dustsheets. Huge stacks of books and newspapers piled high against one wall nearly covered the two octagonal windows, blocking out the warm sunlight. Old trunks of various shapes and sizes rested on the wood plank floor.

One chest in particular drew Anna's keen attention. She knelt before the antique and turned around to call Morgan. "Look, this is a sailor's chest like the captain's and it's identical to the one in the master bedroom." She ran her fingers along the smooth surface as a smile crept slowly to her lips. Gosh, she missed James. Hearing a scuffle on the floor behind her, she turned. "Morgan?"

"Anna, I hate to be the bearer of bad news, but I'm sure someday you will understand." He was nowhere in sight as his husky voice drifted faintly to her.

"Morgan?" Scrambling to her feet, she grasped the stair rail. She leaned over in time to see Morgan's rakish grin from where he stood in the doorway below.

He shrugged his shoulders nonchalantly and stepped back into the sunlit hall. The heavy door swung closed, shutting her in the old attic alone. The lock's click echoed up to her, confirming her dreaded fear.

"Morgan? Morgan!" She ran down the steps and pounded on the door, only to hear his deep chuckle on the other side.

"Have patience, dear Anna. I'm sure he will be here soon." His cryptic words faded as he walked away, leaving nothing but silence behind.

"Dammit!" Anna sat on the last step with a thump.

Her mind whirled in anger. She dug her fingernails into her palms, not even realizing her actions until she felt blood drip onto her bare knees. Her Levi shorts were already stained and dirty, so what was a little blood? Pressing her palms against her thighs to stop the bleeding, she inwardly cursed herself for her stupidity in trusting a man like Morgan the Hawk.

Why would Morgan lock her in the attic? And who was he waiting for? His words drifted through her mind repeatedly. *I'm sure he will be here soon.* The answer came in a cold rush that felt like a bucket of ice water dumped over her head. Alastair! Morgan was in league with Alastair and neither man wanted her to discover what it was they were doing. As a direct result, she was a prisoner in her own house, in her own time. Far, far away from where she truly wanted to be.

~ * ~

Alastair and James stood in the cavern's shadows, silencing their talk as a splash in the time pool alerted them to someone's arrival. Alastair held the captain back. He could not allow him to attack the man they had come so far to find.

Morgan whistled a cheerful tune as he waded slowly from the translucent pool

"Morgan?" Alastair stepped forward.

The squishing footsteps paused. "Alastair?"

"Don't worry about changing into dry clothes, we're going back right now. Both of us." Alastair moved quietly out of the shadows, motioning the captain to stay out of sight.

Morgan snorted a laugh. "Are you nuts?"

"No," Alastair said, "but I have been wondering about your sanity lately."

"All my life I have wanted to be successful at something. I'm about to become very successful. Does that make me insane?" Dripping puddles of water on the cavern floor, he glanced over at the chests stacked neatly on the pool's far side. "All this is mine and you can't make me give it back."

"I don't care about the money, Morgan. Where is Anna?" Alastair moved purposefully toward Morgan when it appeared he was being ignored. "Do I need to repeat my question?"

Morgan reached for a towel lying in a crevice and dried off. "Why, Alastair, I thought you would be happy to meet up with me again to see how well I am doing. Instead, you ask me about a sexy little broad with a hot temper."

"If ye have harmed a wee hair on her bonny head I'll be hanging ye from the yardarm, ye dirty scoundrel," James bellowed, stepping forward from the shadows.

Alastair's arm shot out across the captain's broad chest. "Wait, James. Give us a minute. Morgan, meet my great-great-grandfather."

"Are you crazy?" Morgan planted his fists firmly on either side of his hips. "Why the hell did you bring him here?"

"Because Anna belongs with him. She belongs in the past." Alastair reconsidered his loyalty to their friendship. "This is my heritage, Morgan."

"I know. I locked Anna up in the attic so she couldn't leave until you got here. She's gonna be real upset when she gets out." Morgan's grin spread slowly. "Wait until you experience firsthand your great-great-grandmother's wrath."

"Nothing compared to mine, old friend. You've managed to turn my world upside down over the past few months. My plans went awry when you decided to become a highway bandit. One time for fun, you said. For the thrill of living in the old west, you said. Not to gain a fortune, as you now seem determined to do. Then you pick up that hellion Spaniard as a sidekick, a devil who would rather shoot first and ask questions later." Alastair ran his fingers through his hair in frustration.

"Alastair, you must understand. I don't fit in the future anymore. I don't want to lose you as a friend, but I can't return to a life I hate. There's so much adventure, so much excitement awaiting me here."

"You're losing it, Morgan. Get your priorities straight. You have a medical degree with a promising career and enough money to—"

"I hated my job. I cannot go back to a life studying tubes and slides filled with bacteria and micro-organisms." Morgan rested his hand on Alastair's shoulder. "I implore you, let me remain in the past."

The two men's gazes locked. They were coming to a final parting of their ways. Alastair reached out and shook Morgan's hand. "If that's what you want, then so be it. I won't close off the time pool. You may find you need to escape back home someday."

Morgan smiled. "You're the best, Doc. You always were."

James stepped forward, his impatience overflowing. "Do we *clishmaclaver* the time away, or are we going to find my Anna?"

"*Clishmaclaver?*" Morgan frowned. "What language is that?"

Alastair laughed. "Scots. It means chit-chat, Morgan."

Alastair now understood what had motivated Morgan to be the daredevil individual he had become; living each day for the moment and each adventure for the thrill it gave him. He used robbing as a means of escape from a job and life he had truly despised. But why hadn't he simply come clean sooner? Why all the mystery?

~ * ~

Dust particles floated in the air and flickered in a small sunbeam that tiptoed across Anna's face. She sat with her legs stretched out upon the dirty floor, her tank top and shorts relieving some of the attic's heat. Tears of sorrow flowed down her cheeks as she read an old journal's worn pages.

In a harrowing tale of deceit, theft and murder, she discovered the truth. She had not been born in 1975, as she had previously believed, but in the year eighteen hundred and fifty-six. When Anna was barely four-years-old, her wealthy parents traveled by sea to Boston. On the return voyage to San Francisco, pirates overcame their sailing ship. Her father promised chests of gold to the scoundrels for his family's freedom. He told them the gold was hidden in a cave near some land he had purchased. He guided them to the small sea cove below what would one day be Duncan's Point.

Her father's hidden chests of gold were no longer in the cave. Someone had stolen them. In the pirate captain's uncontrolled rage, gunshots rang out. Her father fell to the sand in a pool of blood.

Crying hysterically, Anna's mother led her deeper into the cavern's darkness in an attempt to hide from the carnage. Shots rang out again. Staggering forward, her mother pushed Anna into the shadows. In doing so, they both stumbled into the time pool.

The soothing waters concealed them from the pirates' wrath by tossing them forward in time to the year 1979. Her mother helped Anna out of the water, and then collapsed upon the cavern floor. She lay gasping for breath and dying from a bullet wound.

Anna swallowed hard as she continued to read the journal's pages. A young couple vacationing along the Mendocino coast that day happened to anchor off shore from the cave. Exploring the cavern, they came across Anna and her dying mother. Anna's mother related the pirate tale to the couple, begging them to raise her daughter as theirs if she died. She lived for only a few more minutes before succumbing to her mortal wound. The couple buried Anna's mother at sea according to her last request.

Tears rolled freely down Anna's cheeks. No wonder she could not remember much of her childhood. She had blocked its horrors from her mind. Reading the journal brought everything back and dear God, how it hurt! At age four, she experienced the harsh realities of life no child should ever suffer. She had caught pneumonia from the water in her lungs and nearly died. When she recovered, the young couple adopted her as promised.

Anna sighed and wiped the tears from her eyes. She had come across her roots at last. Somehow, she wasn't even shocked to learn of her adolescent trip through time. She had never really fit in the contemporary world. Now she understood why. If only she could turn back time far enough to save her birth parents. Alas, she had no control over time travel. The years that appeared to be linked were 1880 and the present, but the reason wasn't clear. Did the captain have the power to pull her through time, or was it some other unknown force?

Hairs stood out on the back of her neck. Her arms broke out in tingly little goose bumps. How did her history get in the attic of this old house anyway? James built this house and it sat above the cavern her father owned. Had her father owned the land so it really belonged to her in the first place? By returning to the past and marrying James, it would be so.

It could be the clue to why she was meant to return to the past, but where were the facts? She needed proof, something solid and written in stone. She must have missed something. Returning to the first journal, she sought a link to information that would settle her doubts.

Thoroughly absorbed in reading the journals, she scarcely heard the disturbance downstairs. The grating creak of the attic door jarred her senses and drew her quickly to her feet. She hurried to the top step and peered down the stairwell in time to see Morgan's blond head appear.

"You big dumb jerk! Why did you lock me in here?" She met him halfway down the steps and hit him over the head with the journal.

"Ow!" Morgan ducked and covered his head with his arms in self-defense.

"Anna! Anna let me explain—" Alastair reached forward from behind Morgan and gripped her wrists to stop her from beating his friend senseless.

"Alastair?" She dropped her arms and pulled away. Her fury subsided at the sight of the man who probably was her great-great-grandson. "What are you doing here? How did you know where I was? Is James okay?"

"Hold on there, not so many questions at once." Alastair chuckled. "Let's get out of this dust haven and go somewhere else to talk." He took her hand and led her downstairs, removing the journal from her grasp.

Anna yanked her hand free. She hurried down the hall to her room, mumbling about the ignorance of men and all their faults when it came to handling women. She slammed her bedroom door, only to hear a light knock a few moments later. She opened the door, surprised to find only Alastair standing in the hall.

"Where is Morgan?" She peeked out the door.

Alastair flashed a slight smile. "Nursing his throbbing headache about now, I should think."

Anna suppressed a laugh. "Serves him right. You know, that was the most awful experience I've ever been through. I could have died up there and no one would have ever found me." Walking over to the fireplace, she flopped down in the overstuffed chair with a weary sigh. "Thanks for rescuing me, Alastair. Now that you have released me from my prison you can leave."

Alastair pulled the ladder-back chair from the desk and positioned himself on it backwards. "You've been crying. Are you okay?"

"No. Go away." She turned away and stared out the window. She felt like a brat after all that had happened, but there were still so many unanswered questions and so little time. She looked back at him. "I've changed my mind. Stay and tell me about the captain."

Alastair leaned forward, cocking an eyebrow. "Morgan was smart to leave. I guess he has experienced your quick temper one too many times."

"Alastair!" She stood, balling her hands into fists. "Either tell me or leave."

"Oh, all right." He grinned, an inherited lopsided grin. "Sit down, Anna. James is fine and well. Of course, I'm not because I realize I overstepped propriety. I owe you a belated apology. I was wrong to think I could change the past. You are my great-great-grandmother, Anna. Or have you found that out already?"

She sat and let the memories of the past day flood her senses. "I read the journals and put two and two together, though nothing states it outright, this land was mine before I was transported into the future the first time. Am I right?"

He nodded. "Yes, that is what I found at the historical society and the county recorder's office. That's why I wrote a will and left everything to you. Just in case something happened to me and I could not return, the house would transfer to you, its original owner."

"Good Lord, Alastair. It was a whole lot to swallow in one gulp." She swiped at a few stray tears that tumbled from her eyes.

"How do you think I felt? My life has always been grounded in reality. I could barely accept the time travel theory. Then to discover you are here, living in my time, was a shock. You belong in the past. I'm not sure what they call it, but I am glad I stumbled upon the cave and the journals. What if I hadn't?"

She shrugged and smiled softly. "I think it is what they call predestination, but don't worry. For all of this to work out you had to find the journals and the pool. It was meant to be. Just as my meeting James and falling in love with him was meant to happen. For Pete's sake! No wonder I am so attached to him. It's kinda like we are caught in a circle and everything has its proper place in time."

Alastair stood and set the chair aside. "You sound a bit prophetic. But I don't mind. I'm just pleased that you believe and understand now."

"There is one more thing, Alastair. How come there is no marriage certificate, no legal documents to confirm all this?"

"Things like that get lost and misplaced over time. But I do have the remainder of the Duncan family journals right here in this old desk." He walked over to the roll-top desk and tugged open the lower left drawer.

Anna scrambled to her feet and pulled two heavy books from the deep drawer where he had hidden them. In her haste to discover what was within, she dropped right to the floor and began reading. She found the wedding entry after turning only a few pages.

"It's here! Captain James Adam Duncan and Anna Bentley," she whispered. A wayward tear rolled down her cheek. "Bound together in holy wedlock...the year of our lord 1880." She looked up, her heart soaring into the clouds. She did belong with James. "Alastair, I can't read the rest."

"Does it really matter? You belong with the captain, Anna. Let me take you to him." Alastair held out his hand. "He's waiting for you. Rather anxiously, too, I would imagine. I didn't think we would be so long."

"Waiting for me?" Her mind captured those three words. "Where is he?"

"I wouldn't allow him to come through the time pool. I promise, he's waiting for you on the other side."

"Are you two ever coming?" Morgan stood in the open doorway. "All we need is an irate Scottish sea captain on our hands." He laughed and winced, holding his sore head. "We already have his wildcat woman."

"Don't push me, Morgan. I still have a few bones to pick with you." She was angry, but she would forgive him—eventually.

A secret smile slipped neatly into place in her heart. She was glad Morgan had locked her in the attic for one reason—she found her roots. All she wanted now was to be with James. She looked up to see both men grinning at her. It was just like Alastair to hide the family journals in such an obvious place. He had originally told her all the volumes were in the attic.

"Maybe, I don't want to go back. Why should I leave a life of comfort and return to one of hardship? Maybe James would like to join me here instead." She watched in mild humor as Alastair recovered himself from shock.

He moved a step closer, looming over her. "You shouldn't mess with the elements of time and attempt to change things."

She laughed. "Take advice from a pro, huh?"

"You are my great-great-grandmother," he reminded her. "You belong in the past and it's into the past you go, my dear."

Alastair grasped her firmly around the waist, hoisting her effortlessly over his shoulder. Anna relinquished her battle. If this helped him think he was winning, she would give him a few minutes of victory. Then she would let him have both barrels for interfering in her life.

~ * ~

A splash in the translucent time pool brought James quickly to his feet. Anna's golden-blond head popped up out of the water. Moments later, Alastair and Morgan appeared beside her. She sputtered as Alastair dragged her from the pool, kicking and cursing furiously.

"Let me go!" Twisting around in Alastair's arms, Anna laid a smacking blow to his wet cheek. She pushed him away.

"Damn!" He staggered backwards and released her abruptly, rubbing the bright red handprint with his palm. "Morgan is right—you are a wildcat!"

"Don't ever throw me in the water again!" Anna wrung out her soaked braid of hair. Her skimpy sleeveless top clung to her full bosom, and her tennis shoes squished when she walked. She heard a familiar deep chuckle and spun around. "James!"

James caught her as she threw herself into his embrace. "Ah, but ye are bonny, lass. 'Tis good to hold ye in my arms again."

He was beginning to think he would never see her again. His heart melted with love for this feisty twenty-first century woman. He knew he had to keep her with him, no matter what the consequences, or his soul would be lost forever.

Anna smiled up at him. "Oh, James, I've missed you so much!" Pulling his head down to meet hers, she placed a long moist but welcome kiss upon his waiting lips. "Ummm, you feel so good." Her damp head rested against his broad chest as she wrapped her arms tightly around his neck.

"Aye, ye are not bad feeling yerself." James accepted a towel from Morgan and wrapped it around her dripping wet form. "Best ye cover up yer charms, Anna. Ye are hardly clothed. 'Twill not be good for the crew to see ye like this." He shook his head in amazement. "Tis a strange manner o' life in the future, this no wearing o' clothes."

She pulled away from him. "James, your ship is here?"

"Aye. She's anchored right off shore, waiting the command to set sail for home." He turned to Alastair, grasping his hand in fond farewell. "Tis very proud ye have made me, lad. Ye are a first-rate doctor and I am honored to be yer ancestor. Are ye sure ye will not sail with us aboard the *Ceilidh*?"

Alastair beamed with pleasure. "No, I'm happy with my life in the future. Thank you for the offer though. If I change my mind I know where to find you." He bent to kiss Anna on the forehead and clipped her under the chin with his knuckle. "You take care of him, sweetheart, and yourself too."

Anna smiled wistfully. "Good-bye, Alastair Duncan." She stretched up and kissed him lightly upon the cheek. "Thank you for everything."

Alastair clapped Morgan heartily on the back. His sad expression said more than mere words. The emotional level was high, but he must return to the distant future where he belonged. Before he could change his mind, Alastair quickly disappeared beneath the pool's glistening surface.

Morgan clasped his hands together and laughed loudly, his voice echoing through the cave. "Well, that's done. You folks better be on your way. I have a rendezvous with Emil in an hour's time." He glanced down at his diving watch, and then shed his wet clothing for the black outfit he wore as Hawk, the notorious highway robber.

James cleared his throat. "Ye will not be undressing in front o' my lady."

Morgan paused from removing his underwear at the captain's warning. "I'll wait."

"You can't be serious about continuing this harmful farce? You want to stay here and rob innocent people?" Anna couldn't believe he would succeed. After all, they both knew who he was now. He couldn't get away with it.

"Aw, Anna, you spoil all the fun." Morgan grinned slyly.

"I didn't know robbing and killing was fun. Excuse me." She backed away from his intense scrutiny and shivered, not because of the cavern's damp chill, but from being close to Morgan. He gave her an uneasy feeling. He was totally unaware he was the model perfect figure of a man, except for his deranged mind.

"Of course I will stay in 1880," Morgan said simply. "I'll just change locations. And I promise not to take any more gold bound for the lumber mill. Deal, Captain?" He offered his hand.

"Do what ye must. 'Tis yer own neck at risk." James took Morgan's outstretched hand in a firm grasp. "Still, ye never want to take from innocent people. 'Twill bring ye naught but heartache. Do ye understand me?"

"I do, Captain, and thanks." Morgan gathered his wet clothes and stuffed them into his leather saddlebags.

Anna shivered again and snuggled back into the comfort of James' warm arms. "Let's go home, Captain."

"Aye, Anna." James kissed her tenderly, slipping his arm protectively around her shoulders. He led her out into the afternoon sunshine, gratefully leaving the mysterious time pool behind them.

Fourteen

The *Ceilidh* lay at anchor in the bay off Gualala, rocking gently on swells that washed endlessly to shore. The cool summer night was clear, an unusual event for the normally fog-shrouded coast. Stars twinkled brightly, like a spattering of diamonds in the heavens above. Everyone sang and danced in celebration of Anna's safe return.

Anna looped her arm possessively through the captain's, while strolling along the polished deck. They laughed as they watched his big burly crewmembers dancing with each other in harmonious merriment. Even George participated with his usual good humor. He danced a jig precariously on top of a large wooden barrel, entertaining the entire crew.

Anna giggled at the silly sight. She was so happy and she wouldn't miss anything from the future. Well, maybe a few modern conveniences, but everything she needed was here with the handsome captain of her heart.

She stole a sideways peek at his rugged profile. "Captain?"

His heated gaze focused upon her. "Aye?"

The message she read in his sapphire eyes sent a luscious thrill deep within. Anticipation tickled her feminine heart. "Don't start that again. We aren't married, yet."

"Are ye saying ye will then?" James positioned himself as close to her as was respectable in front of his men. His body ached to possess her completely, but for the time being he was satisfied with an occasional touch. "I thought ye might have changed yer mind."

She gasped. "You incorrigible sea fox, you've changed the subject again. That wasn't what I wanted to talk about at all. If you get any closer, I may not be able to resist you and you know it."

"Saucy wench." He pulled her close in a quick hug and they continued their stroll along the deck. "Do ye know what a sea fox is, lass?"

"I imagine it's something big and nasty." She blinked innocently. "I've heard the crew use the expression occasionally."

"Oh, aye. Ye see, Anna, a sea fox is a very cunning shark. It catches its prey by thrashing about its powerful tail."

"Really?"

"Would I trick ye, lass?" He chuckled and stole a sideways glance at her. "So ye know I am dangerous do ye?"

She giggled softly. "Aye, captain. Very dangerous." Her eyes reflected the mirth she tried to hide.

James pulled her into his arms and kissed her taunting lips thoroughly before releasing her with a light pat on her bottom. "There's more where that came from," he promised.

Anna sighed in contentment. "I really missed you."

"Did ye now?"

She nodded that she did and laid her cheek against his all-male warmth. No one could ever make her feel the way he did. Her heart, her body, and even her soul cried out to be with him forever.

Unexpectedly, her earlier question popped back into her mind. "I meant to ask you about Jake, before you diverted my attention."

"Jake?" James paused by the rail and faced her in the starlight.

"The gunman on the stagecoach who was shot trying to prevent the robbery. Alastair said he's the one who told you what happened to me." She hoped the brave young gunslinger was still alive. She remembered hearing him offer himself for ransom, so the bandits would leave her behind. He was a good man and she wanted to know what had become of him.

"Och, I cannot say what happened to the man. But I doubt he is dead."

She punched him in the arm. "Dammit, James! This is important to me. Jake was very nice and he tried to save my life. Can't you show some concern for him?"

James chuckled. Ah, but he loved it when she was angry. She sparkled with life and drew him with the lure of a true sea nymph. He had never loved anyone more, nor would he ever love again. He pulled her into his arms. He was about to kiss her when he heard footsteps from behind.

William coughed, before interrupting. "Sir?"

"Aye, William." James released Anna from his embrace. A momentary vagary flashed through his mind—he should thrash the excellent young officer for this unwanted disturbance. His guilty conscience quickly put a stop to his anger. "State yer needs, lad."

Clearing his throat a little nervously, the first mate stood his ground with a broad smile. "The crew got together and—well, sir— we bought Anna a gift."

"How sweet of you," Anna said, her face bright with excitement. "Come on, James. Let's see what it is."

James glanced from William to Anna. Irritation eased from him at her obvious joy. Not being able to resist the lovely sprite at his side, he took her hand in his. "Yer slightest wish is my command, lass."

They followed William across the main deck to where the crew gathered about the mizzenmast. The men parted so she could be in the center. Jock stepped forward and handed her a large, crudely wrapped bundle.

"You've brought happiness to our good captain, Anna. God only knows how ye have tamed him. He is more generous with our pay, more free with his good humor and, although presently preoccupied with yer loveliness, he still runs a tight ship."

Warmth flooded Anna's heart for these rough and rowdy individuals. She smiled. "Thank you, all of you. Quickly tearing open the gift, she squealed with pleasure. "Oh, James! It's a dress. A beautiful dress of my very own!" She twirled about with the dress draped across the front of her. It was the prettiest dress she had ever seen, given to her out of love and gratitude. Warm and fuzzy feelings bubbled up inside her. How could she ever repay their sweet generosity?

James frowned. He had not considered buying her something special. His crew understood how important it was to think of those female things, while he could only think of protecting her. Naught else mattered to him, until her safe return. Now she was here, he did not want to leave her side, not even long enough to purchase her a gift as a token of his love. He regretted his error and hoped she would forgive him.

"Thank you, thank you all so much! It's beautiful and I love it!"

"I think the men would like to see you in it," William whispered in her ear. "They've not seen you in a dress before."

"I would love to model this most generous gift." Anna stood on tiptoe and quickly kissed his bewhiskered cheek. She turned and hurried across the quarterdeck. With a tinkle of laughter, she disappeared down the bulkhead's narrow stairs.

"I am sure she meant nothing by the kiss, sir." William stood in awe, rubbing his jaw where her soft lips had brushed. "You are a lucky man, Captain."

"Ye are wrong, Will. She meant something by it. She was thanking ye. 'Twas a very thoughtful deed ye have done this night." James silently cursed himself again and gazed up at the stars.

He loved to see Anna's eyes sparkle with joy, almost as much as he loved watching them fill with passion. With that exquisite fancy, a burning deep in his loins sizzled to life. He decided he should follow her, hastily muttering something about helping her with the tiny buttons.

George stretched out a hand, grasping his arm. "The lads want to see her in the new dress. Be kind, man. Stay here and let her return. If you go with her we will not see her again this night."

"Ye are thinking I might delay the lass."

"I know you will. Let her be, James. You've time enough later." George released his arm and stepped aside.

James calmed the sudden desire to flatten George on the spot. His friend was right. Blast it all! He hadn't even bedded the lass yet! Remembering that George assumed him already wed, he knew he must deny his passion a bit longer. Sweet Neptune! She was consuming his every thought. He should wed her soon before he ravished her lovely body, with or without God's graceful blessing.

~ * ~

Candles flickered in the cabin as Anna twirled about in her new dress, not wanting to remove it. A soft pink confection with rows of ruffles and lace, the dress was an exquisite Victorian work of art. She glanced over at the captain where he sat at the table, his thoughts buried in business. He was so engrossed in his work that he had not paid any attention to her since they left the upper deck.

"James?" She eyed him carefully. His head raised and his eyes met hers. His thoughtful expression melted into a smile.

James set aside his quill pen and closed the ship's log. He drank in her loveliness. Slowly stretching his sore leg, he leaned back in his chair and continued to admire her feminine charms. Amazing how much better his injuries felt, now that she had returned. She was a true beauty in the dress, but if he had his way he would just as soon see her naked.

"Don't look at me like that," she warned, smiling mischievously back at him. "I feel totally exposed."

"Aye, and ye should be," he said agreeably. "My hands rubbing circles on yer silky skin and my lips tasting yer full tender mouth. Yer lovely body pressed intimately—"

"Stop! My gosh! You have me blushing clear to my toes. It's no wonder you have your way with all the women in this century." Anna turned her back on him to break the spell he so easily wrapped around her. He was too darn sexy.

He was at her side in an instant. "Not all the women. There's only one woman I'll have in my life, or warming my bed. My heart is taken, wee Anna. There is no other. Ye need but accept my love and we'll not wait to consummate our passion." His long bronzed fingers caressed flittering silken patterns on her bare arms.

Her heart soared at his open declaration. She couldn't even swallow let alone move away from him. The time was right to give herself to him, yet one slight obstacle stood in the way. He didn't know about her previous marriage. She had to tell him to clean the slate between them.

"James? I need to tell you something." She dared not look at him. She would lose her courage and her concentration. He must be told the truth before their relationship went any further. How important was it for him to be her first lover?

James felt a sickening thud deep within his chest as his heart drowned in a sea of warning. She did not return his love. That was why she had refused to wed him all along. He walked over to the bed and sat down upon the rumpled quilt, needlessly smoothing it.

"Tis a very sad thing to hear o' one's doom."

"Doom?" She walked over to sit beside him, taking his hands in her own. "I suppose it's all in how you look at it."

"Aye," he agreed quietly.

"What I have to tell you is personal."

He didn't respond, nor did he meet her gaze.

"There's only one way to put it—I've been married—"

James released her hands and jumped abruptly to his feet, bumping his head on the low crossbeam. He yelled out a string of Gaelic curses, not expecting her to understand. Furiously stomping back and forth across the cabin, he flexed his hands in anger as he fought for control. He paused before her, his wild temper barely in check.

"Married? Blast it all, woman! Why did ye not tell me before I made a damn fool o' m'self?"

Words stuck in Anna's throat. She turned away bewildered, blinking back tears. His feelings were hurt, naturally. And when wounded his temper flared dangerously. He didn't even let her explain before he strode quickly from the room, slamming the cabin door with a loud bang that rattled the hinges.

~ * ~

Anna paced back and forth across the cabin floor, finally settling down at the captain's desk. Inspecting the mess strewn carelessly across the top, she began tidying papers into neat piles. She gathered up the quill and inkpots, arranging them neatly along the desk's back corner.

Not having anything else to do until James chose to return, she found cleaning up a distraction to pass time. She discovered a flat brass key hiding beneath a heavy piece of parchment. It was a small drawer key. What did the captain feel was so important that he needed to lock it away?

Upon examination, the desk held only two locked drawers: one large and one small, both on the left-hand side. Anna tried the small drawer first. An array of writing paraphernalia, a few stray coins and what looked like large postage stamps. She slipped the key into the second keyhole. The long deep drawer slid forward easily at her touch. Inside laid an intricately carved wooden box.

She hesitated only a moment, before carefully lifting the box and setting it on the polished desktop. Something seemed familiar about this box, but she couldn't quite put a finger on it. Carefully opening the lid, she gasped in surprise. On a bed of purple velvet lay the captain's brass spyglass, the same spyglass that had brought her back in time.

A shiver ran down her spine and suddenly she felt quite odd. Apprehension filled her soul. What kind of power did this old piece of mariner's equipment have over her? She leaned closer, not wanting to touch it, but unable to resist its lure. The intricate design was unique. A frigate under full sail, beautiful and elegant, surrounded by tiny leaves and flowers delicately carved into the shiny brass instrument.

Again, Anna marveled at the craftsmanship possible in previous centuries. Anything worth its salt cost a small fortune nowadays. Didn't she remember James saying a king had given the spyglass to one of his ancestors? A special treasure, indeed.

Curiosity finally getting the best of her, she reached out to pick up the heavy spyglass. She quickly brought up her other hand for support, holding the spyglass fully within both hands. A strange weakness shot up her legs.

"Oh, no! Not again—"

Blinding light hit her eyes and the cabin faded from view. Dizziness overcame her as her breath expelled forcefully from her lungs. She couldn't move, nor could she breathe. All she could do was pray she would make it through to the other side. Blackness surrounded her. She could do nothing to prevent what was happening. Hearing herself scream, her knees buckled and she fell heavily to the floor.

The world spun around her. Just as suddenly, everything was normal again. Anna blinked her eyes. Even without the slip of moonlight snaking across the wooden floor, she knew she was back in the old house. Dying embers in the stone fireplace glowed faintly in the dark. The woven rug felt soft and thick beneath her trembling fingers.

"My dear God, no! I can't be back. I don't want to be back." She broke into sobs and let the spyglass slip from her hand. "James!" Her scream of agony burst through the midnight silence.

Alastair leaped from his warm bed in sheer panic. "Good Lord! What now?" His heart thumped wildly within his chest. He staggered across the dark room, almost falling over a sobbing form. "Anna? Is that you?"

No answer, just more wailing sobs.

Anna's heart tore in two. She would never see James again, and they had not parted on good terms. She didn't have a chance to finish telling him about being married, and divorced. Damn him! Now he would never know the truth. He would always think she disappeared because she was married to someone else and didn't really care about him. Her wind burned cheeks stung and she rubbed them roughly to wipe away her tears.

"Anna?" Alastair knelt beside her and bundled her into his arms. "Anna? What happened? Why are you back?"

Her tears began anew. She looked up to see concern in his shadowy expression and shook her head. It was hopeless. How could she ever return to James now? She did not even begin to understand the forces that pulled her so ruthlessly through time. A worse notion struck her. If she could return to 1880, would James still want her?

Alastair patiently and gently rubbed her back. He released a weary sigh. "Never mind, sweetheart, you can tell me later. Let me comfort you for a while. Have a good cry. Then we'll go downstairs, raid the kitchen and have a nice long chat."

~ * ~

Stars splattered midnight heavens lighting the *Ceilidh's* freshly swabbed decks as she groaned softly from the sea's rolling motion.

Deep in thought, James leaned against the ship's rail and gazed down into the murky water. Anna was the most beautiful woman he had ever met. She was warm and playful, sexy and sassy, and she was a wee bit stubborn. By knowing her, he had changed his mind concerning his previous ambitions. Uppermost in his mind had always been the desire to avenge his father's death and restore the family's estate in Dundee, Scotland.

For twenty years, he had sailed the world's oceans, starting as a young cabin boy saving his meager earnings with the hopeful dream of being able to return to his homeland. Nothing meant more to him. With enough money, he could rebuild his ancestral home and find the man who had stolen his father's wealth. A heartless act that caused his family to leave Scotland behind and journey to the New World, America.

Lately, however, James thought about a certain saucy wench much more than his heritage. He had never considered settling down before. But she was well worth the sacrifice of his bachelorhood and his hate-filled plans of revenge. He wanted to spend the remainder of time loving her.

Cursed Neptune! How she had played him for a fool! No doubt, she was sitting below in his comfortable quarters laughing at him. He could never forgive her for accepting his heart, only to cast him to sea for love of another. Married, indeed!

Aye, his loins burned for her. Aye, he loved her in spite of her treachery. But he would never be able to fill the emptiness she left him by proclaiming her heart already taken by another. His rival lived far in the future and he could do naught to win her back. She would never return his love.

A slight breeze whipped tendrils of his hair loose from its leather tie. Unconsciously, he began counting stars while his thoughts rambled on over the turn of events. Nay, never would he trust another woman. Maybe he should return to his drinking, wenching ways and ease the burning physical need he still felt for the lovely Anna. His heart lurched in pain.

Gaelic curses filled the peaceful night air, startling the graveyard skeleton crew and echoing out over the ocean waves. James buried his face in his hands and fought the urge to cry, something he had not done since his beloved father died. What was he to do now?

The deck hands had all retired below, filled with enough rum to help them sleep until noon on the morrow. Those few men who had the night watch remained sober and alert as always. He heard their soft calls marking the hour. Across the starlit bay, church chimes played out their haunting tune. From the distant sleepy town the old bell tower tolled the twelve strokes of midnight.

Feeling more wretched than he had ever felt in his entire life, James faced his inner soul. His heart was heavy with shame at the way he had treated Anna. She had not asked to be drawn through time. She did not even follow him from the cabin to curse him to blazes for his unforgivable behavior, and he had not given her a chance to explain.

His gaze shifted to the subtle and sneaky movements of a crewmember, lurking in the shadows. James recognized William, the forever-loyal young pup, attempting discretion by trying not to disturb him in his present state of mind.

"Evenin', Captain." William acknowledged his superior with a nod and a grim expression.

"How goes it, Will?" James straightened and ran his fingers through his unkempt hair. A gentle sea breeze wafted by, messing up his hair again.

"Not good, sir. How should I put this? I'm afraid you will waken yonder town with this news. I hate to deal you another blow."

"Ye are talking in riddles, lad. Speak up."

"Captain, it's Anna. She's gone again."

James released a deafening roar and beat his fist into the rail. "God's teeth, man! Do not tell me this unless it be true!"

"Aye, Captain, it's true." William hastily set about to explain. "I was coming to give report, sir. There was no answer from your cabin. It was wrong of me, perhaps, but I worried for your person. I looked into the room only to find it empty. I checked with George, and then came above to ask the watch. None has seen her since the two of you retired after supper."

"Anna—" A mournful cry escaped his mouth before he turned and strode swiftly toward his cabin with William quick on his heels.

Expecting to find her, to have it all have been a grave mistake, James burst into his cabin with her name hovering on his lips. His hopes shattered at what caught his eye. On his desk lay the open spyglass case. Empty now of its contents, the box was a vivid reminder of what could have been and the spyglass was nowhere to be seen. She was gone. He had forced her to leave by bellowing at her.

Great stars! Why couldn't he control his cursed temper?

Anna was lost to him, possibly forever. Without her, he felt as empty as the velvet-lined case without its brass treasure. He slammed the lid shut and spewed forth a curse or two more, before reaching for a nearby bottle of Scotch whiskey to drown his sorrows.

William backed toward the door and the latch clicked softly into place behind him. James never acknowledged his first mate's departure. He stood totally absorbed in his misery. He loved the mysterious sea, and he loved Anna Bentley. He hated England, and now he hated himself.

~ * ~

Alastair sat across from Anna, sipping a mug of steaming hot chocolate. "We'll think of something, you know."

She didn't say a word. She sat blinking away tears and fighting the trickle escaping down her cheeks. It was obvious she was suffering greatly, and he didn't know how to help. The time pool was there, but the captain and his ship were somewhere farther up the coast in an entirely different century. Would they think to return to the secret cove? If so, when? Anna couldn't very well camp out alone in 1880, miles from the nearest town, in hopes the *Ceilidh's* crew would return for her.

"Alastair?" Anna bit her lower lip with a frown. "I've been thinking...what if we could contact Morgan. You know, leave a note or something? He returns to the cave on a regular basis to stash his stolen gold."

"Morgan's an outlaw and his present company leaves a lot to be desired." He shook his head, folding his hands on the table before him. "We do know the spyglass took you to the captain once. What's to say it won't do it again?"

"I wish it were that simple, Alastair. I've already tried the spyglass again. Nothing—absolutely nothing—happened."

"There has to be a way. A certain place, a certain time. Damn!" Alastair jumped to his feet and ran his fingers through his dark wavy hair. "I've got it." He paced the floor in front of Anna, his mind whirring a mile a minute. "It's you, Anna, you...and the ship, you...and the house. There has to be a connection, we just have to find it."

Anna released a big sigh, then yawned. "Alastair, I'm too tired to think anymore. Let's get some sleep. Maybe the answer will come to us in our dreams." She giggled half-heartedly, trying to make light of an ordeal that was breaking her heart. She felt as though a vital part of her was missing. She was incomplete because she longed for James.

Alastair put his arm around her shoulder and placed a light kiss on her cheek. "Okay, kid, you win. But I want you to know—I'm confident we will get you back to the captain. We have to. You're my great-great-grandmother."

She yawned again. "Thank you, Alastair. Somehow you make me feel so young."

He walked her upstairs to her room, leaving her to settle down in the softness of the captain's huge bed. The same room the captain had shared with his wife, where their children and grandchildren had been conceived and welcomed into this world. No doubt about it, she was extremely depressed.

~ * ~

Sunlight filled the cabin when James awoke to a blinding headache, an empty nauseous stomach and a temper to inflame both. Sitting up slowly, he groaned and fell back to the bed. He covered his face with a pillow. He was in no mood to receive the cheerful attentions of the ship's cook.

"Good-mornin', Capt'n. How's the head?" Cookie set down the food tray and poured a full mug of strong black coffee. "I've got just the thing for what ails you, Capt'n."

James growled. "Leave me be, man!"

Cookie released a low whistle and laughed. "You have a mighty nasty temper this morning, Capt'n, but I've seen you in worse shape. Do you remember—"

"Twon't get any better with yer blasted prattling! So off with ye now." James winced. The slightest noise was like banging pots to his ears. "Where's William? I need me blasted whiskey! 'Tis the only thing 'twill help me pass the hours."

A knock at the cabin door and William entered. "Did I hear you mention my name, sir?"

"Ahh, Will." James turned slowly, raising his aching head slightly off the pillow. "Where've ye been, lad?"

Cookie handed William the cup of strong brew. "I've had my share of the captain's foul mood. Best you brace yourself, young Will." He nodded toward the captain and hastily left the quarters.

George strolled casually in and pulled up a chair to sit beside the rumpled bed where James lay in misery. "What do you say we have a cup of Cookie's great coffee and try to sober up?"

"Blast it, man! If I wanted to be sober, I would not have started drinking in the first place!" He winced and strove to open his eyes wider, attempting to focus on the room's pestiferous occupants.

William pressed the hot mug into the captain's hands and helped him take a sip. "You'll need your wits about you today, sir."

"Och, man! Are ye trying to poison yer captain?" James sputtered and shook his head, then groaned for the pain it caused him. "Ye forgot the barley-bree and still 'tis the strongest brew I have yet to taste."

"Cookie's a smart man, James. We need to have you sober, my friend. We have devised a new plan to find Anna." George spoke bluntly, getting right to the point.

James jerked his head up to peer at George and grimaced. "Are ye mad, George? She does not want me, 'tis as simple as that. She left o' her own free will."

"Are you forgetting what Alastair told us? You two are meant to be together. She has to return, or Alastair won't even be born. I assure you he will work for the same end, which is to return her to our time." George scratched his head in thoughtfulness while standing to stretch his stocky legs. "Trouble is...we need to be wherever it is they come through time. The cavern's pool would be my guess. Can we make it there before they leave?"

Maybe his friends were right. Anna's first slip through time was unintended. Could she have accidentally returned to her own time? He had to find out. He needed her more than he had ever needed anyone in his life. Forcing himself to think helped him sober up and the excitement of finding Anna stirred his groggy senses to awareness.

"Aye, ye are right, George. We need to find Anna, I've a wee bit o' explaining to do m'self." James took a sip of the steamy black liquid.

William walked to the door. "Shall we set sail, sir?"

"Aye, lad. Set a course to rescue Anna. Sure and this seems to be my duty since meeting the fair lass." James stood carefully to his full height and glanced in the mirror. "Bloody hell! I look a sight."

"You finished off at least two bottles last night," George reminded him.

James grumbled to himself about the duty of friends. If they had prevented him from drinking, he would not be in this shape now. There was only one man who could help him. He turned to William, who was about to leave. "Send for Cookie, lad."

~ * ~

Anna slept fitfully in the damp sheets. She threw the covers off her naked form and lay breathing hard. Large hands cupped her breasts tenderly as moist lips caressed her neck in nuzzling nibbles. Her body languished under her lover's weight, responding to his intimate seduction. She sighed dreamily as her eyes fluttered open.

"No, please no—not again." She sat up, covering her face with her hands. It was the dream again. She peeked between her fingers. Her heart raced to discover she was alone in the moonlit bedroom. Dropping her hands to her lap, she searched the shadows. Her gaze lit on the spyglass where she had left it, laying on the mantel. She sighed as memories of a love greater than time flooded her soul.

"James? Is it you?"

No answer. Nothing.

Just as well, he was only a brilliant figment of her imagination anymore. The ocean's fragrant smell drifted into the room, making Anna tremble with yearning deep inside. She released an agonized moan and threw herself back onto the heap of pillows. Tears filled her eyes. She let them roll in lazy patterns down her flaming hot cheeks. She missed the salty rogue! She missed his nineteenth-century mannerisms, his lovable lopsided grin, and his charming Scottish accent. Each memory brought a tingle to her skin she could not ignore. She had to find a way back!

A warm breeze blew in through the open French doors, beckoning her to answer its call. Rising slowly from the bed, she stretched languorously and stepped out onto the balcony. She had no fear of being seen nude. Alastair slept soundly in the room across the hall and she had locked her door before retiring.

Anna stared up at the full moon shimmering down upon the silent grounds below. Closing her eyes, she reveled in the delicate sea breeze cooling her heated body. "Oh, James, my love. Where are you?"

"Anna—"

Her eyes flew open. Was he here? Impossible! Then she recalled her first days in the old house. James appeared in the mirror's reflection and his voice called her name in the arbor. Was it his ghost?

Tenderly, long invisible fingers stretched over her breasts and the pressure of a man's naked form pushed against her from behind in a most familiar way. She would know his touch anywhere.

"James, help me. I want to come back." Was she insane? Whispering into the moonlit darkness as she melted into her phantom lover's arms?

Bristly whiskers tickled her ear and a deep voice hushed her fanciful illusions. "In the arbor, my love. 'Tis the secret."

He was gone. Anna sensed the instant he left her. A cold chill ran up her spine. She must be mad! It was crazy to believe in ghosts. Or was it? The evidence was only in her mind, but she felt it in her heart as well. James was calling to her through time in the only way he could—his ghost—a mere shadow of his former stalwart self.

A smile lit her face. She hurried back inside to pull on a pair of jeans and a T-shirt. To heck with a bra or shoes, she didn't have time. She slipped quietly out the bedroom door. She had to go now, while the spirit moved her so to speak. She giggled softly and felt better already.

The door across the hall remained closed. From beyond came the slightly erratic sound of Alastair's snoring. She didn't need his reasonable advice right now. He would probably laugh, thinking her foolish for believing in ghosts.

Determined to succeed this time, she tossed her long braid over her shoulder and descended the wide staircase, creeping quietly outside to the garden. With a glance at the horizon, she realized dawn would be breaking soon. She followed the well-worn brick path leading down to the grape arbor. Almost stumbling over a low bench, she felt for the seat. Sitting here, in the center of the grape arbor trellises, life seemed pure and serene.

The unusual feeling of being welcomed quickly flooded her senses as the morning sun's first rays flickered across the azure sky and peeked through the overgrown trellises. It was a beautiful summer day. She could feel magic in her very soul.

Something shiny in the thick grapevines directly across the path caught her eye. Lowering herself to her hands and knees, she pushed aside the wide, velvety leaves. She released a strangled cry when she beheld what had been hidden for so long. An old marble headstone, set into the ground, winked up at her with its brass plate as sunlight filled the arbor.

Anna's intrigued gaze scanned the engraving and her heart plummeted in despair. She knelt upon James' grave. She admired the masculine headstone, so typical of the large brawny Scot. Tears filled her eyes, falling unheeded.

Carved into the marble stone above the brass plate was a ship under full sail with the Latin motto he had so proudly quoted her: "learn to suffer."

Anna smiled in remembrance. "Captain James Adam Duncan born December 28, 1848. Died—" She couldn't make out the date of death but the year was plainly visible—1922. He lived for almost seventy-four years! He should have died at sea in 1880, but he didn't because of Alastair. Oh, to spend some of those years with him.

A sudden tenacity filled her. She must get back. There must be a way, a sign she would return. She pulled frantically at the tangled grapevines to the right of the marker and was rewarded a few moments later. She uncovered another marble headstone similar to the first. An engraved spyglass lay across an antique hourglass surrounded by roses. The inscription read: Anna Bentley Duncan, My Beloved, born March 27, 1856. No death date. Nothing more.

Disappointment flooded her heart. But then, did she really want to know? It would be creepy to know when she died. Yet, this was proof she had returned to the past and returned home to James…but how?

A message was here, no doubt. She knelt before the two graves. An eerie feeling overcame her and she rubbed her bare arms to ward off the goose bumps. How could it be she could see her own grave, and still be living and breathing? Maybe she was all but a shadow in this present time, because she really belonged in the past. She tried deciphering the pictorial message to learn the secret to which James had referred.

An hourglass depicted the passage of time…meaning her travel through time? A spyglass being the method that had first transported her into the past, and the most recent way she had returned to the present.

She pushed her mind to recollect her two previous voyages with the spyglass in detail. A simple connection existed, somewhere. Each time she had been completely alone. James was always on board the *Ceilidh*. She had felt the tingling begin as she grasped the legendary spyglass with—both hands!

Fifteen

Stormy seas tossed the *Ceilidh* far off course from her charted destination along the California coast. James stood at the helm, holding the ship's wheel in a death grip as he fought the giant waves threatening to sink her. His hair plastered to his skin with rain that nearly blinded him in its relentless fury.

Never had he met with such a violent storm along the North Pacific shoreline. His experience in crossing the tempestuous Atlantic was another tale altogether. He nearly smiled remembering the fateful journey around the Horn that had brought him to this bountiful and beautiful land.

"Captain! I'm here to relieve you, sir!" William shouted over the fierce howling wind. He wore a heavy canvas hooded jacket already soaked through.

James acknowledged William's worried expression as they changed hands while icy ocean waves clawed across the deck, trying in vain to wash them both overboard. "Aye, lad, I need a bit o' time below," he admitted. He struggled to withdraw the length of rope about his waist that was in turn secured to the deck, and then, with a proud grin, wound it about the first mate. "Hold tight, Will. 'Tis a brave man ye are to take on a strong gale such as this."

William grinned as another wave cast itself across the deck, wetting his long legs to the knees. "Aye-aye, Captain. I've handled many a wicked storm afore and I can manage this one as well."

Secure in the knowledge his ship was in trustworthy hands, James fought his way across the sea-washed quarterdeck. He remembered all too well a violent tropical storm off the Florida coast. Gigantic waves left their ship limping into port two days later to a town that no longer existed. This storm seemed mild in comparison. With the lifeline held securely beneath his arm and blasts of wind whipping at his chest, he wrestled to keep his footing. Relentless waves crashed across the polished deck boards, washing everything not properly secured over the side and into the churning sea.

Cursing his luck for sailing right into a blasted summer storm, James finally reached the bulkhead and ducked below before the next angry wave surged violently across the deck behind him. He left a trail of water all the way to his quarters.

"Ah, there you are at last, James," George greeted cheerfully, offering a length of clean dry toweling. "I was wondering if William could get you to leave the helm. It's mighty nasty out there."

Thankful for the warmth of his cabin, James grunted in response to George's comment and stripped the drenched clothing from his tired body. His only whim now was for a wee bit of whiskey to take away the chill and a short nap before going topside to check on William and Jock.

He stood stark naked, with only the towel about his neck, as he poured himself a mug of spirits and gulped it down in one swallow. Familiar fire warmed his insides, relaxing tight muscles in his bad leg and stiff shoulder.

George sat at the table, staring out the window at the turbulent storm.

"Are ye not listening to me, George?"

"Sorry, my thoughts were elsewhere." George rubbed his fingers through his thick mane of curly blond hair and shifted his powerful thighs on the chair. He struggled to gain composure.

James could not help laughing out loud. "Och, George, sure and it must be Angel on yer mind or my bloody eyes deceive me." He lowered his gaze to George's groin. "Ye are looking mighty uncomfortable. Do ye think yer wife is worrying about ye?"

George answered with a deep resonant chuckle. "I hope so. By the by, it's a good thing Anna isn't here right now. Your response to her feminine charms would be a damn sight more obvious than mine."

James arched his eyebrows in mock surprise. "I'm in need o' a catnap, George, not a woman's charms." He yawned unashamedly. He could no longer deny his weariness. "Can ye find Jock and tell him to wake me in two hours' time?"

George's broad-shouldered figure cast a huge shadow across the lamp lit cabin as he stretched to a stance. He clasped a hand upon James' bare shoulder, a broad smile warming his bearded face. "I'll go find Jock. Rest well, James."

James returned to the cupboard, poured another mug of whiskey and downed it quickly, same as the first. He turned to his bed, stretching his strong muscled torso. Why did George have to mention Anna's name? The dreams had returned since her absence and he hoped he would not have another one. He had enough worry at present with the fierce storm above, a hard-working but exhausted crew and the present danger facing them all.

Och, no! He dared not lose his thoughts to Anna now. His need to find her had grown into a hunger of the most desperate kind. He lay back and forced everything from his conscious mind for the safety of his ship and crew. Collapsing in a worn-out heap across the bed, he drifted into a troubled sleep.

~ * ~

Giant fingers of kelp wrapped around his kicking feet as he watched the dorsal fin approach slowly in a hypnotic swaying movement. Frantic to escape what was sure to be certain death, he beat at the fierce shark's nose. His fists turned blood red from the cursed killer's sharp skin. Thrashing helplessly in the water, he fought with a vengeance until the great sea fox pulled him under. Down, down to a watery grave...

A loud crash awakened James from the terror of his nightmare. He sat up with a start and glanced about the dark cabin, sweat beading on his forehead. Another thunderclap vibrated the ship. Wasting no more time, he jumped quickly to his feet and grabbed for his trousers. He stumbled across to his boots, hoping the ship had not lost a yardarm or mainmast.

The fury of the storm raged on above. The wild wind whipped unmercifully at the rigging. Yet, in listening for the crew's shouts of alarm over damage to the ship, he heard none. James blinked his tired eyes, dropped the tight black trousers he was about to pull on, and turned back to the comfort of his bed.

A rare shaft of sunlight illuminated a small spot across the cabin and he saw what had made the sudden noise. His heart leaped hopefully at the astounding sight. He pinched his naked thigh to make sure he was not dreaming. As he rubbed the sore spot, a female specter appeared. In a mist of pale colors, she slowly took form and he recognized Anna's small figure.

"James! I made it! I'm back!"

Her excited squeals helped speed his long strides to where she sat sprawled on the floor. "Blessed Saints! Anna?"

He gathered her into his arms, burying his face in her glorious golden-blond hair. Holding her silky cheeks between his palms, he covered her rosy lips in a fever of sweet kisses. They stood slowly, wrapped in the moment's ecstasy.

Anna ran her hands over his bare back and down to his hips. James in nothing but his birthday suit made her blush with warmth from her toes to her cheeks. She could feel his arousal through her jeans, pressing at her hips and enticing her to join in his sexual excitement.

Pushing gently away from him, she looked downward at his engorged manhood, standing erect and proud. Her gaze refused to relinquish admiration of so wondrous an object of passion.

"Uh, James?" No matter how hard she tried, could not keep from staring. "You aren't wearing any, umm, any clothes or are you aware of the fact?"

His grin was wide and full of charming enthusiasm. "Are ye telling me ye do not like it now? I remember how ye watched me dress before with desire written all over yer pretty face." He pulled her tenderly back into his arms and placed a teasing kiss upon the tip of her nose, then chuckled at her embarrassment.

Her quick temper flared and she disregarded how much she had missed him. "You enjoy making me drool, don't you? You think I can't resist your great Scottish charm." She pointed her forefinger into his softly furred, muscular chest. "I've got news for you, Captain Duncan. I am not impressed."

He grasped her wrists, forcing her into intimate contact with his body. "Shall we see about that?"

James lowered his lips to brand her with a long demanding kiss, proving conclusively her true weakness for him. Their strong physical and emotional attraction to each other could not be denied any longer. Blast it all! He was in love with this wild, exciting woman, and he had yet to make claim to her luscious body. He wanted much more than to merely satisfy his lust. He wanted her completely, her tender heart and her feisty spirit.

Now was the perfect time, before questions were asked or answers were given. All he cared about at this moment was to make love to the most beautiful woman he had ever known, to hear her cry out his name in the throes of passion, and to watch her lovely face as she reached the heights of fulfillment with him soaring deep inside her lush femininity.

Anna moved out of his embrace and took a deep breath. She inched backward until her thighs brushed against the rumpled bed.

A delightful intoxicating feeling washed over her. James didn't care about her previous husband. Nor did he ask why she had suddenly returned to the future without telling him. He still wanted her and nothing else really mattered. Right now, in his warm comfortable cabin. No interruptions and no more feeble excuses.

She found her fiery desire matched his, leaving her excited as well as a little frightened. Could she really give herself completely to this lusty, nineteenth-century, sea captain without any regrets?

The continual rough ocean swells tossed the heavy ship like a toy, making it increasingly difficult to stay upright. Anna found it hard to stand at all. Quite suddenly, the large sailing vessel listed strongly to starboard, forcing her to fall ungracefully into his powerful arms. She grimaced as her face made contact with his bare chest.

His warm flesh brought fiery flames to her cheeks. He smelled of the salty ocean, a whisper of bay rum and the tantalizing male scent that was exclusively his. She refused to be flustered landing in such a thoroughly compromising position. Pulling herself upright again, she confronted his brawniness and gave him her most innocent smile.

"James? Are we sinking?"

"Tis naught but a wee storm, Anna," he cooed in her ear.

"Oh, a wee storm. Feels more like a hurricane to me." She groaned in total undisguised pleasure as he rubbed his firm body against her.

"Do not worry yerself, lass. William's at the helm." His lips descended upon hers, ending all need for further conversation.

For once in her life, Anna did not argue. James felt much too good. She had to discover for herself just how far this wonderful dream could go. Her heartbeat so hard she thought her heart would explode. His gentle hands slowly removed her T-shirt, letting it fall carelessly to the floor. Her sensitive skin burst into flames at his touch.

"Anna, I'll not wait any longer. Maybe 'tis not a proper wedding, but 'tis bonded we'll be in our hearts. I need ye now."

His husky whispers sent hot shivers piercing her soul. Her response was a muffled groan against his broad chest. She couldn't wait for more as she listened to his tender voice.

"We will be hand-fasted, Anna. 'Tis the Highland way o' marriage." James continued his sensual assault with his passionate words. "I need to feel m'self inside ye, love, for our bodies to be as one. I want to plant the seed o' Clan Donnachaidh deep within ye."

His romantic idea of binding their hearts with an age-old tradition was Anna's undoing. Bearing his children would not only fulfill her dreams of a family, it would surely be a pleasure she did not wish to deny herself. She was whole-heartedly in love with him. There was no more doubt in her mind. She couldn't control what was surely inevitable, nor did she wish to interfere with fate. She would love James forever, no matter what the future held for them.

"James, please make love to me," she whispered. Her request gained an appreciative deep growl from him.

He lifted her effortlessly onto the bed. Levi's flew across the room, joined seconds later by her bikini underwear. Watching him carefully admire each item of clothing before he threw it aside made her smile. At last, she would enjoy this magnificent rogue in the most intimate way, as eternal as time and as sweet as forever, the joining of their bodies and souls as one.

"Ah, ye are so very lovely," he murmured, lighter than a caress of silk slipping past her ears.

Anna groaned in anticipation.

James chuckled. "I know ye will like it, but can ye leave the groaning to me? 'Tis a bit o' sexy whimpering I wish to hear from ye now, lass."

His lips leisurely paved a burning trail down her slender neck, lingering only moments at a tiny sensitive spot on her shoulder before descending between the soft swells of her full white breasts.

He stretched his masculine length out beside her small quivering form, imprisoning her with a powerful leg over her slender thighs.

She sighed, long and lusty, for his touch was heavenly.

Their enraptured bodies melded slowly together, his gaze never leaving her ample charms. His lips devoured every inch of her satin flesh. She whimpered uncontrollably and he smiled. Carefully licking a circle around an attentive nipple, he took the rosy tip between his teeth and tenderly nibbled her sweetness.

Anna squirmed beneath him. Her hands grasped his shoulders for support so intense was her pleasure. He brought his head up to flash a devastating smile, and then lowered his mouth to the other waiting breast. She arched against him as amazing tingles shot through her body, stopping at the core of her desire and making her throb with need. "Ummm, it feels so good, so right."

"Aye, 'tis right, Anna," James agreed, a deep chuckle vibrating his chest.

Wanting to explore every inch of her, his teasing kisses went lower still. She gasped with delight at each touch of his mouth against her fevered skin. The summer storm lashing its wrath topside was no match for the rage of sweet passion tormenting him.

Anna moved beneath him, her skin so inflamed she barely had control of the fire. His hands touched, sought and found places of pure rapture she never dreamed existed. She had never felt such wild pulsating hunger. James deliciously awakened her to her inner self.

Surely, she could take no more. He proved her wrong by carefully sliding a long thick finger inside her most precious place, caressing her gently into intense rapture. She would die soon if he didn't end his heavenly torture and give her release into eternal bliss.

James wanted to make their first time special. He wanted her to crave him, to love him more than she had ever loved any man before. He smiled. She was ready for him and she was getting impatient. He could see her excitement rising. Her urgent hip movements pressed against him. The almost frantic caress of her dainty fingers through his hair told him she had come to the edge.

Anna reached boldly between them and took hold of his swollen member, sending him to the brink of release with gentle little squeezes. James groaned into her soft golden hair as it tumbled loose from its braid in their heated coupling.

"Enough o' that or I will not be able to do ye much good, lass."

"Enough?" Anna made a noise somewhere between a grunt and a sigh. Pushing him onto his back, she straddled him. She rubbed her aching breasts across the furry growth of dark hair spreading like a fan on his muscled chest. "I want him. Now, James."

She giggled as he quickly rolled her over onto her back in his haste to please. He spread her thighs with his own and gently pushed the tip of his manhood into her throbbing wet passage, teasing her with his engorged size. He felt her tighten around him and groaned in pleasure.

Anna astonished him with her eagerness, grasping his buttocks with her small hands. She wrapped her legs around his hips, forcing him deeper still. He gasped as she flexed her feminine self around him, sweetly pulsating, lovingly encouraging him to quicken his leisurely pace. Her immodest actions during intercourse both pleased and amazed him. His confidence in his choice of a wife doubled as he succumbed to her frenzied lovemaking.

Filled with heavenly throbbing desire, Anna lovingly bit at his shoulder and seductively suckled his salty skin as she soared higher and higher. Pulling on his thick wavy hair, she ran her hands up and down his powerfully built body. She squirmed, whimpered, and rubbed herself against him until she could wait no more. Quaking on the edge of ultimate contentment, she lost herself in an exquisite fall over the brink.

James felt her shudder within as she began her long-awaited climax. He swiftly muffled her hungry cry of release with a feverish tongue dueling kiss as he joined her in a soul-shaking journey of pure ecstasy.

They lay tangled together, peacefully sated as the last of their heavy breathing subsided into tender sighs. They did not want to break the magical spell they had woven between them.

Anna nestled her head in the crook of his shoulder, thinking how positively wonderful he was. She loved him so much. She never wanted to leave him again—not for anyone or any place—ever. Though she traveled through time to find him, James was all she ever desired in a lifetime companion. He truly was the man of her dreams.

"James?"

"Aye?"

"Are we hand-fasted?"

"Oh, aye, lass. Indeed we are." A soft chuckle escaped him as he awaited her next question. He knew her well enough to know her curiosity was just beginning to roam.

"James?" She traced an invisible pattern across his stomach, circling his navel with her fingertips, tugging gently at the soft hairs growing there.

"Aye?"

"Is this all? I mean...are we married?"

"Only if we wish it to be so," he confirmed, pulling her back on top of him. "Do ye wish it, Anna?"

She blushed as a minute thought occurred to her and, trivial though it was, she asked, "Is this marriage legal?"

"In the Highlands, aye." James planted a kiss on her chin, hoping to move up to her lips and start the seduction all over again. He missed as she pushed away from him.

"We aren't in the Highlands, James." Anna studied the many emotions crossing his handsome face. Teasing his lips with a wisp of her long hair, she smiled endearingly at him. "If you are asking do I love you—the answer is…yes! I'll be hand-fasted or whatever you want. I just want to be with you—always."

No verbal response was fitting enough to express his joy over her declaration. James placed a hand against the back of her head and pulled her to him in a loving kiss. He held her tight in his arms, frightened she might disappear again. Combing his fingers gently through the long tendrils of her luxurious fair hair, he felt better than he could ever remember feeling before. She had touched his heart in a way that warmed him to his very soul.

Anna was not only beautiful she was intelligent. She humored him with her careless abandon. Decidedly different from most females, she was all he had dreamed of in a woman. He would not be happy without her. She made his life difficult in many ways, but complete in the most important.

Suddenly, he was no longer interested in drinking, wenching or hate-filled revenge. It was a new life James wanted, a life full of carefree laughter and love. He wanted to experience good times and bad, and have children to carry on the family name for his father, as well as for himself. Life with Anna would never be dull. She had shown as much already. She kept him constantly on the edge. Ah, but he loved the exhilaration her presence caused in his life. Aye, he would always crave the excitement she brought with her.

~ * ~

Moonlight sparkled across the dark blue water, a refreshing break from the violent storm that had plagued the *Ceilidh* earlier in the day. Anna stood at the multi-pane window spanning the width of the captain's quarters. She watched waves rippling out from behind the ship as it sailed into the night.

Her heart filled with tenderness and the sweet promise of romance. All brought to her by James—the giver of blissful wonders. How did she ever exist without him? Was he always waiting for her here on his ship? Sailing the seas of time looking for her, just as *The Flying Dutchman* sailed the seas of eternity seeking a safe port in the storm?

She would fight to remain in the nineteenth-century. But he hadn't mentioned her previous marriage. Had his rage on the subject cooled since her return, or was he simply ignoring his feelings on the matter? She hoped he would understand and accept her explanation. After all, it was more important that they were together now.

James stirred restlessly upon the bed.

Anna turned to watch him sleep. Whatever power the spyglass held should be revealed to her so she could prevent herself from accidentally returning to the future. She glanced over to where the spyglass lay upon the cabin floor, forgotten in their joy. She couldn't bear to touch it, for fear she would be drawn forward in time.

Wrapping one of his shirts tightly about her naked body, she shivered in the cool night air. She wanted to snuggle up against James' wonderful warmth as he slept, but he would waken and they would make love again. They found it difficult to stray far from one another's arms, yet he needed sleep to captain his ship properly. Their newfound passion was much too strong and far from spent.

Anna wished James could forget his father's quest for revenge. They had so much living ahead of them; it was a shame to waste it on destructive emotions. James was dedicated to his Scottish heritage. Could he really let go of his past obsession? Would he be willing to give up as much as she had?

She reprimanded herself. She already sounded like a typical wife. No, not typical. Not every woman was loved as thoroughly and tenderly as James loved her. More and more couples drifted apart, torn by social pressures around them and increasing financial difficulties.

"Ah, Anna, ye are a bonny sight to behold standing there in the moonlight," he whispered, his husky words caressing her heart.

She turned and saw him smiling. "Did I wake you?"

"Come here, my love." He stretched his arms out toward her. "Ye did not disturb me, if that's what ye are thinking."

Anna crossed to the bed and knelt beside him. "You needed some sleep." Pushing a long lock of chestnut hair tenderly away from his face, she bent down and brushed her lips to his. "At least the storm has ended. It's beautiful outside.

"Not as beautiful as what sits beside me."

"James—"

He pulled her down on top of him, kissing her honeyed lips. "Let's not talk, lass."

She accepted his kiss, but pushed away when he wanted more. "No, James, I want to talk. We need to talk."

He sat up, running his fingers through his tousled hair. Heedless of the covers falling away to expose his nakedness, he yawned and stretched. "Aye, we need to talk. Ye may as well go first."

She looked away from his nudity. "I want to know what hand-fasting really is."

His hearty laughter filled the cabin and echoed up the long companionway. He had expected another one of her traumatic truths and all she wanted to know was the law of hand-fasting? By gosh, he nearly died in relief. Wiping the remaining tears of humor from his eyes, he faced her and looked her right in the eyes.

"Hand-fasting is a very old custom o' the Highland folk. Ye see, if a young man wants to wed and the lass is willing, they seek the approval o' their elders. If naught is spoken against the couple, they live together for a year. If a wee *bairn* is born at the end o' that time, the man and woman are considered legally wed."

"And if there isn't a child?"

"The choice is theirs. The clan cannot force them apart if they wish to stay together. When ye are hand-fasted 'tis the desires o' the couple that decides what is to be." James leaned against the pillows as he studied the face he had grown to love.

She shrugged out of his large shirt and snuggled up to him. "Then I want to have your child, James. Your wee *bairn*."

James groaned as his loins filled with sweet desire. Pulling Anna into his arms, he smothered her with hungry kisses. 'Twas a bonny time for loving and perhaps to plant a wee *bairn* deep in the belly of the woman he loved.

~ * ~

George burst recklessly through the captain's cabin door. "The storm has blown over, James, I—Ahh—" His fading words floated across the quiet room and he stopped dead in his tracks.

Anna looked up at him from the bed and waved her fingers.

Yanking the sheet up over her naked body, James ground out a furious and unfriendly greeting. "God's teeth, man, can ye never knock?"

George blinked twice and rubbed his eyes. "Anna?"

She giggled. "It's really me, George. Please, forgive James. He has had lots of—" James turned toward her, intense desire burning in his expression. He tugged her gently closer to nibble at her neck.

"Yes, I can see that he has...well, welcome back, Anna." George cleared his throat and coughed to hide his embarrassment. "Just wanted to let you know we're in sight of the cove. I suppose we won't need to drop anchor. No, I'm sure we won't."

James turned back around to acknowledge his partner. "George, Jock can captain the ship for a bit longer. Could we be havin' a wee bit 'o privacy now?

"I'll make sure you aren't disturbed," George said quietly, backing out the door and closing it behind him.

James was wild with unfulfilled desire for Anna. He moved slowly over her, wrapping her petite body in his arms with a deep growl. Her response was a low appreciative groan. He chuckled. She was here to warm his heart, not to mention taking the chill out of the cold night.

What a change in his common ways, for he had not sought to bed another wench since meeting Anna. He was no longer the lusty rogue who had a woman in every port. He had met his match at last. He was in for balmy weather, be it on land or at sea, with Anna as his wife.

~ * ~

James whistled a seafaring tune as he strolled jauntily along the fore deck. The storm had cleared; it was a beautiful day and the ship sat safely at anchor in a secluded cove. He grinned with satisfaction. The *Ceilidh's* exhausted crew itched to explore the cove's bounties. Tonight there would be swimming and fishing, and a big bonfire on the beach with whiskey a plenty.

William was in charge of the crew's daily chores. Jock already had a number of men tarring and tending to the rigging, leaving William free to oversee and call out orders. Several sails needed patching and mending after the recent storm. The decks were greatly in need of swabbing. A wee bit of polish along the rails and companionways was in order, too. Everything must be in tip-top fashion. There was a lady on board his ship.

Thinking of his lady, James hastily returned to his quarters. Anna was wearing what she called a bikini bathing suit, a surprise for him that she had brought back from the future. The bright pink suit exposed her curves to perfection. In fact, the suit barely covered her at all. He restrained himself from throwing her down on the bunk and making passionate love to her.

He smiled as it crossed his mind what a catch she was. Anna had haunted his dreams nightly, luring him ever closer to her, and eventually the time travel was inevitable. They were certainly well suited, both stubborn and adventurous, and definitely of highly passionate natures.

Anna had told him all about his ghostly appearances in the future. She had felt strangely at home in the old Victorian mansion, knowing it had seen love, attention and the long-gone era of better days. Somewhat begrudgingly, she told him about her earlier agreement with Morgan, too. She would clear Morgan's name, in return for Hawk to stop tormenting innocent women along the highways.

"Ye will not become involved with highway robbers and the like," James said suddenly with firm conviction.

She stood before him, her small hands on her shapely bare hips. "A promise is a promise, James. Morgan helped me return to you and that means more to me than anything. Besides, I'd rather die than never see you again." She bent over and gave him a tantalizing kiss. "Or touch you, or..." her voice faded as her passion awoke.

"I thought we were going ashore. We will not get—Ahh, Anna!" He loved it when she seduced him. She was so thorough in her hunger for satisfaction. He groaned while her soft, round body pressed hotly against him.

She pressed him back on the bed with taunting kisses. "Cry uncle," she whispered softly in his ear, while gently nibbling his neck.

"What?" James could not stand much more without taking over this passionate attack on his senses. The bold woman was more than he had ever dreamed she would be, and he thoroughly loved her blatant sexuality.

"You heard me. Cry uncle." Anna suppressed a giggle as she raised his shirt over his head and tossed it carelessly across the room. She kissed his shoulder, moving slowly down his arm, and then switching to his belly and the area below the navel. He was so wonderfully warm and furry down there. She loved rubbing her cheeks against him, listening to him groan in frustration.

Relentlessly, she worked the buttons undone on his snug-fitting pants.

"Sweet Neptune! Uncle!" James bellowed loud enough for his entire crew to hear. "Ye drive me mad with passion, Anna, but I do have a ship to run. The lads have not seen me for hours."

"They know how busy you are, Captain." Her laughter was like tinkling bells and he could never hear enough of it.

"Aye, and 'tis busy ye shall be in a minute." He quickly rolled her over, holding her hands firmly above her head. "Would ye like to see how much ye can take yerself, love?"

"Dare you," she taunted with an alluring smile.

He nibbled her breasts through the silk of her bikini making her pant and arc toward him. She struggled to free her hands, but he held all the tighter. "More?"

"More." Anna wanted to caress his warm, smooth skin with her hands, letting them roam over his magnificent body as they made passionate love. She moaned and sighed, then whimpered in pure enjoyment.

James ignored her seductive little noises and continued to lay siege, paying her back for teasing. Damnation! How many times could he respond to her? She was like sweet magic, a soft whisper on the summer breeze, forever luring him into a lover's tryst.

~ * ~

Two knocks at the cabin door was William's usual signal. James released a sleepy groan and sat upright. Anna snuggled close beside him, deep asleep in the middle of the day. He smiled as he pulled on his trousers, knowing their lovemaking was getting to her, as well. They could not seem to get enough of each other.

James opened the door and peeked sheepishly around it. "I'm sorry, lad. Do ye need me above?"

William grinned. "Have I just imagined all those wonderful giggles drifting up the stairwell, Captain?"

James frowned. The cocky young peacock. "Did ye say ye wanted to swim ashore, lad? I've had enough of yer teasing about my passion for Anna."

William chuckled. "Just finished all duties, sir. The crew asks permission to go ashore. Jock says there's a wonderful abalone patch in the cove just waiting for one of Cookie's pots."

James met his first mate's humored gaze. William turned quickly away when Anna walked up beside James, clad only in her skimpy, twenty-first century bikini. "Anna, I think William's heart cannot take it." Grasping his first mate's shoulder, he turned him back around. "Tis called a bathing suit, William. A bikini. Very common in my time."

"Oh." The blush on William's cheeks lightened, but he still kept his gaze averted rather than look too closely.

"I'm sorry, William. I'll hurry and put on something more respectable."

James could not help chuckling. "Ye think my life will ever be dull, William?"

"Never, Captain." William cleared his throat, a broad smile spreading across his dark features. "Never."

Nor would anyone's life be the same aboard the *Ceilidh*, James mused. Anna had worked her spellbinding magic on them all.

Anna pulled on her blue jeans and T-shirt over the bikini. She fought to untangle her long hair as she glanced over her shoulder toward the men. "I'm decent, James. William can come in now."

The first mate's laughter told Anna he was listening to James tell stories again. Hopefully, they weren't talking about her state of undress. She didn't feel at all uncomfortable in a bikini.

William spoke in low tones. "How are you holding up with this vixen in your cabin, sir?"

"Ye would not think I could, but I'm becoming used to her wanton ways." James turned and looked at her. "Tis tempting ye look, Anna."

Anna put her hands on her hips. "Don't tell me...it's indecent to wear your hair down in front of a man, right?"

Crossing the room swiftly to wrap her into his arms, James placed a quick kiss on her cheek. "Aye, Anna. Ye do look a bit seductive. William here understands, knowing ye are from the future, but ye will not be going about the crew looking as ye do."

"They haven't said anything. Why does it even matter?" She huffed in frustration. "James, you wouldn't believe the freedom a woman has in the twenty-first century. This is all so archaic!" Her eyes flashed with sudden devilment. "I go to the beach all the time to swim—wearing only my bikini." She laughed at William as his jaw fell open in astonishment. "That's what it's for, William, swimming. Shall I demonstrate?"

"Anna—" James reached for her, but she pulled quickly away, laughing as she ran out the cabin door. She threw a flirtatious wink at William in passing.

James shot an anguished look at his first mate. They both bolted out the door after her. He shoved two seamen ruthlessly out of his way where they stood gawking at Anna's fleeing form. Taking the steps two by two, his head rose out of the hatch in time to see Anna peeling off her clothes at the cheers of all the men on deck.

Sixteen

James pushed his way through the group that had gathered around Anna as she stepped up on the rail. Holding onto the rigging, her trim figure a sight for sore eyes in her bikini, she smiled and waved. She turned about and dove gracefully into the clear blue water far below.

"By the Saints, Capt'n! I wish she were mine!" Jock sighed wistfully, his gaze never leaving the near-naked form swimming away from the schooner.

James grunted in exasperation. "Nay, ye do not want a lass as bold as her. She has no fear, no common sense for these times. She will not listen to me."

"Ah, but her loveliness makes up for it, Capt'n. She's no ordinary woman." Jock's expression softened. "I cannot think o' a better man for her than yerself."

"Aye. I've lost my heart to the lass." James studied the incoming tide and noticed a sudden change in the waves. "God's teeth, 'tis the rip tide! Anna is not aware!"

Yanking off his knee-high boots, James climbed the side rail and dove smoothly into the frothy waves. Swimming was not his favorite pastime, but aboard ship, it paid to know how to save oneself in times of danger. It was also something he required of his crew. The men who did not know how were taught in much the same way James had first learned—swim or drown.

Anna swam the breaststroke toward the sandy beach. As she neared, the waves washed to shore in crossing angles. Deciding whether to try to out swim the swiftly moving tide, she paused and glanced back at the ship. Someone was swimming in her direction. A large swell washed over her head, pulling her under the sea. She held her breath until she reached the surface. Before the next wave hit, she took several cleansing breaths.

Her fears were not only for herself, but also for the unsuspecting sailor swimming toward her. She prayed it wasn't James. Did he even know how to swim? She fought the steady current dragging her sideways until the next wave propelled her forward. Going under, her lungs felt as though they would burst. She held her breath, kicking hard for the surface.

James reached Anna as her head popped up suddenly. She gasped for air. His arms slid around her, supporting her so she could breathe easier. Not waiting for the next wave to hit, he pushed toward shore, pulling her along with him. They reached sandy bottom and struggled for footing as the tide nipped unmercifully at their feet. Wrapping a secure arm around her chest, James guided them through waist high water as the waves crashed against their backs.

Anna was breathless and totally exhausted. She fell onto the sand and lay moaning, while soaking in the warmth of the afternoon sun. Her eyes flickered open and she saw a still form stretched out beside her.

"James!" She sat up, dusting fine grains of sand from her cheek. "Are you okay? James! Speak to me!"

Playing possum was not easy, but James held back a grin and groaned mournfully.

"This is all my fault! I shouldn't have dove off the ship. I was only trying to make a point about the bikini. Oh, James!" She shook him and gently slapped at his face. "James?"

Enough was enough. Grasping Anna's arms, James swiftly rolled her over and pinned her down by straddling her legs. "Aye, lass, 'twas all yer fault. Ye are lucky we are not both holding court with King Neptune."

"I said I was sorry." She squirmed beneath him on the warm sand. "What do you want from me?"

His deep chuckles made her look up to meet his blue eyes with their hungry expression. He wasn't craving supper. Well, she would make him work for it.

"James, let me go! You're hurting me." She rubbed her wrists when he released his hold on her, then jumped up and ran down the beach with a lively burst of energy.

James shook his head, causing long wet strands of hair to stick to his face. He laughed heartily. "Ye want to be chased, do ye wench?"

Stretching slowly to his feet, he heard the sound of oars hitting the water and turned to see Jock with six crewmen in the long boat. He cursed under his breath as his well-meaning crewmembers forged quickly ashore. Their timing was rotten for what he had romantically envisioned with Anna. He would simply have to find a way to get them to leave—at least for a few hours. He forced a welcome smile at his second mate.

"Is Anna all right, then?" Jock swiped a big hand across his face and blinked his eyes free of sea spray.

"Aye, the lass is well enough to give me a merry chase." James rubbed the short bristles on his chin. "Do ye think ye could keep the lads down at the cove for a bit, Jock?"

Jock winked and, with a wide perceptive grin, nodded toward the other seamen. "Och, ye say ye will be wanting the lads to fetch enough abalone for dinner then, Capt'n?"

"Oh, aye. To feed the whole ship if need be, Jock." James beamed.

"Good luck to ye, Capt'n. May ye net that lovely sea nymph o' yers." Jock turned and bellowed orders to the crew as he strode determinedly toward them.

~ * ~

Anna stopped running and took cover in the woods. She glanced about and realized she wasn't being pursued any longer. Catching her breath, she waited for a few moments. The sound of trickling water met her ears. Curiosity drove her through the tangle of brush and pines. Tall weeds scratched her bare arms and legs, but she continued her journey. The woods opened up onto a small clearing. A beautiful little waterfall cascaded over the rocks into a deep pool.

The water was so clear she could see moss-covered stones at the bottom and tiny fish along the pond's edge. She heard a movement in the bushes behind her. Thinking it was James, she whirled around with a smile, ready to invite him for a leisurely swim.

"So, Emil finds the lovely señorita once again." The heavyset dark Spaniard swaggered toward her. "What manner of dress is this, belleza amor?"

Anna gasped as his beady-eyed, bleary glare ran up and down her exposed body. Good Lord! If she screamed, James would surely come to her rescue, and face eminent death in the process. This rotten man was a cold-blooded killer. Her gaze went immediately to the shotgun in his hand and the long-barreled pistol hanging from his belt.

"Cat got your tongue, *señorita*?" Emil stood close enough she could smell the strong liquor on his sour breath.

She shivered with disgust. "Where's Morgan?"

"Eh?"

"Ummm...you know." She closed her eyes to grasp for the name floating just out of reach. Why did her memory always fail at a time like this? "Oh, yeah...Hawk. Where's Hawk?"

"What is Hawk to you? Emil can make you feel like the beautiful woman you are." He reached for her, but stumbled on the uneven ground.

Anna quickly stepped aside, folding her arms protectively over her heaving breasts. Why in the world had she brought the darn

267

bikini? And how could she escape from this drunken fool without getting James involved?

"Singing my praises again, Emil?" Morgan stepped out from behind a nearby pine tree, his hand resting lightly upon the gun in its holster.

Emil backed away slowly, and then swung around with surprising agility for a drunk. His deadly shotgun was aimed and ready. "Don't ever sneak up on me, Hawk. I could have easily killed you."

A husky laugh escaped Morgan as he sauntered over to Anna's side. "I doubt it, my friend. Besides, I told you—the wench is mine." Looking down at her, he released a low whistle. "I seem to find you in the most peculiar situations, darling."

Anna looked up at him with a threatening scowl. "Keep your hands to yourself, Morgan."

Emil chuckled. "Eh, Hawk, she is a feisty one this wench of yours. Maybe we could share her?"

Feeling braver, Anna glared at the blackguard. "Not on your life, buster!"

Morgan wrapped a protective arm around her waist and whispered, "Don't push your luck. Just play along with me and I'll help you out of this mess."

Anna wasn't sure she trusted Morgan any more than she trusted his wicked partner in crime, but she had no choice now. She shuddered to think they might have come across James first. She was about to pull away from Morgan, when she heard James call out her name.

"James!" She was half relieved and half afraid to hear his deep voice.

Emil moved quickly for a man his size, with all the cumbersome weapons attached to his belts. Not to mention the alcohol he must have consumed. He emerged from the trees' shelter moments later with James walking quietly before him.

"Who is this, I wonder? *Señorita* are you cheating on the Hawk?" Emil's gun pointed at his captive's back as a merciless grin spread across his evil lips.

"Emil! No more bloodshed!" Morgan sounded as fierce as he looked. "Damn it to hell, man! You've gotten us into enough trouble already. Put the gun away."

The barbarous Spaniard lowered his gun, but did not replace it in the holster. "If I did not know how good a gunfighter you are, amigo, I might question your authority. But I will back-off, rather than attract your anger."

"A wise decision," Morgan said menacingly.

Morgan remembered quite well the first time he met Emil. They had ridden on the same stagecoach to determine its route and the cargo it carried, unbeknownst that they were both crooks. Later, they were each surprised to hear their "stand and deliver" echoed. They quickly became acquainted and decided to join forces in their pliant trade. A good year it had been, too. They had hit upon just the right stage-line to capture their riches in bags of gold and cash payrolls meant for the hardworking lumberjacks up north.

Unfortunately, James was now aware of this fact and Morgan would have to cover his latest tracks. He signaled silently to Emil to back off and turned to speak with James, careful not to release Anna.

Anna glared across at Emil as he stood quietly aside observing Morgan arguing with James. Emil turned his drooling gaze on her. To a man of this era she was nearly naked, and she could see the sexual hunger arise in the Spaniard's dark eyes.

"Hell, why not?" Emil flipped his gun in the palm of his hand, grasping the barrel firmly. He stepped forward and put the butt to sufficient use on the back of the captain's head, ending all need for further argument.

"No!" Anna screamed, pushing away from Morgan's hold. She rushed to kneel beside the crumpled form. "Oh, James—" Glaring upward, she met the defiant flash in Emil's eyes. "How could you?"

Morgan cursed under his breath. "Emil! Enough of this violence!" He yanked Anna ruthlessly to her feet and away from James. "Throw his body into the bushes and let's go before we get the whole damn crew down our throats!"

Anna struggled to get free from his steel grasp. "I'm not doing any favors for you. You can forget it right now. I hate you, Morgan! Do you hear me? I hate you, you dirty rotten beast!"

Emil chuckled as he dropped the captain into the thick underbrush. "Hawk, let me have her for only an hour. I will teach the *zorra* a thing or two."

"I know exactly what you have in mind, Emil. But we have no time for that right now. We need her to clear our good names in Gualala. You can't tell me you like your face on WANTED posters?"

Emil flashed a nasty grin. "The infamous Emil Peligro and his side-kick, the gringo they call the Hawk."

Morgan eyed him with open distaste. "You have that wrong, my friend—and don't you forget it."

"How can I forget who is the better gun, eh, *amigo*?"

Morgan ignored the taunt. "Come on, let's mount up. The woman will ride with me." He struck off through the woods along an unmarked trail, dragging her roughly behind him.

Emil followed quietly.

Two black horses stood tied to a low pine branch not far from the waterfall. Morgan pulled a blanket from his pack and put it around her shoulders, lifting her up onto the saddle in one quick sweep. He mounted with ease behind her and turned to Emil.

"I had better take her to the cabin until I can find her some suitable clothes. You scout the headlands for signs of the captain's ship and crew. Meet me at sundown."

"Promise me just an hour, *amigo*, and I will do your bidding gladly."

Morgan snorted. "What will Rosita say to your dalliance?"

"Ah, Rosita. Now there's a passionate one. You are right, Hawk. What need have I for another wench when I have the lovely Rosita?" His laughter rang out bitterly as he turned his horse and rode recklessly away down the trail.

"You almost gave me to him, didn't you?" Anna clenched her teeth in anger and humiliation. "Where on earth are your twenty-first century morals?"

Morgan's arm squeezed tightly about her waist. "In the twenty-first century, of course." He chuckled, then whispered, "I've just saved your precious lover in the only way I know how. Now shut-up and be a good girl, will you?"

"Damn you, Morgan! Damn you to hell!" She wiped the tears from her eyes as Morgan turned the horse onto a well-worn path which led up into the forest of giant redwoods and far away from the man she loved.

~ * ~

"Capt'n?"

Jock's rugged features came slowly into view as James groaned and put his hands to the back of his head in agony. He found a lump the size of a hen's egg rising through his thick hair. He winced as Jock helped him to his feet. His coherent thoughts returned to Anna and her dangerous situation.

"Jock, have ye found her?"

"Nay, Capt'n. We were hoping ye could shed some light on the matter."

Men's shouts echoed through the dense forest as eight staunch seamen appeared in the small clearing, weapons in hand and ready to fight. Some bore pistols, some knives, and one waved a huge cutlass gripped tightly in his big hand. The afternoon sun danced brilliantly upon the sharp blade of the devil's tool.

"Ahoy, Capt'n! Point the way and we will save the fair lady!" Cookie waved his weapon high in the air.

James grimaced in pain as a laugh escaped him. "Ye will not be telling me ye are going to save her with yer butcher's knife?"

Cookie stepped forward until his beefy face was mere inches away. "Capt'n, I'm as hardy a man as the next. I've grown a bit fond of Anna. I cannot wait to find the blackguard who took her from us. I'd as soon chop them to fine bits as the succulent abalone!"

"Aye, ye are an honest lout, if ever I knew one. Sure and ye will be a braw fighter, too." James clapped the robust cook appreciatively on his shoulder and turned to the rest of his men. "All I can tell ye is the bloody bastard is the same devil who took Anna once before."

"Ye mean 'tis Alastair, Capt'n?" Jock stood at his side, his brow furrowed.

"Nay, 'tis his friend, the one they call Hawk. I met him in the sea cave. He needs Anna to help him out o' trouble with the law. She was to do it when we reached town." He accepted his tartan and weapons from Jock with an appreciative nod. "The man has overstepped his bounds this time."

James threw the length of tartan over his shoulder and strapped his gun holster about his waist to hold the thick cloth in place. His pirating days were long gone. He didn't often carry weapons anymore, but one gun too many had been pulled on him lately. He would not be taking any chances this time.

His heart filled with flaming rage and the sudden overpowering urge to punish someone. He would do what he must to make Anna's tormentor suffer for this treachery. Bending to pull on his boots, he paused and picked up a piece of bright-colored material.

"Tis the silky tie from Anna's braid. She must have lost it in the struggle. God help the man who harms her, for only He can save the beast now."

Jock handed him his dirk. "Ye have the right to champion her, Capt'n. We will all stand with ye, as well. 'Twill be an honor."

James' broad bare chest, his wild long hair and his clan's tartan draped across his shoulder made him look every bit the fierce Highlander. A mean scowl crossed his brow and his heart beat faster. Bloody hell! He would kill the bastard!

"To Anna!" Cookie raised his large knife in the air.

"To Anna!" The cheering challenge was answered in unison.

James gave a nod to begin the ascent uphill through the trees. Only minutes passed before they came upon the place where horses had been tied. Evidence revealed only two horses and each had gone separate ways. James knew they would not find her on foot, the worried expression on Cookie's face told him so.

Cookie stood from examining the hoof prints. "The horse going north carries the most weight. I would say Anna's gone with this one." He pointed his knife northward through the pines where a narrow trail was visible.

"Aye, but 'tis not likely we will be able to catch them without horses o' our own." James ducked when a bullet whizzed past, nearly nicking his ear. "Bloody hell! They have not left at all."

Taking cover in the woods surrounding the hidden falls, James and his crew waited for a sign to show them where the nasty culprit might be hiding.

"*Amigos*, you spoil my fun," a deep Spanish voice spoke out over their heads. "Do you want the *señorita*, or no?"

"Ye bloody bastard!" James bellowed. "If ye treasure yer life, ye will come out o' hiding now." His anger rose faster than the day's boiling temperature as he listened for a reply.

"First we must make a bargain. The *señorita* in trade for my safety," the Spaniard offered.

"Yer life? Aye, we will accept the bargain." James turned to Jock. "It does not mean we cannot torture the man later."

Jock grunted. "Aye, 'tis a sorry bloke he'll be for this dirty deed and I'll make sure o' it."

James stood slowly, keeping hidden behind a large tree trunk. "Ye best be quick, ye Spanish bugger. We're waiting on ye."

"No tricks, *Senór Capitán*." He slowly slid down from a tree branch farther up the hillside.

Cookie was at the Spaniard's side with his butcher knife drawn and the sharp blade pressed against the man's bare neck. "One wrong move and you're the meat for tonight's supper."

James was a little surprised to see the tough robber's eyes water in fear. "Aye, ye best tell us where Anna is, or I'll let Cookie have at ye for the crew's meal."

"I thought the *señorita* belonged to Hawk."

"Hawk has not the right to what's already mine, but 'tis neither here nor there. Enough o' this *clishmaclaver*, where's Anna?" James stepped back from the rancid smelling robber when he snuffled and belched. The clean mountain air around them filled with the stench of cheap wine.

"I will take you—alone. I have but one horse, *Capitán*."

"Ye drunken beast 'twill have to do. As for taking me alone, ye dirty bugger, 'tis I who will have the say in this matter. Jock will go along as well. I do not trust ye at all." James turned to his crew, giving them orders to return to the ship in the cove and sail on to Gualala Bay.

~ * ~

A fine drizzle of rain hampered Jake Hardwick's vision. He stood outside a mountain cabin where he had tracked the highway robber called Morgan Hawk. He could hear voices rising in heated conflict from within the cozy, dry hideaway. One voice was definitely female and he hoped it belonged to Anna.

The woman spewed forth foul words and derogatory comments about Hawk's dangerous and dirty profession. Jake crept closer to peer carefully inside. For all her ranting and bravery, Anna lay snugly roped to the iron bed frame. She twisted and squirmed upon the mattress, wearing only two delicate strips of bright pink fabric that barely covered her female charms. The man who stood over her with his back to the window was Hawk, the man Jake wanted to catch.

Anna managed one more nasty comment before Hawk gagged her and walked out of the room. Ignoring the thick mud clinging to his boots, Jake paused and strained his ears to pick up Hawk's movement from within the adjoining room. A sixth sense told him all was not right. He carefully removed his Colt .45 from its holster and tipped his saturated hat back from his face.

Not bothering to knock, Jake kicked the solid wood portal open. He swung quickly into the room, his gun aimed and ready. Hawk was nowhere in sight, but had undoubtedly returned to the woman in the bedroom. He glanced about the main room and stole forward quietly.

A fire burned low in the grate, giving off just enough light for him to see into the connecting bedroom. "Anna?"

No response, nothing from Hawk, and not even a bad tempered grunt from Anna. Moving with stealth, Jake cursed under his breath when he stumbled over something. Glancing down at his feet, he saw a man's body sprawled face down across the braided rug. He knelt beside the large dark form and felt for a pulse. Dead.

"Shit!" Jumping over the corpse, Jake did not attempt to be quiet. He was anxious for Anna's safety and he knew without a doubt Hawk awaited him. He pushed the bedroom door open. "Anna?"

She lay stretched out upon the bed, her eyes wide with fear. She looked toward the closet and whimpered. Jake understood what she was trying to tell him. Before he could take another step, the closet door burst open and Hawk came out with both guns aimed, one at Jake and the other at Anna.

"Don't push me, cowboy," Hawk said. "I'm a damn good shot."

"So am I, mister. Drop your guns. Your knife, too." Jake moved slowly forward.

"I'll shoot her! Don't think I won't."

Jake didn't flinch. He didn't even stop to think. He just eased the trigger and let his gun do the talking. Hawk staggered backwards, firing off two rounds that flew in wild directions. Jake ducked and prayed the bullets missed their mark. He ran across the room, tackling Hawk and knocking him out.

He removed the robber's weapons and stood staring down at him. He wouldn't be doing anyone much harm for a while. A simpering noise caught his attention and he swung around. Anna's frightened expression quickened his heart. Quickly moving to her side, he removed the gag and cut the ropes binding her to the bedposts.

"Jake!" Her voice was raspy. "You're alive."

A broad smile cracked Jake's face as he lifted her off the bed in a tender hug. "You are definitely a sight for sore eyes, ma'am."

Anna gulped in air. She leaned back from his embrace as her eyes fastened on the man lying on the floor. Her heart raced and her mind blurred. "Is he dead?"

Jake chuckled. "Nope. But he outta be for all the trouble he's caused. He didn't hurt you or anything, did he?"

She shook her head. Thank God! Jake didn't kill Morgan. Or was Morgan supposed to die in this century? She covered her face with her hands and wept.

"Anna, Anna. It's gonna be all right, sweetheart." Jake pulled her back into his arms and stroked her hair in comfort. "Let's get you some clothes, little lady. I've got an extra pair of jeans and a shirt in my saddle pack. Stay here. I'll be right back."

Nothing more could surprise her. Anna sank back down onto the bed with a weary sigh. How in the world had Jake found her? The last time she saw James, he looked much as Morgan did now—still and lifeless.

Dear God, she couldn't take much more! She heard Jake's boots as he re-entered the cabin, and quickly wiped the remaining tears from her cheeks. Life was just one big emotional roller coaster ride and she wanted off right now. She had to get a grip on things. She felt like a ninny, or maybe she was crazy...or maybe both!

"Here you are." Jake strode into the room. "I can't promise they are too clean, but they're warm and dry and they will cover a darn sight more than is covered at present."

"Thanks, Jake."

"What's this? A stinking family reunion?" Morgan's sarcasm cut through the awkward silence.

Like greased lightning, Jake swung around and aimed his gun at Morgan.

Anna shuddered as Morgan's throaty laugh filled the room. The dry clothes Jake had offered her fell to the floor. Her mind filled with dread. This couldn't be happening!

"I remember you now," Morgan said between pain-filled gasps. He struggled into a sitting position. His shoulder oozed blood and it trickled through his spread fingers as he held his hand to the wound. "You're the guard Emil shot when we kidnapped Anna from the stage."

Jake's expression turned hard. His gun pointed steady at its target. "That ain't all you took from the stage—or from a dozen others over the past several months."

"So what's it to you? What the hell are you doing following me here?" Morgan groaned and turned pale.

"It's my job to track down two lousy stealing varmints for Wells Fargo. It looks like I just found one of 'em." Jake took a step toward Anna, standing between her and Morgan. "I've been following that dirty drunken scum out there for a week," he said, nodding toward the door, "...Ever since he came into Gualala asking around for your Spanish friend. I figured sooner or later he'd find the two of you, and he did. He led me straight to you. Careless of him, wouldn't you say?"

"Why should you care? You aren't the law."

Jake laughed, a deep throaty chuckle. "I sure as hell am. I'm a deputy for the Gualala sheriff and a special agent for Wells Fargo. I was hired to find out who was stealing the gold shipments."

Morgan snorted a laugh. "Do you see any gold around here?"

Jake twirled his gun casually. "That don't matter none, you see, 'cause you kidnapped Anna here, and I personally consider that a major offense."

Silence fell in the small room. The air was thick and uneasy with tension and no one spoke a word. The two men glared at one another, while Anna looked back and forth at their equally stubborn faces.

"Jake?" Anna met the question in his dark eyes with what she hoped was sincerity. "Emil is the one you want. He's the only real killer here." Her heart beat faster with danger close at hand. "Believe me, Hawk is okay."

"Let's see...he stole bags of gold from the stage, he kidnapped you, and God knows what else he had in mind to do. I'm sorry, Anna. I have a job to do." Jake turned with a steely glare in Morgan's direction. "I hereby arrest you for the robbery of the Wells Fargo gold shipment stolen near Gualala."

"You can't be serious?" Morgan gripped his bleeding shoulder and staggered to his feet. His face turned deathly pale.

Jake reached into the pocket of his duster and removed a pair of heavy metal handcuffs, never once lowering his gun. "Little lady, would you do the honors?"

Anna looked from the handcuffs to Jake, then across to Morgan. He was Alastair's friend, a fellow time traveler, and a wanted bandit known as the Hawk. This was totally unreal. It should not be happening. Yet, what had been real in her life since the fateful day she first went back in time?

"I can't do it," she said, shaking her head. How could she turn on Morgan when in truth he had tried to save her from Emil? Of course tying her to the bed and gagging her was uncalled for, but he said he'd had enough of her sassing and he had to be able to think.

Jake raised his eyebrows doubtfully. Stepping forward he quickly clasped the cuffs about Morgan's wrists. "Done."

"Are you letting him take me, Anna? Just like that?" Morgan's gaze pleaded with her, an expression of disbelief on his picture-perfect face. "I haven't hurt you, dammit! Tell him! Tell him the truth, Anna!"

Anna grasped Jake's arm. "Jake! He isn't who—"

She got no further in her plea. A sudden commotion erupted outside the cabin. She heard a familiar voice shouting through the rain pattering noisily upon the roof.

"Blast it all, ye lousy bugger! This had best be the right place this time or 'tis to the cook ye will be going, if there is anything left o' ye when I'm through."

Emil stumbled into the cabin, dripping wet. He slid across the bare wood floor and landed beside the table where the dead man lay crumpled on the other side.

"Gonzalo! *Amigo?*" Emil grabbed for the dead man's gun. Before anyone could stop him, he rolled over and got to his knees, aiming directly at Morgan. "Hawk! You *bastardo!*" He screamed in anguish, firing a round of bullets.

Hawk caught one bullet in the side and crumpled to the floor.

Jake pushed Anna down, landing ungraciously on top of her. He heard the "oof" as his weight knocked the breath from her lungs, but knew she was safe beneath him. His body would be her shield. Quickly changing positions, he returned gunfire into the outer room. An accurate single shot winged the Spaniard. He stumbled forward, turned and ran from the cabin, right smack into two brawny men entering the door.

James felt his already drawn dirk puncture Emil's abdomen and noticed the surprised expression cross the robber's face. He deliberately placed his foot in Emil's path. The ruthless killer's cheek hit the porch and the hard wood planks put him out of his misery.

"He'll not be a bother for a wee bit, I am thinking." Jock pushed the limp figure aside on the porch, but kept his dirk ready in case there was more trouble ahead.

James moved quickly, albeit cautiously, into the cabin. He glanced about for any more assailants and finding none, strode directly into the bedroom. Anna sat in the middle of the floor, hugging a dark-haired man. A few feet away lay another man's body.

"Do ye not need rescuing after all, lass?" James leaned against the doorframe, replacing his dirk in its sheath. A smile that belied his true emotions stole across his face. "Who is this ye are holding?"

Jake jumped to his feet, quickly aiming his handgun at the captain. "May I ask who you are, sir?"

"James! I'm so glad you're all right!" Anna struggled to her feet and ran to him. She hugged him and smiled. "It's okay, Jake. I know this man."

Jake slipped his gun into its holster. "If you say so, Anna."

"Aye, she knows me well." James glared at the tall gunslinger. "Jake, eh? Ye wouldn't be the Jake on the stage?"

Jake frowned back at him. "As a matter of fact...I am."

Anna stepped between them. "James, I would like you to meet the man who saved my life. This is Jake Hardwick. Jake, this is James Duncan."

Jake held out his hand. "I've heard of you. You captain the logging schooner that docks often in Mendocino?"

"Aye. I do." James shook his hand, albeit begrudgingly. His scowl grew more ominous. "I thank ye for being so brave, lad. But I do not want ye around my woman."

Jake retrieved his damp hat, dusted his knees with it, and then settled it back on his head. "I understand. Anna...I'll just be on my way now."

"Jake, please don't go." She turned to James. "Why can't you be nice? He's a good man and a lawman. He didn't have to rescue me, but he did. I owe him for what he has done here. He saved me from two really terrible men."

"Aye. I suppose ye are right, lass." James picked up the fallen shirt from the floor and laid it across Anna's shoulders.

Her mind shifted to the shoot-out moments before. "Morgan? Is he okay too?" She attempted to peek around Jake, but was held back by James.

"Ye will not wish to look, Anna. 'Tis not a fit sight to see."

The reality of what had just occurred hit her hard. A shiver of revulsion settled deep in her stomach. Her heart lurched and goose bumps broke out on her skin. Drawn from one bad scene to another, she was trapped in a timeless novel with no control of how the story would unfold.

"Is Morgan dead?" She really didn't want to know. She just wanted to escape this madness as quickly as possible. The room was closing in on her and she couldn't breathe.

Jake's eyes met hers. "Saves me the trouble of taking him alive, Anna. But I still have to show his body to the sheriff in Gualala."

The old west was unpredictable and a little too wild. A wave of nausea rolled upwards from her stomach and she pushed past both men, running smack into Jock as he entered the room.

"Sorry, lass!" Jock boomed.

Not bothering to stop, Anna flew past him and out the cabin door. She stopped at the rail and emptied her stomach's meager contents into the thick bushes beside the porch. She groaned while hot uncontrollable tears burst from her eyes in a torrent of agony. She stepped off the porch into the cool summer rain, closed her eyes and let the drops beat a rhythmic pattern upon her hot upturned face.

Anna listened absently to the deep voices of James, Jock and Jake inside the cabin as they discussed the night's events. Strong arms wrapped around her from behind. Foul breath was a sure give away for who her predator was. Terror seeped into her heart.

"All right, *belleza*, you come with Emil. No games." The Spanish bandit's grip tightened unmercifully, until she nodded her head in silent agreement. He backed her away from the cabin and into the darkness.

"Emil, please, let me go," she whispered. "Hawk didn't kill your friend. He tripped and fell. He came in and started arguing with Hawk, but he'd been drinking and was unsteady. It was an accident...honest! Ouch!"

Anna shut up when Emil gave her a nasty bite on her shoulder. The heartless bastard didn't care about his dead friend. He only wanted revenge. She shivered as they staggered across the clearing and into the woods. Jake's shirt was all she had to cover her nearly naked body, and she never even had the chance to button the shirt over her bathing suit.

Seventeen

"Anna!" James' voice echoed into the night's eerie shadows. "Sweet Neptune, lass! Where are ye?"

Jock grunted a husky curse as he struggled past the captain with the dead Spaniard over his shoulder. "Did ye move the other one then, Capt'n?"

James swung around, his quick mind grasping at the unreality of it all happening again. "Did ye not move him yerself?"

"Nay, I was helping Jake with the body inside."

"Anna!" James pounded his fist into the log post. A violent string of Gaelic curses streamed from his mouth. "Och, that bloody Spaniard has taken her! I feel it in my heart. I left the man for dead and should o' made sure o' it."

Jock dropped his heavy burden on the porch. "Ye mean to say Emil has Anna?"

"Aye, I believe he does at that." James stomped back inside the cabin. "Jake, did ye say Emil was the one to shoot ye on the stagecoach?"

"He was." Jake stood over Hawk's blanket-wrapped body. "He killed a male passenger too, and I know of a few others. Why?"

"The ornery bastard has Anna. I'll not let the man live this time." James pulled his gun from its holster. "Tis not my wish to use violence. 'Tis far too easy to kill a man. Aye, even a man like Red Angus, though I cannot say he did not deserve to die."

Jock came up behind James. "Aye, and ye would not be here this day if ye had let the dirty bugger live. Now let's not talk o' the past, what can we do about Anna?"

"We find her, Jock. No matter what it takes, we find her."

~ * ~

Wild undergrowth tugged at Anna's bare legs, threatening to trip her as she struggled to free her aching wrist from Emil's iron grip. Unrelenting, he continued to drag her farther into the forest wilderness. He was not only a drunk, he was ruthless, and he was a murderer.

A sudden sob escaped her dry lips. She was frightened deep down in her soul. James and Jake were sure to come to her rescue, but would she still be alive when they found her? Her ribs ached from panting. It was becoming increasingly difficult to breathe. Her once smooth skin burned everywhere from cuts and scrapes. Her tired legs were sure to give out at any moment.

Anna did not know where they were headed, or what would happen to her when they got there. There was no one to protect her from this evil man. No one.

She tripped over something in the dark and fell flat on her face, knocking the wind from her aching lungs. Mud and pine needles stuck to her torn skin. Blood oozed into her mouth from a cut on her lip. She spit and wiped her hand across her face.

A drizzle of rain trickled noisily through the dense pines, saturating the forest floor. The moisture soothed her and washed the mud from her skin. She blinked and wondered if she had passed out. Struggling to her feet, she realized her hands were free. She glanced about and couldn't see Emil anywhere. Her chances of escape were increasing.

Emil grasped her long hair and yanked her viciously backwards. "Come, *zorra*."

Anna refused to whimper. She wouldn't give him the satisfaction of knowing he had hurt her again. Tears filled her eyes and pain racked her body as she turned obediently to follow the Spaniard's lead.

~ * ~

Mounting their horses, James watched his second mate ride away from the desolate cabin and into the darkness. Jock headed toward the *Ceilidh* in Gualala Bay. He would find William and alert him to what had happened. Jock promised to wait for word from James, before gathering the crew to form a search party.

Turning in the saddle, James eyed Jake. "What's yer plan?"

Jake coughed. The damn summer fog had a way of irritating his lungs and the cool mountain air didn't help any either. When the sudden attack was over, his eyes watered from the stress. He smiled half-heartedly at the captain. Tired as he was and as long as he had been on the trail, nothing would keep him from finding Anna.

"I grew up in these hills," Jake said softly. "I know my way around the redwoods pretty darn well. There's one place I think an outlaw like Emil would hideout. The only tracks I can find lead in that particular direction, too. It's a long shot, but what choice do we have?"

James nodded in agreement. "Let's be going then."

Jake paused, as though something troubled him. "James, I want you to know I have been a gentleman with Anna. I won't say I'm not interested, because you would know it is a lie. Hell, she's just about the prettiest, most entertaining female I've ever come across."

"Aye, that she is," James agreed, reaching out to shake the young gunslinger's hand. "Ye saved her life, Jake. I must thank ye proper for watching out for her."

The two men stared at one another for a quiet moment. A silent bond grew between them. Their fair minds and strong hearts were a mutual trait. Their shared effort in rescuing Anna from the deadly Spaniard drew them together in comradeship.

Jake turned his horse around and James followed, heading into the dense black forest. Giant redwood trees kept the downpour from soaking them, and though they were damp and weary, neither man wanted to stop the search. Pure physical endurance kept them motivated and both remained hopeful they would find Anna alive.

James did not understand how Jake knew where to search. Everything looked the same. In the logging camps, if one came across a clearing of trees that had been felled, each logger had their mark to tell exactly who and where they were. Here, it was all virgin forest.

The rain slowed to a drizzly mist, but it was enough to hamper their rescue effort. James felt the strain of being in the saddle for so long. He was cold, wet and tired to the bone. Still, he was determined to find Anna, no matter how exhausted he became. He recalled another time when he had become so weary and yet his hatred for another human being kept him going.

James had sought revenge on Red Angus and, given the opportunity, he had ended the evil man's time on earth. Regret was not an emotion James entertained. The pirate had it coming for killing the innocent and ravaging his forefather's land. Anna did not know of this gruesome tale and he rued the day when he would have to share it. There were times when pride was an awful thing.

James studied Jake's back as he rode tall in the saddle a wee bit ahead. Now there was a man who could be proud of his profession. Jake would defend truth and the innocent, even when his own life was at risk. He respected the man. When Jake's horse suddenly slowed to a stop beneath the broad branches of a towering pine, James became concerned. He dug his heels into his horse's sides to catch up.

"Jake? Are ye all right, lad?"

No answer. The confident Wells Fargo agent slumped forward in his saddle. James pulled his horse alongside and grasped the dangling reins. Jake sat fast asleep. A deep snore escaped him, proving his lack of resistance to his body's call for rest.

"Well, ye ornery young cuss. Even the likes o' ye can be bested. Sure and we won't find Anna asleep on our feet." He needed rest as much as Jake, and he prayed the wounded Emil would need to rest as well.

James dismounted and lowered Jake from his horse. He pulled his companion's soundly sleeping form over to rest against the base of a giant redwood. The tree's trunk was as big around as the cabin they had left earlier. Large fragrant pine needles kept the ground dry and provided a thick cushion with multiple layers. James tied the horses to a nearby branch, threw a saddle blanket over Jake and grabbed one for himself before settling down to rest.

He tried thinking about something to curb his impatience over the delay in finding Anna. His thoughts drifted back to the scene they had come upon at the cabin and how it had played itself out. Would he ever have peace with Anna? It seemed she was set on disrupting his life, forcing him to chart a different course.

So much was already changing in his established way of living. Anna was a gift from another time. He was a Scotsman, and he would see this adventure through to the finish. Even if she did alter his lifestyle, she was well worth the change.

Glancing over at Jake, who still slept soundly, James admired the man's determination to solve another's problems. He imagined the poor bloke had been awake for days on end, tracking the men who had kidnapped Anna and stolen the gold shipment. When Jake admitted his attraction to Anna, James' temper had flared, but he knew Jake was a good man and proving himself a worthy friend—if he would only waken.

James cursed under his breath as the moments crawled by and Anna's fate remained unknown. How many seconds were there in eternity?

~ * ~

Emil pushed Anna down to her knees and forcefully shoved her through the large opening in a huge redwood's hollow trunk. "Quiet now, *señorita*, or I will have to slit your pretty little throat."

287

Anna used her hands to feel about the shadowy interior, careful she didn't settle on something alive. Emil crawled into the dry space behind her and squatted on the hard ground. She scooted over and rubbed her cold fingers against her bare legs in a feeble attempt to warm them. At least the ground was dry inside the trunk.

The rain had stopped a while ago, leaving Jake's damp shirt clinging to her shivering body. She never realized how dark the forest could be at night. She almost laughed, thinking how nice a halogen lamp would be about now.

Glancing in the direction of her violent captor, she could barely make out his form. She could smell and hear his ragged breathing, and knew he must be in pain. He was just crazy enough to torture, rape, or kill her, or all three, if he wanted. Check that. He was already torturing her.

Anna swallowed hard and tried not to tremble. She would never live to see another dawn, let alone James. Her heart lurched at the thought. Whatever happened to living happily ever after?

Something crawled across her hand and she bit her tongue to keep from screaming. "There's—there's something in here."

"A few bugs maybe." Emil grunted, and then moved closer. "Give me your shirt." He groped for the fabric, ripping it in his haste to remove it from her shoulders.

"No. Stop it! What are—" She shrugged out of the torn remains, wishing she could throw the shirt in his ugly face. "Just take the stupid thing!"

Emil turned away from her with an anguished groan. He left her alone after that and she wondered what he was doing. She heard him groan again, a more pathetic, injured cry this time. He was hurt badly and probably bleeding a lot, too. Maybe that was the reason he had taken her shirt.

Her idle mind spun tales of escape. If he was really weakening, she could most likely get away from him soon. All she had to do was get him to talk, so she could tell exactly where he was, and then use a self-defense move to disable him. That would give her a chance to run.

"Emil?" She waited a few minutes for his response. "Emil? Are you okay?"

Had he passed out? She listened for what seemed like an eternity. Not a peep. Maybe he had fallen unconscious and saved her the work of knocking him out. Ever so quietly, she made her move toward the opening, dimly outlined by the stormy night sky. Her ears caught a strange sound echoing through the forest, a large dog howling. Hopefully, it was a rescue dog trying to find her. If she ran now it might be even longer before she was found.

Best to stay put, she decided. Let them find her, and the nasty thieving Spaniard. She leaned her head back against the ancient tree with a weary sigh and settled in to wait.

~ * ~

Jake led the way deeper into the forest. He was ashamed that he had fallen asleep, but he had been awake for nearly three days tracking the highway robbers. It all paid off when he caught up with them and found Anna. He had to smile when he recalled exactly how he found her in a state of undress. His thoughts darkened. She was not his to appreciate for she was betrothed to another. Yet, James did not appear upset with him any longer. Thank God! He chuckled as he remembered the interesting stories he had heard in local saloons about hot-tempered Scots and their love of a good fight. He was glad it had not come to that, given the captain's reputation.

Dawn was close to breaking when Jake heard something in the distance. He reined in his horse on the small trail they had been following for the past few miles. What was that? The eerie call of the wild carried on the wind. Wolves—howling wolves.

Jake cursed and turned in the saddle. "Wolves!"

"God's teeth!" Pure fury ignited James' temper like dynamite.

"Where's Anna?"

"Not far, I'm sure. Come on!" Jake dismounted, leaving his horse's reins dangling. "We can be faster on foot!"

James jumped off his horse in a blink of an eye. He shot through the woods as though his trousers were aflame and his quest was ice-cold river water. Passing Jake in a flash, he fired his gun into the air. He was completely horrified at what he saw up ahead.

~ * ~

Startled from an exhausted sleep, Anna opened her tired eyes. It wasn't a dream. She must have fallen asleep, but for how long? She could no longer hear Emil's ragged breathing. Feeling the ground cautiously to her left, she came across his damp arm. He was stiff and cold.

"Emil?" Her voice cracked with denial. "Emil, wake up!"

Wind whistled through the pungent smelling pines, distracting her for a moment. The sky was beginning to lighten and she could make out the shapes of things around her. Listening carefully to every little noise, she knew there was a wild animal scratching at the damp ground nearby.

Suddenly, she heard a deep snarling growl. The noise increased in volume until it drowned out everything else, paws digging in the dirt nearby, several big paws. Rescue dogs? She choked on a laugh, nearly hysterical with relief. It was only the rescue dogs!

Oh dear God, no, not dogs! Wolves! Sniffing, scratching, and howling wolves. Panic hit her insides with mega doses of nausea. A low snarl vibrated from a shadowy form crouching near the entrance to her hide-away. She covered her mouth before she could scream. Staring right at her were the large glistening eyes of a huge gray wolf.

Anna dared not move a muscle. Maybe the animal would go away. She took slow deep breaths, in and out, in and out. Her heartbeat raced erratically with fear. The wolf sniffed cautiously, and then threw its head back in another long eerie howl.

She closed her eyes, squeezing them tight, and tried not to panic. She had lived through a mugging in the big city, hadn't she? She had walked the wild streets of San Francisco at night and survived to remember it. More than once in her life, she had faced death. Yet here she was—lost in the middle of nowhere—with a stinky dead body lying next to her. She was hiding out in a two hundred-year-old, rotting tree, slowly freezing to death in a bikini, and about to be completely devoured by a fierce and rabid creature of the wilderness. Her eyes remained firmly shut, so she wouldn't know when the end came. Oh, where was James?

A deep threatening growl—so close! Her eyes flew open wide, then closed again just as quickly. Bristly wet fur brushed along her cheek and it was all she could do not to scream. The carnivorous mammal was standing half inside the opening, its breath tickling her tepid flesh. Yet, the beast did not attack.

What in the world? She wanted to peek, but was too darned scared.

The wolf licked and chewed at something beside her. Oh God, the dead Spaniard! At least, she hoped he was dead or he was in deep trouble. She fought to hold back a whimper. Don't panic! Emil's fresh blood had drawn the wolf, like the determined shark in *JAWS*. Scenes from horror movies ran rampantly through her mind. If she survived this one, she would never ever read another horror book.

Her stomach rumbled with nausea. She had to escape before the wolf turned on her. Maybe if she could kick Emil's body away the wolf would take it and leave. Letting the wolf eat a dead man was bad enough even though he was a very evil and very smelly dead man. But to sit still and listen—

Anna heard human noises in answer to her fervent prayers. Loud shouts and a primeval scream echoed through the woods. Someone was coming and they were getting closer with every passing second. She could hear them crashing through low branches, their boots stomping over the crunchy needle-laden ground.

Pre-dawn light illumined the scene before her. She could see the lead wolf turn toward the swarming pack that hovered nearby, anxiously awaiting their turn. Lifting its bloodied nose to the wind, the wolf growled viciously. Sharp bestial teeth glistened as the wolf turned toward her. Gunfire echoed in the woods. The wolves paced the forest floor nervously, but still did not leave their easy prey. More shouts and gunshots as Anna heard her name over the din. James! James had come at last!

Biting the back of her hand, the pent up emotions within her shattered and she began to cry. Big tears formed in her eyes when she heard the wolves' retreat. Heavy footsteps rushed toward her hiding place. Strong arms reached in to pull her from the dark hole. She sobbed, and then laughed hysterically. She couldn't stop, not even when her chilled, body pressed into James' warm and loving embrace.

"Anna, 'tis all right ye are, lass. Ye are safe now. I'll not let ye go again," James whispered, tenderly wrapping his tartan around her.

She snuggled against his chest, her sobs changing to hiccups. His virile strength calmed her as nothing else could and she drifted off into an exhausted sleep.

~ * ~

Anna screamed and sat upright in the bed. Her breath came in ragged gasps. James was at her side, lovingly brushing her hair back from her face with his large rough hands. A sensation of peace drifted over her, calming her tormenting fears.

"Tis a bad dream, lass. Naught but a bad dream."

Anna blinked several times, taking in the bright daylight. A small unfamiliar bedroom came slowly into focus. "Where are we?"

"Jake's home was much closer than the ship or town, and ye needed a bit o' rest." James hugged her tenderly and pulled the covers up around her shoulders.

"Oh, my gosh! I'm still in 1880. Did it really happen with the wolves...and Morgan...and..."

"Ye will not be worrying about what happened," James ordered, touching the tip of her pert nose with his forefinger. "Doc said ye are to rest." He kissed her forehead lightly and gazed down at her.

Her heart melted at the comforting sight of him. "James?"

"Aye, lass?"

"I'm sorry for causing you all this trouble."

He groaned and bent over her. His lips met hers and sweetly caressed them. "Tis not been a moment o' trouble."

"Liar."

James pretended to appear shocked, then burst into robust laughter. "I'll not be lying to ye, Anna. Trouble is yer middle name, but I doubt 'twill ever be much different and I love ye just the same."

She smiled. "I love you too, James."

The small ranch house was quiet except for Jake banging around in the kitchen, occasionally releasing a curse or two. James' stomach growled reminding him it was about dinnertime. He had tasted worse cooking than Jake's. He just could not recall when. He was spoiled by Cookie, who claimed to be the best cook west of Texas and his delicious meals testified to the fact.

Anna gazed up at him dreamy-eyed. "A penny for your thoughts, James."

"Hmmm?" He had not been thinking of anything but her for days now.

The first time his thoughts stray to food, she asks what he is thinking about. Wasn't that just like a woman? She looked totally exhausted and yet, he had never seen her look more beautiful. "Ye never finished telling me about yer husband."

She laughed sweetly. "Oh, James. He doesn't even matter to me anymore. I only want you."

"But ye married the man, Anna. How can I marry ye if ye are already wed?"

"I divorced him—a long time ago. Divorce is quite common in the future." She touched her fingertips to his bewhiskered cheek. "You want to know if I loved him, don't you. Well, I thought I did then. I was young and on my own. He was the first man to really pay attention to me. He was handsome and he had oodles of charm. But I found out too late, he was much too charming."

"Do ye miss him?"

"Miss him? Dan deserted me, James. He went out with other women and left me sitting home alone. He wasn't a kind person. He lied most of the time. For a long time I thought all men would be the same, and so I hated them. Then I met you, my first real love. I promise I will go on loving you forever."

"I promise to try to be all ye expect me to be, but I am what I am, lass." He winked and flashed her a devilish grin. "Can ye live with that?"

Anna held out her arms. "Kiss me and I'm all yours." Not waiting for a response, she pulled him to her and met his hungry kiss with fiery passion.

~ * ~

Anna had forgotten how lovely the Stensons' home was even by Victorian standards. She marveled at the luscious surroundings as she soaked leisurely in the deep claw-footed bathtub. The wonderful scent of lavender filled the bathroom. Totally relaxing, she let her mind wander. A wide Cheshire cat grin spread across her face as she visualized James in her mind. He was better than the best hero in any book—and he was all hers.

A tap at the outer door to her suite startled her. "Come in!" She hoped whoever it was could hear her. She sank lower into the warm scented bubbles to hide her scratched and beaten body.

Rosie's kind face peeked around the bathroom door. "It's true, you really is back." She entered to hang fresh fluffy towels on the wooden rack beside the tub. "They told me downstairs that you was back. Why'd you leave anyhow? You 'bout worried your poor young man sick. I heard all about the wolves and robbers too. Land sake's girl, it's a wonder you alive!"

"I wasn't sure I would survive it either. It was horrible!" Anna grimaced.

Rosie clucked her tongue and smiled. "But we're sure glad you is!"

Smiling at the older woman's bold inquisitiveness, Anna tried to explain why she had lied before. "There was something I had to do, Rosie. I had to find out for myself about my heritage."

"And did you find out what you wanted to know?"

"I did, yes. I know where I belong and to whom. I never would have believed it had someone just told me the tale."

"Now that sounds mysterious. Nowadays you young ones always want to sound mysterious. Beats me why you can't all settle for the ordinary." She laughed. "Take old Rosie here…I'm just 'bout as ordinary as a gal can get. You don't hear me complaining none. I like who I am."

"I like who you are too, Rosie. And now I like myself. A darn sight more than I ever did before." She smiled and blew a bubble into the air. "And I am in l-o-v-e!"

"You don't say!" Rosie laughed and placed her work-roughened hands on her hips. "I think we best get you outta this here bath, so you can go tell your man just how much you're in l-o-v-e! Want me to wash your back, honey?"

Wash her back? Anna giggled. She almost gave in to being pampered. No, better not. Learning to get along in these pioneer times would be tough enough without succumbing to luxury. Pretending she was rich might be harmful to her future with James. He had nowhere near George's money. James didn't even have a decent home! Still, he couldn't live aboard his ship forever.

"No thank you, Rosie. I'll get a move on."

Rosie nodded as she picked up the clothes Anna had so carelessly tossed upon the floor. "All right then. Don't let me catch that young man of yours up here washing your back. It's just not proper."

Anna raised both eyebrows. "Rosie, he's my husband."

A deep amused laugh escaped Rosie as she turned around. "In a pig's eye, he is."

"We are handfasted, honest." Anna found herself totally embarrassed. "You know, the Highland way of marriage?

"Now honey, you shouldn't let your man confuse you like that. Marry him legal-like and become an honest woman."

"Rosie—" A familiar sound came from the next room. James was whistling a jaunty tune for the first time in days as he headed straight for the bathroom.

"Anna?"

"I'm in the bath, James." She gasped when he appeared in the doorway, a wide sensual grin enhancing his good looks.

Rosie swung quickly around and blocked the bathroom door. "Young man, you need to marry this girl and quit misbehaving. She has her reputation to consider." She turned James about-face, pushed him back out the door and shut it.

Anna stood up and grabbed a towel from the rack. Dripping wet with bubbles, she stepped out of the tub. "Rosie you do not understand—"

"Blast it all Rosie, let me in!" James beat on the other side of the thick oak door.

"I understand plenty, girl. You got a crush on that fella and he's taking advantage of you." Rosie helped Anna wrap the large bath towel tightly around her body. "Handfasted, indeed!"

"Anna? Ye best open this bloody door before I break it down and we have George up here to see what is happening. Do ye hear?" James beat his fist against the locked lavatory door a final time. "Rosie?"

Rosie opened the door a crack. "You may as well leave, Captain, until you're ready to do right by this girl. She has her future to worry about. Since she has no family to watch over her, I aim to do it."

James shook his head in disbelief. "Rosie, 'tis me, James. Ye have known me since I was a young lad and ye worked for my father."

"I know who you are, Captain. That's why I'm telling you what to do. Here you been single all these years, rutting around like a proud bull. Now you gone and found yourself a wonderful girl. It's time to settle in the right pasture, 'cause it ain't gonna be green forever, boy. If your papa was alive he'd have the belt after your hide, and well you know it too. Now git!"

"Och, I am not a wee *bairn*, Rosie. Ye cannot keep me from the woman I love. She is as much my wife as I am her husband."

Rosie turned to confirm what James had blatantly admitted. "That right, honey?"

Anna gulped. "Well—"

"Do you love him, girl?" Rosie inquired with matronly concern.

"More than I have ever loved anyone before." Anna was shy to admit what was in her heart, but she felt better in having said it.

"Ah, I thought so." Rosie peeked out the door just as James peeked in. "Now none of that. This here's to be a proper courtship from now on."

James cursed under his breath. "Are ye saying I cannot see Anna?"

"Not in her present condition. Now be a gentleman and leave so she can be dressed." The large black woman took his arm, hurried him across the bedroom and out into the hall. "You can see her at supper."

"Who have ye to thank for getting ye this comfy job, eh?"

Rosie patted him on the bottom like she had when he was a boy.

"Captain, you just about the kindest man I've ever known. But no matter how thankful I am for this job, you ain't coming in to see Miss Anna."

"Rosie," James begged, one last time.

"Leave your charming ways to your courtship, Captain. You only making waves here." Turning on her heel, she stepped back inside the room and closed the door in his face.

James did not wait to hear the click of the lock. He knew his old nanny too well. Feeling quite shot-down in his mood, he wandered downstairs to find George.

~ * ~

George sat in his study going over massive piles of paperwork. Dropping down into the leather armchair beside him, James released a final muttered curse. He could not understand why Rosie would champion Anna and turn against him. How in blazes did the old woman find out they were not legally man and wife?

"I am in need o' some advice, George."

George looked up and placed his writing quill in the inkpot. "I see you must have run up against Rosie. She's a stickler for propriety, that one. Marriage is special to her."

"Blast it all, George! How did she find out I was not married?" James rubbed his jaw thoughtfully. "Matter o' fact, how is it ye know as well?"

"Who knows you better than I?" George grinned. "I will never forget Rosie's face when she came in to tell me about it. I understand you talk in your sleep. Well, you must have mumbled a mouthful to old Rosie. She is determined to save both your souls." He laughed heartily and his boyish features reddened.

James frowned and kicked the toe of his shoe against the hardwood desk. "Ye should have warned me! 'Twas the least ye could have done. Now she will not let me see Anna without a chaperon."

George's smile broadened. "The answer is simple, James. Marry the girl. Anna is good for you." He stood with a stretch to his broad shoulders, crossed to the buffet and poured a glass of fine amber whiskey. Handing the glass to James, he returned and poured himself one. "Shall we drink a celebration toast to the engagement?"

"God's teeth! We're already handfasted, George. Ye know yerself 'tis as good a marriage as a piece o' paper will make it. We have pledged our troth to each other." He strangled the glass in his hand and restlessly paced the floor. It bothered him that their secret was well known. "Maybe 'tis for the best after all."

George raised his glass. "To Anna?"

"Oh, aye." James drained half his glass. A sudden horrible thought occurred to him and he lowered his drink. "Does Angel know?"

George smiled slyly and took a long sip of his drink before answering, "I'll leave that rewarding and rather humbling experience to you, partner."

"Ye wish to have me thoroughly shamed, George?" James swallowed the whiskey in one big gulp. "Angel will not understand. She will never let me be."

"Tell her she can plan the wedding, James," George suggested.

"Aye," James agreed wearily, giving in at last. Why should he fight something that would tie Anna to him in a legal way as well?

Eighteen

Early morning sunlight trickled through the lacy curtains as they blew gently into the room from a cool sea breeze. Anna lay comfortably in the large bed, buried under a pile of hand-sewn quilts. She had a few moments alone to think about all that had happened recently.

She shivered from the frightening memories, but she had to face them or have nightmares for the rest of her life. Had she returned to the past for the mere purpose of watching people get killed or eaten by starving wolves?

No, the answer was more complex. She just wanted a quick and easy answer. The emotional turmoil of her innermost thoughts had nearly driven her mad since her tumble into the past. James was the purpose for being called backwards in time. He was her destiny. Over the past two days, she had become hesitant to remain in the nineteenth-century where there were so many unfamiliar things.

She longed to touch her belongings and drive her beautiful midnight blue Camaro. Indulge in an icy cold Mountain Dew, or anything to feel a touch of reality again. How could she stay? How could she leave? If she could only persuade James to return to the future with her…no, he would never leave the past. He belonged in 1880. She yawned and pulled the covers up under her chin.

The bedroom door swung silently open. James entered on tiptoe, closing the door quietly behind him. He turned to see Anna sitting up against a multitude of pillows, a smile on her pretty face. She was the picture of seduction—exactly what he had in mind.

"Morning, lass. Has Rosie come in yet?"

Anna held out her arms. "No, but she'll have your skin if she finds you in here."

"Aye, she will," James said, reaching the bed in two long strides. He tossed back the covers, dropped his robe and climbed in beside her. "I had to see ye, Anna. She cannot come between us this way." Pulling the quilts up around them, he gathered her into his arms. "Ah, but ye smell so bonny."

She giggled. "So do you." Her eyes met his, their message perfectly clear. "I've missed you, James."

A low groan escaped him as his lips descended to meet hers. "I want to wed ye proper, Anna. We cannot put it off any longer. Ye may have a wee *bairn* growing within ye, and I want him to bear my name."

"Him?" Anna cocked a brow as she pushed him away.

"Aye. 'Tis well if ye bear a lassie, but 'tis a son I'll be needing to carry on the family name. And well ye know it."

"I'll do my best, James," she whispered.

"I know ye will, Anna. I know ye will." He chuckled and pulled her close. Collecting on this particular promise would be pure bliss.

~ * ~

James sat in the high-back chair feeling like a disobedient child. It was not that he had to tell the truth. He considered himself a truthful man, but telling the truth to Angel after his deceit would not be an easy task. His stomach went sour as his fingers nervously tapped out a dance on the chair's arm. Angelique had not spoken to him since he had made his announcement. Her face flushed pink and her features were perplexed. He was in for a good lecture any moment now. He wanted this moment in time to be over. Suffering a woman's wrath was not his fancy.

"Tell me I did not hear you correctly, James." Angelique continued to pace the parlor floor in front of him, her normally calm demeanor a bit on the shaky side. Dressed in a soft yellow gown she was the picture of perfection, but it did not make her any more desirable to deal with.

James frowned and rubbed his clean-shaven jaw. "Oh, aye. Ye heard me, Angel. We're not but handfasted."

She stopped in front of him, fury flaming in her violet eyes. "Handfasted? And what, may I ask, is handfasted?"

"Tis marriage." James silently cursed that coward George for disappearing when he could use his moral support. "Tis the Highland way. 'Tis binding in Scotland. My parents were handfasted. 'Tis all very legal, ye see."

"Yes, I see." Angelique shook her head. "No, I do not see. I do not understand at all. To be legally wed in this country you need to have a marriage ceremony performed by a preacher or a Justice of the Peace."

James flinched at her tone of voice. She studied the contents of the tall bookcases in momentary distraction. He waited for the explosion. Dear, sweet Angel. She tried not to show her outrage, or her shame at having housed what she considered "sinners" without morals.

Her face was composed when she finally turned around. "This is a very delicate situation, James. I suppose you have already...Ummm, well...have you?"

"If ye are asking could she be in the family-way, aye. She might be carrying our wee *bairn*."

"I see." Angelique clasped her hands together. "There is no other choice. This must be corrected immediately."

He gulped. "Corrected?"

"Why, by a proper marriage, James," she said succinctly. "You do want to do right by Anna, do you not?"

"Oh, aye. I love the lass."

"Good. I should be able to get Reverend Jones over here by this afternoon." She walked toward the door and paused, turning around on her heel. Her violet eyes flashed mischievously as they met with his. "You should be prepared, James. There is about to be a lovely wedding in our formal garden."

~ * ~

A bouquet of bright pink roses appeared in the bedroom's open door. Anna giggled and rushed across the room, forgetting in her haste it was considered naughty to be seen in only her chemise. She flung the door open and flew into his waiting embrace.

After a lengthy kiss, James handed her the roses and swept her up into his arms, kicking the door closed behind him. "Ah, I have missed ye, Anna."

"And I've missed you." She caught the look of love in his eyes. He made her feel treasured and heavenly in every way.

He dropped her playfully on the bed, took the roses from her and slipped them into a nearby empty vase. He arranged the flowers carefully while slipping seductive glimpses across at her. Completing his task, he crossed to the bed and slowly untied the strings of her lacy chemise.

The silky straps slipped off her shoulders to reveal the swell of her breasts. An emotional tempest flooded her senses as his lips floated light feathery kisses across her bare skin.

James gazed down upon her. "Anna, lass, I love ye more than life itself. I ache to drown in yer softness again."

"James..." Her whisper held a fever of desire. She pulled him down on top of her and kissed him. "I love you, too. You're so special. I don't know why I had to travel through time to find you. Why couldn't you have been the boy-next-door?"

"Eh? Ye are saying ye want a boy now and not a man?"

She giggled so loudly he quickly covered her mouth with his. The lengthy kiss left her lips tingling. "I want you, James, and you are every inch a wonderful man," she said, her gaze taking in all of him. "Should I prove it?"

A deep satisfied sigh escaped his throat as she rubbed that throbbing part of him. "Best we remove our clothes, Anna, or ye will have me in a mess."

Taking his words as a positive answer to her sudden need, she slipped his pant buttons one by one from their holes. Her fingertips lingered just long enough to tease.

"I have never seen a woman take so long," he whispered with a gasp, "...to relieve a man o' his clothes."

"You've never met a woman like me before." Anna looked into his sapphire blue eyes. "I'm a very passionate, very stubborn, and a very randy woman. I want you, James, and if we don't hurry Rosie will be in here with a broom."

James burst into laughter at her bold declaration. "Aye, that she will. I agree ye are passionate and aye, ye are very stubborn. But randy?"

Anna pushed against his chest until he slid off her, then she kneeled on the bed and shimmied out of her flimsy chemise. "Aye, James. Very randy."

He growled playfully and reached for her.

"Oh, no. Not until you're naked too." She moved just beyond his touch.

James jumped to his feet. His clothes dropped to the floor faster than she could pull down the bed's coverlet. He crawled slowly across to her like a lion on the prowl. "Will this be pleasing to ye?"

"Oh I think it might be just fine." Anna's heart leaped when he smiled. She loved his sexy smile. Her whole body ignited from his touch. She wrapped her arms around his neck, pulling him down to lie upon her. She ran her fingers through his hair and writhed impatiently beneath him.

"Ahh. 'Tis been—" his deep voice broke off as a shudder coursed through him.

"Too long?" Her hands wandered down to grasp his firm muscled buttocks. Her mouth sought his. Little nibbles and licks passed between them.

James paused in his kissing and held her face tenderly between his palms as he gazed down into her green eyes. "Aye, Anna, 'tis been far too long."

In one easy movement, he thrust himself fully within her. He held still and felt her quicken around him. He wanted to take things more slowly. He wanted to pleasure her as much as she pleasured him, but she was ready and his need was too great.

"I'm sorry, lass. I cannot wait any longer."

Anna closed her eyes, exhilarating in delightful little tingles echoing from deep within her body. She was almost there, trying to find that elusive point. If he moved at all, she would explode. God, but she wanted him to move—now!

James groaned as she shuddered in release, then with slow rhythmic movements he caressed her most feminine core. The moment she began her ascent for the second time, he made one final thrust and they met the stars in a heavenly climax together.

Panting softly, Anna regained her senses. "If you—were any better—a lover—"

"I cannot do it alone, m'dear." James kissed her moist brow, moving his lips in tiny kisses down to meet her waiting lips. A long silence fell as they breathlessly kissed until they gasped for air.

Anna sighed, a very contented sigh. "James? Are we sinful?"

He struggled to hold back a chuckle. "Tis handfasted we are, my love, and this wedding o' Angel's is only for the records. I want our children, and our children's children, to remember how much we love each other. We need no bit o' paper to bind our hearts for all time, and it would be a sin to deny our feelings for each other."

"Rosie said—"

James jerked into an upright position, sitting on the edge of the bed and running his fingers through his messed hair. "Sweet

Neptune! Rosie cannot live our lives for us. We are doing what is proper and she should not be meddling." He stood and stepped into his trousers, hastily buttoning them.

"Then why are you leaving me? Stay." Anna sat up, tugging the sheet with her.

James wrapped her into his embrace and kissed her swollen lips one more time. "I need to speak with Rosie."

"Ah-hum!" The low female voice grabbed their attention and they both turned around to see who had entered the bedroom.

"What you gonna speak to me about, Captain?" Rosie crossed the room toward them. "Seems you need another scolding. Now, what you doing in here?"

He held his temper and tried to remember how much she cared about his welfare, even though it drove him crazy. "Ye will only blush if I tell ye."

Rosie laughed and her whole plump body jiggled. "Blush? It's you that's standing there red as a fresh summer rose and with your trousers all done up wrong!"

James glanced down and immediately remedied the situation. He ran his fingers idly through his hair. "Rosie—"

"Ah, you two don't fool old Rosie. I remember what it's like to be in love. I just want you to do it right." She wiped happy tears from her dark eyes, smiling all the while. "Now, shoo! You're supposed to be downstairs in an hour. The preacher is already here and we're gonna have us a fine wedding!"

James winked at Anna and grabbed up the remainder of his clothes. He headed for the door, pausing to take a final glimpse of his bride-to-be, clutching the top sheet to her breasts in mock modesty. With a wink in her direction he left the bedroom, ultimately satisfied that soon she would be his to love and to cherish for all time. Nothing would keep them apart.

~ * ~

Sunshine filtered through the mimosa trees, tracing delicate patterns upon the gray gazebo floor. Reverend Jones sat on a cushioned wicker loveseat, patiently listening to Angelique's excited chatter. Guests wandered about the rose garden in idle conversation. All awaited the bride's arrival.

James stood by the balustrade, dressed in Clan Duncan's blue and green tartan kilt. The voluminous sleeves of his white shirt ruffled in the wind. He wore his plaid bonnet cocked to the side. A large brooch emblazoned with a ship under full sail held a length of tartan securely to his left shoulder. His fur sporran hung from a wide belt at his waist and a small dirk tucked neatly into his long, plaid stockings. His black-velvet jacket lay over the rail, for the afternoon was warm. He stared out over the bluff and down to the sea, pondering the turn of events.

George stepped up beside him. His attire was a well-tailored black suit and top hat. "It's a beautiful day."

"Aye," James agreed.

George stared seaward and adjusted his bow tie. "The wind is behaving for once."

"Aye."

"It's a great day for sailing." George sighed dramatically.

James eyed his friend with suspicion. "Are ye by chance trying to get my mind off things to come, George?"

The husky lumber baron chuckled. "Ah, you know me too well, James. I thought perhaps you might want to talk about your honeymoon plans."

"We set sail for the Sandwich Islands at dusk." James stared back out to sea, his thoughts drifting to business. "I plan to look into the lumber trade while there, just to see if our colleague is doing his job. We've not had as many orders from the islands, as I believe we should."

"Kapoho is a loyal subject of his majesty King Kalakaua. He would not aim to purposely cut our trade." George glanced behind them at a sudden commotion in the garden below. "What's this?"

James turned around too, and blinked several times in awe. Dressed in Angelique's frivolous, but very beautiful, white silk wedding gown, Anna stood bent over, fussing with the long train on her dress.

"Wait, Anna. You will tear it!" Angelique rushed down the gazebo steps in a flurry of pink satin to release the dress' train from where it had caught on a blossoming rosebush. She continued to fuss with the long ribbons and flowers in Anna's hair, rearranging them to her satisfaction.

Reverend Jones took advantage of his freedom and moved over by James and George. "Mrs. Stenson is a lovely lady, but quite a conversationalist. Don't you agree?"

George chuckled. "It is her one and only fault."

Reverend Jones smiled. "She is pleased about this wedding."

"So am I," George said with a twinkle in his eye. He turned and nudged James' arm. "I would say it's time, my friend. Your lovely bride has arrived."

James swallowed hard. Anna took his breath away. Covered in lace and pearls, she virtually shimmered in the afternoon sunlight. Her golden hair swept back from her face with little wispy tendrils curling around her cheeks. Delicate pink and white rosebuds entwined with greenery circled her head like a halo, and long soft curls tumbled down her back with slender pink ribbons. His heart skipped a beat. He could not respond to George, though he heard him speaking.

Anna looked up at that moment. A sweet smile danced beneath her rosy cheeks. She waved her bouquet of pink roses high in the air and giggled as she moved toward the gazebo, careful not to catch her gown on any more thorns. The wedding guests grew silent as she passed.

James stood waiting by the altar as she walked up the brick path. Beside him, the reverend cleared his throat and opened his prayer book. James tugged anxiously at his sleeves and carefully smoothed his tartan. He had never felt so impatient.

Jock began playing the wedding march on his bagpipes. George hurried to Anna's side and held out his arm for her. The two walked slowly up the wide gazebo steps in time to the music. George bowed deeply to Anna and took his place beside James as the best man. Angelique moved quietly to stand beside Anna as her matron of honor.

Anna smiled nervously at Angelique, and then reached over to grasp James' hand. He was trembling, too! He was as nervous as she was and somehow it made her feel better. She shivered as a zillion last minute thoughts skipped through her mind. This is it, the real thing. It's too late to back out, too late to run away. What was she thinking? She didn't want to leave James. She was in love for the first time in her life and this is what she wanted more than anything. Now she knew what people meant by the bride getting last minute jitters. Did James feel jittery too?

Her eyes met his and they stared into each other's souls. The time had come to state their vows before God, the reverend, and their closest friends. She turned to look up at Reverend Jones as he slipped a finger in his starched collar to loosen it. The afternoon was quite warm for June, but she had never felt more radiant.

"Dearly beloved, we are gathered here today..." Reverend Jones' deep soothing voice humbly began reciting the marriage ceremony.

Anna knew in her heart this was why she had been sent back in time. She had no regrets. Alastair would take care of things. Her employer might wonder where she had disappeared to, but there were a thousand more eager writers to take her place. The goofy attorney would probably never step foot in the old house on Duncan's Point again. Alastair would be free to claim what was rightfully his. She smiled. Haunted, indeed! How did James do that?

James was about to abandon ship, meaning his old lifestyle. No more careless carousing and no more long ocean voyages, unless he took Anna with him. He planned to have a close, loving relationship. He never wanted her out of his sight again. He recalled the first time he saw her floating above him in his dreams as she comforted his troubled mind. He almost chuckled aloud. How did Anna do that?

Their eyes met and held. James squeezed her hand tenderly. Anna smiled and nodded. However their lives had become crossed, it was their choice to remain together. It was the true mystery of love.

"Do you, Captain James Adam Duncan, take your betrothed, Anna Bentley, as your lawfully wedded wife, to have and to hold, both in sickness and in health, for richer or for poorer, from this day forward, until forever and a day?"

James' gaze searched her face as he listened to the promise. "Aye, I do," he answered in a husky voice.

"Do you, Anna Bentley, take Captain James Adam Duncan as your lawfully wedded husband, to have and to hold, both in sickness and in health, for richer or for poorer, from this day forward, until forever and a day?"

Anna looked up at James with dreamy eyes full of love. "I do."

James barely heard the reverend as he bespoke them husband and wife. He swept Anna into his embrace and kissed her passionately. Tears filled his eyes his love for her was so grand. They separated and he held her at arm's length. Her eyes filled with tears, too. They both laughed and hugged each other.

Reverend Jones cleared his throat. "James, you may present your bride with the wedding ring as a token of your sincere intentions."

James turned to George who handed him a plain gold band. He took the small circle of gold into his big fingers and accepted Anna's upraised hand. Looking deep into her eyes, he carefully slipped the ring into place. He sighed as her tear-filled eyes glanced down at the gold band on her finger and back up to meet his gaze. She did not even have to speak for the love he saw within her eyes.

Anna reached her hand up and placed it on James' cheek. "I love you, James."

His heart soared and his vision blurred with tears. "And I love you, Anna."

Anna moved into his arms for another heavenly kiss. She couldn't remember ever being so happy. She did not want the moment to end. It was pure magic. When he released her, they stared at each other, not wanting to move apart. For a wonderful few moments in time there was only the two of them, their hearts and souls blending as one.

"Great job, James! You've got yourself a wonderful girl." George's congratulations broke the magical spell between them.

Angelique hugged her. "Congratulations!"

"Thank-you. Thank you for allowing me to use your beautiful gown too." Anna reached across to hug George. "Thank you, for everything."

George blushed. "I didn't do a thing, but you have done wonders with my friend. Thank you for saving his life, dearest Anna."

"Congratulations, James." Angelique kissed his cheek. "You take good care of her—or I will never forgive you."

"Aye, Angel. I will." James heard George chuckle in amusement beside him. He took Anna's arm and led her down the gazebo steps into the waiting crowd.

Rosie was first to approach the newlyweds. "You two young people have made old Rosie proud. I wish you the best—always. I'll be waiting in the suite to help you out of your gown, Mrs. Duncan." She hugged each of them in turn, and then hurried off in tearful happiness.

"We're wed, lass," James whispered, a kiss away from Anna's lips. He led them toward the house, so Anna could change into her traveling clothes before the short reception with their guests. "I can hardly wait to get ye alone."

"And I can hardly wait to get you alone, Captain," Anna countered, laughing when he raised his eyebrows. Deep in her heart of hearts this was the man she had waited to meet all her life. She could not wait to begin their journey together.

Nineteen

Angelique stood beside George on the rose garden terrace, waiting for the bride and groom to reappear. "Here they come!" Her excited squeal carried across the lawn to all the guests. "May we present Captain and Mrs. James Duncan!"

Angelique quickly led Anna off to meet a few of her closest friends. James glanced around the crowd, amazed at how many people Angelique had been able to contact in a few hours. She must have had every lad in the stables riding all over Mendocino!

Many of his friends and associates were present. Crewmembers from the *Ceilidh* wandered about, doing their best not to pick fights with men from the logging camp. The loggers in turn cooperated by showing their best town manners. He wondered just how long the peaceful scene would last. Far too much temptation not to enjoy themselves, James mused with a chuckle.

Jock rushed forward and grabbed him in an old-fashioned bear hug. "Ye really did it, aye? Ye made Anna an honest woman. I'm proud o' ye, old man." His hardy clap on the back nearly took the captain's breath away.

"Aye, Jock, 'tis done proper." James beamed with pride. "Thank ye for playing the bagpipes, as well. 'Twas grand."

"Och, I am not very good at the pipes, but anything to see the two o' ye be wed. 'Tis what ye both needed, a proper marriage."

"The American way!" Cookie chimed in as he joined them. "You had to be hornswoggled and nearly hog-tied, boy, but you've made us all proud!"

Cheers went up from the robust men gathering around James. Servants passed around fine-stemmed glasses filled with bubbly champagne and shot glasses filled with the best Scotch whiskey. Toasts were made, one after another, and glasses were kept full. James glanced around at all the smiling faces. It did not matter how much the loggers drank to his happiness, but he wondered how much drink his crew could consume and still safely navigate the ship at sea. They would be setting sail at dusk. That thought had him wondering where his bride had gone.

He espied Anna sitting in the gazebo, surrounded by muscle-bound men. His anger flared when he recognized Michael Burns. Striding across the garden, he arrived in time to hear Anna laugh over something Michael had said.

"Good to see ye, Michael." James swore to himself he would keep his temper in check for Anna's sake. "Good that ye could come to our wedding."

"Congratulations, Jamie," Michael said in greeting, before turning back to face Anna. "Should I tell him?"

Anna smiled, stood up from the wicker chair and looped her arm through her new husband's arm. "Yes. I think it should come from you."

Michael faced James, his big hands on his hips. "I never really wanted to take Anna from you, Jamie. If I did, the law would lock me up for bigamy." He laughed heartily. "That is, if my father-in-law did not hang me from a giant redwood first!"

James eyed him carefully. He could not believe his ears. Michael is married? That was the best news he had heard in a long time! His face broke into a broad grin. "Ye old son o' a sea fox! When?"

"When you were out to sea the last time. I should have told you the day you arrived at camp, but I could see there was tension between you and Anna. At the same time, I could tell you were in love. So I decided to give you a little shove in the right direction." Michael held out his hand. "Still friends?"

James shook his hand. "Ye know me well, Michael. Aye, we are still friends." He rubbed his chin thoughtfully. "Besides, I cannot lose my best fighting partner, now can I?"

"Actually, James, Michael has promised not to fight you again." Anna gazed up at him with her sea green eyes flashing fire. "I told him you would be far too busy loving me to fight him anyway."

"Och! Ye did, did ye? Ye sassy little minx!" James grabbed Anna around the waist and drew her close to him. His love for her overflowed as he held up his glass and made a toast. "Thanks be to Father Time for my bonny bride!"

A servant arrived with a tray of drinks, serving all that stood gathered in the gazebo. The brawny lumberjacks raised their glasses high. "To Father Time!"

Jake Hardwick stood a few feet away with a full glass of champagne in his hand. He did not drink a drop. Consciously, he fought an unruly twang in his heart. Anna would never be his. A sudden commotion in the bushes behind him caught his attention.

A strangely dressed man stepped out onto the walkway. He ran his long fingers through his dark ruffled hair and flashed Jake a lopsided grin. "Good afternoon," he said and with a polite cough, excused himself.

Jake watched him stroll away. His natural curiosity peaked at the stranger's unusual appearance. A few of the robust seamen greeted him with a hardy back clap. Jake watched the newcomer's movements suspiciously when he paused at Jock's side to chat.

Jock swung about to see who had slapped him on the back. He grinned from ear to ear. "Where the devil have ye been, Doc?"

"A long way away...well, you understand." Alastair raised a dark eyebrow. "When did you start wearing dresses, Jock?"

Jock glanced down at his kilt. "Why ye young blowfish! 'Tis the Highland dress, and I wear it to honor yer own great-great-grandfather."

"Shh! Not too loud. I was only joking, man." Alastair glanced quickly around to make sure they were not overheard. "Is the captain also wearing—"

"A kilt? Aye, that he is, and proud o' it too."

Alastair grinned. "Where might my proud ancestor be at this moment?"

"Right over there..." Jock pointed across the garden to the gazebo, where the bride and groom stood arm in arm.

"Thanks. Oh, Jock? You look so—how should I put it—sweet?"

Jock's jaw dropped open and he raised his fist. "Ye nasty wee joker. I ought to hang ye from the yardarm m'self!"

Alastair laughed heartily and strode down the brick path toward the newlyweds, before Jock could come back at him with a rowdy punch. Anna looked radiant in a deep green traveling dress with a small matching bonnet. He bent to place a kiss on her flushed cheek. "Congratulations are in order, I do believe."

Anna threw her arms around his neck and hugged him. "I owe you so much! I'm so very happy, Alastair."

"You deserve to be happy. I'm glad to see you looking so well."

"Why wouldn't I be well?" She saw concern in his brown eyes and a sudden notion occurred to her. "Why are you here? I thought you were done dwelling in 1880."

Alastair grinned down at her. "So did I, until last week."

Anna glanced over at James who was deep in conversation with Michael. Without another word, she took Alastair's hand and led him inside the house to the solitude of the parlor. After making sure they were entirely alone, she turned to face him. "Exactly what is going on, Alastair?"

"I needed to make sure you and James got hitched."

She frowned. "Bull-pucky! Now tell me the truth."

He shook his head and feigned interest in the still-life painting on the wall. "I had reason to believe someone hurt you."

Anna's face clouded as painful memories flooded her. How could she tell him about Morgan? "I'm perfectly fine, as you can see. But there is something I have to tell you, Alastair, and it's not good news, so you should sit down."

He groaned. "Thanks. I prefer to take my medicine standing."

"It's about—"

The parlor door burst open and James blew in like a storm over the open sea. "There ye are, Anna. I thought I lost ye, love." He leaned down for a kiss, and then noticed she was not alone. "Alastair! 'Tis great to see ye, lad."

"James." Alastair shook the captain's proffered hand in a warm grasp. "Anna was about to tell me something." He smiled. "By the way, I love your sassy skirt, James."

James flinched, then laughed good-naturedly. "Aye. Ye should learn to wear one yerself, Alastair. 'Tis yer heritage, ye know. 'Tis not uncomfortable, but it can be a wee bit drafty."

Alastair burst into laughter, and James and Anna joined him.

Anna sobered and stood quietly observing the two men. She still had awful news to tell Alastair. "James, he doesn't know about...well, you know."

"Aye, lass. Ye will need to be telling him now, won't ye?"

She faced her great-great-grandson, wringing her hands nervously. She couldn't think of an easy way to break the news, besides the truth. "Morgan is dead."

Alastair's smile faded, and then suddenly broke into a broad grin. "No, he's not. Morgan is the reason I am here today, but only because he is not well enough for time travel right now."

"Not dead?" Anna swung around to stare at James. "Not dead!"

Alastair took her arm and led her over to sit on the pink brocade loveseat. "It looks as though you are the one who needs a chair. Let me explain what I know about all this and hopefully, you can help fill in the missing pieces."

"Are ye telling us Morgan is alive then?" James joined Anna on the loveseat.

Alastair paced the parlor floor, thoughtlessly tracing a pattern on the flowered rug with his feet. "That's right. Morgan was wounded in that shoot-out at the mountain cabin. You had thought him dead, when he was merely weak and unconscious."

James looked at Anna, then back at Alastair. "Jake told me Morgan was dead. I took his word for it. When Anna came up missing, I forgot all else."

"Wait a minute—how did Morgan get from the cabin to the time pool?" Anna shook her head in confusion. How could a man have looked so dead, but still have made it to the sea cave? One had to be in good health to survive the horrible journey through time. After all, her real mother had died after such a journey.

"I think I can answer that," a deep voice spoke from the doorway.

Anna looked over her shoulder to see Jake standing in the arched framework of the parlor door. His weathered face looked troubled. She hurried over to him. "Jake? What do you know about this that you haven't told us?"

Jake took her hand in his and gazed deep into her eyes. "Anna, I hate to say I lied, but I did. I didn't expect any questions about Morgan, or the business at the cabin, to come up again."

"You must tell us everything—now." She tugged at his hand, leading him over to a wing-backed chair. When he sat down, she rejoined James on the loveseat.

Alastair stood silently, leaning against the sideboard in his twenty-first century suit. "Yes, Jake, do tell us all."

Wiping a hand across his furrowed brow, Jake related what happened after they rescued Anna from the wolves. "When I returned to the cabin to claim the bodies, Hawk was laying across the bed a bloody mess. I checked him out and found him weak, but still very much alive. I remembered what Anna had been trying to tell me. He wasn't the bad guy. He was trying to help her."

Anna met Jake's steely gaze, feeling a little guilty. He knew she was from the future now. Her face flushed with heat. She had told quite a few lies herself just to hide that particular fact from him.

Jake broke the intense eye contact with her, looking instead across at the captain. "Things you said while we were searching for Anna, telling me about her. It was all rather strange. Heck, the whole darn thing—from my first meeting with Anna, clear up 'til today—is all rather strange."

Anna couldn't hold her tongue any longer. "So you do know about me, about us." She pointed across to Alastair.

"Yeah, guess I do," Jake admitted. "That's why I looked you up here in town. We had to settle all this and bring things out in the open between us. I guess I had to get things straight in my mind too."

Alastair coughed into his hand to hide a grin when he saw the captain's face turn stormy. He quickly intervened. "What exactly did Morgan tell you about us?"

Jake switched his gaze from Anna to Alastair. "You look very familiar. Have we met somewhere before?"

"Not likely." Alastair straightened his striped silk tie.

"Alastair is from the future too," Anna hastily explained.

Jake rubbed his fingers over his mustache. "Well then, maybe you should hear my part of the story about Hawk's survival. He told me about the time pool. I thought he was crazy. He told me he was dying and wanted to get back to the future. I felt obligated to help him in any way I could. On the way to the cave he told me about a friend with whom he had traveled through time."

"That would be me," Alastair admitted.

"You're Doc?"

"Yes. I am really a certified physician. Doc is Morgan's nickname for me. I called him the Hawk. When we were kids, I always wanted to be a doctor and Morgan always played the bandit. Many times I pretended to care for his wounds, and this time I did it for real."

Jake smiled, remembering the dying man he had assisted. "Well, I hoped he wasn't lying to me, so I took him to the cavern. I threw him into the water like he told me to do, but I couldn't leave him to drown. I dove in after him and helped him as far as the grape arbor. He told me to go back and take care of you, Anna. I didn't have a chance to tell him you were okay. Someone was coming across the lawn and Hawk didn't want me to be seen. I didn't think about the reason why until later."

Alastair jerked to attention and walked across the room, stopping in front of Jake. "You came forward in time?"

"Yeah, but I was only there less than a quarter hour. Hawk was anxious for some reason. Now I realize he did not want you to find me."

"How did you feel? I mean, after your arrival in the future?"

Jake eyed him curiously. "All right, why?"

Alastair yelped for joy. He continued to move about the room mumbling to himself. He stopped suddenly and turned around to look at all three shocked faces. "Don't you see? It works both ways! People from the past can come forward in time, if they're careful not to change the course of things. We know you came through the first time, Anna, but you were meant to return to the past to complete your destiny." He slapped his fist into his palm. "This is such great news! Why, the possibilities are unfathomable!"

Anna scrambled to her feet and grabbed hold of his arms. "Alastair, you need to calm down. Someone will hear you. It isn't as though we can tell the world about this."

"Right. You are absolutely right!" Alastair's smile turned upside-down. "That rat Morgan led me to believe he had come back on his own! At least he was truthful when he said he didn't know what had happened to you, Anna. He felt concern for your welfare. You have to give him credit for that."

"I felt sorry for Morgan in the end," she assured him. "It hurt to think he died because of my darn bikini."

"Bikini?" Jake's eyebrows rose in curiosity.

James sighed and stood with one big stretch. "Tis a long story, Jake. Just a wee bit o' the Duncan family history."

Anna blushed furiously. "I'll say!"

James looked across the room at his great-great-grandson. "Where is the rascal Hawk now, I wonder?"

"Morgan wanted to come back with me, but he is not strong enough to withstand time travel again so soon." Alastair glanced down at his watch and adjusted his shirt cuff to cover it.

James clapped Alastair on the shoulder. "Aye, 'tis better he does not show his face in the area for a bit anyway. They all think him dead and 'tis for the best."

Jake joined them in standing. "Hawk agreed to stay in his own time for at least a year. And no more highway robbery when he does come back," he added with a chuckle.

Alastair released a long held sigh. "He told me the same, and I plan to hold him to his promises this time." He glanced down at his watch again. "I really need to be going. We have all the stories told. Agreed?"

"Aye, all but one." James pulled his bride into his arms in a lengthy kiss. "Only Anna knows how our story will end, and if I am good she may let me in on the tale."

"Pardon me, Captain, but I have read the journals Anna will one day write. I could let you know all about your long life together, but I think it is best if you simply live it instead." Alastair grinned from ear to ear. "Don't you agree, Anna?"

Anna smiled and took a deep cleansing breath. She had read more about her life in one day than she had ever known existed. Some of the things she learned hurt and some of them eased the pain of not knowing. She had read that James went on to live a full life and she wanted to share it with him. "Alastair is right, James. I read so many things. I cried so many tears. I decided not to read beyond my childhood, other than to find out if I was supposed to return to the past where I belong."

"I am glad to know ye belong here, love." James took her hand in his and gently squeezed it. "I could not bear to lose ye now."

Jake exhaled and straightened his broad shoulders. "Right. Well, that was something I didn't know. I cannot wait to learn more of this interesting subject upon your return to Mendocino. I must be going now. I have a coach to ride." He reached over and shook the captain's hand. "Have a wonderful wedding tour!"

"Thank you, Jake. We will keep in touch, I promise." Anna accepted the light kiss Jake placed upon her cheek and watched as he left the room.

Alastair ran his fingers through his thick hair. "I must be going as well. I have a practice to start up in the future."

Anna giggled. "Now that really sounds strange! Good luck in your life, Alastair. The only thing that saddens me is that I will never know how you fare."

"Are you kidding? I'll send you messages via the time pool, kinda like our own Internet system." He laughed heartily. "Take care, both of you."

"Take care, Alastair!" Anna hugged him and backed up a step so he could say farewell to James. "Say good-bye to the old sea fox," she said with a twinkle in her eye.

"Tis baiting me ye are, my love." James winked at her. "Ye know, at times I may be a sea fox, but still I am not that old. I'll be showing ye soon enough."

Alastair cleared his throat before they could continue their playful comments. "I have enjoyed the opportunity of meeting and getting to know you, Captain. The way things look...well, maybe we will be seeing each other again real soon."

"Aye," James agreed. "I feel the same, Alastair."

"I'll just slip out before Angel sees me, or I'll have yet another story to tell." Alastair held the gaze of his great-great-grandfather a few moments longer, then gave an inherited wink over his shoulder and whistling a merry tune, strolled out the parlor door.

James wrapped his arms around Anna. "Now where were we, love?"

"Oh, here you are!" Angelique walked into the parlor, just missing Alastair's hasty departure. "James? Anna? Jock tells me you need to set sail right away. He says there is a storm coming."

James walked over to the tall French doors and looked out at the cloudless sky. "Aye, Jock is always right about a storm. He's not missed one in fifteen years." He caught Anna's look of alarm. "Nay, lass. 'Tis but a wee storm and ye will recall we made it safely through the last one."

Anna could have dissolved into his arms with the devouring look he cast her. She definitely recalled the last "wee storm" they had experienced. The memory made her shiver in wanton anticipation. She could hardly wait to set sail on their honeymoon.

Chuckling softly, James gathered her to him and kissed her. He would have deepened the kiss, if not for Angelique clearing her throat behind him. He slowly released his lovely bride from his embrace and they walked outside to say farewell to their wedding guests.

~ * ~

Pink hues filled the evening sky as Anna stood on the *Ceilidh's* polished deck, watching the golden sun sink into the blue sea. A soft breeze tugged at her hair. Her long green skirt clung to her thighs. Gripping the extensive length of blue and green tartan about her shoulders, she felt strong male hands slip around her waist.

"A penny for yer thoughts," a husky voice whispered into her ear, before his soft lips nuzzled sweet kisses along her neck.

Anna smiled and leaned back against James. "I'm thinking I never want this wonderful day to end."

"Aye, I feel the same—very special."

"Aye," she agreed, mimicking his Scots burr.

The two lovers stood in the twilight wrapped closely within each other's arms. Her feminine figure fit snug against the captain's curve of steel muscle. This was her ultimate dream with her ultimate lover. He stood beside her in full Highland dress, but for his black velvet-jacket and plaid bonnet that lay discarded on the deck. No matter what he wore, he was the most masculine man she had ever met.

"James?"

For an answer, he nibbled tenderly along her neck. His arms tightened around her, pulling her even closer against him as her body arched in response to his touch.

"Ummm..." she moved seductively against him.

"Were ye about to ask me something, love?" He squeezed her responsive breast with his large hand.

"Captain!" She giggled and moved slightly away from him to lean against the polished rail. "You'll embarrass your crew if you keep that up."

"Tis no offense to them, Mrs. Duncan. They have already seen a bit more o' yer person than I ever intended to show them m'self." He stepped to her side as his arms slid about her waist.

Her gaze scanned the horizon. "It really is more beautiful in your time."

"What, lass?"

"Everything. The land, the sea...even the stormy sky." She wiped a solitary tear from her eye. "It's just beautiful."

James saw the small gesture and kissed her cheek softly. "Are ye sure ye want to stay in my time, now that ye know ye can return to yer own, Anna?"

She turned quickly to face him. "I couldn't live without you."

"That's not what I'm asking and ye know it. Will ye stay with me always?"

"Yes." She lowered her eyes, looking away from him. "I don't ever want to leave. I would be taking the chance of losing you forever, and I couldn't stand that. Sure, I'm going to miss modern conveniences, but Thomas Edison is about to invent the light bulb and then he will perfect the phonograph. So it won't be too bad."

"Ye are speaking poppycock to me, but I am glad to know ye will not be leaving me for all those fancy things in the future." He swung her gently around to face him. "I am afraid I could not let ye go."

His lips slowly descended to meet hers in a kiss that curled her toes. Anna clung to him, breathless, wanting much more than she could have at this moment. Soon they would be under way and they could retreat to the captain's cabin below. She shivered with building anticipation of their first time together as husband and wife.

Snuggling back into the warm security of his strong arms, Anna smiled. She would always remember this day and the precious marriage vows. They pledged their love to each other for forever and a day. James Adam Duncan was her true eternal partner.

James loved holding Anna in his arms. Her passion surpassed that of any woman he had ever known. With Anna, he was complete. Much more than a physical desire bound them. They shared a deep love for each other; so enduring it had drawn them together through time. Aye, they would be together forever, their lives weaving as one like the fine wool threads in his tartan.

The sea breeze whipped her long golden hair about their bodies as he bent to kiss the sweetness of her lips. He pulled slightly away and looked down at the woman who had captured his soul. Their gazes locked as a strong wind picked up and snapped the sails, high in the rigging above them.

William called out orders to the crew, his deep voice echoing on the rising wind. Jock rushed about directing the lads in orderly fashion. Ropes fell to the deck like a tangle of grapevines as the ship prepared for full sail.

James and Anna stood enchanted in each other, far away from the world around them. Only two existed now, a man and a woman, linked by a bond more eternal than time itself. Two hearts entwined forever in a whisper of a tryst.

Epilogue

Alastair carefully hung the heavy-framed portrait above the polished-stone fireplace and stepped down from the stool. He poured himself a shot of Scotch whisky and stood back to admire the beautiful artwork. Though the nineteenth century painter was not famous, his talent was unsurpassed. The canvas colors were clear and bright, right down to the smallest detail. Most importantly, the artist had captured the very essence of his subjects to perfection.

The bride wore a delicate white satin gown with long sleeves and a lacy high neck decorated in seed pearls. A long satin train swirled around her on the floor like a glistening puddle of starlight. Her blonde curls were swept back from her face in a ponytail, accented by tiny pink and white rosebuds, and fine pink ribbons. Her smile was sweet and her green eyes misted with tears of happiness.

The groom stood close to the bride with one arm circling her waist and the other hand holding her hand. He stood in full Highland dress, a tall broad-shouldered man, with a blue and green tartan proudly displaying his Scottish heritage. He had a distinctive dimple in his left cheek and a charming lopsided smile. His eyes were brilliant blue and sparkling with humor as they winked down upon the beholder.

When Alastair found the painting in the attic it was covered in grime from years of neglect. He took the treasured portrait, frame and all, to a friend who restored antiques for the local museum. His friend informed him the painting dated back to the late nineteenth-century, notable from the type of oils the artist had used.

Alastair smiled as he looked up at the wedding portrait. He crossed his arms and stepped back a bit more. What would his friend have thought if he had told him, he not only knew the exact age of the portrait, but that he had met the bride and groom, as well?

"No one would believe me. After all, time travel isn't really possible...now is it?" Alastair chuckled, a deep melodious sound, and raised his shot glass to the portrait. "To my heritage, to Father Time, and most of all...to love."

He tipped the glass back and emptied its contents in one fiery gulp, then walked out of the room and closed the heavy oak door.

Meet

Christine Poe

Christine grew up in California, spent twenty-two years in Utah, and currently resides in Virginia with her devoted husband, a large multi-generational family, lots of Blue Ridge Mountain wildlife, plenty of feline friends, and one Carolina Dog. She began writing at a young age but didn't pursue it seriously until her four children were almost grown. She writes daily about life's adventures and the loves she has encountered...whether they be man or beast.

VISIT OUR WEBSITE
FOR THE FULL INVENTORY
OF QUALITY BOOKS:

http://www.books-by-wings-epress.com/

Quality trade paperbacks and downloads
in multiple formats,
in genres ranging from light romantic comedy to
general fiction and horror. Wings has something
for every reader's taste.
Visit the website, then bookmark it.
We add new titles each month!